JOLT
by
Jodi Bowersox

Special thanks to Vicki Veer for taking me up Pikes Peak that stormy afternoon.

Books by Jodi Bowersox

Interiors By Design
Horses, Adrenaline, and Love

Anonymous Series
Cinnamon Girl Explains It All
The Diamond Diva Vendetta
Red Rabbit on the Run
Blue-Eyed Devil

Rocky Mountain Series
Rocky Mountain Angels
Rocky Mountain Sunrise
Rocky Mountain Redemption
Rocky Mountain Destiny
Rocky Mountain Calvary

Lightning Riders Series
JOLT
JUMP
JIVE

Tripping on Mars Series
Mars Madness
Beware the Eyes of Mars
The Mars Heir

Ephesians: The Plan, The Purpose, and The Power
Chosen and other productions, programs, and skits

Books under the name J.B. Stockings

A Tale of Two Kitties
The Stubborn Princess

JOLT

Chapter 1

"Oh my gosh, this is just like the dream I had last night!" Lalita Torres pivoted three hundred and sixty degrees in the dining room of the Edwardian country house known as Rock Ledge House. "Except in my dream it was my house, and I had just discovered this amazing room I never knew was there."

Nonnie swung the lightweight backpack off her shoulders as she came to Lalita's side. "Only you would have historical house dreams." She dug through her pack until she found a hair clip. "Gads, it's hot in here." She twisted up her honey blond hair and clamped it.

Lalita wiped her own brow and ran a hand through her chin-length black hair. "Yeah, I'm wishing I'd brought my tiny battery-powered fan."

The living history docent nodded. "The coal-burning stove roaring in the kitchen puts out quite a bit of heat."

Lalita looked the woman up and down. "And we're sweating in shorts and tank tops—not multiple layers of clothes that cover every inch below our chins."

Nonnie shook her head. "I couldn't do it. I'd melt clean away."

As the docent led them into the butler's pantry, Lalita gave a final look at the elegant china place settings. As she lingered, trying to memorize every detail, Nonnie grabbed her arm and pulled. "Okay, okay, I'm coming."

Their guide was already in the middle of explaining the "servants gray" paint that was used in all of the servants' areas of the house, and Lalita wondered what it would have been like to be the scurrying mice behind the scenes of this wealthy family's ten course dinner parties. She smiled. *What would it be like to be the ones served?*

Lalita Torres loved history, but it wasn't the big picture wheres and whys that interested her. It was the details of the human story. The minutia of everyday life and living. As the docent explained the electromagnetic bell system for the servants, Lalita scribbled in a small notebook.

"For that book you're going to write someday," Nonnie teased.

"Actually I'm thinking of my doctoral thesis." The docent had moved on, waving them up the narrow, steep back stairs.

"You're really going to keep going after you get your Masters?" Nonnie puffed behind her as they turned to ascend to the third floor. "Aren't you sick of school yet?"

"Not yet. There's so much history to learn."

They stopped at the top to catch their breath. "Who's going to pay for it all?"

A young girl in period dress had followed them up the stairs and directed them to look around the servants' quarters at their leisure. "There are scholarships and grants for Native Americans. That's how I've been going for this long. Plus, I've taken a year off here and there to work and save for it."

Nonnie moved past her to look in the small closet. "Must be nice. I've tried numerous times to get a scholarship and have never gotten more than a couple hundred bucks. And you're not even a full Indian."

Lalita bristled. Nonnie was one of her oldest friends, but sometimes she didn't think before she spoke. "I'm not *Indian* at all, since I wasn't born in India. What I am is one quarter Cherokee."

Nonnie ignored her.

Lalita felt immediate remorse for correcting her. "I'm sorry, Nonnie. I knew what you meant."

Nonnie shook her head. "No, I'm sorry. It's just that—" She waited until the rest of the group had left the room. "It's just that it feels like reverse discrimination. I can't get the money for school because I'm white and have no tragic ancestral story."

Lalita blinked, wondering if Nonnie would really like to have Wounded Knee, the Sandy Creek Massacre or the Trail of Tears in her family history.

Not to mention spending much of your childhood bumping around in foster care.

* * *

"How come you're only staying until Friday when you said you were off work for two weeks."

Lalita pulled her sunglasses off the top of her head and put them back on her face. "I want to get some painting done in my apartment before classes start. Then my parents are going on some kind of family reunion cruise, and they want me to house sit and watch their dog."

The two left the blacksmith demonstration in search of the Chambers House that was built in the 1870's. "What? They aren't taking you with them?"

"It's okay. I mean, they really aren't my family anyway. You know I've always felt like an outsider."

Nonnie shuffled her feet on the dirt road, making fat snake-like tracks. "Why did two white people adopt an In— a Native American kid anyway?"

Lalita stopped, forcing Nonnie to turn back. "Please tell me you're kidding."

Nonnie looked confused for a few moments before breaking into a grin. "Yeah, I'm kidding. Of course I'm kidding." She turned back to the road and continued shuffling, though now in zigzags. "You've gotten really touchy."

Lalita shook her head as she jogged to catch up. "And you've acquired a weird sense of humor."

They walked in silence for a while with Lalita wondering what had happened to the easy friendship they used to have in high school. Nonnie finally spoke. "Well, what else do you want to do while you're here? We've hit most of the historic places that I know of—Garden of the Gods, the Pioneer Museum, old buildings downtown. . . "

"I don't know. I definitely want to tour Glen Eyrie and go up Pikes Peak."

"You have to call ahead for Glen Eyrie."

"Okay, so we do that tomorrow. Shall we go up Pikes Peak today?"

Nonnie looked at her watch. "I'm not driving it—too scary—so we'll have to take the cog rail. There might be time if you don't dawdle all through the rest of the Ranch. There's a house and a homestead to see yet."

Lalita started to walk faster. "Well, let's get moving, then!"

The Chambers House wasn't as elegant as Rock Ledge House, but Lalita found it fascinating, nevertheless. Her eyes drank in the carved wood furniture, the ornate standing wood stove, and the small pipe organ.

She lingered in an upstairs bedroom full of smaller beds. *The kids' room.* She knelt down to take in the details of a china doll, and she smiled imagining the little girl in long blond curls that might have played with it. She sighed. If there was anything she loved even more than history, it was kids. She spent most of her summers working at a daycare.

Nonnie was moving on, so she followed her into the master bedroom. Everything in her wanted to slip into the lacy, high-collared dress that was on display. "Wouldn't you love to play dress-up for just a day?"

Nonnie wrinkled her petite nose. "Maybe an hour. In the winter. These clothes are too hot."

"I know, but I'd like to give it a try."

Nonnie headed for the stairs to go back down. "What's stopping you? You know how to sew. Make yourself a fancy Victorian dress and go shopping at Safeway."

Lalita followed her down the narrow stairs. "That's the problem. I'd want to wear it in an appropriate setting. Wouldn't it be awesome to be a part of a historical ball where everyone dressed in the time period and knew all the dances?"

Nonnie stopped at the bottom and looked back, her blue eyes staring blankly. "Yeah, that would be a hoot. While you're there, I'll go to the bar next door."

As the two moved back through the house to the exit, Lalita wondered what had happened to her old friend. *We used to have more in common.*

*   *   *

"Why oh why did you make me drink so much water!" Lalita was squeezing her legs tightly together on the not-so-comfortable bench of the Pikes Peak Cog Railway.

Nonnie gave her a sympathetic smile. "I'm sorry, that's what you're supposed to do when you travel from 7,000 to 14,000 feet to prevent altitude sickness. I assumed you wanted to enjoy your time at the top once we got there."

Lalita looked at the rain beating on the windows. "I'm not sure 'enjoying ourselves' is gonna happen anyway." The lightning illuminating the thunderheads seemed far away, but their tour guide had warned them of the danger of running around on the highest point in a lightning storm—no matter how far away it seemed.

Lalita's last-minute idea to go up Pikes Peak had earned them the last two spots on the last run of the day and the fold down jump seats at the front of the second car.

Now they were sitting at the top of the mountain, not allowed to exit the rail car until the light show stopped. The next bolt seemed less intense and farther away, and Lalita reached out and tugged the sleeve of the twenty-something tour guide. "Do you think it will be much longer? I really really have to use the bathroom. There's going to be a puddle here very soon if you don't let me off this car."

The young man with a high-lighted blond faux hawk grimaced. "I'm sorry, but no one gets off until the lightning stops."

Lalita nodded, thin-lipped, and closed her eyes. She was shivering as well. It had been eighty-eight degrees at the bottom, but it was in the thirties at the top. The shorts and tank top she had on was like wearing nothing at all. Nonnie, who was similarly dressed, put her arm around her, and the two huddled together for warmth.

"So much for my brilliant ideas," Lalita spoke through chattering teeth. "I'm gonna pee right here and freeze to the seat."

"Give me fair warning," Nonnie growled.

After a few silent moments where Lalita did nothing but pray for bladder control, Nonnie nudged her arm. "Oh look, Lita! A rainbow."

Lalita opened her eyes and craned her neck to look where she was pointing. "It's a beauty, alright." Her pressing need kept her from further excitement, however, until she realized what the clearing skies meant. She breathed a sigh of relief when she noticed the blue-eyed guide heading their way, smiling. She and Nonnie rose, as their seat actually had to fold up so the door could be opened.

"I know you're in a hurry, but please don't run to the building," he warned.

Lalita nodded, took two steps at a slow pace, then sprinted to the gift shop.

*   *   *

After their emergency bathroom stop, Lalita and Nonnie met up at the check-out counter, each with articles of clothing and blankets in their arms. Lalita held up a red union suit that sported "Pikes Peak or Bust" on the rump.

"There must be more idiots that come up here inadequately clothed to be selling long johns and blankets," she observed, looking around at the milling crowd from the cog rail. "But today, I think we get the prize."

Nonnie snorted. "Some 'prize.' This stuff isn't cheap."

Lalita took a few steps forward as the line started to move. "Of course not. They know we'll pay anything once we're up here and freezing our butts off."

After paying, Lalita went to the bathroom again to slip into her long underwear. She'd hoped to put it on over her clothes, but there was too much bulk. Slipping out of her shorts and tank top, she stuffed them into her shopping bag before pulling on the outfit that was guaranteed to garner her a few stares. "Thank heavens I have on my hiking boots rather than my rhinestone-studded sandals."

Making her way back through the gift shop, she found Nonnie in front of the "World Famous Donuts" sign and snapped a selfie of them sampling the wares. She checked the time. The lightning storm had eaten up some of their allotted minutes, but she was determined to see something of the view before she had to climb back in the rail car. "Come on, Nonnie, we need to go have a look while there's still time."

Pulling their woven wool blankets tight around them, they headed out and snapped another selfie in front of the Pikes Peak Summit sign before jogging to the rocky edge. There were still dark clouds in the south, but the north was clearing.

Turning her attention outward, Lalita marveled at the massive boulders close to the top and the distance she could see. The view across the mountains was indescribable. "Wow."

A whistle sounded, and Nonnie turned. "Time to go."

"Wait. I haven't taken any pictures of the view yet."

Nonnie continued back to the cog rail car. "Well, hurry, you don't want to get left up here."

Lalita snapped pictures in several directions, and when the whistle sounded again, she turned in resignation, sliding her phone back into her soft leather shoulder bag while gripping the blanket closed at her chest. A sudden breeze blew a wisp of her dark hair into her eyes, and she stopped a second to work her hand out from under the blanket to clear her vision.

A moment later, her hair lifted, her skin tingled, and the brightest flash she'd ever seen sent her into darkness.

Chapter 2

The pounding on Tate Cavanaugh's door was relentless. He had just settled into a hot bath when it began. He'd gotten caught in the rain while out on a call and hoped to ward off the chill with the steaming tub, but it seemed that there was to be no rest for the weary. Or at least no hot bath for the doctor this evening.

He had already sent Mrs. Kettler home for the night, so unless he wanted his 5-year-old daughter to jump out of bed and answer the door after dark—which she just might do, being a rather impulsive child—he needed to haul himself out of the tub and answer the door post haste.

Wrapping a towel around his waist, he dripped down the stairs to the door and at the last minute considered that whoever was on the other side might be female. He wavered. "Who is it?"

"Martin and Alfred Hill. We've got someone who needs your help."

Tate unbolted the door and pulled it open to the dark night that was only illuminated by the lantern held by one of the Hill brothers. The other was carrying someone bundled in an Indian blanket, and all of them looked as though they had gotten caught in the rain as well. A sizable puddle was forming on his covered front porch.

He stepped back. "Bring him in. What's the trouble? Illness or injury?"

Martin shook his head as he set the lantern down just outside the door, and Alfred stepped through with Tate's new patient. "We don't really know. He was found at the top of Pike's Peak when the cog rail train made its final run of the day. He's breathin', but nothing seems to wake him. He even slept through the downpour we got caught in. With just the buckboard, we couldn't give him any shelter."

He paused and just seemed to notice the doctor's lack of dress. "Sorry we interrupted your bath, Doc."

Tate shook his head and waved the two men down the hall toward the stairs rather than his examination room at his right. "Bring him this way, Alfred. We better get him warmed up. The man doesn't need a case of pneumonia on top of whatever else is ailing him."

Alfred hesitated and gave a quick glance to his brother. "There's something you might want to know first."

Martin pulled the blanket away from the dark-haired bundle's face. "His features ain't real strong, but he looks like he might be a young Injun. Ute, maybe, or Cheyenne."

Tate studied the face surrounded by hair as dark as midnight that had been plastered to his head by the driving rain. The bronzish skin was paler than usual due to cold, but he could definitely see the high cheek bone structure common to the Colorado natives. He wondered what could have befallen this young Indian and felt a chill run up his spine, but shook it off as being due to his current state of near nakedness.

"Duly noted. Now let's get him undressed and in the tub. If you two wouldn't mind doing that, I'd like to put something on that's more suitable to the occasion."

Striding upstairs with the Hill brothers following, he nearly ran into his daughter standing in the hallway. "Nellie, what are you doing out of bed?"

She pulled on his towel, wide-eyed, and he had to make a quick grab for it lest he'd be standing there in nothing at all. He stroked her curly blond head as he guided her back to her bedroom. "You haven't answered my question yet, Miss Nell."

She whispered a reply that Tate didn't catch, but didn't have the time or inclination to ferret out. "Well, whatever your excuse, it just won't serve. Back to bed with you. And stay there."

He gave her a little push into the room that should have been filled with all the frills that girls love, but instead was as practical as the doctor himself. Turning into his own room, he quickly got dressed while the Hills took the bundled young man to the room next to Nellie's. Donning trousers and shirt, he decided to forgo footwear until he had his patient in a better state.

He padded across the crewel-carpeted hallway to his bathroom and was surprised to see the brothers kneeling in front of the young man, who was laid out on the floor next to his clawfoot bathtub. As he entered the room, they both turned, their slack-jawed expressions only puzzling him further. "I thought I asked you to get him undressed."

Tate took in the boots that were small even for a young man, his gaze traveling up the red union suit to where the Hills had started to unbutton it. They rose and stepped back, allowing the doctor access. His brows rose at what could only be a bright pink support for what he didn't need to be a doctor to know were obviously breasts.

Chapter 3

Tate watched his patient, wondering if he should take her to the hospital in Denver—a journey that would take him away from his practice for several days. She was still out after twenty-four hours, and he feared a full out coma. He and his housekeeper, Mrs. Kettler, had been monitoring her around the clock, and even little Nell had stayed with her, giving her droppers of water and broth at regular intervals.

After the discovery that "he" was a "she," he'd sent the Hill brothers to fetch Mrs. Kettler but proceeded to undress her himself down to her underthings—the strangest, skimpiest underthings he'd ever seen. If she hadn't been in desperate need of warming up, he would have waited for his housekeeper for the sake of propriety, but he'd told himself that the young woman's health was more important, and he was, after all, a doctor.

Mrs. Kettler had arrived in time to remove the last of the girl's wet clothes and get her dressed for bed in one of his late wife's nightgowns.

As surprising as her underclothes had been, the colorful flowered tattoo that covered her right shoulder and upper arm had captured his attention the entire time he had been warming her in the bath, and even now his eyes drifted to the spot, even though he couldn't see it through the long-sleeved gown.

He couldn't help but appreciate the artistry—he'd never seen a tattoo like it—but was shocked that a woman would have such a thing permanently done to her body. Not to mention the piercings on her earlobes. One of her earrings was missing, but the hole was still plainly there. With such bodily decoration, he feared that she had spent time in a house of ill repute. The cross necklace she wore at least spoke to the possibility of redemption.

He sat back, letting his gaze rest on her peaceful face, her long dark lashes resting against her high cheek bones. *Perhaps it's all merely for tribal distinction.*

Another curiosity was her hair. Not even the Ute men wore their hair so short. His eyes narrowed remembering the union suit she'd been wearing with the prospector's slogan on the backside. *Was she trying to pass for a miner?* He smiled. *Better remove the other earring, then, missy.*

He was just about to make himself a cup of coffee, when her nose twitched and a sigh escaped her lips. Pulling his stool closer to the bed, he was hopeful that his wait was over.

Lalita couldn't open her eyes for the pounding in her head. She groaned and almost immediately felt a hand on her forehead. A deep voice resonated an "Ah" that sounded miles away, ringing in her ears for several moments before there was silence once more.

She tried to turn her head, but light sparked around her eyes, sending her hands in search of her face. They seemed to be under something heavy and cloth-like, and she panicked to get her hands out.

The weight lifted off of her arms as the voice spoke again, sounding closer this time. "Shh, it's all right. Can you hear me?"

Lalita tried to swallow, but her mouth had absolutely no spit. She gave a small nod as she licked her dry lips in vain.

A strong hand slid under her shoulders and lifted, and she felt a glass against her lower lip. "See if you can take a sip for me. You've been out quite a while."

Lalita gripped the quilt as she sipped the water. She had a vague remembrance concerning water, but it slipped away before she could grab onto it. The last thing she remembered was watching the blacksmith at the history farm. *It was really hot by the forge. Did I faint?*

When the glass was pulled away, and she was laid back down, she was determined to see where she was. Putting a hand to the eye that was throbbing, she managed to ease the other one open.

A very serious man was looking at her intently. She shut her eye tight and opened it again, trying to gain better focus. Dark brown eyes stared back.

Suddenly aware that she was no longer in her clothes, both eyes snapped open, and despite the pain in her head, she looked down to see what exactly she had on. She seemed to be in a lightweight, though long-sleeved granny nightgown of some kind, and she was pretty sure she didn't have anything on underneath. "What the hell's going on?" she squeaked out, covering her right eye with her hand once more.

The man reached for her hand, easing it away from her face. "It's all right. There's no need to be frightened." His mouth hinted at a tiny smile. "Or any need to swear. I'm a doctor. You've been injured somehow, but I'm at a loss to know just what happened. You don't appear to have any abrasions, contusions, bruises, or broken bones."

Lalita closed her eyes again. "My head hurts something awful. Do you have any extra-strength Tylenol?"

Instead of answering, the man who claimed to be her doctor pried open the eye closest to him and held some kind of lantern up to it. "You speak very well for a Ute woman."

She pushed his hand away. "A what woman?"

He took her hand and pulled it to the bed. "A Ute woman. The natives of this area. Or did you come from elsewhere?" He then proceeded to examine her eye once again.

Once again, she pushed him away. "Hey! That's really annoying right now when my head feels like someone's hitting it with a cricket bat."

"I'm terribly sorry, but if you've had a head injury, I need to examine your eyes—see how they respond to light."

He started his hand toward her other eye, and she slapped it. "Just wait a minute. I'll do it myself."

It took a lot of effort, but she managed to flutter the other eye open. "Why would you assume that I'm descended from your local tribe? People travel all over, you know."

Lalita wiped the watering corner of her eye as the doctor sat back on the stool he had pulled close to the bed. He seemed to be trying to contain a smile. "That they do, Miss. My apologies for my assumptions. You have obviously been well educated."

She stretched out her arms in front of her. "So what's with this funky nightgown, and is Nonnie here?"

"The nightgown was... I let you borrow it, since your clothes—such that they were—were soaking wet. Two men brought you to my door last night, and no one has inquired about you."

"Last night!" She bolted upright, only to fall sideways with sudden vertigo.

The doctor caught her. "Careful. Take it slow. You are most certainly short on sustenance."

Lalita clung to him as the room spun, her thoughts spinning with it. *Last night? Nonnie must not know where I am.* "I need to let Nonnie know what's happened, although I don't really understand what's happened. She was with me at Rock Ledge Ranch, so where is she?"

He held onto her stiffly, his breath tickling her ear. "What were you doing at Rock Ledge Ranch?"

Lalita was perplexed by his tone that almost sounded accusatory. "Taking the tour like everyone else. What do you think?"

He didn't speak for a moment. "You were not found at a ranch. You were found on top of Pikes Peak."

The spinning in her head stopped, and she pulled out of his arms. The scent of his strong aftershave seemed to come with her. "Pikes Peak? But Nonnie wasn't with me?"

He shook his head, looking more than a little concerned. "I've heard nothing of a Nonnie."

"I don't understand..."

"Neither do I, Miss... I guess I should inquire your name."

"Lalita Torres," she answered, on the verge of tears.

"Well, Miss Torres, I'm Dr. Tate Cavanaugh, and let's not panic just yet. I'm sure more will come back to you as time goes on, and I promise, we'll find your Nonnie."

Her stomach rumbled, and the brown-haired man gave her hand a pat. "Mrs. Kettler has left for the day, so I suppose it's up to me to find you something to eat."

Lalita looked around the room, and for the first time, it dawned on her that she was in a house rather than a hospital or doctor's office. A very stylish house. A very stylish Victorian house. She looked back to the man who was heading out of the room in high waist slacks and suspenders over his crisp white shirt. *I don't remember going up Pikes Peak at all... Maybe I never left Rock Ledge Ranch.*

* * *

While Tate warmed some broth on the stove, he pondered his new patient. He was relieved that she was awake, and the need to take her to the hospital had diminished. Along with the arduous journey, he feared that she might not receive the best care due to her heritage. Many folks bore animosity toward Indians.

He stood straighter, his chin ticking up. *Many do, but I will not.*

Her level of education was more than a little surprising given her gender and background, but her colorful way of speaking wasn't likely to land her in the best of social circles. There were certain society rules that most young ladies were schooled in at a very young age. He thought of his late wife's struggle to fit into Denver society, and he grit his teeth.

Dipping a spoon in the broth, he tested its warmth with a sip before setting it on the spoon rest. Satisfied, he poured the broth into a bowl and turned to retrieve a clean spoon from the drawer, when he heard a crash.

Running down the hall to the examination room, he found his patient on her knees, trying to pick up pieces of a broken lantern. He quickly moved to lift her up by the shoulders "Careful, girl, you'll cut yourself." Scooping her up, he carried her back to the bed and examined her feet before pulling the quilt over her once more.

She looked mortified. "I'm so sorry. I'm sure that was an antique. I can pay you for it." She looked around the room. "That is, if I can find my purse. That's what I was looking for when I got dizzy. That and my clothes."

Tate waved a hand in dismissal. "Nonsense. It was an ordinary lantern. Nothing special about it. Now stay in bed while I fetch your broth and a broom."

Returning moments later, he helped Lalita to prop herself up in bed and left her to the eating of the broth while he swept up the broken glass and mopped up the spilled oil with an old rag.

He straightened from the task just in time to see her lift the bowl to her lips. His eyebrows rose of their own volition. "Well," he stuttered, trying to pretend he hadn't witnessed her lack of social graces, "how do you feel after a bit of broth?"

She wiped her mouth on the napkin he'd given her. "I'm still starving. Could I have something else before I leave?"

"Leave? I don't think you're quite ready to strike out on your own yet. Besides, it's getting dark. We should probably see how you feel in the morning." He set the broom behind the door. "I'll give you a thorough exam then, and hopefully, your full memory will have returned."

Her mood seemed to shift in an instant. "Look, I appreciate the fact that you've taken care of me for a day, but it's time to cut the crap. You're just a volunteer at the Ranch pretending to be a doctor for the sake of realism. I should just give Nonnie a call and have her come get me. Since I can't find my purse, and my phone is in it, would you be so kind as to let me borrow your cell?"

Tate had no idea what the woman just said, and he feared she might be having a stroke. Moving swiftly to her bedside, he sat on the stool. "Can you repeat that?"

Rolling her eyes, she flung the quilt back and attempted to get out of bed. Tate put out a hand to stop her. "Miss Torres, I'm going to ask you to stay in bed. Even though I can find no evidence of it, I believe you've had a head injury that could lead to further serious complications. Can you understand what I'm saying?"

She sat down, clearly exasperated. "Of course I can understand what you're saying, but *I'm* saying I need to leave now. The show's over. You've done a marvelous job of staying in character, but I really need to go."

Tate blinked, wondering how to proceed. He needed to calm her down before she fled and injured herself again. He tried smiling. "Thank you, Miss Torres, for your sincere compliment, but I'm going to ask you to stay here with me just one more night."

The girl's lips went into a thin line, and her agitation was evident. "Why don't I have anything on?"

Tate wondered if this was more gibberish. He put a hand to her forehead to check for fever but found her to be cool to the touch. "What do you mean? You very plainly have on a nightgown."

"Underneath, Sherlock. I've got nothing on underneath."

He had no idea why she'd call him Sherlock when he'd told her his name quite plainly, but he did understand the rest of her sentence and despite being a doctor, he blushed. "Miss Torres, I can explain."

Lalita crossed her arms over her chest. "So talk."

"When the men brought you to me, you were soaking wet from a rain storm and nearly blue with cold. It was important to get you warmed up, so... so my housekeeper got you undressed for the bath. Not me." He moved to a free-standing wardrobe and opened the doors. "Your clothes are right here. Mrs. Kettler laundered them today, and you are free to put them back on if you like, although I think the union suit may be a bit warm for this time of year down here in the valley."

He wasn't sure why he'd felt the need to cover up the fact that he had, indeed, undressed her down to her undergarments. As a doctor he had dealt with much more embarrassing facts.

Lalita rose and walked across the room. Her boots, socks, underwear, and bra were stacked neatly on a shelf, along with a pair of red long johns that were obviously not hers. "Where's my tank top and shorts?"

The doctor's brow furrowed. "I don't know about those items. This is what you were wearing when you arrived."

She shook out the long johns and held them in front of her. "Are you kidding me? I was wearing this?"

She read the backside's slogan— *Pikes Peak or Bust*— and had a flash of a memory that was there for just a moment and gone. She swayed, and he stepped forward to steady her. She felt fear rise up again, but it was squelched by the appearance of a small blonde holding a china doll in a nightgown almost identical to the one she was wearing.

The doctor followed her gaze, his manner shifting gears. "Miss Nell, what are you doing out of bed?"

"Papa, I heard a noise, and I wondered..." she whispered. She stepped into the room and pulled on his arm. He bent his ear to her lips, and Lalita had to strain to hear her. "I wondered if she was awake."

Before he could answer, Lalita stepped forward, forgetting her earlier fear. "I am awake."

The girl closed the gap between them, and Lalita squatted down to her height, still holding the long underwear. "Did you help take care of me while I slept?"

The little blonde nodded, her long curls bouncing. Lalita put a hand to her shoulder. "Well, I appreciate it very much."

Nell cupped her hands around her mouth, and Lalita turned her head to receive the intended message. "I'm also hungry."

Lalita smiled and looked up at the man who was smiling down at them both, looking a bit mystified. "Me, too. I believe your papa was about to make me a bedtime snack. You can join me." She rose and stuffed the long johns back in the cupboard. "Isn't that right, Doc?"

"I suppose we could try a bit of bread with some broth this time." He turned his attention to his daughter. "Nell, go wash your hands."

He waved a hand toward the door. "Miss Torres, would you care to join Nellie in the dining room?"

"In a minute. If you don't mind, I think I'll at least put on my underwear."

Nodding, he reached for the door knob. He hesitated before closing it behind him, however. "Does this mean that you'll be staying until morning?"

"Apparently."

"May I ask what made you change your mind?"

"Well, I just figured this all out. My two passions are history and kids, and here I am in a cool Victorian house with an adorable little girl." She smiled. "And you're totally hot." She took her clothes off the shelf. "I'm still sleeping, Doc, and this is just a really fantastic dream."

Chapter 4

Tate watched Miss Torres interact with his daughter, the two of them laughing over a silly show that the animated young woman was relating. It must have been the most fantastical stage production ever produced, being set under the sea. *Or perhaps this Sponge Bob Square Pants is just another product of her head injury.*

He smiled at Nellie's laughter. Joviality had been too far removed from their lives the last few years.

As his patient reached for another piece of bread and proceeded to mop up the last of her broth with it, Tate thought about her pronouncement that she believed she was merely dreaming. He'd not had a lot of experience with head injuries—at least not where strange delusions were involved. *I may need to consult with other physicians on this case.* For the time being, her dream idea was keeping her calm and happy until he could figure out some way to help her.

Nellie yawned, and Tate checked his pocket watch. *After eleven.* He rose to put the rest of the bread in the larder. "All right, Miss Nell, it's back to bed with you."

He hesitated at the dining room doorway, loathe to leave his patient unattended while he tucked Nell back in bed. Then he had an idea. "Miss Torres, would you like to assist Nellie with her toilet and putting her to bed? She can show you the way."

Taking one last gulp of water, she pushed back from the table. "Sure, no problem."

She followed Nellie up the stairs while Tate carried the bread and dirty dishes to the kitchen. He didn't want to leave a sink full of dishes for Mrs. Kettler in the morning, so he washed them himself and placed them back in the cupboard, using the time to ponder what kind of treatment would help Miss Torres gain back her memory and sort out the confusion in her speech. *Of course you are assuming that she wasn't confused before.* He turned and leaned against the counter. *Perhaps she is just mentally disturbed.*

He immediately regretted sending her upstairs with his daughter. Running through the house and up the stairs, he opened Nellie's door. By the light of a nearly full moon, he could see that she was in bed. He walked quietly forward until he could detect the sound of her breathing.

Letting out a breath of his own, he went back out to find Miss Torres. Looking further up the hallway, he could see that the bathroom door was closed. He went to his bedroom to wait for her to come out.

After fifteen minutes had passed, where he'd nearly fallen asleep in the chair, he jumped up and strode to the bathroom door. He knocked lightly. "Miss Torres, are you all right in there?"

He heard a thump and pictured her on the floor, passed out. Without thinking, he opened the door.

His patient was leaning out of the tub trying to retrieve his safety razor that was now on the floor. She gasped when she saw him, ducking back down, her forearms along the tub's edge, her chest pressed against the side. He moved swiftly and swept the razor up. "What were you doing with this?" His eyes slipped to her tattooed shoulder, then to the curve of her hip his vantage point afforded. He backed up to the doorway.

Her face was the picture of indignation. "What's the point of knocking, if you don't wait for a response?"

"I'm sorry, I heard a noise and... and..." He watched her hook a longer strand of hair by her face behind her ear, causing the bouquet on her shoulder to shift. He took another step back, putting him out in the hall. "And I thought you might have fainted."

Her face relaxed. "I guess I should have asked if I could use your razor. I was feeling pretty fuzzy; I was just shaving my legs. I'm sorry."

Tate was having a hard time gathering his thoughts. "Your le— limbs?" He then noticed the cup of shaving cream on the floor by the tub. "Why on earth would you shave your limbs?"

She hitched a brow. "I'm not a tree, Doc. And while I appreciate the natural look, I draw the line at shaggy. I'm no wookie."

Wookie? She might as well have been speaking Russian. "So you didn't intend to harm yourself."

"Well, I gave myself a few knicks, but I assure you it wasn't intentional. The 'safety' part of your razor is a bit of a stretch," she said, using air quotes.

He just stared, unable to formulate a response.

Finally, she reached out a hand. "Can I finish? I only got one leg done."

Still he tarried, frozen in place.

She blinked at him. "Since this is my great dream, maybe you'd like to do the honors."

Shaken out of his stupor, Tate reached for the door knob and pulled, suddenly wondering if he were the one dreaming.

Chapter 5

Lalita found she couldn't sleep. Every time she closed her eyes, she pictured the doc's face when she had suggested he finish the job on her legs. And best of all was his reply, looking shell shocked— "I don't believe it would be in your best interest to return it to you at this time"—before he closed the door.

She laughed out loud then slapped her hand over her mouth, shaking with silent giggles until her face started to hurt. *This is the best dream ever.*

She had to admit that she had never had a dream that lasted so long and that didn't fall completely apart at some point with the people turning into rabbits or something. It was also weird that when she wanted to find a bathroom, she did, and the toilet even worked, in all its high tank Victorian splendor.

She turned to her side, pondering the fact that she was dreaming about dreaming, but she'd had those kind of dreams before, as well. Sometimes when a dream was particularly interesting, the rest of the night's imaginings was all about telling everyone about that dream.

She thought of her dream doctor with the chestnut brown hair. She let her mind meander over his straight nose, brown eyes, and bow lips. When he'd been leaning over her, she'd noticed a small scar shooting up from his lip on the right side. She had a crazy urge to kiss that scar. *Maybe if I think on it long enough, my mind will work it into the storyline.* She smiled in the dark. *The very best dreams always involve kissing.*

*   *   *

Tate found he couldn't sleep. Every time he closed his eyes, he saw her breasts slipping back into the tub—her bare arms with that flowered shoulder... Her reason for having the razor seemed a fabrication, and yet, he was no expert on women's fashion. Perhaps it was a new trend since his wife had passed. He thought of the women for whom he'd delivered babies. *It does not seem to be a trend around here.*

He thought it ironic that he had probably seen the legs of his female patients more often than he had seen the legs of his own wife.

Tate had never actually met his wife's family as they were killed in a railroad derailment accident, but Augusta had described them as strict, with a puritanical bent. Augusta had seemed reserved before they were married but downright fearful after. Their intimacies were always after dark, in the dark, and under the covers. She had been completely scandalized at his suggestion that she remove her nightgown.

With the addition of little Nell, Augusta had become even more withdrawn and melancholy. Tate had thought to help by getting her invitations to social gatherings, but that seemed to only make things worse. Bringing a hand to his head, he rubbed the spot between his eyes. *It was my fault. I pushed too hard.*

His mind returned to the day she died, but he shook his head, unwilling to hash those events over again. Flinging off his sheet, he mused on his patient's wild ramblings. *Well, she was correct in her assessment about one thing; I certainly am hot. There's nary a breeze this evening.* Finding his slippers beside the walnut sleigh bed and his dressing gown on the chair next to it, he headed downstairs.

After drinking a snifter of brandy to aid in his sleep, he checked on Miss Torres, surprised to find her still awake, although looking sleepy. He set the lantern on the table and sat on the stool beside her bed. "Having trouble sleeping? Does your head still ache?"

She shook her head, smiling. "One doesn't really sleep in dreams. Otherwise the dream ends, or you have a dream in a dream, which I suppose is theoretically conceivable."

Tate just stared, wondering how it was possible for her to seem well-educated and completely unbalanced at the same time. "Well... I suppose I'll let you get back to it then. The dream, that is."

He made to stand, but she reached out and caught his hand. "But this is the dream. You came to me, and I want my kiss."

Tate's eyebrows flew up, his voice delayed for a few moments. "Miss Torres, that would be highly unethical. You're my patient. I... I could lose my license to practice medicine were I to kiss you while you are under my care."

Her smile sagged. "Dang, this is the strangest dream— almost too realistic." She released his hand and rolled over, sighing. "Good night, Doc."

Tate sat a moment or two longer, wondering about her fragile state of mind, and he prayed that another night's sleep would clear her head.

Leaving the room, he couldn't account for the tingling on his palm, his suddenly dry mouth, or the way he couldn't seem to catch his breath. "I hope I'm not coming down with something," he mumbled, climbing the stairs.

Chapter 6

Lalita woke to the same bedroom in the same house, the small child she'd dreamed about sitting on the stool looking at her with expectation. "Are you Nellie?"

The little blonde smiled and nodded.

Lalita bolted out of bed and ran across the hall into the parlor. "Doc?"

As she came back out, she was met by a woman coming down the hall who looked to be around her mother's age, but her mother wouldn't be caught dead wearing a long-sleeved dress that went to her ankles covered by an apron. The woman, whose hair was in an updo, was smiling. "Miss Torres, I'm so pleased to see you up and about. I'm Mrs. Kettler, Dr. Cavanaugh's housekeeper. The doctor had to step out for a few house calls. Is there anything I can help you with? Some breakfast, perhaps?"

Lalita turned toward the door, and Mrs. Kettler moved with speed to head her off. "Oh, Miss, I wouldn't advise stepping out in just your nightwear!"

Lalita took a step to the right and a sidelight window. "I just want to look out." With her knees on a small upholstered stool, she brushed the sheer curtains aside and bent to look beneath the long, swagged velvet drapes. She saw more Victorian houses, but what made her suck in a quick breath was the horse-drawn carriage passing by. "Mrs. Kettler," she began without turning, "am I dreaming?"

Mrs. Kettler came to her side and spoke quietly. "I don't believe so, dear, unless I'm dreaming too."

Lalita watched a couple strolling by in period costumes and a boy in knickers riding a bicycle. Nellie appeared at her other side, and Lalita took the time to look her over. She, too, wore a long-sleeved dress. But while Mrs. Kettler's was sage green, Nellie's was China blue. The two-tiered ruffled skirt attached to the slim bodice hit her above the ankles, each ruffle trimmed in ribbon. Part of her long curls were pulled back behind her head, where a big blue bow was attached. If she had been in black and white, she could have been a picture from the 1890's Smithsonian archives Lalita had been looking through the previous week.

Lalita turned and plopped down on the stool. "If I'm not dreaming, then I don't know what the hell is going on."

Mrs. Kettler's shock at Lalita's language was obvious, but at the moment, Lalita was too distracted to apologize. Pushing up, she looked at the housekeeper with determination. "If I can't go out in nightwear, then what can I go out in?"

"I don't know." Mrs. Kettler gave a nervous glance to the stairs, and Lalita jumped to her feet, immediately heading that direction.

Mrs. Kettler followed. "The doctor said you were not to go out. He told me to play along with your dream notion," she mumbled as they reached the top, "but it seemed wrong to lie to you."

Lalita strode down the hall to the master bedroom. "The doctor has a little girl but doesn't talk about a wife." Lalita stopped in the doorway. "Is she dead?"

Mrs. Kettler put a hand to her arm. "Please, Miss Torres, Dr. Cavanaugh won't like you looking through her things."

Lalita didn't really care at the moment what Dr. Cavanaugh would or would not like. As she approached what she assumed to be the closet, she noticed a small adjoining room with numerous hat boxes on shelves. *A dressing room.* She moved toward it. *Just like Rock Ledge House.* Opening the closet in that room with Mrs. Kettler fretting behind her, she found what she was looking for. She shifted the dresses until she found what she recognized as a "day dress" with long mutton leg sleeves and a high collar. *It looks close to my size.*

She laid it on the bed while Mrs. Kettler stood looking solemn, her hands on Nellie's shoulders in front of her.

Stripping the nightgown off with one fluid motion, Mrs. Kettler gasped and turned herself and Nellie around. "Oh good grief," Lalita lamented as she pulled the dress over her head. "We're all girls here."

The dress hung on her a bit and was several inches too short, but it would have to do. Returning to the closet, she found a pair of shoes. More digging through drawers while Mrs. Kettler huffed and puffed, produced stockings. Unlike the dress, the short boots fit perfectly. She was grateful that they had laces—she didn't have the time or patience to figure out a button hook at the moment.

Looking through a few hat boxes, she found a simple, round, flattish, tan hat with a single black feathery plume and set it on her head. She knew that hat pins were usually used to keep them on, but that would require more hair than she had, piled high to pin it to. It didn't seem like a particularly windy day, so she hoped for the best.

Heading back downstairs, Mrs. Kettler was still trying to talk her out of leaving the house. "You're welcome to come with me, Mrs. K., but like it or not," —she opened the door while looking back— "I am going out."

"Are you, now?"

Lalita turned to see the doctor blocking her way. She pursed her lips with determination and narrowed her eyes. "I am."

He looked her up and down, and she was surprised when he turned and extended his elbow toward her. "May I accompany you?"

Miss Torres took the arm that Tate held out to her, and the two stepped out onto the wide front porch. She seemed to hang back at the top of the steps. "Are you sure?" he asked quietly, placing his hand over hers on his arm.

She took in a breath and let it out. "We're so close to the mountains."

"We're in Manitou Springs. Where was the ranch that you remember?"

"Colorado Springs. Right next to Garden of the Gods."

The two started down. "Ah, yes, an amazing, enchanting place."

Tate guided her over the cobblestone walkway to his waiting buggy and helped her climb aboard. He couldn't help noticing how Augusta's dress hung on her slim form, and he remembered that after giving birth, Augusta never quite got back to her pre-pregnancy size. Even with a corset.

He settled in beside her and started the horse forward. "I see you found my wife's dresses."

Miss Torres looked down at what she was wearing, her hands smoothing the skirt. "I'm sorry I dug through her clothes... Does it bother you?" She looked at him sideways, and the hat tumbled off her head.

He reached between their feet and picked it up. "A little."

"I'm sorry." He handed her the hat, and she put it back on.

He smiled. "If you were going to venture out, I don't know what else you would have done." His smile grew bigger. "Parading around in that red union suit would likely land you in jail."

His patient was indignant. "I don't care what you say, those long johns are not mine!"

He decided to let that slide. "You can come with me to my next appointment. I only stopped at the house to check on you—to see if you were up yet." He gave her a reassuring smile, but she was lost, looking around as if she'd never been out of the house before.

When another horse and carriage passed them going the other way, he thought she was going to hyperventilate. "Breathe, Miss Torres. It's just a buggy—just like ours. Nothing to be afraid of."

She looked at him wide-eyed. "It's so quiet. There are no car sounds—no jets." She looked up. "There's not even any jet streams."

There she goes again. He reached over and patted her hand clenched in her skirts. "Most people like the quiet. It's peaceful, don't you think?"

"Peaceful, but wrong. All wrong." She turned more toward him on the seat. "Okay, Doc, it's time to level with me. If I'm not dreaming, then where am I? Is Manitou Springs one big living history town?" She deliberated, looking down at her lap. "Nonnie would have told me about something like that so close to Colorado Springs... unless... Did Nonnie set this up, somehow? As a surprise?"

Tate couldn't keep the look of concern off his face. "Lita, as I told you last evening, I know nothing about your friend Nonnie. My job is merely to see that you recover from whatever happened to you."

"Ah ha!"

Tate blinked in surprise. "Ah ha?"

"Yes, ah ha! Only Nonnie calls me Lita!"

He looked at her blankly.

"And you just called me Lita!"

He shook his head. "A slip of the tongue, I assure you. I have not been in collusion with Nonnie to confound you. You have my word."

"Why is it your job to look after me, then? Why do I need looking after? I don't think you're a real doctor. I think you 'just play one on TV.' "

More gibberish. He pulled back on the reins. "Whoa, girl."

"Is this your house call?"

He stepped down and tied his buggy to a post close to the street. "Yes. I'll be 'playing doctor,' as you put it. Although I won't be on any 'teevee,' whatever that is."

Even though the doctor's frustration was evident, he still helped Lalita down from the buggy and escorted her to the house. She was in awe of the styling details on the wraparound porch, and inside, the furnishings weren't just elegant, they were opulent. While they waited in the parlor to be received, she stared open-mouthed until she caught the doctor smiling at her.

He leaned toward her on the sofa. "Be careful, you're going to catch flies with your gaping."

"How many houses are like this?"

"In Manitou? Only a few this rich. Most are like mine. There are a number of wealthy individuals in Colorado Springs, however."

A woman appeared at the doorway, and the doctor stood. Dressed similarly to Mrs. Kettler, but with a bit more style, she talked with him a moment then moved toward the stairs. He looked back to Lalita before following. "Come, Miss Torres. I'd like you to see just exactly how I play at being a doctor."

She smiled and followed. *Well, at least he's finally admitting it.*

They moved through a foyer with a chandelier suspended from a vaulted ceiling then went up a carpeted stairs with an elegantly carved banister railing. The housekeeper led them into a large master bedroom with expansive windows in the east. She remembered from her Rock Ledge House tour that houses of this era were built facing the east because they believed the morning sun to be more healthful than the evening sun. *No mountain views for you, Mrs. Rich.*

The doctor moved to the bedside of what appeared to be a very pregnant woman. Lalita smiled. *That's one big foam baby.* While the doctor performed his exam, recording information in a journal he pulled out of his medical bag, she feasted on the details of the elegant bedroom. The wallpaper print was cabbage roses and the heavy wood furniture was elaborately carved. Rich velvet was draped on the windows edged with brocade trim and gold tassels.

Dr. Cavanaugh interrupted her inspection and waved her over to where he sat in a chair by the bed. "Mrs. Pilson, this is Miss Torres. She's... assisting me today." Lalita greeted the woman whose long, blond braid hung off the edge of the bed and hit the floor, and she pondered the weariness that shone out of her green eyes. *They have certainly got some great actors for this little drama.*

Pulling the sheet back, Dr. Cavanaugh felt the pregnant woman's belly in numerous ways, then placed the bell of his stethoscope to her abdomen. He listened in several places, and Lalita smiled at how thorough he was in his playacting. She sidled up behind him. "Waddya hear, Doc?"

Removing the stethoscope from his ears, he rose and offered it to her. "Have a listen, yourself, Miss Torres."

Lalita was surprised but took the antique apparatus and placed the ends in her ears. He pointed to a spot on Mrs. Pilson's rounded belly, and she placed the bell there. She immediately heard an unexpected heartbeat. She carefully placed her hand on the woman, her eyes connecting with the doctor's. "It feels real," she confessed, barely above a whisper.

He took her hands and guided them to the sides of the woman. "It is real, all too real. Tell me what you feel."

Mrs. Pilson groaned, and Lalita pulled her hands back.

"It's all right. You're not hurting her; it's a contraction." He guided her hands once again to the woman's belly.

Lalita felt the distension on the sides, and although she wasn't a doctor, she knew that wasn't the correct position for birth. "It's sideways."

He nodded.

"You should call an ambulance—get her to a hospital."

He shook his head and took hold of her arm, guiding her to the far end of the room. "The closest hospital is Denver," he whispered. "The journey is too long, too hard for her condition. She'd never make it."

"Nonsense. Maybe Manitou Springs doesn't have a hospital, but I know a city the size of Colorado Springs has to have one."

He shook his head again. "Not yet."

"Bullshit!" He squeezed her arm, and she lowered her voice. "You're just going to let her die when you know this is all a charade."

"I have no intention of letting her die, but I will need your cooperation, your assistance, and maybe a bit of your trust. Hard labor just started within the hour. We have time to turn the baby. But," he emphasized with a downward tilt of his chin, "I'll need you to be for me and not against me."

Lalita couldn't believe what was happening. If this was some kind of "Truman Show" set up for a paying patron's historical whimsy, then surely this was all a very elaborate fake, and the woman would be all right. *Isn't this what you've always wanted? To be a part of an era gone by? To play dress-up for just a day?*

She squared her shoulders and looked deep into his eyes. "I'm in."

Chapter 7

Dr. Cavanaugh took off his jacket and draped it over an
upholstered red velvet armchair in a seating arrangement by
the fireplace, then proceeded to roll up his sleeves. Lalita
removed her own hat and flung it on the chair as well, then at
the doctor's direction, pulled Mrs. Pilson's nightgown up above
her belly. He coated it with petroleum jelly while he explained
what he was about to do. "I'm going to be pushing pretty hard
on your abdomen, and I know it will not be comfortable, but it
will be more pleasant than a delivery that goes nowhere."

Mrs. Pilson nodded with a knitted brow.

The doctor put his hands on either side, pressing in and
rotating. Mrs. Pilson gave a little gasp, and Lalita took her
hand in a firm grip. The woman gave her a worried smile then
gasped again as the doctor readjusted his hands. She cried
out as a contraction came over her, and the doctor released
her. "There's no point trying to fight with a contraction. Miss
Torres, take note of the time."

"I don't have a watch."

Dr. Cavanaugh looked at his pocket watch, unfastened
it from his vest and handed it to her, then removed his vest
as well. When Mrs. Pilson was once again breathing easier.
He placed his hands on her and blew out a frustrated breath.
"That's what I was afraid of. The contraction let the baby slide
back to where we started."

He began again, more vigorously this time, which had Mrs.
Pilson gasping and moaning, holding Lalita's hand so tightly,
she was about to lose circulation.

Sweat was running into his eyes, but he wouldn't release his hold on the infant to wipe it away. "Almost there, Millie."

He'd no sooner said it than the next contraction was upon her. Tate stopped, wiping his brow with his sleeve, and Lalita prayed that the baby would stay in its new position. The woman's pain was obviously increasing, but with the baby out of position, the contractions were doing nothing to speed delivery.

After Mrs. Pilson relaxed once again, he felt her belly and smiled. "We only lost a little bit of ground this time. Miss Torres, if you can assist me, I want this done before the next contraction hits." He moved around to the other side of the single bed, and she released Mrs. Pilson's hand and moved hesitantly to her belly. "Put your hands here." As she reached forward, he took her hands and positioned them. "You'll be pushing the rump, and I've got the head. Ready? Push."

Lalita visualized a tiny baby's bottom under her hands, and with the two of them working, they moved the baby the last few inches that would allow it to enter the birth canal. Lalita removed her hands and the doctor examined his patient, a grin spreading over his face. Lalita clapped, feeling victorious, but then another contraction hit the laboring mother, and Lalita realized that there was still a long way to go before they reached the finish line.

*   *   *

"Why don't you get something to eat? I promise you the baby won't be born while you're gone."

Lalita was lurking just behind Tate's shoulder while Mrs. Pilson rested in between contractions. Her nearness was... unsettling.

"I'm not hungry."

Her stomach picked that moment to growl, and Tate looked back at her. "You were so wound up this morning, did you even eat breakfast?"

She put her hand on his shoulder and leaned in to his ear, her breathy whisper tickling the back of his neck, causing all manner of sensations to wing through his body. Instead of answering his question, she asked questions of her own. "What happens if something goes wrong? If the baby is in trouble, you'll call for an ambulance, right?"

He swiveled on his chair to face her. "You have nothing to worry about. As far as I can tell, labor is progressing as expected. I don't anticipate any trouble."

She crossed her arms so tightly, her shoulders rose. "But... what if there is? What's your plan? You can't do a C-section here, can you? Are there surgeons waiting somewhere?"

Rising, he led her a few steps from the bed. "Miss Torres," he began in low tones. She pursed her lips with eyebrows raised, and he corrected himself to the name she insisted he use. "Lalita, as I said, I don't anticipate a problem, but your anxiety will most certainly be transferred to our patient. I suggest you go downstairs and partake of the offered meal."

He tried to move her toward the door, but she latched onto his hand. "Please, just tell me you have a plan for an emergency."

Her worry was so evident that Tate's other hand came to her cheek without thought. "Yes, I can perform a C-section if necessary, but—" Mrs. Pilson began to moan with the next contraction, and both moved back to her bedside. "You really should go eat, Miss—Lalita."

Tate sat as Lalita wiped Millie's face with a damp cloth. "In a minute, Doc."

Tate turned, smiling. He didn't know why he was proud of this woman he'd barely known for a day, but he was.

*　*　*

Lalita came back to Tate's side after grabbing a bite to eat. "Your turn."

Tate pulled his stethoscope from Mrs. Pilson's rounded belly. "I'm fine."

"You said yourself this could go on all day. Better to eat now before the real show starts."

He rose and took the woman's pulse. "I'm used to going without."

Lalita waited until he laid the woman's hand down on the bed. "But that's because you do this alone. You don't have to today. I'm here, and I can sit with her for the ten minutes it will take you to eat."

He looked at his watch. "I think you were only gone five."

"I'm a college student; I eat on the run a lot." He tilted Mrs. Pilson's chin until she opened her eyes, seeming to study them. "Is everything all right?"

"Her pain level shot up considerably with that last contraction, and she has requested chloroform. I'm just check—"

"Chloroform! You mean you're going to knock her out?"

"Yes, we've found that it is less traumatic for the mother." He moved toward his medical bag sitting on a dresser by the door and pulled out a small bottle.

Lalita followed. "But. . . how will she help push the baby out? Won't it take longer—be more dangerous for the baby? Why do you insist on doing everything old school?"

He placed his hand on her shoulder. "Miss Torres, the use of chloroform is relatively new, and you said you'd trust me. I am a doctor."

"But," she scrambled, following him back to the bed, "nobody puts women out for childbirth anymore. Sometimes they do a spinal block or use other pain meds that help her relax, but nobody puts them clear out. They use breathing techniques to help with the pain." He looked at her blankly. "You know, the Lamaze method?"

His brows rose, and he stood a moment staring at her. Finally, he gave her a patronizing smile. "I think maybe your head injury is causing some confusion. Why don't you go downstairs and rest in the parlor?"

Lalita felt as if she could scream, when Mrs. Pilson did it for her.

The doctor moved back to her bedside, and Lalita was determined that this woman would be awake for her baby's birth. "Doctor, you need to go eat now before you give her the chloroform. Afterward, you won't want to leave her side, I'm sure." He didn't move. "I ate in five minutes, and I bet you can too." When he still didn't move, she added, "You need to keep up your strength to help her."

Finally he set the bottle down on the bedside table. "Perhaps you're right." He patted Mrs. Pilson's hand as she relaxed back onto her pillow. "I'll just be a few minutes."

She nodded, and the doctor strode out of the room. Lalita didn't waste any time. "Okay, Millie, we are going to handle this pain so you can stay awake. It's better for you both." She paused and tried to remember all the chatter of the pregnant mothers who frequented the daycare where she worked. They talked nonstop about breathing methods and birthing balls and massage. She swept the sheet off of the woman. "Do you have any lotion?"

*   *   *

Tate stopped abruptly as he came back into Mrs. Pilson's bedroom, unsure of what he was seeing. His patient was on her knees on a pillow beside the bed, resting her head and arms on the bed itself. Her lower half was swathed with the bed sheet and her nightgown was rolled up, exposing her lower back. Lalita was on her knees behind her, her hands rubbing and kneading.

"What is going on? Miss Torres... Mrs. Pilson..."

Lalita looked as though caught in the act but brought a hurried explanation forth. "Doc, I know you all like to do everything the old-fashioned way for some reason, but sometimes you just have to use some modern techniques. The massage is making her more comfortable, and when a contraction starts, I'm helping her focus on breathing. That helps shift it away from the pain."

The doctor squatted down to look into Mrs. Pilson's eyes. "Is this helping?" The woman nodded. "Do you still want to use the chloroform?"

"Let's give this a try," she panted. "Edwin didn't like the idea of the chloroform anyway."

He covered her hand with his. "Where is Edwin today? I assume someone called his office."

"He's out of town," she puffed as another contraction came over her. She began rocking back and forth on her knees while Lalita pressed the sides of her hips and encouraged her to breathe in a series of "hee hee hee hoos."

Tate was fascinated. "Where did you learn this?" he asked after the contraction had passed.

"I work with little kids, and little kids have young mothers and pregnant mothers." She swept up the hem of her skirt and wiped her brow. "They talk a lot."

Whatever Lalita was doing, it seemed to be a comfort to Millie, and he could see no harm in it. Most of the job of baby delivery was a matter of comfort, anyway, until the woman became fully dilated. He rose and sat in the chair by the bedside, watching. "So you're not a midwife."

She laughed. "No. I just listen and read." She suddenly stumbled back and to her feet. "Oops, we've got a sudden flood happening here."

Tate looked down at the sheet turning wet. "Ah, her water broke." They both helped the woman to her feet, and Lalita walked her to her dressing room to find another gown while Tate buzzed for the maid to bring them another pillow and more linens.

Tate and Lalita assisted the now contracting and groaning woman back to bed, and Tate checked her progress. He had hoped for more. Forcing a smile, he tugged her night gown down. "Not quite there yet."

As the woman rested, Lalita came to his side and squatted down to his ear. "What does that mean in real time?"

He tried not to think about how near she was and looked to the foot of the bed. "It's hard to say. Every delivery is different. Sometimes progress just stops."

"Completely or just for a while?"

She straightened, and Tate let out a breath. "Either could happen."

She looked at his pocket watch laying on the bedside table. "She's already been in labor for more than six hours," she whispered, "but that's not unusual, right?"

"No, that's not unusual." Tate smiled at his patient turned maternity ward assistant. "If you are tired, I won't think any less of you if you'd like to go down to the parlor and rest."

A look of indignation came to her face. "Although I might look it, I'm not a wilting violet, Dr. Cavanaugh. Millie can't walk away from this, and neither will I!"

He couldn't keep a smile from spreading over his face, which seemed to bring a blush to hers. Their eyes held for a

moment before the birth pains were upon Mrs. Pilson once
again, and the two turned their focus to her comfort.

* * *

Tate adjusted the reins in his hands, more than a little bit
worried. Lalita had spoken hardly a word since the baby
delivery.

He had been surprised at both her stamina and her very
real assistance. She hadn't been squeamish or faint of heart as
many women seemed to be and had not only followed his every
instruction precisely, but brought new comfort techniques that
he had never heard of to aid the laboring woman.

He wasn't really sure what to think about her ideas of
massage and breathing, hot water bottles and comfort positions,
but there was no doubt that Mrs. Pilson had been helped, and
she got through the birth without chloroform. *Maybe I've
missed some new developments in childbirth since leaving
Denver.* He vowed to write his colleagues at the earliest
opportunity.

His thoughts returned to the moment when the infant
had finally made its way into the world. Lalita had held the
screaming newborn with tears streaming down her face, but
ever since, she had been quiet and withdrawn. He hoped he
hadn't pushed her delicate mental state too far.

He glanced over at her on this cloudless night and saw
that her chin was bobbing toward her chest. *It was a long day.*
Taking the reins in one hand, he swept an arm around her with
the other, pulling her head to his shoulder.

*Who are you, Lalita Torres, and where has your friend
Nonnie gone?*

He suddenly realized that he should have gone to the
marshal's office to see if anyone had reported a missing person.
Without thinking, his fingers sifted through her short hair. *First
thing tomorrow.*

He pulled into the carriage house and was met by Mrs.
Kettler's son, Harold. A bright boy who was eager to work,
Harold took care of Dr. Cavanaugh's horses and kept a good
polish on his buggy.

He'd sent word that he'd be arriving home late, and he'd half expected the care of his horse to fall to himself after his long day of caring for Mrs. Pilson. Seeing Harold ready to take on the responsibility warmed his heart. Tate smiled at the boy's disheveled appearance as he unhitched his horse, Maisy. *He was probably sleeping in the hay.*

Tate handed Miss Torres down to the strapping teen. "Thank you for being here so late, Harold. You've certainly earned yourself an extra nickel tonight." He jumped down and took her back into his arms.

"Is she the Injun they found on Pikes Peak half dead?"

Tate gave a weary smile. "She is the *lady*, Harold, that was found knocked out on Pikes Peak and who still has some memory loss. Right now, she is merely exhausted after helping me with a birth." He turned to leave. "Good night, Harold."

"G'night, sir."

Carrying her in, he laid her on the bed still in his late wife's dress and realized that somewhere along the way, they had lost the hat.

Mrs. Kettler looked in the door as he finished unlacing Lalita's high top shoes. "Do you want me to get her dressed for bed?"

"No, I don't want to wake her." He pulled off the shoes gently and placed them on the floor beside the bed.

"Did going out do her any good?"

Tate rubbed a hand around his weary face. "Time will tell."

"Did she make more sense today?"

"Yes." He sighed. "Mostly. It's late. Harold has probably settled Maisy in for the night, and I'd think you'd like to be heading home." He tacked on a small smile, knowing she'd had a long day as well.

With a curt nod, she headed for the door. Tate knew he'd been brusque. "Take tomorrow morning off, Mrs. Kettler. I appreciate you staying late."

She nodded again and let herself out.

Tate's stomach rumbled, and he headed for the kitchen. He found a bit of left-over beef in the ice box and ate it with one of Mrs. Kettler's yeast rolls.

Before turning in, he looked in on Lalita. He let his gaze wander over her face. A face that was altogether lovely. He thought about the previous night when she had asked him for a kiss, and he found himself moving toward her bedside.

Holding a hand out, he studied the difference in their coloring. He had a summer tan on his hands that came close to her complexion, but pulling his sleeve up revealed a much stronger contrast. He let his hand fall to his side. *Respectable white doctors don't kiss Indian women.* He watched her sleep another minute or two, old memories pulling at his emotions. "Until they do," he whispered, leaning down and placing a gentle kiss on her forehead.

Chapter 8

With Mrs. Kettler taking the morning off, Tate was left with a little fair-haired shadow that followed him everywhere he went. He had finally put his ledgers aside and let her crawl up on his lap for a story. He didn't have the incredible imagination of Miss Torres, however, and had to rely on the written word.

After several books, he and Nellie looked through the rest of Augusta's dresses to see what else might fit Lalita, all the while acknowledging she might not be with them much longer if the marshal had some knowledge of her or her family. Still, she needed something to wear for the trip to the marshal's office.

Opening a trunk of dresses that Augusta had packed away, he found her smaller sizes. He was flooded with remembrance of the earlier years of their marriage, but there was no real longing for days past. Their life together had never been all that he had hoped.

He hung a couple dresses out on the balcony to air out and had just come back into his bedroom, when Lalita sailed by on her way to the bathroom.

He and Nellie went down to the kitchen and had a hearty breakfast of ham and eggs ready for her in the dining room when she returned. His brows rose at the sight of her in *his* dressing gown.

She slid into a chair at the table across from him. "I hope you don't mind my wearing your robe, Doc. After yesterday's sweaty business, that dress reeked. I don't suppose you have any lady's deodorant around the house, or would that be historically inaccurate?" She scooped up a too-big bite of eggs and washed them down with a swallow of tea. She lowered her voice. "I really need some clean undies, as well." She grinned. "Does Manitou Springs have a Victoria's Secret?"

Tate's surprise had turned into embarrassment, then utter shock, and finally confusion. He counted himself among the enlightened, intelligent men of his time, but one conversation with Lalita had him wondering if he had spent his life thus far with his head in a hole.

With a glance at Nellie, who was offering her doll a cracker, he wondered how best to rein Lalita into the rules of respectable society. The thought that she needed reined in, however, took him back to another time—another woman he'd tried to make fit in to no good end. And yet, there were basic manners that even Nellie understood.

Sitting straight, he gave her a slight smile. "Miss Torres..."

She waved a hand as she skewered a bit of ham with her fork. "Please, Doc, I can't take another minute of this 'Miss Torres' business. Please call me Lalita."

"Lalita," he continued, "while I would never try to suggest that you need to please someone else with your... manners, there are a few society rules that preserve the boundaries of good decorum." He took a deep breath, hearing his own voice raised in anger at a young woman who had been unable to negotiate the often murky waters of social interaction. "If you wish to fit in... what I mean to say... you must try to... to..."

She stared at him fumbling for words and set down her fork. "Okay, I get it. If I'm going to be a part of the show, I need to get into character, but that's why I'm asking about deodorant and underwear and such. So I can do it like you all do it here in 1892—that's what the calendar says in your kitchen, right?"

Tate nodded slowly, more frightened than ever for her mental state. "Yes, the year is 1892. Did you forget that along with your visit to Pikes Peak?"

She grinned. "Yes. Yes, I did."

"You have made quite a change in attitude over the last several days. From wanting to flee to believing me to be a quack doctor—"

"Oh, I'm sorry about that, Doc. You are obviously a real doctor, and that was obviously a real pregnant lady with a real baby coming out of her." She laughed. "A billionaire must be financing this reality show! It doesn't seem like Warren Buffet's style or even Bill Gates, but maybe Steven Spielberg. And you! You're amazing! You never break character even for a second. Makes me wish I'd taken some theatre classes in college."

"Theatre. So you now believe that you are part of some grand production." Tate leaned forward, his forearms on the table. "Tell me, Miss Torres, what does real life look like where you're from?"

She smiled, looking from corner to corner in the room.

Tate turned in his chair, following her gaze but could see nothing out of the ordinary. "What are you looking at?"

She leaned toward him. "Just wondering where the cameras are," she whispered.

Then she sat back, stiffly taking her cup of tea in hand and taking a sip. "Well, Dr. Cavanaugh," she began with a wooden gesture, "the time I come from is very different than yours. For instance, we have—"

"Excuse me, did you say the 'time' you come from?"

She nodded.

"The time. Not the place."

"Well, the place is different, too, since I'm not from around here."

"Where are you from?"

"Missouri. Close to Kansas City."

He leaned in again. "*When* are you from?"

She spread her hands dramatically. "The early 21st century."

Tate just stared.

Lalita nodded. "That's right, man from the 19th century," —she gave an exaggerated wink— "you're looking at a 21st century woman."

Suddenly she pushed back from the table, rose, and struck a pose with one hand in the air and one on her hip. Then she started to sing. "I can bring home the bacon" — she moved her hips a quick left and right— "fry it up in a pan" —she slinked toward him, spinning the cord tie at her waist— "and never ever let you forget you're a man," —she sat right on his lap, throwing her arms around his neck— " 'cause I'm a woman."

Tate was speechless, but Nellie clapped, and Lalita was biting her lip, trying to keep from laughing. She put a hand to the side of her mouth as she whispered, "I don't know how much competition there is for airtime, but that should keep us off the editing room floor."

Tate's heart sank. This beautiful, young woman was absolutely off her chump.

Chapter 9

Lalita had read about woman's Victorian fashions and had studied pictures and museum displays, but it was another thing entirely to put it all on.

Mrs. Kettler had assisted her through the chemise and the corset cinching—which was way more uncomfortable than any underwire bra she'd ever complained about—then the silky corset cover and bustle pad, and finally the dress itself.

Nellie helped her choose one in a lovely shade of lavender from among those Tate had laid out for her. It fit perfectly.

The matching hat was much fancier than the one she had worn the day before, with gathered silk and several plumes in a deep purple. Normally, she loved having shorter, easy-care hair, but today, she wished for long locks to pile up on her head to make the picture complete.

She stepped down the stairs in ivory lace-up boots, hoping that Tate would be there to see her descend, but he was nowhere to be seen. Halfway down, she sent Nellie to find him and went back up to the top.

When Nellie pulled him out of his exam room, Lalita started down again, acting as if the timing were mere coincidence. She sought his eyes, which at first smiled at her, but the closer she got to him, she could see what looked like sadness, and it dawned on her: *I'm wearing his dead wife's clothes.* Then as he extended his elbow to her, she squinted in thought. *But he's merely an actor in this drama. He's a real doctor, but surely the back story is made up.*

Escorting her down the hallway, he grabbed a brown bowler off the standing hat rack by the door before leading her out and down the porch steps. *He should be in movies.*

After a short ride, the doctor stopped the buggy once again at the Pilson's mansion to check on mother and baby. Both seemed to be recovering well from the exhausting delivery of the day before. Lalita was given another opportunity to hold the new little one, and after fifteen minutes, the doctor had to nearly pry her out of Lalita's hands so they could leave.

"You seem rather fond of children," he observed as he helped her up into the buggy.

She sat and tried to get comfortable with corset boning digging into her sides. "I am. I work at a daycare back home."

He started Maisy moving once again with a shake of the reins. "A daycare. I'm going to take a leap and guess that a daycare is a place that takes care of children during the day?"

She nodded, in awe of how he never slipped up in what he should and shouldn't know.

The day was heating up, and Lalita was starting to feel the effects of being cinched tight and covered neck to foot with multiple layers of fabric. She hoped she could make it back to the doctor's house without fainting. Then she noticed they weren't going back the way they came. "Where are we going?"

"I'm taking you to the marshal's office to see if Nonnie has filed a missing persons report."

"Here in Manitou Springs?" She suddenly found taking in a normal-sized breath more difficult.

"Yes, it's not too far."

She felt a trickle of sweat drip down the side of her face and popped the fan out of the drawstring bag Nellie had found in a dresser drawer. "But wouldn't Nonnie have reported it in Colorado Springs," she asked, fanning herself in a way she assumed was lady-like, "since that's where she lives?"

She fanned more vigorously, and the doctor gave her a side-long glance. "Perhaps, but the marshal here can call the marshal there."

"Ah, that's right. There are phones. That way you don't have to take me to Colorado Springs yourself, and shatter the fourth wall of this production." She was whipping the fan through the air but was barely stirring a breeze with the pretty, but mostly useless, device. "I remember now seeing a phone on the wall in your hallway." Her lips were tingling, and she was starting to feel faint, her breath coming in short puffs. "I haven't... studied... telephone history."

The doctor pulled Maisy to a stop. "Are you quite all right, Miss Torres?"

She shook her head, her vision starting to blur. "I believe Mrs. K. overdid it on the corset. I can't... I can't breathe... and I'm so hot."

Throwing an arm around her, he turned her away from him on the seat and began to unbutton her dress close to her waist. She knew she should probably put her head between her knees—if bending were at all possible. She felt the doctor pulling up the corset cover, then finally, loosening the corset ties. Sweet breath returned to her lungs.

As he re-buttoned her dress, she almost lost her breath again thinking about his fingers working their way up her spine. "Thanks, Doc," she managed to squeak out. "I'm not very good at this."

He squeezed her shoulder, and she turned to face forward. "It's quite all right. Women's fashions are ridiculous. I don't know how you stand them."

"I'm beginning to agree. I wanted a day to dress up, Nonnie said an hour, and I don't think I made it thirty minutes. It was easier yesterday without the corset."

The doctor was silent, but fidgety. Finally he spoke. "Miss Torres, I hesitate to correct you, but women don't usually speak of their unmentionables in mixed company."

"I'm sorry," she said quickly, irritated at herself for not realizing that. She had studied the Victorian age at least somewhat. "I'm going to be the first to get kicked off, aren't I?"

"I beg your pardon?"

"Of the show. These reality shows always narrow down the competition somehow." She could feel her head sweating, so she swept the hat off her head and held it on her lap. "So what's the gimmick with this one, or are you allowed to tell me?"

"I'm not sure what 'gimmick' you are referring to, and I promise I won't kick you out until I feel you are ready. My plan today is to see if anyone is looking for you, whether that be your friend Nonnie or..."

She was now using the hat as a fan, which worked much better. "Or who? The only one I know in the area is Nonnie."

The doctor adjusted the reins in his hands and led Maisy into a right turn. "Would Nonnie, by any chance, be a... nurse?"

Lalita laughed. "Now that would be the day. She's too busy feeling sorry for herself. No, she's in a dead-end job with no motivation to better herself."

Although Tate wasn't familiar with the phrase "dead-end job," the meaning was easy enough to grasp. He wondered if the other oddities of her speech would be understandable, as well, to someone from her region.

His forehead furrowed. *That doesn't explain her fimble famble about the 21st century.*

The "or" he had been thinking of that might be searching for her was a psychiatric sanitarium. He prayed that wasn't the case, as many were known for overcrowding and generally deplorable conditions. And Tate didn't agree with the current fads for treating ailments of the mind.

When his own wife had needed treatment for melancholia, he had only trusted his friend and psychiatrist Dr. Jeremiah Fischer, who preferred using hypnotism and relaxation techniques over spinning chairs, electroshock treatments or, heaven forbid, near-drowning therapies.

Lalita interrupted his thoughts. "You've gone all gloomy. I'm still trying to figure out the rules. Is this a made-up scenario, and I should just improvise with you?" She looked up. "Is there a buggy-cam? Or are we free from the cameras out here, and we can be ourselves?"

Tate gave a little laugh. "Please, by all means, be yourself."

She put a hand on his arm. "What about you? Are you being yourself? Are you really sad about something?"

He looked into her dark eyes, returning to solemnity. "Yes, I am." He turned back to look at the street. "I wish I could fix that which I cannot."

There was silence between them for a moment; then Lalita spoke again quietly. "When I feel like that, I try to just focus on something I can fix. It's a broken world with so much sorrow, one can hardly fathom the pain and suffering on this one planet, and fixing it isn't really possible on a global scale. All we have is our little corner of the world. We have to find that which is fixable there."

Tate pulled Maisy to a halt once again and turned to face her, wanting to take advantage of this moment of surprising lucidity. "Lalita, there is no theatre happening here. It really is 1892, and I am a doctor in my own part of this broken world trying to fix the sick and the hurt. I believe that you have had a head injury, and that is making your speech strange and giving you the fantastical idea that you are from a different century. I promise to help you all I can, but if I find someone who can help you more than I, I will have to relinquish you to their care." He placed a hand on her cheek. "And that, Lita, is why I am feeling sad."

Lalita held his gaze, tears forming in her eyes. "Wow," she breathed. "Are they feeding you lines somehow, or do you just make this stuff up?" She wiped her eyes. "If I had an Oscar, I'd give it to you."

Chapter 10

After visiting the marshal's office, where they learned that no one had yet made any inquiries about a missing woman fitting Lalita's description, she had spied a photographer's studio and begged Tate to pose with her. She hung onto his arm and her hat as they crossed the dusty street, and despite Tate's fear for her sanity, he felt something swirling inside he hadn't felt in a long time.

They stood a moment inside before a tall, thin man with a long, thick mustache waxed into two perfect curls emerged from a back room. Tate approached him about the cost of his services while Lalita went to look at his backdrop and furniture possibilities.

The man pointed to a sign with prices but looked at Lalita then down at Tate with disdain. "I don't take photographs of Injuns."

Tate narrowed his eyes and lowered his voice. "And why is that?"

"Injuns killed my grandparents."

Tate glanced at Lalita, who was trying out poses in the various chairs. Taking hold of the photographer's arm, he pulled him as far away from her as he could. "This particular lady—who is obviously not even full Indian—this petite wisp killed your grandparents?"

The man snorted. "I didn't say that."

Tate crossed his arms over his chest. "Then this woman is innocent of the crime."

"Course she is. She wouldn't have been much more than a child." A smug smile was creeping onto Tate's face, but the man went on. "I still ain't taking her picture. It's bad luck."

Tate very nearly turned and walked out, but one look at Lalita's bright eyes as she sat on the white wicker chair, waiting for him, put determination into his negotiations. "I'll pay you twice your usual rate."

"Ten times."

Tate's brows flew up. "Ten times!"

"It's that, or you take your half-breed out of here."

Tate tried staring the man into a more enlightened attitude, but no glimmer of redemption showed in his eyes. He finally retrieved a dollar bill from his wallet and held it out. "You, sir, are no gentleman."

The lanky man took it and smirked. "Never claimed to be."

Tate spun on his heels to join Lalita just as she started toward him, looking concerned. "What's the problem, Doc?"

He waved her back toward the chair, forcing a smile. "Nothing. It's all worked out."

She continued toward him, however, reached up, and took off his hat. "I'm not a fan of the bowler."

He was getting more out of sorts by the minute. "You're not."

She wrinkled her nose and tossed it toward the standing hat rack then tugged him toward the setting she'd created in front of a draped curtain. She sat, and he stood behind her as the photographer took his place behind the camera. "It's new, you know."

She looked back at him over her shoulder—"It looks new"—then faced forward.

"What don't you like about it?"

She adjusted her hat and folded her hands in her lap. "The shape. It makes you look old."

Striking a pose, Tate placed a hand on her shoulder. "Old. The word the salesman used was sophisticated."

She reached her hand over to his. "Please, Doc, don't scowl about the hat. You'll ruin the picture."

Her hand on his did unexpected things to his heart rate, and he pulled away. "Face forward, Miss Torres. I believe our photographer is ready."

Lalita turned and folded her hands on her lap. Tate didn't know what possessed him, but he rested his hand once again on her shoulder.

The photographer lifted the cloth at the back of the camera and poked his head out. "Is that the pose you want? Because you're going to have to hold it for thirty seconds."

"Yes," Lalita blurted out. "Just like this."

Tate knew what they were doing was nothing short of decadent, but it was the best thirty seconds he'd experienced in a long while.

*   *   *

"So I've been noticing that most of the men have these huge mustaches, and you don't have one at all. Why is that?"

Tate had taken her to Cliff House for afternoon tea, and she was drinking in the elegant setting along with her beverage.

Tate set his coffee cup back on the saucer. "They're unhygienic. As a doctor, I simply can't bring myself to grow one."

She closed one eye and held a crooked finger up in the space between them to see what he might look like with his upper lip—and maybe even his whole mouth—covered in hair. "I think that's probably a good call." She lowered her hand and reached for her cup of tea, emboldened by the moment they had shared in the photographer's studio. "I like your lips."

He gave her a lift of his eyebrows, but Lalita could tell he was trying hard not to smile. "And," she went on, thoroughly enjoying the blush that had come to his face, "a mustache just makes these men look old. It's a whole town of old men. Even the young men."

Tate finally gave in to the smile. "So now you know why I wear the bowler." He tilted his head toward the hat setting on the side of the table. "I'm just trying to fit in without growing a mustache."

She leaned forward, "My dear doctor, why would you want to fit in when the good Lord has given you everything you need to stand out?"

She held his gaze, his eyes blinking with what seemed like revelation before simmering with something new. The spell was broken by a waiter carrying a tray of pies. Tate took a cherry piece, but Lalita didn't think pie and her corset would get along.

As he ate, she looked around the room, surprised to be getting an unusual amount of stares. *They shouldn't be staring at a contestant. These extras need to take lessons from Tate; he never breaks character.*

Then she thought of his hand on her shoulder and wondered if that was just part of the script. *Maybe he was told to throw in some sizzle.* She giggled inside. *Well, sizzle for Victorian times.* She took another sip of her tea. *The picture will still make a great souvenir. I hope it turns out.*

She smiled his way, and he smiled back. "Would you like a bite?"

"No, I was just thinking that I can't believe our pictures won't be ready until tomorrow. Yowzers, my generation is spoiled. We can take a picture with our phones and have it on FaceBook or Instagram in a matter of seconds."

Tate didn't respond, his eyes dipping quickly to his pie, and Lalita felt as if something had shifted between them.

"You're suddenly quiet," Lalita mused after taking a sip of tea.

Tate pushed aside his plate that still held a few bites of pie. "I'm trying to decide the best course of action."

She dabbed politely at her lips with a napkin. "For what?"

"For your treatment—to get your memory back."

She squinted in thought. *That is a puzzle. Why can't I remember getting into the show?* "I don't know, but it seems weird that you're concerned about it. I mean, far be it from me to suggest that you don't know how to play your part—you're a master—but shouldn't you just involve me in your world? Like you did yesterday?"

All she got in return was what she was starting to think of as "the Tate stare."

Finally, he blinked and spoke. "I need to drive you to Colorado Springs."

She picked up her fork and helped herself to a bite of his pie. "Why? Won't that kind of ruin everything?"

He pulled his pocket watch out of his vest pocket and clicked it open. "No, I'm hoping it will fix everything. If we leave right now—"

"Doc!"

They both turned to see two men weaving through the tables, heading their way.

Tate rose and put out his hand to the elder, who had piercing blue eyes and sandy hair, sun crinkles at the corners of his eyes. "Mr. Dickson, is there a problem?"

The man nodded, trying to catch his breath. "It's Max. A horse threw him off. William thinks his leg is busted."

Lalita leaned to see William standing behind the two men. He looked to be around eighteen, the spitting image of his father.

Tate dug in his pocket and produced a coin that he laid on the table. "Miss Torres, come. Young Max needs a bone set."

Lalita rose and followed, doing her best to keep up with the long-striding men.

* * *

Lalita wanted to be of help, but she just couldn't in the dress she was wearing. It made her feel as if she should be in a store window. She ran up the stairs to see what else she could find in Augusta's trunk.

Mrs. Kettler was down in the exam room, changing the sheets on the bed, so she nabbed Nellie to unbutton all the buttons going down her back.

Pulling off the dress, she caught a whiff of herself. *Eww. Victorian deodorant evidently sucks.* She picked up a diffuser bottle of perfume off the dressing table and gave herself a few squirts.

It felt so good to be out of all the layers, she went in the adjoining bedroom and lay on the bed in just the chemise, reveling in the breeze from the open window. Nellie crawled up and laid beside her. "What did you do today, kiddo?"

She shrugged. "Played with Arabella."

"Is that your doll?"

Nellie nodded.

"Is that what you do most days?"

She nodded again.

"Hmm, don't you have a bike or something? You should be out enjoying the summer sun." She rolled over to face her.

"Playing a part in this 1890s... thing would be pretty boring after a while. Do you get to leave sometimes and go home?"

Nellie giggled. "This is home."

Lalita looked around and lowered her voice. "Is the doctor really your papa? You can tell me if he's not. Your secret's safe with me."

Nellie turned to face Lalita. "Of course he's my papa!"

Lalita's curiosity was rushing ahead of her brain. "And your mama... died?"

Nellie's brow knitted over sad eyes. "One day she went in the bathroom and didn't come back out. I knocked and knocked. When papa came home, he broke the door to pieces. She fell—"

"Well, here you are, Miss Nell." The two females jumped at the sound of Mrs. Kettler's voice. "I've been searching all over for you."

Nellie scrambled off the bed and stood facing Mrs. Kettler with her hands behind her back.

Lalita rose more slowly. "She's okay, she's with me."

Mrs. Kettler raised an eyebrow at Lalita, leaving her to guess what was running through the woman's mind. She didn't have to guess long.

"It is my understanding, Miss Torres, that you are a patient, not a guest. This room belonged to the doctor's late wife, and I imagine he'd be quite displeased to see you lying around on her bed barely dressed in the middle of the afternoon."

Lalita bit back the retort that was on her tongue. She did, after all, want to stay in the game. "My apologies, Mrs. K. I was just at a loss as to what to wear. I was going to go down to see if the doctor needed any help. Is there something simple I can put on?"

Mrs. Kettler left the room and returned a moment later carrying another dress that looked nearly identical to the one she'd taken off, only in a different color.

"What's simple about that?"

"You won't be wearing a hat."

* * *

"Careful, Dickson, watch the leg." Tate was carrying Max Dickson under the arms while his father, Seth, and brother carried his legs, one of which Tate had confirmed broken before they brought him in. What his father hadn't told him right away was that the tumble from the horse had also rendered the young man unconscious.

They laid the blond-haired boy on the bed, and Tate split the leg of his pants up the side. Swelling had turned his calf into a balloon, and he sent William to the kitchen to chip ice off the block in the ice box.

Tate knew the boy shouldn't have been moved before being thoroughly examined, but since his father and brother had already thrown him in a wagon and jostled him all the way through town, they couldn't do much more harm bringing him on into the house.

Probing the site of the break with his fingers, he was happy that it appeared to be a clean break. He did a quick exam of his head, finding a fair-sized bump on the back. Holding a lantern close to each eye, he found the pupils responsive.

Seth came up on his elbow. "What do you think, Doc?"

Tate stepped back and moved toward the foot of the bed. "His eyes look good, but we'll know more about his head injury when he comes to. As to his leg, we need to control the swelling." He lifted his chin toward the head. "Get behind him and grab him tight. It's time to set this leg."

Taking a firm grip on the ankle, Tate saw Lalita in the doorway just as he was about to pull. "Miss Torres, could you assist William in the kitchen with the ice and wrap it in two towels from the cabinet beside you?" He looked to Seth. "Ready?"

The man nodded, and Tate pulled hard. Max's eyes shot open and the cry from his lips could probably be heard for several blocks.

"Welcome back, Max." Tate felt the break again, and another yell commenced, followed by a string of curses.

Tate smiled. "Good boy, Max! Show us you're alive." He allowed the boy to grip his hand as he fought through the pain.

Lalita returned with the rolled-up towels, and Tate took one from her hands, walking to his head. "Now, Max, there is a lady present, so we must try to control what comes out of our mouths." He gently lifted his head and laid the towel over the pillow. "Miss Torres, the other one goes on the leg."

Going to a locked cabinet, he produced a key and pulled out a blue bottle, then came back to the moaning young man. "And now for a bit of pain relief."

Lalita came to his side. "Where were you with your magic pain medicine when my head was pounding?"

"It's quite addictive, so it's best to use it only when absolutely necessary."

William reappeared while Tate was pouring out a spoonful. "I put what's left of the ice in the ice box, but you'll be needing more."

"Thank you, William, and I imagine Max would thank you, as well, if his every thought wasn't bound up in pain."

"Doc, we hate to run out on you, but we're in the middle of a big saddle order for the cavalry..."

Tate waved a hand. "Go. I still need to splint his leg, and with the head injury, he'll need to be watched for a while. Come back in the morning."

Lalita sat on the bedside stool. "Do you use plaster casts at this point in history?"

Tate scowled at her phrasing. "Yes, but not right away. Some of the swelling needs to go down first. I'm just going to immobilize the leg with splints and wrap it for now."

"Doc," Max groaned, "you must not have given me enough pain medicine. I'm still hurtin' somethin' fierce."

Tate gave his shoulder a pat. "I know, Max, and I'm terribly sorry, but that's the best I can do for now."

While Tate got the splints and bandages ready, Lalita took Max's hand. "It's going to be okay. I've seen the doctor birthing a baby that did not want to come out. He's going to fix you up, too."

Max turned his head to look at her, and he almost smiled. "Are you an angel? You sure are pretty enough to be one."

Lalita blushed, but before she could reply, Tate interrupted. "There. The laudanum is starting to do its work."

Lalita swiveled, her mouth open. "Are you saying this guy needs to be high as a kite to consider me pretty?"

Tate stopped wrapping and looked at her in surprise. *High as a kite.* He chuckled at this particular turn of phrase. "No, I was not saying that at all. I wasn't even insinuating that. It was the declaration, itself, that was a sign of his near delirium."

Lalita still looked hurt.

He resumed wrapping the leg. "Only a fool spouts everything he's thinking, Miss Torres."

She looked back to Max, another Seth Dickson clone, who wasn't quite asleep but was blinking excessively. "What are you thinking, Max?"

He grinned. "I'd like to kiss—"

"Max. Hush." Tate decided it best to get Lalita out of the room before Max embarrassed her further. "Miss Torres, you may want to rest before dinner. It has been another long day for you."

She rose. "Longer for you. I don't need a rest. How can I help?"

As she drew near, Tate got a whiff of a scent that seemed familiar. "Well, I... don't..."

She took a step even closer. "What are *you* thinking, Tate? Or are all your feelings dictated by the script."

The room suddenly felt very small. He tied off the bandage and turned to place his scissors back in their place. "My feelings are my own, Miss—"

"Lita. You called me Lita in the buggy. You jump back and forth between the formal and the... the not. 'Miss Torres' puts distance between us, but 'Lita' pops out when you forget that's required."

Tate glanced over at his new patient, who seemed to have slipped into a more peaceful place, and back to Lita's big, brown, beautiful, imploring eyes. Just like Max, he could see how pretty she was, and thoughts of kissing her easily sprang to his mind. He pushed them aside. "I apologize for using your familiar name. I..." That same scent wafted up to his nose again, and he couldn't explain the anxiety that came over him.

He stepped back. "Could you... please tell Mrs. Kettler that our patient will be needing some broth soon? Then I would appreciate it very much if you could entertain Nellie this evening while I keep an eye on Max."

Lita stared, looking thoughtful. "Sure, Doc." She headed toward the exit but turned back at the door. "I thought I had the plot figured out, but... I'll just follow your lead, shall I?"

Tate acknowledged her words with a small nod and a tight smile, then turned and blew out a breath as she left the room. His emotions were suddenly as mixed up as she was.

Chapter 11

Around midnight, Lalita was awakened by rain on the roof and wondered how Max Dickson was doing in the bed she'd slept in the past several nights. She had been given a guest bedroom across the hall from the one Mrs. Kettler had informed her to be Augusta's.

She pulled on the lightweight robe Mrs. Kettler had found for her among Augusta's things—she'd called it a wrapper— and after having visited the bathroom, which was now right next to hers, she tiptoed downstairs and down the hall to the front of the house and the exam room.

She nearly tripped over Tate dozing in a formal, upholstered, though uncomfortable-looking chair he'd dragged in from the parlor across the hall. She didn't want to turn on the overhead light, so she turned on the small lamp on the table giving a soft glow to the room, and studied the man who she'd like to get to know a whole lot better.

Quietly pulling up a stool, she pondered what Nellie had told her about her mother while they had played dolls and jacks and pick-up-sticks and a number of other boring games—that her mama had died in the bathroom that day. That her papa had turned and carried her quickly to a neighbor's house after breaking down the door. That her mama was buried in her favorite blue dress.

A tear slid down Lalita's cheek as she thought about a little girl losing her mother so young—she knew what that was all about—and about a man losing his wife after only a few years of marriage. She looked over at Max, who couldn't be more than sixteen with a real broken leg, then thought about the baby

delivery that she'd seen with her own eyes. And suddenly she
knew.

This is real.

She had to admit that no one man, or even one whole TV
network, could finance a whole town that functioned in every
way like a real community but set in another time. *It would
take millions–maybe billions—to get this many people to give
up everything modern for some kind of past experiment.* She
sucked in a breath with a new idea. *Unless you're Amish. Then
no one pays you; you just want to live that way.*

She looked around the room, and her eyebrows did a slow
lift as she considered the possibility that Manitou Springs was
like an Amish community, only the folks chose the Victorian
age rather than a more rustic, pioneer way of life. *It's really not
a lot different, except for the electricity and the extravagance.*
She looked back at her dashing doctor. *A simpler time but with
perks.* She smiled, feeling confident that she had finally put the
puzzle together.

Max groaned in his sleep, but the doctor didn't so much
as twitch. Lalita rose to get a new towel from the cupboard
to wrap around more ice. On the shelf next to the towels was
the pair of red long johns that Tate had insisted she had been
wearing when she had been given over to his care. She took
them off the shelf and let them unfold as she held them out in
front of her.

As she stared, she had a memory of Nonnie holding two
blankets as Lalita crossed a space crowded with clothing,
jackknives, mugs, jewelry, and a rack of 3D post cards. She
remembered holding up the red union suit while Nonnie
laughed as she read the butt. Then she remembered looking at
a selfie she'd just taken of the two of them. They were wrapped
in the blankets, but red fabric was clearly seen at her chest. And
behind them was a sign that read "Summit Pikes Peak."

Lalita sucked in a breath, stumbling backwards. She ran
into the arm of Tate's chair and sat down hard on his lap. Tate
jumped up gasping, sending her to the floor with a thump, and
Max sat up straight in bed, then howled in pain. Tate blinked
and stepped toward his patient, treading on Lalita's fingers. She
cried out, sending Tate jumping sideways, his hand brushing

the lamp, and he yelled out with the burn as Lalita scrambled to her feet. "Tate, I'm sorry! Are you hurt?"

She reached for his hand, and Tate finally seemed to come fully awake. "Lita, what are you doing here, and why were you on the floor?"

Max had laid back down and seemed to be asleep, so she pulled Tate's hand toward the glow of the light. A red, shiny spot was already forming on the back of his hand. "I... I fell when I came down to check on you and Max. I thought maybe you needed me to watch him for a while. Do you have anything for burns?" She shook her head. "Of course you have something for burns, being a doctor and all."

Tate was just staring at their hands.

"Right, Doc? Something for burns?"

He looked to the medicine cabinet across the room. "Yes." He started toward it but didn't pull his hand out of her grasp. Instead he wrapped his fingers around hers and pulled her along with him.

Opening the cupboard, he pulled out a jar of salve. Lalita released him to open the jar, and swiping a bit out with her finger, she took hold of his hand again. Before she put the cream on the burn, however, she hesitated. "There's an old remedy I remember my mom using," she whispered without looking at him. Then she lifted his hand to her lips and laid a gentle kiss there.

She heard Tate take in a breath, and she looked quickly to his eyes. "I'm sorry. Did I hurt you?"

He merely shook his head.

She rubbed the salve over his hand, wrapped it with gauze, and reluctantly turned him loose.

Suddenly feeling awkward, she turned to go, but he put a hand to her shoulder. "Lita, I think I hurt you as well." He give her a sheepish smile. "What part of you did I step on?"

She lifted her hand and wiggled her fingers. "They're okay, though. Nothing broken."

He raised an eyebrow. "I think the doctor should have a look."

While he inspected and bent every digit, she told him what she remembered. "I *was* on Pikes Peak. I remembered at least some of it. Nonnie was there with me, and that's where I got the long underwear—in a shop at the summit. I bought them because I was cold."

Tate laughed. "That's wonderful! I had hoped that your memory would return in time. And now maybe you'll... well maybe some other things will become clearer as well."

She knew what he meant. "Yeah," she began quietly, "I realize that this whole town couldn't be part of a reality TV show. You are all living very real lives full of very real, and sometimes very painful, events."

Tate's smile grew. Then he looked down at her hand. "Nothing broken."

He stared so long, she wondered what he was thinking. "Doc?"

Max groaned behind them, and Tate let go of her hand to move to his side. "I think Max could use some new ice. Lalita could you—"

He stopped abruptly mid-sentence as Lalita gave him a pinch on the butt as she headed for the kitchen. "I'm on it, Doc."

Chapter 12

Tate should have been dragging the next day, but for some reason he had a spring in his step. He attributed it to a cooler morning, even though his mind kept returning to the middle of the night with Lita's hand in his and her lips pressing so lightly to his skin. He shook his head as he climbed into his buggy, trying to dislodge the memories, but they refused to give up their purchase. *It's been over a year since Augusta died. You're just feeling...*

The problem was, Tate didn't know what he was feeling. He had no right to feel anything at all toward the confusing female under his roof and in his care, even though he knew he had very nearly kissed her hand. He tried to deny it, but her sweet kiss had buoyed his spirit through his early morning calls, despite his inner admonitions.

As Maisy trotted briskly toward home, he wondered that he could be attracted to someone else so out of touch with societal standards. Someone who seemed as if she came from a far-off country. *Wasn't once enough for you?*

He had to concede that Lalita was more complicated than that. She wasn't socially reserved as his late wife had been. On the contrary, she had an out-going, exuberant nature that charged forward rather than hang back. And her assistance with Mrs. Pilson had shown him that she was tougher and had more endurance than most women.

He chuckled, however, recalling her near-fainting expression in the buggy the next day. *It wasn't the blood of childbirth that nearly took her down for the count but the corset.* His hands tingled, reliving their slide up her back to loosen the ties. Though she seemed to be a somewhat unconventional woman, she was obviously a woman.

He slipped one of the portrait prints he'd picked up from the photographer out of his breast pocket and looked at it again. His gaze traveled up her figure to her lovely face, her Indian heritage giving her just a touch of an exotic look. He found her beautiful, but he knew others would not. Some would only see a race of people they hate whether from personal loss or the fear stirred up by newspapers, dime novels, and wild west shows. He knew all too well about the fear that caused ordinary good people to do the unthinkable.

His eyes drifted to his hand on her shoulder, and he felt so many things at once, he couldn't begin to sort it all out. He stuck it back in his pocket. *I must warn her not to show it to anyone.*

As he approached his home, he saw the Dickson wagon parked out front. Pulling into the carriage house, he left Maisy and the buggy in Harold's hands and strode to his back door. He was met by Seth Dickson coming out. "Doc, Max seems improved." He stuck out his hand, and Tate shook it. "Thank you."

"Yes, the swelling reduced somewhat overnight, and he seems more himself." He continued toward the house with Seth by his side. "I had a few calls to make this morning, but I left him in the capable hands of Mrs. Kettler and—"

"And the prettiest little squaw I've ever seen." The man was grinning. "I was wondering if you got yourself a new woman, but Max says she's just your new nurse. If I were a younger man..."

Tate stopped before reaching the back steps. There were so many things wrong in that sentence, Tate hardly knew where to begin. He lowered his voice and started at the beginning. "Mr. Dickson, the term 'squaw' is not welcome in my house."

Dickson looked offended, but Tate pressed on, a mix of emotions wringing anger out of him faster than it should. "Second, Miss Torres isn't just a woman, she's a lady, and as such, should be treated as one." He remembered the pinch he'd received on his posterior by her hand, but he had explained the inappropriateness of that at the time—never mind her non-repentant grin.

"And third, while she has been an able and willing assistant the last few days, she is, herself, still my patient."

Dickson's expression transformed into surprised recognition. "Is she the one they brought down off the mountain? Martin Hill said by the time they brought her to you, she was as soaked as a drowned rat."

Tate sighed. *The grapevine of a small town...* "She was."

Dickson smiled again. "She don't look like a drowned rat now. She's mighty—" The back door opened, and Lalita appeared with a water bucket in hand.

"Mighty helpful," Tate threw in, taking the bucket full of water from her hand.

She smiled. "Why thanks, Doc. I gave Max a bit of a sponge bath." She gave a nod. "Good day, Mr. Dickson."

She turned and closed the door behind her as Tate moved to pour the water on a rosebush. When he turned back, Dickson was still staring at the door. "Mr. Dickson," he said, setting the bucket on the steps, "please do remember that you are *not* a younger man."

* * *

Lalita paced the parlor, waiting for Tate to finish up his conversation with Mr. Dickson. She thought Max was a sweet young man, but his father gave her the creeps.

Just seeing Tate had sent butterflies winging through her belly. She had relived his hand holding hers so many times she had lost count. She was sure if Max hadn't woke up, Tate would have kissed her the same way she had kissed him. Her mind had been a torrent of activity since waking, wondering if he'd be open to at least visit the modern world outside Manitou Springs. *Maybe once he sees all the medical advances, he'll realize how silly it is to not take advantage of them.*

She knew she was getting ahead of herself— *He just held my hand, for Pete's sake* —but she couldn't help hoping that he wanted to kiss her the way she wanted to kiss him.

When he finally came into the house, she heard him discussing something with Mrs. Kettler in the kitchen. *Rats! Mrs. K.! He'll never be real with me as long as she's here.* She sat on the upholstered tapestry settee, nervously chewing a nail.

66

Nellie came into the room carrying the pick-up-sticks, and Lalita let out a groan. "Nellie, we have to find something more interesting to do today."

Nellie stopped, looking puzzled. "What?"

"I don't know, but I'm seriously having video game withdrawal. It has to be something good. Come up here, and let's brainstorm." She patted the spot beside her.

Nellie approached the settee but didn't climb up next to her. "Mrs. Kettler says I'm not allowed on the good furniture, and I don't know how to brainstorm." She put a hand to her head. "Does it hurt?"

Lalita laughed. "Well, not usually!" She pulled her up beside her. "Let me take care of Mrs. K. Now, all brainstorming means is to throw out ideas, no matter how silly or impossible they sound. For instance, my idea is bicycling."

"Papa has a bicycle, I think, but he hasn't ridden it for a long time."

Lalita's eyes popped wide. "So that's a possibility then."

Nellie's lips quirked to the side. "I never saw Mama riding. There may not be any dresses that are split."

Lalita mulled that over, really wanting to get out and get some exercise, but knowing that she could never ride in what she currently had on without hiking it up above her knees. Then she remembered something. "Nellie, didn't I see a sewing machine in your mama's room?"

Nellie's eyes lit up. "Yes!"

Tate entered the room, and Lalita put a finger to her lips.

He stopped, smiling down at them with his fists on his hips. "So what are you two up to?"

His eyes lingered on Lalita's, and she felt that flutter again, sure that she was turning red.

Nellie jumped up and stood on his feet, taking hold of his wrists. "Papa, Lalita and I have been brain... twisting."

Lalita laughed at Tate's bewildered expression. "Not brain*twisting.* Brain*storming.*"

His puzzlement only deepened.

"You know, throwing around a lot of suggestions, no matter how nonsensical, to break through old, overused ideas into something fresh."

"Brainstorming." He chuckled, taking Nellie's hands as she leaned back as far as she could. "Where do you come up with these things?"

"She probably brainstorms them, Papa!"

Tate laughed again, and Lalita couldn't help seeing the fun right before her. She stood up. "Nellie, do a little brainstorming right now. What could you do starting right where you're at on your papa's shoes and holding his hands that would be fun."

"We could dance," Nellie proclaimed, looking back at Lalita over her shoulder.

"Have you done that before?"

"Lots of times."

Lalita made a sound like a buzzer. "Wrong answer. Think again."

Nellie closed her eyes tight. "Papa could pull me up into the air and catch me."

"Has he done that before?"

Nellie stood still a moment before she opened her eyes and frowned. "Yes."

Lalita made the buzzer sound again. "Keep thinking."

Tate was fascinated with this concept of "brainstorming" and reluctantly amazed that another of Lalita's odd phrases had actually turned out to be more than mere nonsense. He looked down at Nellie's determined face, wondering how long he'd have to stand there, when to his surprise, she walked up his legs and flipped, releasing his hands as she did so.

Mrs. Kettler gave a gasp in the doorway.

Nellie jumped up and down. "I did it! That was new, wasn't it, Papa!"

Tate smiled down at her. "It certainly was, Miss Nell, but—"

She bounced over to Lalita. "Did you see me?"

Lalita grinned. "I sure did! That was awesome!"

Mrs. Kettler harrumphed from her side of the room. "Hardly ladylike behavior, Nellie. I'm sure your papa would agree that you are not to do that again. Little girls need to keep their feet—"

"Little girls need something more fun to do than pick-up-sticks. She's only five." Lalita stepped toward her. "She'll have lots and lots of years to be stuffed into the confines of your society. For heaven's sake, let her have some fun while she can."

Mrs. Kettler looked to Tate, her chin lifted in expectation. Lalita gave him a look that was much the same, and he realized that both women were expecting him to join their position. He licked his lips. He hadn't really decided how he felt about it himself yet. His initial reaction was to side with Mrs. Kettler, who had a narrow and strict set of rules for lady-like behavior, but he knew those same rules had vexed his late wife to the point of despondency.

He looked down to his daughter's shining eyes. "Miss Nell, I think your new idea was a marvel to behold," —he glanced up to see Lalita's satisfied smile— "however, we can only do it right here when it's just you and me and Miss Torres. Showing your bloomers would not be suitable for company." He shot a look at Mrs. Kettler, who nodded curtly and turned to leave the room.

"Breakfast is ready, Dr. Cavanaugh," she threw back over her shoulder.

He smiled at Lalita. "After you."

She gave him a lop-sided smirk as she moved ahead of him toward the door. "You know," she said looking back over her shoulder, "you missed your calling. You should have been a diplomat."

He pulled Nellie along toward the dining room with a thin smile, knowing that any diplomacy skills he might now employ had been forged in the fires of grief and self-castigation.

* * *

Tate was in a quandary. This being Sunday, he would normally take Nellie to church, but he had two patients in the house of different genders, both single. Propriety would state that they should not be alone in the same house, despite the fact that one of them was immobile.

Lalita, however, had recovered much of her memory, so perhaps she was moving out of the patient category, but that created other problems. If she was no longer a patient then *he* shouldn't be alone with her either. He leaned back in his desk chair in the study. *But where else would she go?*

Mrs. Kettler had offered her services as chaperone, but Tate couldn't stand the idea of having her hanging about all evening and all night as well. He locked his hands behind his head. *We don't need a chaperone.* He remembered how close he had come to kissing her hand and blew out an ill-tempered breath as his forearms came to his desk.

His thoughts were interrupted by Lalita's appearance at the door. "Doc, Mrs. Kettler just asked me if I'd like to accompany her family to church, but... I'd rather go with you and Nellie. If you're going, that is."

Tate couldn't stop the smile that spread over his face at the suggestion that she would prefer his company. He rose, stumbling over his words. "I was just wondering... well, there's the issue of Max, you see, and I couldn't figure out—"

"I'd be glad to stay with him while you go," she volunteered.

He came around the desk. "There are certain difficulties with that. I should probably stay here."

The disappointment on her face warmed him more than it should.

She had just turned to leave his study, however, when there were unexpected voices in the house. He passed Lalita in the dining room and moved on into the front hall to find Mrs. Kettler admitting William Dickson.

Tate walked down the hall and threw out his hand to Max's older brother. "William, how goes the saddle business?"

"Pretty busy, I guess."

"Did you come to see Max?"

"Pa thought I should come sit with him this morning so you all could go to church."

William looked a bit nervously past Tate's shoulder, and Tate glanced behind him to see Lalita there. He smiled. *Do they all have eyes for her?* "Thank you, William, I'd appreciate that very much. Max is feeling better, so you two can sing a few hymns before you pull out the checkerboard."

William let out a smirk as Tate threw an arm around his shoulder and opened the door to the exam room.

*   *   *

Lalita inhaled the fresh mountain air, glad that she was riding to church with Tate and Nellie instead of Mrs. Kettler and her family. "What church do you go to?"

"There's not much choice yet. We go to the Congregational Church."

"What's it like? Are there very many people?"

Tate laughed. "It's not big enough to hold very many people."

As she gazed at the mountains, church bells rang out through the valley, and Lalita was entranced. "Oh, Tate, it's beautiful!"

Tate drove toward the bells and soon stopped in front of a small stone structure. The double doors were topped by a pointed arch window, and three tall slim windows featured stained glass to their right. It was a historian's dream.

Tate lifted Nellie out of the buggy, then offered his hand to Lalita. She felt a tingle as he touched her, but when she looked to his face, he looked all too serious. She stepped down. "What's the matter?"

"You don't have gloves. I completely forgot."

"Gloves? Surely not in July!" She looked around at the ladies walking toward the church and saw that Tate was right. Every woman had gloves on.

She looked to Tate anxiously as they moved forward. "Will they still let me in?"

His expression was still stern, and he lowered his voice as they approached the steps. "If they don't, the Reverend and I will be having words."

For the sake of clothes that fit her better, she had opted to wear the corset again, but as soon as she walked into the stuffy building, she regretted it. She adjusted the blue straw hat with its own bouquet of flowers that matched her skirt and shirtwaist, hoping someone would crack a window.

Tate walked them quickly to a pew on the right side and stood as she and Nellie slid in first. She knew that everyone in this tiny congregation was well acquainted with Tate, and she knew they'd be dying of curiosity about the woman sitting on the other side of his daughter in his wife's old clothes. She hoped that no one actually remembered his wife's old clothes. With that thought she was immediately aghast and wondered what had possessed her to leave the house. She looked Tate's direction, but he was looking to the front where a large pipe organ was playing.

"Good to see you again, Miss Torres."

Lalita jumped with the whisper that was so close to her ear, she felt the heat of it. Turning, she saw Seth Dickson sit back in his seat with a wink. She almost didn't recognize him with his hair slicked down and dressed in his Sunday best, but those piercing blue eyes were unmistakable. Lalita blinked and turned back, glancing again at Tate, who was oblivious to Mr. Dickson's attentions.

After stumbling through several hymns she didn't recognize, the song leader bid them sing "A Mighty Fortress Is Our God," and she sang out loud and clear, giving Tate a smile when he looked her way.

The sermon, delivered by a dark-haired minister as clean-shaven as Tate, was dry as the Sahara, and with the heat, she started to get drowsy. The corset wouldn't let her slump, but her eyes started to drift closed. All at once she felt a poke to her elbow, and she startled awake just in time to hear "Amen."

She looked out of the corner of her eye to see Tate's arm draped around Nellie, who was leaning against him.

Feigning an itch on her arm, she kept her hand there, just a hair away from his. Like a magnet, his fingers brushed hers before he pulled his hand back and set it to the task of flipping through the hymnal for the final song. She smiled.

Four long verses later, the threesome was moving to the back of the church. The minister had made a hasty departure down the aisle and out, and Lalita guessed that he was probably as eager for some fresh air as the rest of them. Lalita couldn't wait to get out in the breeze, but just as they were about to reach the doors, she felt a hand on her arm pulling her to the side.

Pulled off balance she stumbled sideways, watching Tate and Nellie heading out without her. She looked to the one who waylaid her, already suspecting whose hand was still wrapped around her arm. Seth Dickson grinned down at her, his blue eyes shining.

"I say, Miss Torres, you're looking prettier than a picture this morning."

Lalita swallowed. "Mr. Dickson, if you'll excuse me, my ride is leaving." She pulled her arm from his grip.

He put his bowler on his head. "Aw, the doc won't leave you. You can talk a minute with me."

The crowd had mostly gone out the door, and Lalita turned to follow. "I'm sorry, but—"

Dickson caught her arm again. "Now hold on, there's no reason to be afraid. I don't hold any grudges against your people." He grinned again. "Especially when they're as fine as you."

Lalita's brows knit together as she tried without success to pull away again. "My people?" Her volume was rising. "What are you talking about?"

"Seth, I don't believe the lady appreciates your attention." Lalita looked to the door, so relieved to see Tate striding toward them.

Seth let loose of her arm and backed up a step. "Now, Doc, you said she wasn't your woman, and I don't mind if she's a bit addled."

Lalita's jaw dropped. "I am not addled, you over-bearing asshat!"

Tate's eyes grew wide as he tried to move her toward the door. "Lita, this is a church."

Dickson just grinned as he followed them out of the building and down the steps. "She's got spunk. That comes from the Injuns."

Tate spun on the bottom step, fire in his eyes. "Dickson, you've said enough today."

Lalita took hold of his sleeve and pulled him down to the ground, trying to keep him moving toward the buggy. The minister, who was talking to a couple along their route was blissfully unaware of the volatile situation just a few feet away.

"Come on, Doc." Dickson followed, seemingly unable to stop talking. "My wife's been gone longer than yours. Most men here won't give this girl the time of day, being a squaw, but I don't—"

Lalita saw it coming but couldn't stop it. Tate turned and swung. Dickson dodged but took his own swing. Tate ducked as the minister finally clued in to what was happening on his church lawn and moved to break it up. For his trouble, he got a fist in the jaw.

And Lalita really, really wished it hadn't been Tate's.

Chapter 13

Lalita fixed another towel with ice, but instead of taking it to Max in the exam room, she took it to Tate, who was sitting in the parlor. She stood in front of him, and he held out his hand while she wrapped the towel around his knuckles. She noticed the red spot that still lingered on the back of his other hand.

She sat beside him. "I think I'm bad for your health."

Tate shook his head. "I shouldn't have let him goad me."

"He totally deserved the punch you intended to give him. What an ass—"

"Lita, please watch your language. Nellie's in the house somewhere, and she doesn't need to witness any more bad behavior."

She sat quiet a moment. "You're too tough on yourself."

"I've worked hard to become a respected doctor here, Lita. That didn't happen by brawling on the church lawn."

"Of course not, and those who know you will not give it a second thought."

He gave her a side-long glance with eye-brows raised.

"I didn't say they wouldn't discuss it. This is a small town. The fact that you punched the preacher will be all over it by mid-afternoon, but I'm betting most folks will give you the benefit of the doubt and believe that you must have had a very good reason for throwing a punch on the church lawn not ten minutes past the service."

Tate didn't look reassured. " 'The benefit of the doubt' is something I've found lacking in the general population."

She took hold of his hand on the pretense of adjusting the ice-filled towel. "Well, anyway, I appreciate what you did, and the fact that you may suffer for it gives it even more meaning."

She caressed his fingers with her own, and Tate stared at their hands before slowly pulling away and rising. "I should check on Max."

Lalita looked up at him, her disappointment evident. "Yeah, I suppose you should." She jumped up and hurried past him. "I'll see what I can find in the kitchen to have for lunch."

Tate called after her down the hall. "Mrs. Kettler makes extra on Saturdays, so there should be something in the icebox."

He watched her walk away, her bustle swinging with her obvious irritation. He closed his eyes, his right hand clenched around the ends of the towel. His attraction to Lalita was hard enough to keep under control without having to deal with her forward ways. Every time she caressed him with those tender touches, he couldn't think straight. *Except it was me that touched her in church.*

He walked across the hall to the examination room. As much as he'd like to blame his behavior on Lalita, he knew that Seth Dickson's use of the word 'squaw' had touched on a personal bugbear that always sparked his temper. *Always will.*

He examined Max's leg while Max told him how he'd spent the morning with his brother. "We played a few games of checkers; then he read to me from a new book, *Treasure Island.*" He waved a hand toward the side table. "He left it for me to read on my own."

"Ah, that's a good one." Tate pulled his split pant leg back over his wrapped leg.

"So how does it look, Doc?"

"Good. The swelling has gone down considerably, so I should be able to cast it in a day or two, and you can go home."

Max almost looked disappointed. Now that Tate had dealt with his father on a more personal level, he thought he might know why. He patted his shoulder. "I imagine you're sick of this bed. Would you like to join us in the dining room for a meal?"

Max grinned from ear to ear.

* * *

Treasure Island had been the topic of conversation over the dinner table, with Lalita throwing in insights not only about the book, but Robert Louis Stevenson himself. Tate was impressed with her literary knowledge and amazed that her Missouri university had such in-depth information about the author.

After everyone had finished their meal and eaten a piece of Mrs. Kettler's lemon cake, Lalita offered to read, so they all trooped into the examination room, and Tate brought in chairs from the dining room. Lalita helped Max get situated in the bed once again, which seemed to please him to no end. Sitting and pulling Nellie onto his lap, Tate wondered what Max would think of his own father's interest in his "angel" nurse.

As Lalita dove into the story, Tate couldn't help smiling. He had never experienced a reading like hers. Full of animation and employing different voices for the characters, she made the experience almost like watching a play. When her voice grew tired, he had tried to take over, although he knew he didn't come close to her talent.

When he started to grow hoarse, even Max had taken a turn, although he stumbled over the words. Frustrated, he handed the book back to Lalita. "I'll just ruin the story. Can you read any more?"

She tried, but Tate could hear the wear in her voice and suggested they stop for the day.

Nellie ran upstairs to find her doll, and Lalita rose to lay the book back on the side table. "Thanks for sharing your book with us today, Max."

He grinned. "No, thank you for reading. You are… wonderful."

Tate smiled as he picked up a chair to take back to the dining room. *I'm afraid Max is smitten.* He walked down the hall feeling almost smitten himself, and for a moment, he allowed himself to feel pride in the punches he'd thrown to defend her honor.

Lalita appeared after him with the other chair and put it in place. He was surprised when she gave him but a small smile and turned to go.

"Lita, Max isn't the only admirer of your talents. You keep surprising me with your skills."

She gave him a half smile. "Thanks." She turned to leave again. "I guess I better go wash the dishes."

Tate was bemused by her short response. "Lita? Did I say something wrong?"

She stopped a moment before turning back, her expression bordering on peeved. "I'm just trying to figure you out. You seem to run hot and cold. Sometimes I think you really... like me, and sometimes you pull away. You have me baffled, Doc."

He took a step toward her, trying to formulate an explanation. "I do like you, Lita. You're good with Nellie, good with patients, a talented reader..."

Her expression didn't change. "Tate, stop talking like an old man. I'm not a kid you need to build self-esteem in. You can't be too much older than me." She stepped close. "I'm talking about attraction. Attraction between a man and a woman."

He swallowed. "It's not proper... we're alone in the house... you are still my patient," he stammered.

"Am I still your patient?" She searched his eyes. "I swear you nearly kissed my hand last night. And we're not alone; Max is just down the hall."

Tate looked down into her bright eyes. "I admit, you do seem quite a bit better, but I probably need another day... or two to" —she stepped closer still—"observe you."

"Observe me, how?"

His eyes slipped to her lips, and he took a step back.

She followed and reached out to take hold of the ends of his fingers. "I feel fine."

Being a doctor, Tate noticed things like rapid breathing and sudden sweating. He usually observed it in his patients, however, and not in his own person. "Lita, it's not prop—"

She pulled his hands around her, and he found himself touching her lower back. She slid hers up his chest and rested them on his shoulders. "I've never been too concerned with what's proper, Tate. I know you want to kiss me. Just do it."

He couldn't keep himself from leaning toward her. "Aren't you worried about your—"

"No," Lalita whispered, letting her hands slide to the back of his neck.

Tate hadn't felt such wanting in years, and though her lips had grown silent, they called to him like a siren. He allowed his head to bend forward, his lips so close to hers, he felt her breath.

Then the doorbell rang.

* * *

Lalita knew she shouldn't be eavesdropping, but she was, after all, the whole reason for the minister's visit. Reverend Niemeyer said he had just come from Seth Dickson's place, and now he wanted to hear Tate's side of the morning's "disagreement." She wouldn't miss that for the world.

Holding the tray of lemonade on one hand, she knocked on Tate's study door. There was a moment of silence before she heard Tate's, "Come in."

Opening the door with a smile, Lalita brought the tray into the room and slid it onto the desk. "I thought you two might like a bit of refreshment."

Both men stood as she entered, and the reverend thanked her warmly, although Tate looked a mess. His face was red, and he'd obviously run his hand through his hair a few times, leaving it sticking up in a few places. When the reverend turned his attention back to Tate, she tried to catch his eye, smoothing her hair, but he seemed to be avoiding looking at her.

"Well," she announced, "I guess the dishes aren't going to wash themselves." She stood a moment, bouncing on her toes before turning with a sigh and heading toward the door.

She was almost there when the minister turned. "Miss Torres, maybe you should join us, as this seems to involve you."

She turned and looked to Tate, who looked like he was about to have a heart attack. She smiled at the minister. "I'll just pull in another chair."

After they were all settled, the reverend asked her to relate what had happened between her and Seth Dickson before Tate had gone back in the church to find her. She detailed his advances and emphasized how grateful she was for Tate's assistance.

"So am I to understand, Miss Torres, that you would not be open to having Mr. Dickson court you?"

"Nope. I don't even live here. As soon as I can, I'll be heading back to Kansas City to finish my degree. This has been a really interesting experience, but I'm not sure I could do it for the rest of my life."

Niemeyer squinted, blinking, "Do what, Miss Torres?"

"Live here in your quaint, historic, little Manitou Springs."

The reverend gave her a tight smile. "I imagine it is a might smaller than Kansas City, but we do have something that Kansas City does not have." He turned in his chair, gesturing to the window and the mountain view.

"You're absolutely right about that Reverend." She looked to Tate while the minister was gazing out the window. "There are a few other things I'd regret leaving as well."

Tate's chest rose under his white collarless shirt.

"But," she went on as Niemeyer brought his attention back from the window, "Seth Dickson is not one of them."

He nodded. "I understand." He looked to Tate. "Doctor, would you be agreeable to meeting with Dickson to work out the animosity between you two?"

Tate shook his head. "I'd hardly say there's 'animosity.' "

The reverend rubbed his chin. "It certainly felt like animosity."

"Again, I apologize, Reverend. Miss Torres, will you please get the man some ice?"

Niemeyer waved a hand at Lalita as she started to stand. "That won't be necessary, but thank you for the offer." He grew serious. "I can't have this kind of conflict in my congregation. I really think you should talk—"

"I don't think there's anything to talk about, Reverend. He and I have different ideas about... " His eyes flicked to Lalita and back again. "About certain things. I don't believe that will change with a 'talk.' "

"I understand you have Max here with a broken leg. Will you be able to deal with Dickson over your fees?"

Tate nodded tightly. "I believe so."

The minister paused and seemed to be holding something back. Finally, he gave Lalita a small smile. "If you wouldn't mind, Miss Torres, I have something I'd like to discuss with the doctor of a more personal nature."

"Oh, certainly." Lalita rose and let herself out. She did not go far, however. She put her ear to the edge of the door.

"Doctor, surely you realize that you shouldn't have Miss Torres in the house alone with you."

"We're hardly alone. Nellie's here, and so is Max, or are you implying that I'd act indecently in front of my daughter or a patient?"

"Of course not, but you must realize how it will look to the community."

"The community can mind its own business. Miss Torres is a patient."

"She seemed quite well to me."

"She still has some memory loss."

Lalita didn't need to hear more. She moved swiftly to the dining room cabinet and pulled out the silver tea set. Then she dropped it with a loud clang. It was only a moment before Tate's study door was thrown open. Lalita quickly put one hand to the table and the other to her head, her eyes closed tight.

Tate was at her side in an instant. "Lal—Miss Torres, are you all right?"

She opened her eyes to see a concerned minister in front of her before clamping them shut again. "You'd been in that room for so long, I wanted to make you some tea. I... I got dizzy." She fluttered her eyes open again.

The minister gave a slow lift of his chin. "You just left us, Miss Torres. Surely you remember bringing us lemonade."

Lalita blinked. "Did I?" She looked to Tate. "I guess I'm still having some memory problems, Doc. I hope I didn't damage the tea set."

His eyes narrowed almost imperceptibly. "No harm done." He put an arm around her, guiding her toward the door. "I think you should lie down."

She nodded with a hand to her head.

The minister moved out of the room ahead of them and started down the hall. "I'll let you take care of your patients, doctor. I can see my way out." He pulled his hat from the standing rack and turned back at the door. "I'll be in touch."

Tate nodded, holding up Lalita, who had slumped against his side, but as soon as the door closed, he looked down at her, his expression a mixture of admiration and unbelief. Even biting her lip, she couldn't stop a smile.

He slowly released her and stepped away as she straightened. "You would lie to a minister."

"You needed me to be a patient. I convinced him I still was one."

He shook his head, his jaw going slack.

She put her hands on her hips. "Well, what would you have done? Do you want me to stay with someone else when I can only stay a few more days anyway?"

Tate watched her devilry turn into defiance. Then when he didn't answer, into sadness. He reached out a hand to her cheek. "No, I don't want you to stay somewhere else. I... I enjoy your company."

With her eyes smiling into his, he stepped toward her and pulled her to his chest. It wasn't allowed—wasn't at all proper for him to be holding her—but nothing in his life had ever felt this right. He had to concede, he didn't know what he would have done had the minister pushed his point. Socking him in the jaw by accident was nothing compared to defying his authority over his flock.

"Why can you only stay a few more days? You haven't found your friend yet."

She pulled back to look at him. "I have a job I need to get back to, and my classes start in just a few weeks."

He released her and stepped back, sliding his hands into his trouser pockets. "Ah, I see. And do you have a plan for getting home?"

Her eyes registered his withdrawal. "You have a train depot, right? I know I'd have to borrow some money for a ticket, but I promise I'll mail you a check when I get home."

"As you wish."

He turned, and Lalita caught his arm. "Tate, it doesn't have to be goodbye—at least not forever. We can write letters... trade visits, and if I can figure out how your phone system hooks up with the rest of the world, we can call."

Nellie appeared on the stairs, and he knew the rest of this conversation would have to wait. "Of course." He gave Lalita a weary smile. "I think I'll lie down before dinner. If you don't require rest, perhaps you can entertain Nellie for a while."

Lalita smiled and reached for the little girl's hand. "It would be my pleasure, Doc."

*   *   *

Tate spent most of the evening in his study. He needed to think, and he needed to be out of Lalita's presence to do it clearly.

He could not deny the attraction he felt for her, but he owed it to his daughter to think everything through carefully before he made decisions he might regret.

He rose from his desk and went to stand at the window, gazing at the bright half-moon. Since Augusta died, he'd never been attracted to another woman. He'd never thought about marrying again, and probably wouldn't be thinking about it now, but he felt the press of time. He turned to stare at his bookcase, not seeing it at all. *She's leaving.*

He hadn't expected the panic that thought put in his heart, but he also felt panic at the thought of watching her rejected by the society matrons of the town. *She's far too spirited. They'll never accept her.* And even though, at one time, he had tried to push a woman into society's mold, he would never do it again.

He sat on the edge of his desk, trying to separate his emotions from rational thought. She had the qualities that most men look for—beauty, intelligence, mothering skills—but Tate knew she had something more. "She's confident, bold," —he shook his head, thinking of the embrace she had created for herself out of his arms— "but far too forward."

Her pursuit of him, however, was exciting. Something that could not be said of his marriage, and after Augusta's lack of affection, he found that he appreciated being... appreciated. *Lita's different. A new kind of woman.* He rubbed a hand around his jaw, mumbling under his breath, "And she thinks nothing of creating a fabrication in front of a minister."

He pushed off his desk and paced, thinking about his position in the community and how Lalita would affect it. *Have the attitudes shifted enough that a woman with Indian ancestors would have a place here?* He'd been aware of the stares when they'd been dining at Cliff House. He had ignored them for her sake. *"My dear doctor, why would you want to fit in when the good Lord has given you everything you need to stand out?"*

A knock on the door interrupted his thoughts. "Tate, Nellie wants you to tuck her in."

Tate huffed out a breath and tugged on the hem of his waistcoat, before pulling the door open to the woman he'd been puzzling over, her bright eyes stripping all reason from his head. "Yes, I guess it is that time."

She walked with him through the dining room to the hall and the stairs. "Are you okay? You look a bit... befuddled."

Tate smiled. In one word, she had quite captured the state of his mind.

Chapter 14

As morning dawned, Lalita sat up in bed, wondering why she hadn't tried to call Nonnie on Tate's wall phone. She'd seen Tate talking on it, so it wasn't just for show. Sweeping up her robe off the end of the bed, she flew down the stairs. Standing in front of the wooden box in the hall, she smiled thinking of her smart phone, so slim it would fit in her pocket.

She carefully picked up the part she knew she was supposed to put to her ear and gave the crank on the side five or six turns as she had seen Tate doing.

The operator came on the line. "May I help you?"

Lalita moved her mouth to the small black funnel, suddenly realizing the problem with her smart phone. Without it, she was dumb. "Oh, rats, I was going to place a call, but I realize I don't know the number by heart. Can you look it up with a name? She lives in Colorado Springs. Nonnie Slowensky."

"Just one moment." Lalita heard pages being turned. Real physical pages. "I have a Charles Slowensky on Cascade Avenue."

Lalita frowned. She knew Nonnie had a large family and had lived in the area all her life. "That's it? You have one Slowensky?"

"Yes, ma'am."

"And there's absolutely no Nonnie Slowensky on Flintridge Drive."

"No, ma'am. I can't say as I've ever heard of that street. Is it new?"

Lalita's brow furrowed. Flintridge was in the middle of town. "Not particularly."

She was about to hang up when she had an idea. "What's the date on your directory?"

"I can assure you, we have the most recent edition."

"But what's the date?"

"1892, ma'am."

Lalita blinked. "You are all taking this thing a bit far, don't you think?"

"I'm afraid I don't understand, ma'am... Would you like to make a call?"

"I do, but it appears that I can't. You don't happen to have a directory from 2015, do you?"

"The *year* 2015?"

Lalita couldn't help her irritation. "Yes, the year 2015; the year that it is everywhere other than here."

There was a moment of silence, then the woman came back on the line. "I must inform you, ma'am, that the telephone company takes a dim view of pranks and crank calls. Good day."

Lalita replaced the ear piece in the clip as Tate started down the stairs. He looked over the rail at her. "Good morning, Lita. You're up early." She turned, and he raised a brow as he came around the newel post to the hallway. "Are you planning to dress today, or do you have another fainting spell planned?"

"Ha ha. I just woke up thinking about trying to call Nonnie. I don't know why I didn't think of it before now."

"And?"

She sighed. "And nothing. I ran into the brick wall that is Manitou Springs. I will be able to leave when I want to, won't I, or will a big, bouncing Rover block every exit?"

The phone rang, and Tate gave her a quizzical look as he moved toward it. "Rover?" He plucked the receiver from the clip and moved to the mouthpiece. "Dr. Cavanaugh... Yes, Bertie... Ah... Is he feverish?... Coughing up anything?"

Lalita studied her handsome doctor as he continued talking into the old-fashioned phone, alternating questions with sounds of affirmation, and she realized that it wouldn't just be hard to leave him behind when she left, it would be heartbreaking.

His tone grew more serious. "Bertie, there may not be anything I can do, but yes, I'll be around as soon as I check on a patient here."

Tate hung up the call with an exhale of breath. "Bertie Gwynn. Her husband has spent his life abusing his lungs, and now they are failing him. And I'm afraid the dry clime here has not helped him as it does the tuberculars."

He started down the hall toward the exam room, then turned back. "Lita, I should like to take you out for a drive when I get back, so see what you can find upstairs to wear that's suitable for a picnic." He lingered, his eyes sparkling. "I have something I wish to discuss with you."

She didn't miss a beat. "So what's wrong with what I've got on? Where I come from, a picnic means casual, and you can't get more casual than a nightgown."

He turned with a smile that lit up his whole face and continued down the hall. "I trust your humor doesn't reach burlesque."

He disappeared into the exam room, and Lalita was left to ponder what Tate might want to discuss with her and what she could find among Augusta's dresses that said "picnic."

* * *

"All I can do is keep him comfortable, Bertie." Tate had his arm around the older woman's shoulders as they stood beside the large, four poster bed where Ralph Gwynn lay, sleeping soundly. "I've given him enough pain medicine to knock out a small horse."

The woman in a simple, brown day dress gave a small smile as she dabbed at her eyes with a handkerchief. "I knew he was failing, but I didn't expect him to go so fast. Will he last the day, do you think? I should contact the children."

Tate rubbed her upper arm before releasing her. "It's hard to say, but I imagine it will be today or tomorrow."

Moving to his medical bag, he put away his stethoscope and medicines. "Do you have anyone who can sit with you?"

She thought a moment before shaking her head. "Not really. We haven't been here all that long, and I've spent most of that time taking care of Ralph."

Tears started to run down her cheeks again. "I think I'll go back to Springfield after he... passes. Bury him with his family."

Tate nodded. "I have a few more calls to make this morning, but I'll come back and check on him." He moved toward the bedroom door. "It should be before noon."

Bertie sat in a Queen Anne chair by the bed. "Thank you, Dr. Cavanaugh, I'd appreciate that."

Tate trotted down the stairs and let himself out the door. This was the part of his vocation he wished he could avoid. But one can't dedicate one's self to saving lives without dealing with death.

*   *   *

After breakfast, Lalita and Nellie were left once again to figure out their day's entertainments. They'd played with paper dolls for a while and took turns trying to fling a ball on a string into a cup. Finally, Lalita plopped down on Nellie's small bed and flopped backwards. "I'm bored, Nellie. There must be something more fun we can do."

Nellie sat down beside her, Arabella in her arms. "Well, we never did go on a bike ride."

Lalita popped up. "That's right. I forgot all about it."

Pushing off the bed, she headed down the hallway to Augusta's room with Nellie close on her heels. "Let's see what we can find that could be made into riding bloomers."

They decided a skirt and shirtwaist would work the best and found a charcoal gray set that she considered rather homely and wouldn't feel badly cutting into.

It really didn't take all that long to split the skirt and restitch it into pants, even with the learning curve of the treadle machine. She tried it on, and Nellie tied each skirt "leg" around her ankles with ribbon.

She was admiring herself in the full length, standing, oval mirror, when Mrs. Kettler appeared in the doorway. One look at her scowling face, and Nellie took a step back. Lalita took a step forward. "How do you like them, Mrs. K.? Nellie and I are planning on taking a bike ride after my picnic with the doctor."

Mrs. Kettler's nostrils flared. "Dr. Cavanaugh just called and asked me to convey his regrets, but he will be detained, so there will be no picnic today."

Lalita's heart fell, but she wasn't about to let a packed picnic lunch go to waste. "Nellie and I will have a picnic then."

Nellie jumped up and down. "Can we really?"

Mrs. Kettler's face pinched unbecomingly. "Well, I don't—"

"It's all made, right?" Lalita swept up the hat she'd added a ribbon to, so it would stay on her head.

"Yes, but I don't think—"

"That, Mrs. K., would be best. I'm sure Tate won't mind."

Mrs. Kettler's expression was nothing short of appalled. "I'm certain that Dr. Cavanaugh would be scandalized by such a familiar use of his name, Miss Torres."

Lalita had a retort in mind but bit her tongue. She had an image to keep up. She smiled, rolling her eyes. "Oh yeah, you are so right, Mrs. K. Ever since that bump I took on the head, I'm having trouble remembering my P's and Q's. Thanks for the reminder."

Mrs. Kettler seemed satisfied, if not a bit wary of her sudden reversal. "Well, then, I would also suggest that you take your meal in the dining room instead of—"

"Nope." Lalita grabbed Nellie's hand and pulled her past Mrs. Kettler and out the door. "I'm sticking to my guns on that one. Nellie and I are taking a bike ride and having a picnic."

Before Mrs. Kettler could sputter another protest, they had run down the stairs, grabbed the lunch basket out of the ice box, and headed out the back door.

Using stealthy moves—more for fun than need—they made their way to the carriage house. They found the bike back in a corner, covered with dust, but since it had been kept out of the elements, it was free of rust. Lalita was surprised but delighted by the elongated seat. "This is perfect. This way we can both sit on the seat."

They found a rag and wiped it off; then Lalita wheeled it out into the light of day. Stepping over the bar, she instructed Nellie as she slid the basket over the handlebars. "Okay, climb up on the seat and hold onto me as I sit in front of you. There's really no place for you to put your feet, so make sure they stay clear of the wheel."

After Nellie was sitting securely, she put her feet on the pedals and started forward. The slope of the carriage house driveway helped with momentum, and she moved out into the street. Nellie laughed with delight as they went faster, passing slow-moving buggies and waving to people on foot. It had been a long time since she'd ridden a bike, but she guessed the old adage about riding was true.

They sailed down the hard-packed dirt hill toward the main part of town and found a patch of grass by the clock that had a statue of a Greek woman on top.

Sitting in the grass, Lalita opened their basket to find cold fried chicken, apples, rolls, a wedge of cheese, and a jar of lemonade. She grinned at Nellie. "Mrs. K. may be a bit of a sourpuss, but she can cook."

The two ate until their picnic site was discovered by ants, then moved to sit on the fence around the clock, the basket hanging on the bike parked close by. They laughed trying to balance on the metal rails and eat at the same time. "Picnics are seriously over-rated," Lalita said, flicking an ant off of her roll. "They are always better in theory than real life."

Mrs. Kettler had packed the basket with the doctor's appetite in mind rather than little Nell's, so they found themselves full long before the basket was empty. Lalita offered the rest to two passing boys, who took it with hearty thanks.

She looked to Nellie as she walked the bike toward her. "Well, where to now?"

Nellie spun around with her eyes closed, her arm extended. She stopped suddenly and opened her eyes. "That way."

Lalita nodded and helped her climb on. "That way, it is."

* * *

Tate was weary. It had been the kind of day one dreads. The kind of day where you feel helpless. The kind of day where you watch someone die.

Ralph had been much worse when he returned, gasping for his every breath, and Bertie was beside herself. Tate had stayed with her till the end, which had made for a long, solemn afternoon. He recorded the death at 3:45 and had called the undertaker. Then knowing that Bertie shouldn't be alone, he

had called Reverend Niemeyer and had waited until he and his
wife arrived.

He let Maisy set a slow, even pace toward home, hoping to
shake off some of the melancholy before getting there. He'd
had such grand plans for the day this morning—a picnic lunch
where he had intended to ask Lalita to stay with him in his little
mountain town.

And to let him court her.

He had lain awake most of the night, a wrestling match
going on between his head and his heart. His heart had won
when his head grew so tired he couldn't think straight. In the
hour before dawn, he knew he wanted her to stay, no matter
what the society mavens might say about her heritage. He'd
fallen asleep, finally, only to wake again in an hour.

Throughout the day, he had rehearsed his pitch. The clean
mountain air, the college nearby—he had even thought of
letting her start a daycare if taking care of Nellie wasn't enough
to satisfy her. But mostly, he intended to tell her that he wanted
her to stay because he simply wanted *her.*

Her dark eyes, her warm heart, her joy-filled spirit.

He pulled into the carriage house and released Maisy into
Harold's care. Yawning, he decided a nap was in order before
dinner. He hadn't taken two steps into the house, however,
before Mrs. Kettler was spouting like a teapot about Lalita
cutting up Augusta's clothes and taking Nellie to her sure death
sailing down the hill toward town on his bike.

Tate wasn't concerned about the clothes or Lalita taking
his bike for a ride, although Mrs. Kettler's description of Nellie
perched on the back "precariously" did give him a moment's
pause. He'd set quite a few bones since bicycling had become a
fad. "How long ago did they leave?"

"Noon! Miss Torres insisted on taking the picnic lunch
for her and Nellie. With that basket hanging off the front and
Nellie on the back, wearing those ridiculous riding bloomers
she made out of one of Augusta's skirts, she probably ended up
in a ditch somewhere!"

Tate sighed, put his hat back on, and headed back out to the
carriage house.

* * *

Nellie had gotten them started off in one direction, but before the afternoon was over, they had toured every byway of the small burg. Even though not more than a village in size, she noted that most of the buildings were large, and some leaned toward gargantuan. *No tiny house trend here.*

The afternoon sun was heating up the day, and even though she had on practically nothing under her shirtwaist and bloomers by Victorian standards, Lalita was starting to sweat.

After she was drenched and completely parched, Nellie directed her to where several natural mineral springs were located. They came to one she called the soda springs, although the sign on the spring house said Cheyenne Springs. It actually shot into the air like a geyser every so often and had an effervescent quality like carbonated water.

Lalita didn't much care for it, however, so they walked to one called the Navajo Springs that Nellie insisted was sweet enough to make lemonade. After tasting it, Lalita wasn't convinced, but it was better than the soda springs. She and Nellie drank until their thirst was quenched then splashed cool water on their faces.

Looking to the west, Lalita saw that the sun was heading toward the peaks. "Well, Nellie, I guess we better head home before Mrs. K. gets her bloomers in a bundle."

Nellie laughed and climbed back up on the bike seat. "I hope she made a big dinner; I'm starving."

"You're starving?" Lalita climbed onto the pedals. "I'm the one doing all the work."

Nellie giggled. "I don't know why, but having fun makes me hungry!"

Lalita smiled and put what strength she had left into making good time before they had to tackle the big hill that led to home. Building up speed on the straightaway, she dodged the occasional pedestrian, biker, and buggy. She sailed around the corner to scale the elevation with as much speed as she could muster, not anticipating the slow-moving horse-drawn wagon that had just pulled out in front of her.

Swerving to go around would put her heading into a horse and buggy coming down the hill, so she made the split decision to pass on the other side. "Hold on, Nellie!"

It was the large rock hidden in the weeds that unseated them, sending the bike flipping and the girls flying.

Lalita landed on her back with the wind knocked out of her, while Nellie made a splash in the standing water from last night's rain. While Lalita struggled to draw breath, a scowling man appeared over her. A clean-shaven man in a brown bowler.

*   *   *

"I don't know why you're so grumpy. We got a bit wet and dirty." She looked at the mud-covered girl beside her. "Okay, we got a lot wet and dirty and got a few scrapes. So what? We had a blast today, didn't we, Nellie?"

Seated between Lalita and Tate in the buggy, Nellie's forehead wrinkled in thought. "I don't remember a blast, but I had a lot of fun." Mud dripped off her nose onto her soaked pinafore.

Tate refused to look at her. "I told you, Miss Torres, that we will discuss this in the parlor after you two have had a chance to bathe."

Lalita sulked the rest of the way, mad that one rock had so easily changed the course of their day.

After Tate had lifted Nellie to the ground and given her the admonition to take off her dress on the wash porch, he handed the reigns to Harold and headed toward the house himself.

Lalita called after him. "Aren't you going to help me down?"

Tate turned. "I'm always happy to assist a lady should there happen to be one nearby."

Fuming, Lalita jumped to the ground and hurried after him. "I see you're wearing your old man hat again today."

He continued up the steps to the back door but hesitated before opening it. "Someone has to be the older one in the household, Miss Torres. Now I'm sure you don't want to continue this conversation in front of Mrs. Kettler. She'll be out of sorts already with having to give Nellie a bath in the middle of the week at a time when we should be sitting down to eat. I will be glad to speak to you later after she has gone home. Am I clear?"

*   *   *

"There are certain things that society expects from its citizens. . ." —Tate was pacing back and forth in the parlor while Lalita and Nellie sat on the settee— "a certain level of decorum that sets us apart from the rabble of the world."

He stopped and looked at Lalita, who was sporting an attitude a mile wide. "And while bike riding has become an accepted activity for men and women alike, it should be a leisure activity, where a lady doesn't push herself to the point of perspiring unduly."

Lalita was about to protest that statement since she was sweating just sitting still in the stuffy parlor, but Tate turned and continued his pacing and yammering. "I can't speak for you, Miss Torres, but I would very much like my daughter to grow up with a sense of what is lady-like behavior and what is not."

He stopped to take a breath, and Lalita stood, her ire rising. "I'm very sorry, Doc, to not fit into your mold for what a lady looks like, but I won't apologize for giving Nellie something to do today besides playing jacks. I understand your desire for a simpler time, I really do, but unfortunately, the time you picked is very confining for women. Your society rules are a complete bore."

He narrowed his eyes. "The time I picked. . ."

She waved a hand. "Well, probably not *you* personally, but whoever set this all up. Or maybe it's been going on since 1892; the people back then just decided they didn't like the way the world was progressing and dug in their heels."

Tate just stared.

"You know, like the Amish."

"The Amish. . . in Pennsylvania. What do we have to do with the Amish?"

She walked toward him. "You know, this whole. . . town is. . . is set apart from the rest of the world—the rest of progress and technology." He continued to look at her as though she were speaking Swahili. She blew out an exasperated breath and began pacing herself. "I mean, over a hundred years of advancement—computers and cars and mammograms and and and video games and microwave ovens and mini skirts and..." She spun to face him. "Tate, I'm sure you remember that out there, there are refrigerators that *make* ice, not just hold a huge block of it!"

Tate swallowed and turned to his daughter. "Nellie, run on upstairs. I'll be up in a minute to tuck you in."

Nellie, whose eyes had gone round during Lita's discourse, slid off the settee and walked swiftly to the stairs.

He turned back to Lita, scolding himself for not seeing that she was still unstable in her thinking. He forced a smile and waved a hand toward the settee. "Please, sit. There's no need to get upset."

She didn't move. "I'll sit if you'll sit."

He moved to the settee and sat, and she slowly joined him.

Tate licked his lips, wondering how to proceed. "Lita, two nights ago you said you understood that I'm a real doctor, and the people here aren't just acting in some grand production..."

She nodded. "Not a production, but definitely a different way of life."

"Different like the Amish."

"Yes. I would think that is obvious. You do know something about the Amish and how they live, don't you?"

"They are bound by common religious convictions in a tight-knit community."

"That's not the only thing that separates them anymore. As the world progressed, they didn't—just like here."

"So aside from the Amish and Manitou, the rest of the world has moved on?"

"Big time. While you're trotting around in your horse and buggy, the rest of the world is driving 75 miles per hour down the interstate and jetting around the globe."

Tate leaned back, one arm across his abdomen and a hand to his chin. "This world 'out there'... does it include Colorado Springs? Are they driving 75 miles per hour in Colorado Springs?"

She rolled her eyes. "Well, not through town, but on the highway, yeah."

"So one could drive to Denver from Colorado Springs in about... an hour?"

"Yeah, thereabouts. The traffic was really bad when I flew into the airport, so it took us a bit longer than that."

Tate tried not be distracted by the idea of heavy traffic and flying into an airport, and only focused on what he knew about driving a buggy to Denver— it was easily a seven to nine hour journey, depending on the horse.

He looked back into her eyes. Eyes that seemed so sure of her delusions. And he made a decision.

He rose and offered his hand, and she took it with a perplexed expression as he escorted her out of the parlor and down the hall. "I think you'd better turn in; we will have a big day tomorrow."

"Why? What's going on tomorrow?"

He stopped at the bottom of the stairs. "Tomorrow, I'm taking you to Colorado Springs, so you can show me all the progress that has passed us by."

Chapter 15

Lalita woke early with the first rays of sun, even though sleep had been hard to come by. She was both elated and saddened to be leaving the Cavanaugh residence today.

When Tate had planned to take her on a picnic, she thought it meant something—maybe even something like a date—but his indignation at her "unlady-like behavior" spewing like the Cheyenne Soda Fountain had her questioning his feelings. She wondered if they were just too different to have a relationship.

She had never intended to get Nellie in trouble. The poor girl had been near tears before her papa had wound down. The tumble into the ditch had been unfortunate, but no bones were broken and both they and the clothes could be washed. *Good grief, you'd think we'd robbed a bank instead of going on a bike ride.*

After a trip to the bathroom to brush her teeth with the coarse toothbrush and horrible tasting tooth powder that Tate had provided her, she made her way quietly across the hall and through Augusta's bedroom to the dressing room to find something to wear. *It needs to be lightweight.* She dug through the open trunk. *And it can't require a corset to fit.* She pulled out a pale blue number and gave it a shake. "It's time to go home."

* * *

After Lalita said a cordial goodbye to Mrs. Kettler and an emotional goodbye to Nellie, Tate helped her up into the buggy, and with a snap of the reins, they were off.

She thought leaving would be easier, but she had grown attached to Nellie in the last few days. She looked to Tate and felt a tug. Despite his old-fashioned beliefs about women's behavior, she still felt incredibly sad to be leaving him. *And we never got to have our picnic.*

She looked around at the town, wishing she could see it at Christmastime, blanketed in snow. She admired the residents for their strength, even as she couldn't fathom making a decision to live more than a century in the past technology-wise. She had to admit, though, having the mountains at her back gave her an empty feeling.

When they reached the edge of town, Tate glanced her way. "I don't think you've been this quiet since you woke up in my examination room."

Lalita tried to smile but found she just couldn't. "I know. It's weird, huh?" She realized her hands were twisting her skirt into wrinkles, and she tried to relax. "You put the cast on Max this morning?"

"Yes, and his father was supposed to pick him up within the hour." He adjusted the homburg hat on his head to keep the sun out of his eyes. "I think Max was quite sad to be leaving your company."

Lalita smiled. "He's a sweet kid. I'm happy to be missing his father today, though."

Tate nodded. "Stay away from men like Seth Dickson."

Lalita's mouth quirked to the side. "Aw, Doc, you do care, after all."

He sat up straight, his chin ticking up. "If I did not care, we wouldn't be making this trip."

"I thought after you yelled at me last night that... well, I mean, you said I wasn't a lady, and I know how important all that is to you." She turned her face away, trying to keep her composure.

His hand pulled her chin back to him.

"Lita, I'm sorry. I over-reacted. It was a very long day yesterday, and I was tired. I hope you can forgive me." Lalita felt a shudder move through her as his fingers left her chin and settled over her hand on her lap. "If you leave me today, I hope you will think well of me, and not as I was last night."

Lalita's mouth had gone dry. "I will miss you."

He smiled, squeezed her hand, and returned his to the business of holding the reins. Lalita wished for it back on her hand, her chin, running through her hair. She swallowed. "How far until everything gets back to normal?"

Tate shifted the reins in his hands. "That's a rather difficult question."

She frowned. "Not really. How many miles before we run into a paved road or a highway? Maisy won't be frightened, will she?"

"Maisy will be fine."

She noticed he didn't answer the first question. "Tate, how—"

"Lita, just relax and enjoy the ride. We'll get there when we get there."

She huffed out an anxious breath. "Patience isn't my strong suit."

Tate chuckled. "Isn't it."

That pulled a smile out of her. "Oh, so you think you know me so well, do you?"

He shook his head. "No. The more I try to decipher you, the more baffled I get."

"Hmm, if you've been trying to decipher me, then I must have been on your mind quite a lot."

He smiled, keeping his eyes on the road ahead.

Lalita studied his profile. She hoped Nonnie would be home when she got there, so she could take their picture together. All at once, she remembered their portrait. "Oh, no! You never picked up our pictures from the photographer! Promise me you'll mail me one."

Tate slipped his hand into his jacket's inside breast pocket and pulled out a stiff-backed picture. She took it from him, and unexpected tears came to her eyes as she saw for the first time the expression on Tate's face. She could almost feel how fast his heart was beating with his hand on her shoulder in that exhilarating thirty-second pose.

Pulling open the drawstring purse at her wrist, she slipped it inside beside the picture of the wild bike ride that Nellie had drawn for her. Tears slipped down her cheeks, and she tried to wipe them discreetly on her sleeve before Tate offered her a folded white handkerchief.

As the dusty road went on, taking them lower in elevation, Lalita couldn't help the sigh that escaped her. Tate noticed. "Would you like to drive the buggy?"

Lalita perked up. "I've ridden a horse, but I've never 'driven' one."

"There's a first time for everything. Do you want to try?"

She took off her hat and threw it under the seat. "Sure. Is there more to it than snapping the reins to go and pulling back to stop?"

"A bit. First of all, look how I'm holding the reins."

The left rein went over the top of his left hand's fingers, his thumb holding it tight. The right rein went between his third and fourth fingers. His right hand rested easily between them.

"I use my right hand for signaling a stop or a turn. I grab both reins and pull back for a stop, and I pull on either the right or left for corresponding turns." He reined Maisy in and helped Lalita position the reins in her hands. "Relax and give just a small flick of the reins to give her the go-ahead."

The arrangement of the reins felt awkward in her hands, but she put some slack into them and flipped them the way she'd seen Tate do it, and Maisy started forward. Lalita grinned and looked to Tate. "You'll tell me if I need to turn, right?"

He smiled back. "Don't worry, I'll let you know."

As the morning started to heat up, Tate slipped out of his jacket and laid it on the seat between them, rolling up his shirt sleeves and unbuttoning the top button of his shirt.

Lalita glanced his way. "Goodness Tate, Mrs. K. was right." She looked back to the road, a smile tugging at her lips. "You do need a chaperone."

His hand stilled. "You heard that conversation?"

"How could I miss it? She was quite loud... and very insistent." She laughed. "Oh my heavens, I haven't had a chaperone since I was sixteen!"

Tate straightened, his surprise evident. "Your parents let you go unchaperoned at such a young age?"

"Most parents are less strict than mine. Some have no idea where their thirteen and fourteen-year-olds are most of the time. Then they wonder why their daughters end up drunk and pregnant."

Tate's eyes grew wide. "Missouri must have turned into a veritable den of iniquity."

"Not just Missouri. You should leave Manitou once in a while, so you know what's going on."

Tate finished rolling up his sleeves, wondering if her assessment of life outside his little town was really so dire, or if this was more of her unfettered imagination. It's true he hadn't ventured from Manitou for four or five months, but surely the world outside it couldn't have slid so fast into wanton immorality.

While the morals may have slipped in Missouri, he was certain that Colorado Springs was not so much different than Manitou. He wondered how she'd take it when she saw that no one was racing around at 75 miles per hour.

He knew this whole jaunt was a risk. Her mind would either accept reality or reject it, but rejecting it could push her further into her self-deception. Her mind could shatter utterly. He considered again the need to seek out professionals in the field. Only his fear for her care in one of the state sanitariums kept him from stopping her and turning the buggy around.

"So why did you reject Mrs. K.'s advice? She said you would compromise my virtue taking me out alone through the countryside. That was important in 1892." She lifted her brows as she gave him a teasing look. "Don't you care about my virtue?"

He clasped his hands between his knees. "I most certainly do, but as I told Mrs. Kettler, as a respected doctor in the community, I should be trusted to help one of my patients as I think best."

Lalita gave him a sly smile. "Good one. See, even you feel pinched by the Victorian society rules."

Tate gave a little snort. *Lita, you have no idea.*

Taking the reins in one hand for a moment, she laid her hand on his leg, speaking softly. "If you want to stop a minute before we get there and give me a kiss, I wouldn't mind," she teased. "No one will ever know."

Tate swallowed, unable to take his eyes off her hand on his thigh. "If there is to be a goodbye, I'll kiss you then."

She looked at him, surprised. "Really?"

He thought about his plans to court her—plans that were no longer viable—and brought his eyes to hers. "Really."

"On the lips?"

Tate's heart skipped at the thought. "Lita, you should at least try to be a lady." He smiled, knowing full well that Lita would be Lita.

* * *

Miles down the road, buildings became visible in the distance. "Seriously, we're this close and still on dirt roads?" Lalita leaned forward, squinting. "Wait. Is that Colorado Springs or some other little town?"

Tate had taken back the reins. "That's Colorado City. It will take us another half hour to reach Colorado Springs."

"Oh, yes, I read about that. It was founded first, right? But General Palmer found it too rowdy for his taste and started Colorado Springs further east. I read that he was a real visionary—created beautiful parks and talked up the place to all his wealthy friends."

"Not only that, he provided funds for the college and brought the railroads to the area. Did you drive by his fabulous castle home?"

"Glen Eyrie? No, but it was on the list for this week. Such a shame that his wife couldn't stay in the area and enjoy it. She was so young to have a heart attack, and to die at only forty-four..."

Tate hadn't heard anything about Queen Palmer's death. *Surely it would have been in the newspapers.* He was about to question her further, when Lalita gave a little gasp.

"Tate, it looks just the same as Manitou!"

Tate chose his words carefully. "What exactly were you expecting?"

"Not this! Is it more of your Victorian community project?"

Tate scowled. *No accepting reality here.* "I don't know what to say, Lita. It is... what it is."

She slumped back against the seat, looking agitated. "Another half hour."

He drove Maisy carefully through the town; then when they were out in the open once again, he felt the need to draw Lita out—to learn more about her. "Tell me about your family."

Lita's breath leaked out in a hiss. "My parents died in an accident when I was little—even younger than Nellie."

Without thinking, he laid his hand over hers. "Oh, Lita, I'm sorry."

She rolled her shoulders and looked at the sky. "I had no other living relatives that would take me, so I was put in foster care, and eventually, I was adopted. My new parents never seemed to understand me, however. We were always at odds." She looked at Tate's concerned face. "Even now. I haven't spoken to them in a month. That's when my mom called to see if I'd watch their dog while they go on a family reunion cruise this weekend."

Tate was shocked. "They have the money for a cruise, but they want you to watch their dog? They're not taking you along?"

Lita gave him a lop-sided smile. "It always sounds worse to say it out loud. I don't mind, really. I just wish..."

She trailed off and looked at the horse rigging.

Tate spoke softly. "What do you wish, Lita?"

Her eyes stayed on Maisy. "I wish that they'd call when they didn't want something from me. Just to talk, you know?" She let out a heavy sigh. "And that's why it's been a month since we've spoken. I stopped calling them. I just wanted to see if they'd call to say something other than, 'honey, we need a favor.' "

Tate squeezed her hand, then throwing caution to the wind, he flung his arm around her and pulled her to his chest. He wondered if this early trauma and continued family tension could be the reason for her flights of fancy rather than a head injury. "I'm sorry, Lita." Caught up in her dejection, he pressed a kiss to her head.

"I thought you were saving that for goodbye."

Smiling, he ran his hand up and down her arm. "So I was."

He knew he shouldn't continue to hold her. He knew he was setting himself up for an unbearably lonely return trip home, but he couldn't bring himself to release her. He was both relieved and bereft when she sat up out of his embrace, appearing to have something else on her mind.

She swept her hair behind her ear. "Nonnie was my best friend, but now even she seems changed. We don't really have a lot in common anymore."

Tate wondered that her "best friend" hadn't made much of an effort to find her, and suddenly he had a discomfiting thought. *Perhaps Nonnie isn't real. Maybe she was an imaginary friend to help Lita through a difficult time.*

Tate wanted to know more. "Tell me about school. You said you were completing your Master's Degree. That's quite an accomplishment. What is your field of interest?"

"History."

"Ah." His perceptive inflection slipped out without thought.

"What do you mean, 'Ah'?"

He shook his head with eyebrows raised. "Nothing. Go on."

She suddenly switched gears. "Tate, I know you're attracted to me even though you try so hard not to show it." She grabbed her reticule off the seat and pried it open to pull out their portrait. "This picture proves it. You bent the rules because you wanted to touch me, and just a minute ago you did what Mrs. K. would have scolded you for because you want me close to you."

He considered his words. "Max was right. You're very pretty, as well as intelligent, and you're good with Nellie. I was also quite impressed with your baby delivery assistance, and I thought maybe we could... but... well, you tell me you're leaving today."

She sat back. "Just because we're saying goodbye today doesn't mean it's forever. We can write letters until I'm finished with school. I only have one more year."

Tate forced a smile. "Of course."

The minutes passed with Lita growing more agitated. Over and over she marveled at what she called ancient-looking electrical lines and inadequate roads so close to Colorado Springs. She asked if Tate were taking back roads for Maisy's sake, and he assured her that he was taking the most direct route.

When buildings came into view again, she put her hand to her mouth, her eyes growing wide. She turned to him, clearly panicked. "How far are we from the Broadmoor?"

Tate narrowed his eyes in concern. "The Broadmoor Casino?"

"No, it's a resort. A really famous resort."

He just shook his head. "The only Broadmoor I know is a casino, and no place for a lady."

"Okay, how about..." She squeezed her eyes shut. "What was the name... Antlers! The Antlers Hotel."

Tate nodded and turned Maisy at the next corner. With every street sign, Lalita would cry out, "It can't be. It just can't be."

He wanted to pull her back to himself, but he needed both hands on the reins in city driving. "Lita, what's different than you remember?"

She looked at him, her lip quivering. "Everything. I mean the downtown is the older part, so some of the buildings are the same, but the streets are dirt, there are horses instead of cars and trucks and SUVs and jeeps and motorcycles." She gawked at all the buggies they passed. "And everyone looks just like us."

Tate set his jaw, almost certain that he should just turn around and take her back home with him. *I'll find her good doctors. I won't let her be taken away.*

He pulled Maisy to the side of the street intending to break the news of his intentions gently, when Lita leaned forward standing right up out of her seat. "Oh my gosh. What's happening?" She looked to Tate, her hand holding on to the side of the buggy top.

Tate reached for the hand near him. "Lita, I was hoping when you saw the town, you'd, well, you'd snap out of your delusions. You seemed to think that Manitou was somehow behind the rest of the world. I brought you here today to show you that it's not."

Tate had stopped the buggy within view of the Antlers Hotel, and while it was an imposing structure, it didn't compare to the high-rise Antlers *Hilton* Hotel Lalita had driven past with Nonnie a week earlier.

She sat down hard, her mind whirring with the possibilities even as Tate droned on without her hearing a word. Suddenly, she felt the need to get out and walk. She jumped out of the buggy with Tate yelling after her. Walking briskly toward the hotel, she waited only a moment at the busy corner of Pikes

Peak Avenue before walking right out into the middle of the extra wide street.

She looked toward the ancient, yet nearly new building. Buggies were passing her from both directions as her gaze lifted to the mighty mountain above that wore only the tiniest scrap of snow at this time of year. Without warning, a flash of light seared her memory, and she cried out, crumpling to the hard packed dirt.

Chapter 16

"Lita! Wake up, sweetheart."

Tate had been just a few feet away from Lita in the middle of Pikes Peak Avenue when she cried out and collapsed. He had carried her quickly back to his buggy and set her beside him on the seat, her head lolling with unconsciousness. He feared the worst—that he had pushed her too far into accepting something she couldn't, and her mind had opted for oblivion rather than facing the truth.

Reaching under the seat for the medical bag he never went anywhere without, he dug through it one-handed until he found the smelling salts. Waving the small bottle under her nose, he prayed for her consciousness to return, as well as her sanity. *Heavenly Father, please undo any damage I've done by bringing her here.*

Without warning, Lita's eyes popped open, and she pushed the strong-smelling ammonia away from her nose. She blinked, and Tate held his breath.

She sat up straight and looked around. "What are you doing, Tate? Why were you trying to pour that horrible stuff up my nose?"

Tate smiled and let out a heavy breath, recapping the bottle. "I wasn't trying to pour it up your nose. You fainted. It helped to revive you."

She ran a hand through her hair, looking to the spot in the street where she collapsed, then turning to look at the hotel. He watched her eyes track upward to the mountains. "Wow," she breathed out.

He took her hand with both of his. "Lita, tell me what you're thinking."

Her gaze connected with his, but he couldn't read her emotions. She seemed in shock. Finally she licked her lips and words came out in a rush. "Tate, I know what happened up on Pikes Peak."

His chin ticked up in surprise. Why she had been on Pikes Peak and what happened there was the furthest thing from his thoughts. "What happened?"

"Nonnie and I went up on the cog rail, but it was really stormy at the top and cold. That's why I bought the long johns."

He caressed her hand with his thumbs. "Yes, you said that the other night. Is there something more?"

She nodded and seemed reticent to speak. He waited. Her lip quivered, and Tate began to fear that she had been attacked—perhaps even violated—while on the mountain. He brought a hand to her cheek. "It's all right. You can tell me. Whatever happened, I'll help you through it."

She bit her lip a moment longer before speaking. "I'm afraid you won't believe me." She choked on a sob. "I'm not sure I believe it myself."

Wrapping her in his arms, he pulled her head next to his, feeling even more certain that a horrific attack on her person was responsible for her spotty memory. She had blocked out the terror. He turned his lips to her ear. "Sh, I think I understand. You don't need to speak of it if you don't want to."

She clung to him a moment longer, then slowly pushed away. "I don't know what you think happened, but I. . . I was struck by lightning."

Tate's brows flew up. "Lightning! Lita, if you were struck by lightning, you would have had far worse things to deal with than just memory loss."

"Well, I probably wasn't struck directly, but close enough to cause unconsciousness."

Tate squinted in thought. "I suppose that could be possible. You actually remember the lightning flash?"

"Yes. I was taking pictures of the view—"

"You had a camera up on top." Tate feared they were heading down the same confusing road.

"Well, I was taking pictures on my phone. Almost nobody carries a camera around anymore." She stopped, taking in a small breath. "Oh boy, no wonder you have given me that stare for days. Most of the time, you've had no idea what I've been talking about, have you?"

He nodded. "I did mention that you were a cypher."

Lalita looked deep into Tate's worried eyes. *What if I can't make him believe me?*

She'd seen his eyes filled with professional concern, but today they held something more—genuine caring. She knew that no matter the consequences, she had to tell him the truth.

She took hold of both of his hands. "Tate, I know this is going to sound impossible, but I simply have no other explanation." She took a deep breath and let it out. "When Nonnie and I went up Pikes Peak, it was the 21st century. 2015, to be exact."

Tate blinked, and Lalita rushed on. "The bolt of lightning that knocked me out also knocked me back. In time, that is." She got to experience the Tate stare one more time. "That explains why Nonnie has never tried to find me. She's still there in 2015."

Tate didn't say anything, and Lalita felt tears forming. She gave his hands a squeeze. "Please, Tate. Please say that you believe me. I lost my phone, so I can't give you any proof."

Finally he seemed to shake himself out of his catatonic state. "You're probably hungry. I believe they serve meals at the Antlers Hotel." With that, he jumped down and untied the reins from the hitching post. Climbing back up, he gave the reins a snap. "We'll just put Maisy in the livery while we eat to give her a chance to rest." He looked over at her, smiling, but Lalita's heart felt like a stone.

* * *

Tate watched Lita pick at her mashed potatoes and gravy with her fork. She'd barely eaten three bites and hadn't even touched her roasted chicken. He guessed that he was probably responsible for her lack of appetite, but he'd been unable to give her what she wanted—acceptance of her next wild fantasy.

"So you don't want to even look for Nonnie's house?"

She shook her head and laid down her fork. "There's no point. It's like the phone operator tried to tell me, Nonnie's not there. Her street doesn't exist."

"You're coming back with me then."

She looked into his eyes, her own glistening. "What choice do I have? I have nothing. No money, no clothes other than what I'm wearing. You're the only friend I have in the whole wide world, Tate Cavanaugh."

His heart broke at the pain in her voice, yet he couldn't be sad that she was coming home with him. He would do all in his power to help her come to her senses.

He reached across the table to cover her hand with his, pushing his own feelings aside. "And I'm honored to be so." Love and marriage had been taken off the table, but he would not abandon her. He sat back, looking again at her uneaten meal. "Now, be a good girl and eat something. It's a long drive back. I don't need you fainting for lack of food. Please, eat."

She took another bite before setting her fork down. "I'm just not hungry."

"Well, you know Mrs. K., as you call her, won't indulge you with a crumb before the proper time."

She lifted the napkin from her lap and laid it beside her plate. "That's fine."

Tate couldn't stand to see her so... so blank. He set his fork down. "Lalita, I know I'm the cause of your sadness, but I can't tell you that I believe something when I don't. If I did that, you would never know if what I'm saying is truth or a falsehood."

Lita picked up her cup of tea. "Ironically, that's the very reason I told you." After a sip, she set the cup back on the saucer. "I pondered just keeping the revelation to myself."

Tate didn't know what else to say. He reached for his hat sitting on the chair next to him. "Well, if you're truly finished with your meal, we should start back."

She pushed away from the table and rose, not waiting for his assistance. Tate ground his teeth, his old self fighting with the resolution he'd made after Augusta's death. He kept his jaw shut tight as he followed her through the restaurant. Finally, his upbringing forced its way out of his mouth. "Miss Torres, a lady waits for her gentleman to assist with her chair and offer his arm."

She looked up at him with watery eyes. "Are you *my* gentleman, Dr. Cavanaugh?"

He was silent as they walked through the lobby, composing his thoughts, but at her exasperated expression outside, he strove to put them into words. "Miss Torres—"

She stopped. "Don't you dare. Don't you dare 'Miss Torres' me. Not after you've called me Lita for days." Her voice was rising and passersby were staring. "Not after you put your arm around me and kissed me."

Taking her arm, he strove to pull her toward the livery and away from gawkers. She pulled free and sped ahead.

Tate strode with purpose after her but did not run. Thankfully, he found her sitting in their buggy. After paying the livery hand for Maisy's care, he jumped up beside her, and she scooted to the far end of the bench. Gathering the reins, he sighed and moved the buggy out onto the thoroughfare. Expecting a long, silent ride home, he was surprised when she suddenly turned to him and spoke. "Can we go to the Garden of the Gods?"

Tate thought a moment. "It will add an hour or more onto our trip home to drive up there."

She reached out a hand to his arm. "Do you have to get back? I'd really appreciate it if you would take me there."

Tate did want to get back. The trip so far had not been what he'd hoped, but he found he couldn't say no. "If you can stand my company for that long, I'll be glad to take you. It's been a long while since I've been there myself."

"Thank you." She removed her hand to her lap, and Tate wished for it back. He knew he'd hurt her, but if she was still to be his patient, he couldn't let his feelings rule. He couldn't do that to Nellie. *One unbalanced mother in a lifetime is enough.*

* * *

Lalita saw the red rocks jutting up out of the earth long before they got to the famous garden. This time there was no vehicle-filled parking lot with tourists descending on the trails like a plague of locusts. There were no paved walkways, no split rail fences, no visitor's center with a gift shop and 3D movie about the history of the park. There were only one or two other buggies driving the dirt roads between the massive natural rock sculptures.

It was so quiet, you could hear the birds— a number of different calls that she had never taken the time to identify with its owner. She squinted at the passing brush, but most of the time she couldn't land her eye on the bird responsible.

The sky behind the wondrous rock formations was bright blue with a few wispy clouds slowly changing and reshaping with the gentle breeze. It was so peaceful, Lita almost cried.

"The kissing camels, praying hands, and balanced rock are still here in a hundred years, Doc, and while it's still beautiful, in a way, it's been defiled. In becoming a tourist attraction, I doubt it's a place for 'gods' anymore. The Father, Son, and Holy Spirit probably moved on to a more tranquil setting long before the 21st century." She turned to her confused doctor and smiled, a tear running down her face. "But today, they're here." She shut her eyes and leaned her head back. "Close your eyes and breathe them in, Doc. They're here."

*   *   *

It was a quiet ride back to Manitou. Lalita had much to process. If the realization that she might be stuck more than a hundred years in the past wasn't enough, she was slowly beginning to feel the loss of those she loved. And while she didn't always get along with her family, she still loved them. *Why didn't I just call them? Why did I have to prove something?*

If she lived to be an old woman, she might be alive when her parents and adoptive parents were born. She'd never see Nonnie again or any of her friends back in Missouri. It was as if they'd all died in some horrible catastrophe, and she was the only survivor. Knowing that they were still living out their lives without her was only a small comfort in the midst of the grief sweeping over her.

As the tears fell, Tate patted her arm or hand, but he didn't offer to hold her again—didn't let his fingers slide through her hair—didn't kiss the top of her head. He'd pulled away, leaving her feeling completely alone.

When they were approaching Manitou, the dam of her emotions broke utterly, and she began to weep openly, unable to stop. Tate pulled over but still didn't reach for her. "Do you want to talk about what's troubling you?"

She shook her head. "Why?" she hiccuped "You won't believe me anyway."

"It doesn't matter what I believe. I want to help you."

Lalita couldn't fathom how obtuse men could be. "Seriously?" She could feel herself heating up from more than the mid-afternoon summer sun. "You don't have a clue why I might be upset?"

He shifted the reins in his hands. "I'm sorry. I know I've hurt you. I—"

She gave a high, little laugh. "Oh my, Doc, I hate to be the one to break this to you, but not everything is about you." She bit her lip, fighting for control. "I've lost everything— everybody I knew. Everybody I loved. All my education was for nothing. In this time, women can't even vote. I'm a liberated fish out of water, and I'm so hot right now, I want to tear this ridiculous dress off my body and jump in the creek."

For the second time in one day, Tate found himself watching as Lita jumped from the buggy unexpectedly. *Surely she wouldn't.* He quickly wound the reins around the arm rail and jumped to the ground, following her briskly down the creek bank to the water's edge.

He was glad to see that she was not undressing but had dipped his handkerchief in the stream and was wiping her face and neck. He moved beside her, sliding his hands into his trouser pockets lest he be tempted to take her in his arms. "I'm sorry to have been so insensitive to your feelings. We can send a letter to your family in Missouri, and perhaps they will want to make the journey out to get you."

The look she gave him could have smelted iron. "My mom was born in 1961—my dad in 1962. My *grandparents* haven't even been born yet."

He opened his mouth and closed it again, and Lita spun and climbed the bank. "I'm going to find a way to prove it, Tate. I don't know how yet, but I'll think of something."

Tate blew out a breath and followed her to the buggy.

Chapter 17

It was nearing midnight and every now and then, Tate still heard Lita crying. She had wept all evening.

Flinging off his sheets, he got out of bed, pacing in his nightshirt. Every fiber of his being wanted to go in and console her. Every bit of reason told him not to.

The doctor could check on her, but it was the man who wanted to hold her. He'd reasoned his way into being stoic on the drive home, but the longer she cried, the less resistance he had.

Ever since their trip to the Springs, he'd been thinking about her—the side of her that seemed to have lost touch with reality and the side of her that seemed to feel reality deeper than he'd ever felt it. The words she spoke in the Garden still resonated inside him, and even though she couldn't possibly know the things she claimed to know about that place, he felt distress at just the possibility of it being changed in any way.

But it was nothing compared to the distress he felt now, knowing she was hurting and not being allowed to help. He stopped his pacing as a question formed in his head. *"Who says it's not allowed?"*

He spun as though speaking to someone in the room. "Everyone would say I shouldn't go to her. Everyone. I'm a widower, and she's a single woman in my house."

And then it occurred to him. "Everyone" was not there.

Grabbing up his dressing gown from the chair, he strode to her room. He paused just a moment, catching his breath, before knocking lightly.

The crying stopped, but no one came to the door.

He knocked again, louder. He was about to knock a third time when the door opened. He pushed into her room and turned on a lamp. Then without a word he took her in his arms. The weeping started anew as she clung to him, and he swept her up, carried her to the edge of the bed and sat, pulling her head to his shoulder. He didn't let go until her crying was reduced to quiet shudders.

Finally she pulled back and braved a smile. "I like this new treatment, Doc."

He smiled back, wiping the tears from her cheeks. "I'm always on the lookout for new medical advances."

Her expression grew serious. "If you are a part of this, I think I can do it."

He wasn't entirely sure what she meant. "A part of what?"

"Living. Here. Now. Without you, it's too hard."

He pulled her back to his chest, his heart and his head once again warring over words. "I'll take care of you, Lita."

Chapter 18

Tate approached his house long past noon, stopping for something to eat before heading out again to check on Mrs. Pilson's infant. He hoped to take Lita along. *If she's still feeling down, holding the baby might cheer her up.*

After all her tears of the night before, he was completely unprepared for the laughter that floated on the breeze as he left Maisy with Harold in the carriage house.

Coming around the corner, he saw that two quilts had been thrown over the clothesline, the corners weighted down with bricks to form a V-shaped tent.

Tate walked to the open end and peered in to find Lita and Nellie stretched out on their backs atop a quilt covering the ground, their stockings and shoes in a pile nearby. The two were giggling uncontrollably.

Crouching down, he tickled the bottom of Nellie's feet, and she pulled her legs up as she sat in surprise. "Papa!"

Lita pushed up on her elbows, still grinning. "Do you want to join our comedy club, Doc? We're offering free memberships for a limited time."

Tate chuckled. "No doubt you two are quite entertaining, but I only stopped by home for something to eat."

Lita sat all the way up. "Mrs. K. went home not feeling well about mid-morning, so I made lunch. There's quite a learning curve with that stove, but I managed to make some fairly decent biscuits and gravy."

Tate grimaced. "How not feeling well?"

"Stomach ache."

He took off his hat and ran a hand through his hair before replacing it and standing. "Well, that fits with about half the town. I'm trying to decide if it's just a touch of the flu or something else."

"What other reason could there be? It wouldn't be food poisoning if half the town has it." Lita scooted to the end of the tent, and Tate offered his hand and pulled her up. "Or could it be a water issue? Most of your 'healthy springs' taste awful."

Nellie bounded ahead to the back door as Tate walked with Lita. He noticed that both had left their shoes behind. "It's most likely flu, although one can never rule out the possibility of drinking water contamination."

He held the door for her. "You seem... better today."

"I'm not going to get over what I've lost in a day, Doc, but Nellie doesn't need to feel it, too." She gave him a small smile as she passed him into the house. "I'll always try to put on a smile for her, and if this is where I'm... stuck, then this is where I'll have to learn to be happy."

He frowned at her use of the word "stuck" but was proud of her attitude. "You have emotional adjustments to make, and I'll try to be understanding."

She cocked her head at him. "But that doesn't mean you believe me."

Tate took off his hat, struggling to find the right words. He took too long.

Lita blinked back tears and gave him a weak smile. "No, I thought not." Holding his gaze, she swallowed. "So how do I go forward in a century that is way behind?"

His hand came up without thought to smooth her hair, ruffled by laying on the quilt. "I'll help you."

She smiled. "Well, I am living proof that you have to be careful what you wish for." She turned abruptly, moving through the wash porch to the kitchen. "I always loved this style of dresses, but looking at them and living in them are two different things. And I'm just not used to the lack of air-conditioning in all these layers." She stopped at the ice box and pulled out a bowl covered by a plate. "I'm sure they will feel wonderful in winter, but right now, and especially in this kitchen, they are nothing short of torturous."

Tate wondered about women's fashions in Missouri. From what he'd seen advertised in the papers, he had assumed they were pretty much the same all over. He took the bowl from her hands and waved her on through to the dining room. "Well, don't let it be said that I am a torturer of women. I'll warm up my own lunch."

"Knock yourself out, Doc. The biscuits are in still in the pan."

She left the kitchen, and Tate was left to ponder the term "air-conditioning" and how knocking himself out had anything to do with cooking.

As soon as he had the gravy warmed and spooned over two fluffy biscuits, Tate carried his plate and coffee into the dining room to find Lita writing in a small book.

Curious, he sat next to her. "May I ask what you are composing?"

Instead of answering, she handed it to him. The first page was a list of names: Thomas Edison, Oscar Wilde, James Naismith, Lizzie Borden, Mark Twain, Sir Arthur Conan Doyle.

He laid it down on the table as he cut into Lita's meal and took a bite. He was momentarily distracted by the savory flavors in his mouth. "Mmm, this is good. I believe your biscuits rival, if not surpass, Mrs. Kettler's."

"Thanks. I'm glad you like it." She pointed to the book. "These are all names you know, right?"

"Some of them."

"Which ones?"

He paused to take another bite. He could see that she was impatient, and he remembered her declaration of the previous day that patience wasn't her best suit. He smiled, swallowed, wiped his mouth on his napkin, and turned his attention back to the list. "Let's see, well, I know Thomas Edison, of course, and I believe Oscar Wilde is a playwright. And everyone knows Mark Twain. The other three I'm not familiar with."

"Okay, well, Lizzie Borden was famous for being accused of killing her parents quite brutally with an axe, but I'm not exactly sure of the date. Maybe it's happened already, maybe not. The same goes for James Naismith. He is credited with

inventing basketball, although I'm not certain exactly when—
sometime in the late 19th century. And Sir Arthur Conan Doyle
was just getting his Sherlock Holmes character off the ground
around this time. Turn the page."

Tate had gotten side-tracked, by "maybe it's happened
already, maybe not," and hadn't heard much of the rest.

She turned the page herself. "Okay, now here are a few
things I'm pretty sure of. Unfortunately the big things like
World War I isn't for another twenty-two years, and I can't wait
that long to convince you I'm not totally looney tunes."

World War I?

"Women in Colorado got voting rights way before it was
a national law. That happened in 1893, and here's a tidbit I
learned up on Pikes Peak. Katharine Lee Bates wrote a poem
entitled *America the Beautiful* also in 1893 while looking off
the mountain. It wasn't published, however, until several years
later. Then someone set it to music, and it became a patriotic
classic." She paused. "I hope it doesn't take two more years to
convince you, but just in case..."

He couldn't help smiling. "Well, I won't be surprised about
the women's vote. Almost anyone could predict that... So how
does the song go?"

She didn't miss a beat. "Oh beautiful for spacious skies..."
She kept singing until a very dramatic "from sea to shining
sea."

It was a good song—a beautiful song. And no, he had never
heard it before, and if Lita were to be believed, he wouldn't
hear it for another couple of years.

He stared into her eyes, wishing he could believe her, but
he couldn't help thinking that she was making all this up in
some part of her fractured mind. He longed to hold her again,
but he couldn't allow that until she was well. Her eyes were
asking for his acceptance, but all he could offer was truth.
"That was beautiful. And you have a lovely voice. I look
forward to hearing it more often."

He turned back to his meal, vowing to write a letter to a
colleague about her case as soon as he was done seeing patients
for the day. He didn't trust the phone system when it came to
confidentiality. He had a feeling those operators listened in.

She leaned toward him, determination setting her jaw. "Tate, you know that hotel we ate in yesterday? It burns to the ground sometime before the next century."

He froze with his fork in his mouth then slowly withdrew it. After swallowing, he turned to her. "Lita, I know to let most of what you say go by because of your... head injury, but other people may not. You need to watch what you say. If by some chance that hotel did burn down, and someone remembered your ramblings, you could be blamed."

"Ramblings. Tate, I'm telling you what I know of history to prove to you that I've been in the future."

"Well, so far you've proved nothing."

"I know that. Unfortunately you'll have to wait, but when they do happen..." She patted her book.

Tate sipped his now-cooled coffee. "So who's the next president?"

"I know all the presidents, but not the dates so much... Who's the president right now?"

It seemed impossible that one so intelligent and well-educated should not know the current president. *Must be another gap in her memory.* "It's Benjamin Harrison."

Lita closed her eyes and started to sing another song. "James Garfield someone really hated 'cause he was assassinated. Chester Arthur gets instated. Four years later he is traded for Grover Cleveland, really fat, elected twice as Democrat. Then Benjamin Harrison—" She stopped singing. "That is, of course, where the song isn't quite right because—"

"Grover Cleveland was only elected once."

"No, it's not quite right because Benjamin Harrison was in between Cleveland's two terms."

"So you're predicting Cleveland to win the next election."

She smirked. "I'm not *predicting* anything. It's already happened. It's a done deal. I'm just telling you what the history books say."

Her eyes were shining with confidence, and if he were a weaker man, he might have been persuaded.

"And Tate," —she laid her hand on his shoulder— "there's an economic downturn coming next year; don't put your money in silver. Gold is going to be the standard of the nation, at least for a while."

He pushed his plate away while she continued to talk. "I wish I knew something major that happens in August or September of this year, but I just don't."

As was so often the case since Lita's arrival, he found himself without words. People make predictions all the time about the economy, but they usually don't speak with quite this much confidence. "I guess time will tell."

She closed her book and held it to her chest, smiling smugly. "It will indeed."

She looked so sincere, sitting there hugging her names and dates in his late wife's pinstriped, green dress as if they were some kind of lifeline. His mind strayed to what he knew of the mysteries underneath the dress—bright pink underthings she washed out in the bathroom sink every night, unlike anything he'd ever seen, and a tattoo that no respectable woman would have commissioned. And for a moment, what she was purporting almost made more sense than what an injury could explain.

Almost.

"Lita, what you are suggesting simply isn't possible. People aren't thrown through time by lightning."

She rose and moved quickly past him to the door. "There's a first time for everything, Doc."

Chapter 19

Lalita drank in the mountain scenery as she and Tate traveled to the Pilson's house with Nellie in between them on the buggy seat. She had persuaded Tate to take them both to see the baby. After a quick call to confirm that the stomach flu had not hit their household, he had agreed, and Nellie had been ecstatic.

While Tate lectured Nellie on the dos and don'ts of a house call, Lalita let her mind wander. She still felt a certain emptiness at the thought that she'd never be going home, but the adventurer in her was starting to return. Had she been able to choose a time period on her own, she might have very well chosen this one, although she hadn't been kidding about the clothes. She was so over Victorian dresses.

She looked to the handsome man still yakking at his daughter, who was nodding every few sentences. The man who thought she was flat out crazy. The man she was falling for. She also knew he was falling for her as well, but he wouldn't admit it as long as she appeared "ill."

That left her with two options: pretend to have come to her senses and do everything possible to fake it in this century or prove to Tate that she is from a different time and only have to fake it when she left the house. Both had their difficulties, but she still believed the latter was the best course of action. She would then at least have one ally who understood her.

For the thousandth time, she regretted losing her phone. *Maybe it couldn't come through time with me. Maybe it's still laying there on the mountain in 2015.* She winced. *It was probably fried by the lightning.* She pictured the headlines: *"Freezing Female Disappears on Mighty Mountain. Unidentified Melted Technology Left Behind."*

Nellie poked her in the ribs, and she brought her attention back to her companions in the buggy. "I'm sorry, did you say something?"

Tate smiled. "I said, 'a penny for your thoughts.' "

Lalita laughed. "Wow, a penny is actually worth stopping and picking up in this time, so I'm flattered that you're interested. You would, however, not appreciate hearing my thoughts at the moment."

She glanced at Nellie, and Tate gave a tiny nod of acknowledgment, although his expression seemed to show surprise as well.

They arrived at the Pilson's a few minutes later, and Millie herself received them in the parlor. After Tate checked the baby girl over and declared her fit and growing, he handed her back to Millie, who deferred to Lalita, smiling warmly. Tate laid the baby in her waiting arms, and Nellie leaned in beside her on the small sofa.

Millie pushed a button by the door, then sat across from them. "I want to thank you again for all your help with the delivery, Lalita. You'll make the doctor a fine nurse."

Lalita looked at Tate, surprised. "Do you hear that, Doc. Maybe I've missed my calling as a history major, and the universe adjusted my course to send me to you."

Tate smiled warily. Even when Lalita didn't say something completely ridiculous, she said it in a different way than most. He looked to the blond woman who was now giving her maid instructions, wondering how she would take Lalita's comments. She appeared not to notice anything amiss, and Tate scolded himself for being touchy. *Stop looking for trouble.*

The maid returned a few minutes later with a tray of iced lemonade. Tate, who was sweating profusely on what must be the hottest day yet this summer was grateful for the cold beverage instead of the hot tea women seemed to indulge in no matter what the temperature.

Tate took a drink then nearly bolted out of his seat when Lita seemed to be handing the baby to Nellie. "Miss Torres, I don't think that Nellie—"

"It's okay, Doc, I'll help her." She looked to Mrs. Pilson. "That is, if it's all right with you."

Mrs. Pilson waved a hand as she took a lemonade off the tray. "Goodness, yes, Nellie looks to me to be up to the task. That baby has three older siblings, so she's been handed about a good deal."

Tate settled back in his chair but kept his eyes on his daughter. It wasn't until he realized that Lita was holding her hands in such a way on her lap as to be ready for every contingency that he relaxed enough to give Mrs. Pilson his attention. "Are you having any problems post delivery? No trouble with nursing, I assume."

She blushed and seemed reticent to speak. "I do have something... I noticed it just this morning."

He leaned forward. "What is it?" He noticed her glance toward Lita. "We can talk about it in another room, if you'd like more privacy."

She hesitated a moment longer, then spoke. "I hope it won't offend you, Doctor, but I was wondering if I could talk to Lalita about it."

Lita looked up at the mention of her name, and Tate's eyebrows rose along with his hackles. "Lalita! Even though she was a fine assistant in Anna's delivery, she does not have any medical training."

"Nothing beyond basic first-aid and a CPR course," Lita agreed.

Tate's brows converged. "CPR?"

"You know, cardiopulmonary resuscitation. Or are we too early for that?"

"Are you talking about chest compression following a heart attack?" She nodded, and Tate blinked. "You know how to do chest compression?"

"Sure, it's standard for working at a daycare. We all have to know how to do it."

Mrs. Pilson cleared her throat. "Uh, I don't want to cause a fuss; I'd just feel better talking to a female about this particular... problem."

Tate's feathers were not just ruffled, they were in a twist. "You will allow me to treat you if treatment is necessary?"

She nodded and stood, looking expectantly to Lita, who looked questioningly to Tate. He gave her a small nod as he moved to take her place beside Nellie. "Nellie and I will watch the baby then, until you return."

Lalita had seen Tate confused. She'd seen him disgruntled. She'd even seen him downright mad, but she'd never seen the kind of indignation he was wearing on his face as she followed Millie out of the room. She turned back and shrugged; he answered with a muscle jumping in his very tight jaw.

After the door was closed on Millie's bedroom, she turned and asked Lalita to unbutton her shirtwaist. After pulling it and her corset cover off, she turned, pulling the neckline of her chemise down to reveal a red spot on her breast. "I just noticed this last night, and now it's bigger, and I can feel a hard lump there."

Lalita raised her hand. "May I?"

The worried woman nodded, and Lalita gently laid her fingers on the spot. Millie winced. "Hurts, too, huh?"

"Yes. I've nursed three other children and never experienced this before."

"Well, like the doc said, I've not been medically trained, but I'd say you've got a clogged milk duct. You need to put warm compresses on the spot and just let Anna nurse, nurse, nurse on this side first. Make sure it gets all drained. It might hurt for a bit, but that's the only way to get rid of it."

Millie blew out a breath in relief. "Oh, thank you. I was afraid it was something more serious."

She reached for her corset cover, and Lalita laid a hand on her arm. "Millie, you should probably take off the corset. Plugs can happen if you're too... compressed."

Millie frowned. "But I'm hardly back to my normal size. None of my clothes will fit."

"Have Mr. P. spring for some new clothes. You've just had a baby; you deserve to let it all hang out for a while." Then she gently turned her around and started to undo the lacing.

* * *

Tate was pacing the parlor with a now wailing baby, and Nellie was holding her hands over her ears. He breathed a sigh of relief when the two women finally made a reappearance. Mrs. Pilson rushed toward him no longer wearing her dress, but her wrapper. "I'm sorry, Dr. Cavanagh, and thank you so much for lending me your fine assistant again. I know what to do now."

A maid joined them in the parlor, and after she spoke with the lady of the house in low tones, retreated while Mrs. Pilson walked them to the door, the baby still screaming.

Tate could hardly stand not knowing what Mrs. Pilson and Lita had spoken about, but he could see the youngster needed to eat. "We can see our way out. If you have no further need of my services today…" She was bouncing on her toes and hushing the bundle at her shoulder, and Tate sighed. "Go take care of the little one. Call if you need me."

Ushering Nellie and Lita out, he managed to get everyone seated in the buggy before his curiosity got the better of him. "So, Dr. Lalita, what was it that Mrs. Pilson could say to you but not to me, her trusted physician for over two years."

Lita laughed. "Now don't get your underwear in a tangle, Doc. There are some things that women can just ask other women more easily."

She didn't say any more, and Tate could see she was enjoying the fact that she had been Mrs. Pilson's confidant. "So are you going to tell me what the problem is?"

Lita put a finger to her lips. "Hmmm, I guess she didn't sign a HIPAA form, so I suppose it will be all right."

"Sign a what?" She grinned at him, her eyes sparkling, and Tate nearly forgot what he wanted to know.

"Okay, I'll give you a break. She has a clogged milk duct. I told her how to take care of it."

Tate reined Maisy into a left turn. "And how did you know how to take care of it?"

"I work—worked—at a daycare. Remember the blabbing pregnant mothers? Well, there are blabbing nursing mothers, too. Nursing mothers are obsessed with breasts and milk and nursing habits, schedules, poop, pumps and pumping, so believe me, I've heard about the dreaded clogged milk duct and how to treat it more times than I care to recall."

He wasn't completely satisfied. "So what did you tell her?"

"I told her to use warm compresses and let the baby nurse that side first to make sure it gets all drained out."

Tate was surprised. That's just what he would have said.

"Oh, and I told her not to wear a corset. That could have caused the problem in the first place."

"And how did you know that? You seemed to imply that you had never worn one before."

Lita laughed. "I thought we weren't supposed to have a conversation with 'unmentionables' in it, Dr. all-about-the-rules Cavanaugh?"

Tate blushed and urged Maisy to a trot.

*   *   *

At Lalita's request, Tate drove them to the grocery store. If she was going to fill in for Mrs. Kettler, she wanted to see what her options were for cooking. She had no idea what kind of convenience foods were available, if any.

She found a variety of canned goods, but the extra fudgy Duncan Hines brownie mix she was hungry for was not to be found. It seemed she would have to settle for Jello.

Next she searched for dried pastas and spaghetti sauce in jars but struck out again. Tate finally asked if he could help her find what she was looking for. "I don't know how to cook in this era. What does Mrs. Kettler make other than meat and potatoes?"

"She makes a variety of meat pies—robin, squirrel, rabbit... sometimes even bear if the bigger game hunters have been busy in the area."

Lalita couldn't stop the grimace that came to her face. "Oh! Ugh!" She turned, still making a face. "Okay, I'll try making spaghetti from scratch. I know how to make noodles, even though it will be more difficult without my pasta machine, and all I need is tomatoes and seasonings to make a sauce."

Tate followed, pulling Nellie along by the hand. "Spaghetti. All right. I haven't had that since I left Denver. You're right, Mrs. Kettler isn't a very imaginative cook."

After Tate paid for the produce, they headed back to the buggy, but Nellie pulled Lalita to look in the clothier's window next door. Lalita knew that had she looked at this display of mutton-sleeved dresses and elaborate hats a week ago, she would have been dying to try them on. Now they just looked hot and uncomfortable.

Nellie looked up at her, grinning. "Which one is your favorite?"

Lalita smiled back. "For looks, the salmon one with the embroidered underskirt, but seriously, I can't wait for the flapper dresses to come into style."

Tate appeared by her side. "Pick one out, and I'll buy it."

She looked to him, surprised. "I couldn't. I mean, Augusta's dresses are fine." She looked down at the hem that was two to three inches too short and the waist that was probably two to three inches too large.

Tate spoke what she was thinking. "No, they're not. Augusta was a shorter woman, and later, a plumper woman. If you plan on staying with us for a while, you need clothes that fit."

A while. Lalita smirked. *Doc, you're stuck with me.*

He cocked his head at her. "Did I say something funny?"

She shook her head at him, wide-eyed. "No, not at all." Then she grinned. "Let's shop!" Grabbing his hand she pulled him to the door as she waved Nellie forward.

She was glad to see that the newer fashions had not yet moved on to the ridiculously puffed sleeves that were yet to come, but skin showing was still for the most part a no no. "They all still look so hot."

Nellie tugged on her skirt. "What about those? They're beautiful!" She was pointing to a display of dresses in embroidered silks that actually had swooping necklines and small cap sleeves, obviously designed for a very special occasion.

"It wouldn't do to stand over a stove or wash the clothes in something like that, though, would it? I wonder why it's okay to be more bare at a party but not when you're slaving in the kitchen?"

Nellie shrugged.

A clerk approached, and Lalita asked to see her lightest weight dresses. Frankly, she didn't care what they looked like as long as they were cool.

Tate watched the two females perusing the ladies' fashions a moment before heading to the gentlemen's side of the store. He looked over the selection of hats, remembering Lita's assessment that his bowler made him look old. He tried on a fedora or two, wondering what she'd think of them before putting them down and pulling his own thoughts down to earth. He couldn't start dressing with her in mind, or he'd never be able to keep a professional distance.

He shook his head, knowing that a "professional distance" had flown out the window the moment he'd held her on his lap the night before in her bedroom... on her bed. He sighed, wandering along the glass case, looking at cuff links, embroidered handkerchiefs, suspenders, and collars. He didn't really need anything himself, so he kept moving, thinking he might pick up a new hair bow for Nellie.

Before he got to the hair accessories, however, he ran into the perfume. He picked up a sample atomizer bottle and held it under his nose. He was immediately struck with a sick feeling, not unlike what had happened to him several nights before. Determined to ferret out the mystery, he took another whiff, and it came to him. The bathroom had been full of this scent when he broke down the door to find Augusta dead.

Suddenly sweating, his pulse rapid, he stepped back from the counter just as the females in his charge appeared at his side. He turned to see Lita carrying several bolts of fabric, a pattern, and sewing notions. He pulled his racing heart out of the past. "You'd rather sew a dress?"

Lita put a fist to her hip. "Not really, but the dresses are designed for the one who wants to wear a cor— that which cannot be named—necessary to squeeze one down to an eighteen-inch waist. I hope that's one society trend you don't mind that I buck."

He smiled at her defiant expression. "No, I don't. As a physician, I have recommended to many women to loosen their... undergarments for the sake of proper digestion."

"Good."

Tate pointed her toward the counter then noticed Nellie with a spool of ribbon. "And what do you have, Miss Nell?"

"Lalita said you would buy me some ribbon if I asked you sweetly."

The corners of Tate's mouth twitched, but he didn't crack a smile. "And do you plan on asking sweetly?"

She nodded with her eyes wide, and Tate laughed, certain he knew who had schooled her in these shenanigans. He took the spool and moved toward the counter beside Lita, grateful for joviality to wash away pain.

*   *   *

"Nellie, today I'm going to teach you how to make noodles. Could you get me two eggs, please?"

Even though the kitchen was hot without the stove even lit, Lalita was determined to cook the spaghetti she'd bought the ingredients for. She switched on the small electric fan that only brought a slight improvement to the temperature of the room.

After stirring and rolling out the dough, she had sweat through her dress and felt drained. "Ugh! Damn these dresses straight to hell!"

At Nellie's gasp and wide-eyed expression, Lalita bit her lip. "Oops. Sorry. Forget I said that." She wiped her forehead and neck with a dish towel. "I may have to set up a swear jar, although I don't know what I'd put in it, since I have no money."

She leaned against the counter, dreaming of walking through the refrigerated section of a 21st century grocery store. "Nellie, I'm going to expire in this kitchen before we get the sauce even started." All at once, she remembered something she'd seen in Augusta's trunk—swimwear.

She headed out of the kitchen. "Come on, Nellie, I'm thinking beach party."

Chapter 20

"Everybody's gone surfing—surfing USA."

Lalita was belting out a tune quite unfamiliar to Tate as he walked into the house inhaling the most delicious aroma—a spicy, tomato scent that made his stomach growl as he hung his hat on the rack.

With the closing of the door, the singing stopped. "Tate, is that you? Would you mind terribly not coming into the kitchen just yet?"

Tate slowed his gait down the hall. "Why?"

"Um, it's a surprise."

He stopped, his brow furrowing, but the sound of pots and pans clanging to the floor had him moving again. He reached the doorway to see Lita scrambling to pull a skirt over a short navy dress with a square collar— *Augusta's swimsuit?*—and Nellie pulling her dress on over her petticoats. "What in the name of God's green earth is going on?"

Lita spun, buttoning her skirt on the side as she did so. "Tate, you couldn't wait just a minute for your surprise?" She grabbed up her shirtwaist and slipped her arms in the sleeves. "And you say I'm impatient."

He stepped toward her. "Actually, I believe you owned up to that all by yourself." He looked from one to the other with eyebrows raised. "Was the surprise that you're cooking in swimwear and bloomers?"

Lita was reaching behind her back at her waistline, buttoning buttons. "Well, no, the surprise would have been that the spaghetti was made by two fresh-as-a-daisy girls in a sweltering kitchen."

"Ah, I see. A lie by appearances only. Is that your specialty, Lita?" He turned her around to finish buttoning her buttons.

"Would you have rather walked in on us in swimwear and bloomers? We'd be happy to oblige."

He finished, and she turned to face him, Tate's nose picking up something other than the tomato sauce. *Augusta's perfume. Lita's been wearing it.* Backing up, he shook his head. "No, I... so when will this feast of yours be ready?"

She rushed to the stove and stirred the pot of boiling pasta. Looping a strand on a spoon, she pulled it off with her fingers, blew on it, and sucked it up. She smiled as she chewed. "Just a minute or two more."

Tate nodded and headed out the back door.

Lita walked after him, calling through the screen door as he headed toward the carriage house. "So where are you going?"

He turned, but kept walking backwards. "Just need some fresh air. You're right, that kitchen is too... close." He spun, calling over his shoulder. "I'll be back in a few minutes."

Entering the carriage house, he took in a big breath, letting the odors of horse, leather, and manure replace the scent of old memories.

Lalita watched Tate jog to the carriage house, pondering his sudden flight. Nellie brought her attention back to the kitchen. "Can we use the special dishes? The ones with roses?"

Lalita turned back into the kitchen. "I don't see why not."

After the two had set the table, drained the pasta, and ladled sauce over it in a tureen, Tate reappeared and followed them to the dining room. Lalita sat and blinked when Tate sat down as far away from her as possible.

He raved about the spaghetti, however, and when Lalita pointed out that Nellie had helped with everything on the table, he had compliments for the cherry Jello and lemonade as well.

She wondered at Tate's distance and strove to eat with perfect manners. Spaghetti didn't give itself to this plan easily. Finally, frustrated with dangling ends, she just cut it all up into tiny bites. "I'll have to have Mrs. K. teach me how to bake bread. I'm spoiled with my bread machine. I don't know how to knead it by hand."

"You have a machine that does the kneading for you?"

"The stirring, the kneading, the rising, and the baking."

Tate twisted his fork in his spaghetti. "Well, what will they think of next?"

"Nobody's going to think of it for about a hundred years, though, so..."

Tate's smile slid, and Lalita regretted highlighting the fact that he still regarded her as being off her rocker. "Forget I brought it up." She spooned a second helping of Jello into her bowl, discouraged with her inability to prove the truth about her lightning time travel.

Tate seemed to sense her mood shift. "I just realized we are using different dishes than usual. They're very pretty. We should use them more often."

"It was my idea, Papa!" Nellie chimed in. "Mrs. Kettler always says they are too good to use for everyday."

"Nonsense! What's the point of having pretty dishes if you don't use them. What do you think, Lita?"

She couldn't help the smile that slipped out. "I think someone is bucking society rules."

He helped himself to more spaghetti. "I don't strictly adhere to the rules that dictate things that just don't matter. Fashion for instance, or which plates one uses on what occasion. Those rules change with the winds of time. Basic propriety, however, is ageless."

"So which rule was I breaking by cooking in swimwear," she teased, "fashion or propriety?"

He considered with a forkful of spaghetti in front of his mouth. "Probably both, but as long as you don't hire yourself out as a swimsuit wearing cook, your secret's safe with me."

Nellie sipped her lemonade and wiped her mouth on her napkin. "It was much cooler. Who invented swimwear? Maybe we should write them a letter and ask them to invent cooking wear."

Lalita grinned. "Maybe we should invent it, Nellie. We could be trend setters."

Tate hitched a brow. "I hate to be a wet blanket, but the fashions you left behind in Missouri might not be acceptable here."

Lalita quirked her lips to the side. "Actually, you love being a wet blanket, but I wasn't planning on jumping from this" — she motioned down her body— "to halter tops and cut-offs. It will have to be a subtle change." The gears in her head were turning. "Do you have any paper I can draw on?"

Tate pushed away from the table and strode to his study, returning with several sheets and a pencil. Lita thanked him, set her plate to the side, and began to sketch.

Nellie leaned forward across the table, so Tate excused her to go watch Lita draw. He set to work clearing the table, sure he hadn't eaten so much in a great while. He was glad to help with the clean-up, smiling as he set the empty tureen in the sink. *And if I force her back in here, she may strip down to that swim dress again.*

He shook his head as he filled the sink with water and rolled up his sleeves. He never knew what to expect anymore when he walked through the door to his own home. He couldn't imagine what Mrs. Kettler would think of their unconventional dress in the kitchen—or the meal itself, for that matter— but one thing was obvious—Nellie was blossoming under Lita's care.

Mrs. Kettler made sure Nellie was dressed and fed and safe, but Lita engaged her mind and her spirit. If only he could loose her from her time traveling fantasy, he'd gladly welcome her into his home and into his heart. He scrubbed a few strands of stuck-on spaghetti off the bottom of the pot. *And I would not try to force her to be something she's not.* He bent his head back, looking up at the ceiling. "I promise," he whispered.

As he went back to the dining room to gather the rest of the dishes, he wondered about the fact that he'd never actually seen Augusta in that swim dress. He supposed she had worn it on the beach back east before she moved to Denver. He hadn't really thought about it before, but it seemed a very bold move for one so reserved, to move to Denver all by herself after her parents' deaths.

Pausing with plates in hand, he looked over Lita's shoulder and was surprised again at her skill. "You have a talent for drawing."

Lita didn't look up. "I just goof around." She added a final flourish to her model's hair then sat back. "What do you think? Some of the formal wear of the day doesn't seem to be concerned with a bit of décolletage showing or going practically sleeveless, so why not in the kitchen where we're frying while we're frying, if you know what I mean." She went over the lines of the skirt with the pencil. "And the walking skirt will hit stores before long anyway—maybe five or six years."

Tate inwardly sighed at yet more future predictions as he studied her design. He had been afraid to see what she would come up with, but her new design wasn't as immodest as he expected. The fitted bodice had a scooped neckline and short sleeves with no fullness at the shoulder. The skirt still extended to the toes but employed a simple A-line shape with only slight gathers in the back.

He pictured Lalita in it, her cross necklace laying against bare, bronze skin, and Augusta's perfume once again wafted up to his nose. He wondered if she'd used the whole bottle. He turned and escaped to the kitchen, throwing his comments back over his shoulder. "Lengthen the sleeves and raise the neckline, Lita. Those in the kitchen shouldn't be enticing the men of the house."

As soon as it was out of his mouth, he realized that he had just broken his vow. He hung his head as he set the plates in the dish water. *But how far can I let her go? There has to be a limit, doesn't there?*

Lalita scowled at Tate's criticism. *What a prig.*

She sketched a slightly longer sleeve down to the elbow and gave it a little bit of a poof at the shoulder to fit in more with the style of the day. She took the neckline up a bit, then added an apron that would hide the "enticing" servant's shape. "What do you think of that, Nellie?"

She nodded. "Are you going to make it out of your new fabric?"

"No, I think I'll practice on one of the old dresses. We can take one apart, and I bet we'll have enough fabric left in the skirt to make you a dress also."

"Arabella, too?"

"Is she going to help cook?"

Nellie nodded.

"Well then, I suppose she'll need one. Why don't you go give her the news?"

Nellie turned and ran for the stairs, nearly running into Tate as he came out of the kitchen. "Slow down, Nellie. Ladies don't run."

Lalita rose and stepped away from the table, feeling peeved at Tate and uncomfortable with the beach wear under her clothes. "Sometimes they do, Doc. Sometimes they run really fast and win Olympic medals."

A crease appeared between Tate's brows. "Olympic? As in the ancient games in Greece? Women weren't allowed in the Olympics. What would they do?"

She frowned. *Seriously?* She thought a moment about what she knew of the history of the Olympics. "Oh yeah, the modern games haven't started yet," she conceded. "Well, it won't be long." She snatched her drawing off the table, feeling cross, and moved past him toward the door.

"Did you make any changes to your design?"

"Yep."

He followed her out. "Can I see?"

"Nope." She started upstairs.

"Lita..."

She stopped and sighed, turning. "I'm tired, Tate. I'm going to take a cool bath and head to bed. We can talk about it tomorrow."

He nodded up at her. "Excellent idea. Thank you for the meal, Lita. I appreciate it."

He waited until he heard the bathroom door close, then tiptoed up the stairs and made his way to her room. Finding the perfume bottle on top of a chest of drawers, he gave it a small sniff, then held it away from him before he lost his very delicious spaghetti supper.

Heading back downstairs, he disposed of the offensive liquid down the kitchen sink, all the while thinking about her latest conjecture about the Olympic games. He'd heard no rumblings of gossip concerning their reinstatement.

Leaning on the counter, he ground his teeth, wondering how to proceed. He thought of his old friend in Denver, who had been a doctor to Augusta, and while he might be willing to come for an evaluation, he probably wouldn't be able to stay for any extensive treatment. *But maybe he could advise me on how to proceed.*

He pushed off the counter with an exhale and headed to his study to write a letter to Dr. Jeremiah Fischer.

* * *

Lalita slipped between her sheets in just a thin chemise. The chilly bath she'd taken had helped, but it was still hot in her room.

She'd been pondering Tate's avoidance of her since leaving him standing at the bottom of the stairs. *As if I stank to high heaven.* Her eyes flew wide and she sucked in a breath. *Maybe I did.* Flinging off the sheet, she stumbled to where she'd left the shirtwaist hanging over a chair. Lifting it to her nose, she was instantly repulsed. "Oh! Eww!" Embarrassed, she cursed this century for its lack of adequate deodorant, and she wondered if the blouse should just be burned rather than washed.

Casting it aside in disgust, she stomped back to the bed, feeling overwhelmed with the weight of this century—from clothing to society norms to basic hygiene. She plopped down on the edge, wondering how she'd ever fit in, or if she even wanted to.

She looked to the mirror, frowning at her hair that had all but lost its shine with the harsh soap available. Her gaze headed down to her hairy legs and back up to her hairy arm pits, and her frown deepened into a scowl. *I wonder where Tate hid his razor.*

Her eyes roamed over her colorful shoulder tattoo, and she felt suddenly bitter, knowing she'd spent hundreds of dollars on something she had to keep hidden. She rubbed her earlobes. *My pierced ears are even healing shut.*

Feeling as if she were losing herself with each passing second, she leaped up, grabbed her robe, and headed out of her room, determined to feel human again.

* * *

Tate ascended the stairs with mixed emotions. Laying out Lita's delusions and fantasies on paper gave them extra weight, and he wondered if he should even try to keep her here in his house. *Nellie is already attached. If Lita's mind slips further...*

As he reached the top of the stairs, he became aware of noise in his room. Ready to scold his daughter, he strode forward to the doorway and put his hands on his hips. It wasn't Nellie, however, it was Lita. He was surprised to see her rummaging through his drawers. "Can I help you find something?"

Lita jumped, and Tate caught a flash of silver in her hand before she thrust it behind her back. He knew what it was. He walked forward with his hand out, his heart jumping to a faster rate. "Lita, give it to me."

She backed up, looking defiant. "Tate, I just want to shave my legs. Please. I can't stand them another minute."

Tate wouldn't let her disappear into the bathroom with a razor. He couldn't. He kept walking toward her, backing her up, his hand out. "No, Lita. I can't. Not when you're—"

"What, Tate? What am I? Crazy? Ready for the looney bin?"

"No, honey," he placated sweetly. "Like you said, its safety is overrated. You'll hurt yourself." She had moved into the dressing room, and Tate followed.

Her heels ran into Augusta's trunk, and she sat down hard. Tate sprang toward her, but she didn't fight him. He pulled the razor easily from her grasp and took a big step back. What she did do was hang her head and cry. Tate's heart broke. "I'm sorry."

"I... I," she blubbered. "I just wanted to feel like myself again."

"And shaving your... your..."

"Legs, Tate, legs! Legs is not a bad word!" She pulled up her robe to her knees. "These things I walk with aren't that risqué!" She looked at them with disgust. "Especially now."

Tate didn't want to upset her further. "How can I help?"

She looked up at him with a new spark in her eyes. "When I asked you before to finish what I started, I was teasing." She rose and came toward him. "Now I'm not. You're a doctor. You see women's legs all the time. You do it. If you don't trust me, then you do it."

Tate looked into her determined eyes then down at her bare feet. He'd seen her legs when he was warming her in the bath. Doctors deal with the unclothed body because they're doctors. They set aside personal sentiments and shame for the sake of the patient. *But would shaving her legs be seen as a medical need?* He looked back up to her face, still damp with tears. It seemed absurd that this aberrant behavior should be so important to her, but there was no denying her depth of feeling. "Go wait in the examination room. I need to put Nellie to bed first."

*   *   *

Lalita lay in bed, smiling. She slid her silky-smooth legs over the sheets, feeling as if she'd just been to the spa.

She had stood on a towel in the center of the exam room with her robe hitched up and tied below her butt, while Tate daubed the shaving cream on her legs with the brush. She could tell that he was nervous, but he had been so gentle and careful, she hadn't received one nick from his hand.

She rolled to her side and closed her eyes. *Oh, Tate, I'm falling for you hard. Now to convince you I'm not a lunatic.*

*   *   *

Tate lay in bed, staring at the ceiling. He'd left Lita fifteen minutes ago, but his heart rate was still not quite under control. He'd started out keeping his medical perspective, but as time went on, he began to appreciate her shape as a man—as a man who had been without a woman in his life or in his bed for over a year.

Setting his mind abuzz were the tan lines on her legs— nearly to the top—as if her legs had been completely uncovered for most of the summer. He recalled her desire to find her "shorts" when she first awakened, and he shook his head trying to comprehend the styles that must be popular for young women in Missouri.

He closed his eyes, trying to put her and her now smooth-as-a-baby's-bottom legs out of his mind, but he realized it was fruitless. He couldn't unsee them, unfeel them, anymore than he could deny the way she'd lit up his life and crept into his heart.

He tossed his sheet off, feeling overheated, wondering how long he could really keep her under his roof. Part of helping her recover was protecting her from those who would not understand. But keeping her close to himself without revealing that he was falling in love with her would be the hardest thing he'd ever done.

Augusta never gave me her heart, and now I must deny Lita mine. He slipped out of bed and after pacing back and forth in his nightshirt until he feared he'd wear a path in the carpet, he knelt down at the side of his bed to pray.

Chapter 21

Mrs. Kettler was still not back on the job Thursday morning. Lalita made bacon, eggs, and pancakes, wishing for her waffle maker. Tate didn't eat all that much, though. She thought maybe he was still full from last night's spaghetti.

After breakfast, he suddenly announced that Nellie would be spending the day with a friend and that Lalita would be accompanying him should there be calls to make.

She looked at him over her shoulder as she walked dirty dishes to the sink. "I was going to try creating my new design today. Do you really need me to go with you?"

Tate nodded a bit too vigorously, following her to the kitchen. "I do. Extra hands are always helpful."

Lalita set the dishes in the sink and started the water running. "Now who's lying?"

He sat on a stool by the window. "Not at all. Having you with me for the Pilson delivery was very beneficial." He smiled. "And who knows, maybe I could train you to be a true medical assistant."

"Maybe." Lalita suspected it had more to do with keeping an eye on her.

The phone rang, and Tate got up to answer. Within fifteen minutes, he had loaded Nellie up in the buggy that had come for her and Lalita in his own heading toward a building site where a man had taken a tumble from a roof. Lita wrote in her book as he drove Maisy at a swift trot.

It didn't take long for Tate's curiosity to be aroused. "What are you writing? More predictions?"

"Just jotting down the rest of the presidents. The last one I know was the first black man to be president. It took a hundred and forty-five years from the Emancipation Proclamation for a black man to become president. And his mother was white."

Tate smiled, obviously just playing her along. "How about Indians?"

"Somewhere in the 20th century, we became Native Americans, Tate. It's no longer PC to say Indians unless you are referring to people from India."

He slowed Maisy and turned. "PC?"

"Politically correct. We've become a very offendable people in the 21st century."

Tate pulled Maisy to a halt in front of a new house going up, and Lalita could see a small crowd gathered on what would someday be a lawn. Tate jumped down and offered her his hand. She took it while she stepped down, wishing she could keep hold of him, but she released him when her feet hit the ground and let him rush ahead to see to the injured man.

As she joined the crowd, several men stared with admiration in their eyes, while one or two gave her another look altogether. Tate was squatting in front of a man sitting on the ground with his shirt off, holding his side. Tate waved her over, and she squatted down beside him. "Paul, here, was testing out gravity today. He informs me that it is still working."

Lalita smiled. "And what was the fruit of his scientific research?"

Tate reached for his bag at his side. "Several cracked ribs."

Paul chuckled, then winced. "Doc, stop joking around and fix me."

He pulled out a roll of bandages and stood. "If you wouldn't mind helping him up, boys."

After the man's chest was wrapped, and he was given instructions on his physical activity for the next several weeks, Tate and Lalita walked back to the buggy.

"I think that's one treatment that hasn't changed over the years," Lalita mused as Tate gave her a hand up. "There's still not much one can do for broken ribs in 2015 except wrap them and let them heal."

"You're implying that other treatments will change." He climbed aboard and took up the reins.

"Oh, yes, Tate, you would just... I wish I could show you."

Tate didn't know whether to cut off her wild speculations or let her talk. His inquisitive nature won. "So tell me."

"Well, you've gotten a start in this century with vaccinations, but there will be more—so many more— for diphtheria and tetanus and mumps and measles and chickenpox...

"And the equipment, oh my heavens, Tate, there are x-rays and MRIs and EKGs... for looking at things going on inside the body without cutting into it.

"In the next century there will be treatments for all kinds of things—diabetes, cystic fibrosis, heart disease, high blood pressure... And there will be new diseases too. It seems one new one pops up for every one we conquer. Now there's Alzheimer's, Parkinson's, Multiple Sclerosis, Reflexive Sympathetic Dystrophy, Marfan's, Fibromyalgia... the list goes on and on."

She paused, and Tate couldn't explain the crazy excitement that was coming over him. He knew it had to be just more of her ramblings, but the way she spoke these things—with no hesitation whatsoever, no stopping to think—gave him a shiver up his spine.

Lita went on, breaking into his thoughts. "They've made artificial hearts, Tate, and they've sequenced the human genome, and they're just getting started with stem cell research. That has the potential to cure all kinds of things."

Tate felt short of breath, but thankfully Lita had become distracted as they drove through downtown. She changed topics rather abruptly. "Tate, would you buy me something?"

He was still feeling off balance. "What... what would you like?" Pulling his handkerchief from his jacket pocket, he wiped his brow.

"The perfume I've been using suddenly disappeared. I think Nellie borrowed it. Maybe she didn't want me to use it up since it was her mama's. I didn't much care for it, anyway, but I need something." She turned her attention from the shops, lowering her voice. "The deodorant that was in Augusta's dressing room is somewhat... inadequate."

Tate opened his mouth to confess but found he didn't want to go into the reasons he'd thrown out the perfume himself.

She was looking at him with anticipation. "It doesn't have to be expensive."

The thought occurred to him that he was about to commit a lie of omission, besides letting her believe a falsehood about Nellie, but he plunged ahead. "Yes, of course. I'd be happy to."

He found a spot to park the buggy, and the two walked to the dress shop they'd been in the day before. At the perfume counter, she sniffed them all and let Tate smell them as well. He said no to several that were too much like the one he'd gotten rid of, and she said no to one that made her sneeze.

When they were finally in agreement, and she had tried some out on her wrists, Tate told her to go look through the other women's toiletries, certain that buying her perfume he actually liked was probably a mistake.

She came back with an armload of bottles and bars, along with a sheepish grin. "All of this stuff seems really cheap to me, since the last face cream I bought was literally a hundred times this price, but you tell me if it's too much."

He waved her to the cash register. "I haven't had to buy anything like this for over a year."

She grinned, setting it all on the counter. "Thanks, Doc, that soap of yours was about to ruin my hair."

Tate hadn't noticed any difference, but now that she had brought it to his attention, he wanted nothing more than to run his fingers through it by way of inspection.

The woman behind the counter brought him back. "Do you want to pay cash today, Doc, or just put it on your tab."

Tate smiled. "Thank you, but I prefer not to have a tab." He pulled out his wallet and handed her enough to cover the cost.

When he turned, Lita surprised him with a kiss on the cheek. "Thanks again."

Tate blushed. "Lita..." He looked around and hurried her through the store and out. "It's hardly suitable—" He stopped and tipped his hat to a passing woman and her daughter, biting his tongue against further correction.

They walked in silence to the buggy, but Lita refused his hand and climbed up herself. Sighing, he ran around to the other side. After starting Maisy down the street, he tried to form an apology. "Lita, I'm sorry. I'm just concerned about the gossiping tongues of a small town."

"Oh pooh, you're no fun at all. It was just a little peck. I didn't take you into a dip, for Pete's sake."

"Nevertheless, a 'little peck' between two single people in a small town like this will start rumors. You have your reputation to consider." Tate started Maisy back on the road to home.

"Is that really all you're worried about? What was it Seth Dickson said?... 'Most men won't give her the time of day because she's a squaw.' Now, I know you would give me the time of day because you let me stay in your home, and you just bought me a lot of nice things, but is that how you think of me too—as a squaw? Did my little kiss embarrass you because I'm part Native American?"

Tate's head jerked toward her. "No, absolutely not."

She lowered her voice to almost a whisper. "How do you think of me?"

Tate swallowed. "I... I think very highly of you. You have many talents." He flashed her a smile, somewhat surprised that she was not smiling back.

She turned her stony stare to the road ahead. "I took you for a braver man, Tate Cavanaugh, but I was wrong. You're a coward."

Tate flinched. "How do you figure that?"

"You're scared of me."

"Nonsense," he blurted. "You've just... read more into our relationship than is there."

"I don't think so. What did you want to discuss with me the day before we went to Colorado Springs?"

"Discuss?"

She pursed her lips. "Don't play dumb with me. The picnic you invited me to go on—you said you wanted to discuss something with me. And you had a real sparkle in your eyes when you said it. What was it, Tate?"

Tate felt a drip of sweat run down his neck. "I... I don't recall."

She snorted. "For someone so concerned with truth, you are quite the liar."

He turned Maisy onto the hill heading home, knowing she was right. "All right. Here's the truth. You spoke the night before about leaving, and I... well, I was going to ask you to stay."

"Just... stay. Was there more to it than that?"

Tate was gripping the reins so tightly, his knuckles were turning white. "I wanted to court you, Lita."

"But after I told you I came from the future, you changed your mind because you think I'm crazy."

"No, well, I don't know. I'm not that kind of doctor. I can't make that diagnosis on my own. That's why I—"

Lalita was watching her handsome, strong doctor turn to jelly before her eyes. "That's why you what?"

He looked at her with what seemed like regret, or perhaps it was just sympathy. "I wrote a letter to a doctor that deals with illness of the mind about your case."

"I'm not a *case*, Tate, I'm a woman out of place."

All at once, Lalita saw the future all too clearly, being questioned and probed by psychiatrists and psychologists. Maybe even locked away. Away from Tate. She blinked back tears. "How long until he gets the letter?"

"A week or so, I imagine."

She wiped a tear from the corner of her eye. "You said you'd take care of me."

He reached over and unclenched her hand from her skirt. "I will, Lita. I promise."

* * *

"Ugh! How did people live before microwave ovens? This stovetop warming is for the birds." Lalita was trying to warm up the spaghetti and sauce in a pot without it getting burned, her mood continuing a downward spiral.

Tate turned the page on his newspaper, where he sat on the stool across the room. "What's for the birds? Are you making something for the birds?"

She gave him a look, still fuming from their earlier conversation. "No, I really am making lunch for us, not the birds." She couldn't help the scowl that came to her face. "If only I could take you back with me, but standing out in a lightning storm on the off chance I'd go time hopping again instead of being fried is probably pretty risky." She stirred with great vigor, continuing to mutter. "And who says I'd go back to 2015? Maybe I'd jump back to Shakespearean times. The plague would be fun."

He didn't answer, seemingly absorbed in The Daily Gazette. When she had been talking about advances in medicine, Tate seemed different—like he was starting to believe her, but talking about her "illness of the mind" on the way home disobliged her of that thought. She found she was getting pretty weary of his distrust. She set the pot off the stove and walked to stand in front of him. He brought his gaze slowly up to her. "Can I help you with something?"

She took the paper out of his hands, folded it and tossed it on the counter. "Tate, after all I've told you today, how can you still not believe me. Nobody could make all that stuff up."

Tate didn't speak for a moment, and Lalita wanted to slap him. Finally he rose and crossed his arms. "I grant you, it all sounded very… natural, but since I didn't recognize a good deal of what you were talking about, I have no idea if you were making it up or not."

"But," she continued, putting her hands on her hips, "Don't I sound rational whenever you do know what I'm talking about?"

He smiled before maneuvering around her to divide the spaghetti onto the two plates she'd brought from the dining room. "So what you're saying is that you sound perfectly rational when you are rational."

She grabbed a spatula and slid a biscuit onto each plate, her ire building. "No, that's not it at all. What I'm saying is how can someone who sounds rational to you most of the time, sound completely crazy to you at other times?"

"That is, indeed, a very good question."

Tate carried his plate to the dining room, and Lalita felt like screaming. "Oh, you are just not trying to understand me!" She grabbed her plate and followed, sitting down across from him.

"On the contrary, Lita, I've been doing almost nothing but trying to understand you from the time you woke up here a week ago."

He bowed his head for prayer, and Lalita followed suit, but as soon as the "amen" was said, she was right back after him. "Okay, what I'm saying, I guess, is that I'm not prone to irrationality, so why would you assume that just because you can't understand what I'm saying at the moment, that I'm irrational and crazy."

Tate chewed and swallowed, not sure if he wanted to pursue this conversation or not. "So last night... that felt rational to you."

Lita blinked. "Perfectly. I'd been suffering for a week with your awful soap for my hair and deodorant that doesn't work— don't think I don't know why you were avoiding me all last evening—and my itchy, hairy legs were just the last straw." She stared down his skeptical expression. "Maybe not rational for a man, but completely rational for a woman."

He couldn't help it when a smile slipped out. "So are there two different scales for rationality? Male and female?"

Her expression was bordering on dangerous. He ducked his head and went back to eating, but it was impossible to ignore the fury being directed his way. Finally, she set her napkin beside her plate and rose. He caught just a glimpse of her acerbity before she strode from the room.

He sighed and followed her down the hall and to the parlor. "Lita, I'm sorry. I didn't mean to upset you. You're right. There are things that women are concerned about that men are not."

She spun to face him, tears forming in her eyes. "I just need someone here to believe me, Tate, and you're all I have."

He plunged his hands in his pockets once again when he'd rather pull her to his chest. "I wish I could."

She rolled her eyes and pushed past him, speeding down the hall and up the stairs.

Tate sighed again and walked back to the dining room. He sat back down but found that his appetite had left him, as well. He rubbed a hand around his jaw, wishing he could make the leap to belief in her tall tale. *Would it really hurt anything to play along?* He looked across the table to her barely-touched meal, wondering if he should take it up to her, when the doorbell rang.

He found Rand Allen and his wife, Mercy, standing on his porch. Though they loved to espouse their distinction as founding members of the Congregational Church, Tate thought of them more as the town's biggest busybodies.

He slapped on a smile. "Mr. and Mrs. Allen, to what do I owe the pleasure?"

Rand Allen spoke even though his mouth couldn't be seen behind his graying mustache. "Dr. Cavanaugh, might we have a word?"

Tate opened his door wider, and the large man and his thin wife stepped inside. He waved them into the parlor. "Be my guest."

When they were all seated, Tate smiled thinly. "Well, what can I do for you?"

*   *   *

Lalita lay on her bed listening to her stomach growl. She really was hungry. She'd heard the doorbell, but all she had been able to see through her window was a buggy parked out front. Now she didn't know if she'd be able to sneak back down and finish her lunch without being seen, and she scolded herself for her temper that had taken her from the dining room table in the first place.

He's not going to believe you without proof. You're just going to have to accept that. Agitated, she rolled off the bed and began to pace. "Such a frustrating man!"

With her hunger pangs increasing, she opened her door and listened. The voices were muffled, so she assumed Tate must be entertaining whoever had stopped by in the parlor.

She was half-way down the stairs, when the voices suddenly grew quite loud.

"I don't see how my medical practice falls under the jurisdiction of the church, Mr. Allen."

"Dr. Cavanaugh," a deep voice was appealing, "do you deny buying her dress goods, perfume and the like? That hardly seems like something a doctor does for a patient."

"They do when the patient has shown up with nothing but a head injury that has left her memory full of gaps. She's been wearing my dead wife's ill-fitting clothes for a week, and I have no idea how long her recovery will take."

Lalita took a deep breath and continued down the stairs. Her stomach would have to wait. Tate needed backup. She lingered a moment at the doorway, catching Tate's eye before she stepped into the room.

Tate gave her a nervous smile as she entered, rising from a heavy leather chair. "Mr. and Mrs. Allen, I'd like you to meet Miss Lalita Torres," —he gave her a pointed look— "the reason for your visit."

Lalita sucked in a tiny breath as the man pushed his overweight body back up to standing. *Wow, I thought obesity was a modern problem.* Lalita saw his eyes crinkle, but no smile could be seen under his mustache. She wondered how on earth he ever got so fat with his mouth unavailable.

"Miss Torres, Dr. Cavanaugh was telling me and Mercy about your recent injury that has put you here in his care." He waved her toward the settee. "Now that you're here, you can tell us yourself."

Both men sat, and Lalita lowered herself to the velvet couch. Sitting as ram rod straight as Mercy, she considered the incongruity of this woman's sour face together with her name. On the outside, though, Lalita kept a serious, though pleasant expression. "Mr. Allen, I'm most certain that the good doctor can probably explain my condition better than I can." She gestured toward Tate. "My memory is still quite sketchy."

Mercy leaned forward. "And yet you were seen riding a bicycle all over town just a few days ago." She turned her attention to Tate. "Shouldn't someone who has suffered a head injury be abed?"

"In the case of Miss Torres," Tate jumped in, "I am assuming an injury as I could not physically find one at the time she was brought to me. She was unconscious and—"

"But I'm certain, my dear doctor," Lalita interrupted, "that my unconsciousness was caused by the lightning strike I experienced up on the mountain."

Tate inwardly cringed, wondering if Lita was going to go into one of her incomprehensible speeches.

Mercy gasped. "You were struck by lightning?"

Lita shook her head. "Not directly, but a big flash in the middle of a lightning storm on the highest mountain around is the last thing I remember before waking up here."

Mr. Allen rested his elbows on the arms of the chair, his hands clasped over his prodigious belly. "What were you doing up there?"

"With the cog railroad, it's becoming quite the tourist attraction," Tate threw in from his side of the room.

"Yes," the large man said, stroking his mustache, "but they say she was all alone. Did you go up alone, Miss Torres?"

Lita gave a tiny glance toward Tate before answering. "That's part of my memory loss, Mr. Allen. I don't remember that part."

The man and his wife exchanged a look before Mercy spoke. "Miss Torres, surely you realize that as a single woman you should not be here living in the same house as a widower."

Lita opened her mouth to speak, but Tate jumped in, leaning forward in his chair. "I assure you, Miss Torres is in no danger from me. We have a doctor/patient relationship only." He looked to Lita, who, praise God in heaven, had schooled her face to complete agreement. "And until such time as she regains her memory enough to return to her family," he continued, "she is welcome to stay here."

Mr. Allen lifted his double chin. "Welcome, yes, and you are to be commended, doctor, for your kindness, but we have to think about what is best for Miss Torres. You must agree that the two of you under the same roof—"

"Will come to nothing," Tate threw back. "I've been through all this with Reverend Niemeyer. Surely I have lived in this town long enough to earn a bit of trust in my person and in my medical knowledge. If I say that it would be best for Miss Torres to be in my house until she fully recovers, then I would think that should be good enough."

Mercy scowled, rose, and went to sit beside an obviously surprised Lita, taking her hand. "Miss Torres, we would just like to offer you another alternative. You can come and stay with Mr. Allen and myself while you recover. Doctor

Cavanaugh can still see you as often as he thinks necessary, but your virtue would not be in jeopardy by staying alone with an unmarried man."

Tate ground his teeth, wanting to tell this busybody to mind her own business, but he knew he didn't dare. He also knew that one day listening to Lita, and the Allens would be calling the sanitarium in Denver.

Lita was making a show of pondering the nosy woman's words. At least he assumed it was a show. He had a flash of her earlier anger. *Maybe she wants to leave.* The room suddenly felt devoid of air, and he jumped up to open a window.

"It's a very kind offer, Mercy, but I think the doctor's right," Lita was saying as he turned to sit back down. "Besides, to help me earn a bit of money to get back on my feet, the doctor has hired me as a governess for Nellie."

Tate didn't blink, and he strove to contain the smile he felt twitching on his lips.

"I can hardly do that job if I'm staying with you," she went on sweetly. "If the doctor gets called out at night, who would be here for Nellie?"

"We thought that Mrs. Kettler. . . " Mr. Allen muttered into his mustache.

"Oh, no, dragging Mrs. Kettler out of her house in the middle of the night was just a temporary arrangement until the doctor could find someone more suited to the task. You see, Mr. Allen, the doctor told me that the first time he saw me with Nellie, he knew that God had answered his prayers for a governess." She looked directly at Tate. "Isn't that right, Doc?"

Oh, Lita, we've moved way beyond lying by appearances. Tate cleared his throat as he shifted in his chair. "I couldn't have said it better."

Mr. Allen and his wife continued to implore her to consider coming home with them, but Lita was adamant that Nellie's needs came first.

Finally they rose, handing their calling card solemnly to Lita, leaving Tate feeling like a lecher for even considering letting her stay in his home unchaperoned. They all walked to the door, Mercy reminding her husband to call Fall River when they got home.

"Oh, yes, I suppose I must." He turned back at the door. "I don't imagine you've heard, Doctor, about the ghastly business that happened in Fall River, Massachusetts, this morning."

Tate sunk his hands into his pockets. "No, the newspapers here don't often cover the East Coast."

Mr. Allen nodded. "The only reason I know is that Mercy is distantly related to the deceased."

Mercy shook her head, looking near tears. "If it had just been a death, but the way she died... and her husband, too." She put a hand to her mouth, unable to go on.

Her husband put a hand to her back. "A heinous crime, and the prime suspect is their daughter Lizzie."

Lita's eyes went wide, and she took a step back. Tate understood her repulsion. "The daughter murdered both her parents? That is a nasty bit of news," he agreed. "My condolences, Mrs. Allen."

Mercy found her voice, although it was a ghost of what it was earlier. "She didn't just murder them, she nearly chopped them to bits. With an axe."

Tate felt horror a split second before something else flashed in his remembrance. He licked his lips as Mr. Allen opened the door and ushered his wife out onto the porch. Tate followed them out. "Mrs. Allen, if I might ask, what was the surname of the woman suspected of this murder."

Mercy turned back. "Borden. Lizzie Borden."

Tate put a hand to his porch's pillar, feeling reality spin. He didn't know how long he stood there with the laws of the universe changing around him. When he finally turned back to the house, there was Lita standing in the doorway, her "prediction" book clutched to her chest, her eyes bright.

"Do you need to see it in writing, or do you remember?"

He slowly walked back to her. "I remember."

He backed her into the house and shut the door behind him, still feeling dazed. "So... I guess you're from... the future."

She nodded.

Tate ran his hand down her hair, all pretense and proper boundaries gone. Then he took his new governess in his arms and kissed her.

Chapter 22

Lalita's heart was soaring as Tate kissed her over and over, his hands in her hair and sliding down her back. She held him tight, never wanting to let go. Finally, he pulled away, smiling. "My Lita," he breathed.

"My Tate," she countered. "I think you've been holding back for a while, huh?"

He nodded, desire unrestrained in his eyes. "Yes." He pulled her head to his shoulder and kissed her forehead.

Lalita reveled in his embrace. "Oh, Tate, thank you. Thank you for believing me."

He shook his head. "I was left with no real alternative. Only a fool denies the evidence when it hits him squarely between the eyes."

She pulled back to look at him. "So what now?"

He ran his fingertips through her hair, looking thoughtful.

"Tate? Do we tell Nellie?"

He brought his attention back to her face. "No, I don't think that would be wise. Little ones do not have wisdom in what they say. Best to be careful around her."

"Sooo..."

He slowly moved his hands to her arms and set her away from himself. "We must continue to practice restraint in front of others—including Nellie. If anyone gets the idea that we are more than a doctor and a patient, you will have to move out."

She hitched a brow. "You're okay with that—a lie by appearance?"

He raked a hand through his hair as he turned and walked a few steps down the hall. Facing her once more, he nodded. "We don't have a choice. Even if you don't tell anyone you're from the 21st century, you're not proficient in the 19th. Most of what you say sounds like gibberish, and people will label you..."

She took a step toward him. "Crazy. Just like you did."

He closed the gap between them, taking her in his arms once more. "I'm sorry."

"It's okay." She nuzzled her nose into his neck, smiling. "I'm willing to overlook your flaws," she teased.

He leaned his mouth toward her ear, chuckling softly. "Are you. Good thing I'm willing to do the same."

She pulled back slightly, her mouth agape. "Dr. Cavanaugh, I'm pretty sure it's ungentleman-like to insult a lady by bringing up her flaws." Then her lips quirked to the side. "But I'm pretty sure I've failed at being a lady this week."

"Perhaps in the conventional sense." He kissed her nose. "But I find" —he whispered against her lips— "that I still want to kiss you."

She pressed her lips to his, and he responded so slowly and gently that she nearly wept with his tender soft lips on hers.

Lalita knew they should stop before they both got carried away. Tate was right—if they were going to live together, they had to practice restraint. She knew it, but nothing in her life had ever felt this perfect. Then she thought of something and pulled back a few inches. "Tate, how did you get this little scar right here." She put her index finger to the spot just above his lip.

His eyes met hers with a look of contrition. "I'm afraid there's something you should know about me. The church lawn wasn't my first fight. I..." He sighed. "I just can't stand to see an underdog bullied. It just does something to me. It—"

"It pushes your buttons."

A perplexed look came to his face, followed by a slow grin, and *that* did something to *her*. "I love you, Tate Cavanaugh," she whispered.

He put a hand to the side of her head, his thumb caressing her cheek. "I love you, Lalita Torres."

Kissing resumed.

*   *   *

"Something's different," Nellie announced over dinner.

With wide, innocent eyes, both adults looked to the blue-eyed blonde and spoke at the same time, pulling their feet apart under the table.

"Wh–what are you talking about, sweetheart?"

"Different in what way?"

Nellie swished her long curls back and forth that had been gathered together at the back of her head. "Polly did it, although I have to give her ribbon back to her the next time I see her."

Tate let out a sigh with a nervous chuckle. "I see. She's tied it into a queue. It's very pretty, Nellie."

"A 'queue'?" Lita raised her eyebrows. "Where I come from, that's called a ponytail."

Tate paused, nodding his head. "A good name, although I've never seen one on a real pony so curly."

"You don't have enough hair for a ponytail, Lalita. Why is your hair so short?" Nellie looked completely baffled, although it had taken her a week to notice or care. Tate wanted to know the answer to this one himself.

"Well," Lita began after taking a sip of the wine that Tate had pulled out of the cellar," I used to have really long hair, but after I went to college, I started getting it trimmed a little shorter every time I went to a salon." She gave her short layers a shake. "Finally I ended up with this, and I decided I liked it."

Tate smiled. He liked it too. Most women's elaborate hairstyles were completely untouchable. He could slide his hands through her hair all day and never mess it up.

"But you look like a boy! I don't think you should get it cut anymore."

Tate wondered at his daughter's worried expression. "Nell, Lalita has been with us for more than a week and you haven't been concerned about her hair until now. Why?"

"Polly said it. She said Lalita looked like a boy." She hung her head. "And she laughed at her."

Tate looked to Lita apologetically, but she didn't seem fazed at all by the child's taunt. She laughed. "A boy, huh? Well, I've been called worse." She sliced off a piece of ham and chewed on a bite while Tate looked at her in surprise. She blinked at him. "What?"

"It doesn't bother you one bit to look different from everyone else, does it? That's why you haven't complained about the dresses that don't fit you or the hats that won't stay on your head."

"Don't forget cooking in a swimsuit, Papa. Polly thought that was queer, even when I told her how much cooler we were making noodles."

Both the adults looked to her then, all smiles gone. "Miss Nell, what goes on in this house is nobody's business but ours alone, do you understand? You will not discuss what I do or what Lalita does or even what Mrs. Kettler does with anyone else. And I believe I've told you this before."

Nellie's lips went into a pout as she fought tears. "I'm sorry, Papa."

"I think you're finished with your meal. Go up to your room and think about what I've said."

Nellie slid off her chair, sniffing, and a moment later sobs could be heard as she went up the stairs.

Lita rose, her brow knitted, tears of her own threatening, but Tate grabbed her hand. "No, Lita. She needs this time to consider her actions."

"But Tate, she's just a little girl. She didn't know any better."

"Like I said, I've warned her of this before. The first time was just that—a warning. Now more is required. A bit of thought in her room won't hurt her." Tate stroked the back of Lita's hand with his thumb. "There must be true repentance to give meaning to forgiveness."

"But I know what that's like." Tears were running down her cheeks. "To be sent to my room to wait for the hug of acceptance." She turned to face him, and his heart clenched at her tears. "I waited and waited, Tate, on many occasions, for absolution that never came."

He rose and wiped the tears from her face. "I promise I won't let her cry long."

She nodded and turned into his arms, and Tate had to keep reminding himself that this was real. He was holding a woman who wanted him to. They stood there whispering exchanges

of love and caring, a little bit of the past breaking off of them
both.

Chapter 23

Lalita walked down the stairs once again with Tate's gaze on her, but this time she was wearing a dress of her own design, and his eyes couldn't be rounder or his jaw more slack. "Lita, you can't be serious. You're going to church, not the Burly-Q."

She couldn't help grinning, stepping down each step slowly and dramatically. Her new creation was a light blue, sleeveless dress with a midnight blue overskirt that split in the front and was pulled back to gather into a small bustle. She carried the matching fitted shirtwaist hooked over a finger behind her shoulder just so Tate knew she didn't intend to go into church with—heaven forbid—her arms showing.

But what really had captured his attention was her legs. The skirt in front was pulled up with fabric tabs in three places, higher in the center than the sides, giving it a scalloped effect and taking the hem to a few inches above her knees. She'd covered one of Augusta's hats with the light blue fabric and added some feathery plumes for good measure.

He brought his eyes to hers as she stepped down to the floor. "Lita, you can't possibly..." he sputtered. "You told me about the miniature skirts of your time, but this is not..." He trailed off as she reached down to unbutton the tabs, letting the hem fall to the floor. Then she slipped the mutton-sleeved jacket on, buttoning it up the front to a modestly scooped neckline.

Tate just stood there staring, his brows frozen in a raised position.

She did a slow turn, and he finally found his voice. "Well..."

She laughed. "I think I've rendered my favorite doctor speechless."

"Quite. Where's Nellie?"

"Still in her room, I believe."

He pulled her quickly into the dining room, lifted her chin, and kissed her. Lalita wanted to melt into him, but they'd already been nearly caught several times by Nellie and had a very close call with Mrs. Kettler, who had come back to work two days ago. Showing restraint was proving difficult.

He pulled back, looking into her eyes, then gave her another quick peck before pulling her back out into the hallway and calling up the stairs. "Nellie, are you ready, sweetheart?"

"I'm putting on my shoes."

Tate let his fingers slide between Lalita's, and she smiled. "I think you're going to have a tough time sitting through church this morning with me sitting two feet away."

He sighed. "That I am."

Nellie's footsteps were heard in the hall, and Tate released Lalita and stepped away. Tate smiled at his daughter as she descended the stairs in a green and gold frock with a big grin on her face. "Look, Papa! See how Lalita braided my hair?"

"I see." It was loosely French braided around the crown with Nellie's long curls hanging down. "It's quite beautiful." The deep green ribbons intertwined matched the sash around her waist.

She looked at Lalita then tugged on her daddy's sleeve until he bent his ear to her. "Did you see what Lalita's dress can do?" she whispered loudly.

Tate blushed, and Lalita stepped in. "Now, Nellie, remember that was to be our secret."

She put her hand to her lips. "Oh, I forgot." She looked back to her dad, who had straightened to full height. "Most of those buttons on Lalita's dress are just for decoration." She hastily shook her head. "Only three are for buttoning, and I promised not to say what."

Lalita watched Tate's mouth strain against a smile. "I'm proud of you, Nellie, for keeping your promise." He looked back at Lalita. "And now I think we best be going. You two beauties will attract enough attention without walking in late."

Lalita followed the two out the door, smiling at the sunny day that greeted them along with the fresh mountain air. So much had changed in the Cavanaugh house since the news of Lizzie Borden had proven her true. As much as she hated to be grateful for a thing like that, she couldn't be sorry that Tate now believed her.

She still got the Tate stare on a regular basis, but at least now, he asked her to explain, and she tried to use terms he'd understand. She couldn't resist, however, throwing in some modern slang every now and again just for fun.

* * *

Tate whistled a hymn while Maisy trotted through town. The last several days had been like something out of a dream. He'd been busy with an outbreak of chicken pox, mining injuries, and another baby delivery, but in between he'd spent every minute with his daughter and the woman who'd stolen his heart. He and Lita had even shared a few evenings on the settee, after Nellie had been put to bed, with the shades drawn and the lights low, his arm around her.

After Augusta's cold, touch-me-not personality, he savored every stroke of Lita's hand on his and every stolen kiss. He knew it wasn't proper, and the whole community would decry their behavior if they knew, but he also knew that Lita needed to stay with him. She didn't fit in even when she thought she did. She was too bold and outspoken for this time. She was even different from the suffragettes, as she wasn't angry, protesting, or demanding; she was simply sure of herself and all that she could do or become. She just didn't see the limitations.

And because of that, Tate worried. *Her beauty and heritage already puts her in a spotlight. And once they're looking and listening, eyebrows are bound to raise.* He sighed. *I tried to make Augusta fit into society, and now I want to keep Lita out.* It was a shift born of experience, but he wondered if the latter was really any better than the former.

"What ya thinking, Doc? You stopped whistling, and that was an awful big sigh you let out."

162

Tate smiled at the nickname she only used now when they weren't alone. "Sorry." He ignored her remark about the sigh. "Would you like me to continue?"

"Sure. Since we don't have a buggy radio."

He looked at her questioningly, and she winked—a promise for a later explanation. He took in a big breath, looking into her eyes over Nellie's head. His daughter's upward tilt told Tate she could "feel" their nonverbal exchange above her, and that got his eyes back on the road. The longing remained, however, and he wondered how he could marry this woman who had his heart racing without starting scandalous rumors.

Society demanded a certain amount of courting, and courting demanded she be out of his house. No one married without the proper passage of time and observance of the courting rituals by the church and the community as a whole.

Usually there were two families involved that made sure it was all done correctly, but since his was in Denver and hers even more remote, being distanced by time as well as miles, they were completely on their own. Lita seemed non-plussed by this. She said women made their own decisions about who to marry and when in her time, but he knew that would not work here.

The church bells began to peal as he guided Maisy to a hitching post. He lifted Nellie down and couldn't help but swell with pride as Lita took his hand and stepped down beside him.

She leaned in and whispered. "Tate, if you don't get that look off of your face, everyone is going to know our little secret. You're looking at me like you want to eat me up."

He turned and tucked her hand at his elbow then reached for Nellie's. "That, Lita, is a fair description."

She squeezed his arm as they walked to the church. "Well, think about something else," she hissed while smiling at another couple converging with their path.

Blowing out a breath, he put his mind to the task of thinking on something solemn or at least less cheerful. Luckily, he was a doctor and had a fair repertoire of those kinds of memories to draw upon.

* * *

As Tate ushered them toward the same pew they'd occupied last week, Lalita caught sight of the backs of all the Dickson men and pulled Tate to a halt. He followed her gaze and leaned toward her. "Do you want to sit in the front?"

She looked around then back to him. "Why the front? There are lots of open spots."

"No one ever sits up front, but the other spots will probably be filled eventually."

"Assigned seats?"

Tate tried to guide her toward the aisle. "Not exactly. People just usually sit in the same place."

"But they don't have to."

"No, but—"

"Then this one will do." She slid into a pew in the center of the right side.

Tate reluctantly pulled Nellie toward it and slipped in after her. "This is the Calvins' pew."

Lalita shrugged. "They can sit where you usually do."

Tate looked around, getting red. "They are a group of six; we are a group of three. We can't just switch."

Lalita put a hand to her mouth. "Oh my heavens, they might have to split up. How horrible for them," she whispered.

An usher tapped Tate on the shoulder, wanting to know if he could move them back two pews. Lalita knew that would put them right back where she did not want to be—in front of the Seth Dickson clan. She leaned forward and caught the man's eye. "Excuse me, but this spot is just fine, thank you."

Tate gave her a look that was not at all like he wanted to eat her up. The minister took his place behind the pulpit, and Lalita pressed her lips together while pointing discreetly toward the front. Tate slowly turned his head.

The minister looked over the congregation, smiling, his gaze doing a little hiccup as his eyes lit on the Cavanaughs. Lalita watched him work out the reason for the switch, and his chin rose just for a moment before speaking. "Good morning and welcome." The organist began to play. "Let's lift our voices in song."

The first hymn was a cheery song in melody, but the lyrics proved to be quite a dire warning.

"All deceived and deceiving, see the city and her
lords
Riot in their carnal pleasure, heeding not Jehovah's
words;
For He speaks, now revealing mystic Babel's utter
fall,
And the holy read the writing of their God upon
the wall."

The next, called the Fount of Purity seemed to continue on the same track...

"Behold the fountain near,
By faith, oh, plunge today;
Oh, sin-sick soul, draw near—
'Twill purge thy stain away."

And by the time they'd finished singing

"O poor sinner, come to Jesus,
Hasten, come, before too late;
Lest the Spirit cease His wooing;
Sad, then, sad will be your fate."

Lalita was pretty sure she knew what was coming. The good reverend did not disappoint. It was a fire and brimstone sermon for the ages, and although he addressed his admonitions, exhortations, and warnings over the whole congregation, she couldn't help feeling that he focused a great deal of his verbal energies right on their pew. She set the fan she'd brought along to work, moving the stale air, and she noticed Tate wiping his brow with a handkerchief.

When the final hymn was rolled out—Don't Resist the Holy Spirit—Lalita was starting to feel bruised. She leaned toward Tate over Nellie. "Can we leave?"

He gave her a tiny smile of understanding but tried to signal patience with his hand over the hymnal. Lalita's patience meter, however, read empty. She released her end of the song book and eased her way past half of the Calvins to the aisle. Seth Dickson gave her a grin and a tilt of head as she marched by, and the reverend himself seemed to plead through the song for her to return.

"Don't resist the Holy Spirit,
He has called you oft before;
This may be His final visit,
If you open not the door."

Lalita opened the door, all right, and stepped out into a gale that nearly took the hat from her head. Grateful that she had thought to sew in hair combs, she hung onto it with both hands as she made her way down the steps and to Tate's buggy.

Waiting for Tate and Nellie, she watched the clouds. Dark thunderclouds had formed while they were in the church, and she couldn't help remembering the last storm she had experienced. *What if lightning strikes nearby? Will I jaunt through time again?* Fear seized her, and she jumped back out of the buggy and ran to the church just as a spitting rain began.

She just reached the top of the steps when the doors opened. Tate and Nellie were coming out but stopped at the sight of her. "Lita, you're white as a sheet. Are you ill?"

She shook her head, pushing past them and the rest of the throng heading out.

Tate turned and pulled Nellie back into the building. After weaving through the crowd, ironically, he found her sitting on the front row. He sat beside her, pulling Nellie onto his lap. "Lita, tell me what's wrong."

She looked to the windows that were now being pummeled by rain. "It's the storm." Her eyes were filled with fear. "Lightning brought me here. Maybe it could take me away, and who knows where I might end up." As if on cue, thunder rolled, and she jumped.

Tate wanted to take her in his arms, but a pat to the shoulder would have to do. "Don't worry, you're safe in here. And I very much doubt you would be in danger even outside." He suddenly scowled as he remembered consoling Augusta through many a storm. Lightning had been one of her irrational fears as well, although he had to admit, Lita actually had reason to be afraid after what she'd been through.

Nellie broke into his thoughts, looking bewildered. "Lightning brought you here?"

Tate and Lita's eyes met, both realizing their error at the same time. They were saved from either a difficult truth or spinning a yarn in the house of the Lord by hands on their shoulders. They both looked up into the face of Reverend Niemeyer.

"Riding out the storm? That seems like a good plan, and I was hoping to have a word with the both of you." He turned his attention to Lita, and Tate held his breath. "Miss Torres, the Allens relayed your hesitance to reside with them while you recover from your head injury, but I'd like to make the appeal once again. I—"

Lita's chin ticked up. "I believe you've been making it for the last hour, Reverend, and while the whole room may have heard your sermon, you seemed to be preaching to just a few of us."

Reverend Niemeyer's brow furrowed. "I assure you, I never meant to single anyone out in particular..."

Tate rose, setting Nellie on her feet. "Reverend, if you wouldn't mind having a word with me in your study."

The reverend slipped out into the aisle. "Certainly. Right this way."

Tate looked into Lalita's flaming eyes. "Wait here with Nellie."

"Tate, don't let him tell you—"

"I'll handle it."

"But—"

"Lita. Please."

She sat and folded her arms, and Tate followed the minister, pondering whether he could be an Episcopalian.

Lalita was a mixed-up mess. She was still fuming about the church service, irked to be left out of the conversation with the minister, and a good deal of fear from the storm was hanging on as well.

Nellie sat beside her. "Lalita, what did you mean when you said that lightning brought you here?"

Lalita threw an arm around her. She had hoped that Nellie would forget all about that remark, but no such luck. "I don't have any idea if your papa would want me to tell you this or not, but since he saw fit to have a discussion with the minister without me, I guess I'm on my own." Lalita looked around the room, but those who were waiting out the storm were at

the back. Still, she lowered her voice. "Well, Nellie, I know
this may be hard to believe, and you have to swear not to tell a
soul..."

* * *

"I'm sorry you feel this way, Dr. Cavanaugh, but perhaps
you're taking my sermon upon yourself because you feel some
guilt for having an unmarried woman under your roof."

Tate's jaw was set. "No, Reverend, I do not. I know that
you and the church and maybe even the whole town would
like me to feel guilty, but I've had enough of society rules for
a lifetime. I've put one wife in the ground because of them. I'll
not let them think for me again."

The minister leaned forward in his desk chair. "Tate,
Augusta took her own life. Surely you can't think that anyone
wanted that."

"It doesn't matter what anyone wanted. She killed herself
because she couldn't fit in, and I helped her do it by insisting
she find a way to conform." Tate rose and paced. "I shamed
her in Denver, Reverend, when she scorned society functions,
sinking deeper and deeper into melancholia. When we moved
here, I tried again to make her fit in because as a doctor, I
thought I needed to achieve a certain status."

He stopped and faced the minister. "But when the dirt
was being shoveled onto her coffin, I saw it all so clearly. She
needed understanding, and because she had been a cold wife, I
mocked her instead. And I made a vow that day. I would decide
which rules of society and propriety would fill my home. Miss
Torres is in my home and needs my help, and as God is my
witness, she will not be harmed or taken advantage of. She
will stay there until she no longer needs it or decides herself
to leave."

Reverend Niemeyer was silent for several moments as Tate
tried to slow his breathing. Finally, he rose and came around
his desk, putting a hand on Tate's shoulder. "I can understand
how you feel, but I believe you are letting your past cloud this
issue. If she stays with you for much longer, looking as fit as
a fiddle as she does, rumors are bound to start." He tightened

his grip on Tate's shoulder. "She'll be ruined, and no man will have her. Is that what you want?"

Tate shook his head, grinding his teeth. "There are... mental issues that can't be seen." He strove to explain without lying. "Her... thinking is... different. It makes her... vulnerable."

Niemeyer released him and crossed his arms. "And are you qualified to deal with these issues?"

"I'm as qualified as anyone here in town."

The minister smiled and returned to his desk chair. "That may be true, but perhaps in Colorado Springs or Denver, she might find better help than you can offer."

Tate swallowed. "I've considered that and have written to a psychiatrist in Denver. I've not received a return post yet."

The minister nodded. "Ah. Well, perhaps this will all be resolved soon then."

Tate was starting to sweat through his jacket. "Perhaps."

Chapter 24

It was a silent ride home.

Tate kept his eyes on the wet road, trying to avoid muddy ruts, not saying a word. His silence bugged the heck out of Lalita, but she knew she wouldn't find out about his time with the minister until Nellie, who had been strangely quiet ever since Lalita had explained about taking a ride into the past on a bolt of lightning, was in bed.

Lalita let out a sigh as they turned onto their hill, wondering if the rest of the day would be like this, when they were met by a buggy coming down. The man in the seat waved and shouted to Tate as he approached.

"Doc, there's been an accident with a wagon overturning up the mountain. The man driving was pinned. He needs you right away."

Tate handed the reins to Lalita as he pulled his bag out from under the seat. "Can you drive Maisy up the hill?"

Lalita took them, trying to remember what he'd taught her. "I think so."

"Good. I'll go with Mr. Winley then, to save time." Jumping down, he made his way across the muddy street and climbed into the buggy. They took off at a brisk trot, the horse's hooves sending mud flying. Lalita eased Maisy forward slowly, and they arrived at the carriage house without incident. Harold, however, didn't usually work on Sundays. "Now, what do we do, Nellie? Your papa never taught me how to unfasten the carriage."

Climbing down, she tied Maisy to a post and studied the carriage straps and fittings. Not wanting to damage her

new outfit, she took off her hat, shirtwaist, and overskirt and
handed them to Nellie, leaving her standing there in the simple
sleeveless dress. "Can you please take those into the house for
me?"

She took the large bundle of fabric. "Can I come back out
and watch?"

Lalita began gathering up the front of her skirt. "Sure. Just
change out of that pretty Sunday dress first." Grabbing hold
of the tabs hanging underneath, she buttoned them to keep the
skirt off the ground and out of her way.

It seemed a simple matter to disconnect the horse from the
carriage but more complicated to get the elaborate harnesses
off the horse. As she was unfastening buckle after buckle, she
heard a noise at the door and assumed that Nellie had returned.
"Do you know where the horse feed is? I'm sure Maisy's
hungry."

"It's most likely in the room over yonder, kept closed to
keep the rodents out."

Lalita spun at the sound of a man's voice.

Seth Dickson stood just to the back corner of the buggy,
grinning as he looked her up and down. "My my, but that's
the kind of Sunday dress a man only dreams about." His
eyes widened still further, "And what's that you got on your
shoulder? Real pretty." He moved closer, and Lalita stepped
back. "I knew you were a wild one. I could see it in your eyes
the first time I seen ya." He kept walking until he had her
pinned against the stall fence.

Lalita tried to stay calm. "If you're looking for the doctor,"
—she tried to ease past him— "I'll just slip inside and get him
for you."

Dickson caught her arm. "So the doc makes his patients
unhitch his buggy while he lounges in the house?"

Lalita swallowed. "No, not usually, but he... he... "

Dickson tsked as he rubbed his thumb over her tattoo.
"Now there's no need to lie to me. I seen the doc heading out
of town at a fair clip."

Lalita squared her jaw. "What do you want?"

He trailed a finger up over her flowered shoulder. "To put it
bluntly, I want to court you." His finger continued up the side
of her neck. "So I can marry you."

Lalita licked her dry lips. "I'm sorry Mr. Dickson, but I don't wish to marry you."

He looked down at her bare shins. "There's some that would say being together here with you in this state of undress would make it mandatory."

She batted his hand away. "No one tells me what to do, Mr. Dickson, and nobody can force me to marry you."

He hitched his thumbs in his front pockets but still blocked her way, looking perplexed. "I'm not a bad-looking man, Miss Torres, even if I'm a might older than you, and I have a successful saddlery. I promise I'll take care of you."

Lalita wondered if she might get out of this with an appeal to his vanity. She attempted a smile. "Of course, anyone can see that. I'm just not in need of anyone's care."

He squinted. " 'Cept the doctor's. Or is your noggin better?"

She put a hand to her head. "There are still some things I can't remember."

"That don't much matter, though, does it? Seems to me the doc is keeping you to himself unnecessarily."

"I do what I want. The doctor isn't 'keeping' me at all." She shoved past him, but he spun and caught her shoulders, pulling her back against him.

His breath was hot behind her ear. "So you're one of those spinster suffragettes, are you? What's your story? Were you ruined, so you think you've got no more chances?" He turned her to face him, careful to keep his arms around her. Lalita's hands were on his chest, her nose inches from his chin. "I don't care what you've done in the past. The Lord forgives, and so do I."

Lalita smiled as sweetly as she could muster with her heart beating in her throat. "That's mighty nice of you, Mr. Dickson. I hope you can forgive me for this, as well." She clutched his shirt and brought her knee up sharply and swiftly. Dickson released her with a howl and bent over as she flew out of the building. She met Nellie coming out the back door. "Quick, back inside!"

Nellie, confused, turned, and Lalita hurried her up the steps and into the house. Locking it, she pulled the shade, then ran to the front door. It was still locked, so she pulled all the shades on the ground floor before stopping and trying to catch her breath.

Nellie's eyes were round. "What's wrong?"

Lalita sank to the settee in the parlor. "Do you remember Mr. Dickson?"

Nellie nodded.

"Well, he's taken a liking to me, and he doesn't give up easily."

Nellie sat beside her. "I bet he doesn't like you as much as Papa does."

Lalita looked to Nellie with eyebrows raised. "What makes you say that?"

Nellie giggled. "He can't stop looking at you."

Lalita blinked. "So you know that we've been—"

"Sneaking kisses." Nellie nodded, giggling some more.

Lalita put a hand to her chest. "Well, your papa isn't quite as covert as he thinks." She gave Nellie a serious look. "This has to be another secret, though. If anyone knows, I'll have to move out."

Nellie threw her arms around her. "I promise not to tell. Are you going to be my mama?"

Lalita returned the hug. "That's the plan. Your daddy hasn't figured out how just yet."

Nellie pulled back. "Just tell Reverend Niemeyer you want to get married."

Lalita looked down into Nellie's adamant expression. "That's what I thought, but evidently it's more complicated than that. And anyway, we should probably get to know each other a little bit better before saying 'I do.' "

"He loves you, and you love him. What else is there to know?"

Lalita smiled and pulled Nellie to herself once more. *Out of the mouths of babes.*

* * *

Tate unlocked the front door as quietly as he could. The house was dark but for a lamp in the parlor, and he found Lita curled up on the settee, covered by a quilt. If he had any strength left, he would have carried her upstairs, but the day had been too long.

Walking to her side, he squatted down beside her and combed his fingers through her hair. Her eyes blinked open, and she gave him a sleepy smile. "You're home."

He smiled back, grateful that this woman was now a part of it. "How did you do with the buggy? Has Maisy been taken care of?"

She sat up, and he rose to sit beside her. "Yes, although I had to call Harold."

He nodded. "All the harnesses can be a bit overwhelming."

She rubbed a corner of her eye. "I could have done it, but Seth Dickson showed up, and—"

"Dickson!"

She pulled the quilt tighter around her. "That man just won't take no for an answer."

Tate's pulse jumped. "He didn't touch you, did he?"

Lita covered his hand resting on her knee and told him everything that had happened.

Tate tried to remain calm during her retelling, even while she admitted to stripping down to indecent exposure of her limbs, but when she told him that Dickson had caressed her shoulder, he leaped up and walked across the room. "Lita, why would you expose yourself like that outside of the house?"

Lita stood, still clutching the quilt. "I didn't want to ruin my new dress. It's the only one I have that fits. And anyway, why are you blaming me for Dickson's bad behavior? He had no right to touch me, whether I was covered head to toe or stark naked."

Tate turned back to face Lita's righteous anger. "Not everyone sees it like that. Many would say you provoked him by your exhibition."

Lita strode toward him. "Exhibition? I was inside the carriage house! If anything, he was trespassing." She scowled. "You don't even care that he had me trapped against the fence, breathing on me like a randy teenager."

He stepped toward her and took her in his arms. "Oh, I do, Lita. I care very much. And believe me, I am going to have a talk with that man first thing in the morning."

Lita giggled against his shoulder. "Well, don't be surprised if he's walking a bit funny."

He pulled back, taking hold of her shoulders, knowing the answer to his question before he asked it. "Why?"

She was grinning. "I put my self-defense class into practice and gave him a good knee in the—"

"You didn't!" Tate stepped back, horrified.

Lita was defiant. "He totally deserved it."

Tate ran a hand around his very tired face. "Maybe so, but it will be your word against his. Did he try to kiss you? Tear your clothes? Anything that would suggest he planned to ruin you."

"Well, no, but he thought I was already 'ruined' as you Victorian troglodytes put it, so who knows what he had in mind. I wasn't about to wait around to find out. I let him have it and ran to the house."

Tate took hold of her shoulders. "Lita, the laws don't favor women."

"I just. . . he wouldn't press charges for something like that, would he? Especially when he said he wanted to marry me."

Tate's brows rose, and this time he was the one seeing the future. Filled with a sudden foreboding, he turned Lita out of the parlor and headed her down the hall. "You need to get to bed. Bright and early tomorrow, we are driving back to Colorado Springs."

She stopped at the base of the stairs, bemusement etched on her face. "Why?"

He urged her forward with a hand to her back. "We need to get married."

Chapter 25

"Tate, I still think you're being ridiculous." He had awakened Lalita at dawn and was now hurrying her down the hall toward the bathroom so they could leave for Colorado Springs the moment Mrs. Kettler arrived. "I'm really hungry; I've got to eat breakfast before we go."

"I'll pack us something to take along."

She turned back at the door. "Tate, are you serious about getting married today? I know you think I need your protection, but I don't have a dress or anything."

He gave her a little push into the bathroom. "If you need something special, I'll buy it there." He pulled the door closed in front of her. "And don't take as long in there as you usually do," he said louder through the door.

Lalita stood a moment, staring, feeling overwhelmed. *This is not how I envisioned my wedding day.*

She turned to run a tub of water, wondering at Tate's urgency. She had an anxious feeling rising up, but she didn't know how to express what she was feeling. *I love Tate, but this is going too fast.*

Slipping out of her robe and chemise, she stepped into the bath, hoping to wash her anxiety away.

* * *

Come on, Lita, we need to get moving. Tate had Maisy hitched to the buggy waiting out front, their breakfast packed, and now he had nothing to do but pace the upstairs hallway. Finally he strode to the bathroom door, ready to knock, when it opened to a startled Lita with wet hair.

He grabbed her by the arm and pulled. "Come, Lita, we need to go."

She drug her feet all the way to her room, obviously not feeling the same urgency that he was. "Tate, what is it you're afraid of? I love you, but I'm not sure I'm ready to get married today. I know we've been together a lot in the past several weeks, but really, we just met. I'm not all that easy to live with. What if you regret—"

He cut off her speech with a kiss. A kiss to let her know exactly how he felt. His hands roved over her back as his lips claimed her as his own. When he broke it off, they were both out of breath. He framed her face with his hands. "Lita, I love you. I want to marry you. That won't change if we court for a day or six months. I feel the connection with you I never felt with Augusta. Things are so different in your time that you don't realize when you're stepping over the line. You need my protection, and I can't give that to you fully without being your husband." He caressed her cheeks with his thumbs. "Now please hurry. If Dickson decides to make trouble for what you did to him yesterday, I want to be way down the road."

Lita stepped backward into her room. "Okay, well, I'll be as fast as I can." She closed the door and Tate blew out a breath before pulling out his pocket watch and clicking it open. *Mrs. Kettler should be here any minute.* He trotted down the stairs to make sure the back door was unlocked.

At the bottom of the stairs, however, footsteps on his front porch made his heart leap into his throat. He stood still, waiting, and when the doorbell rang, he prayed that it was just someone who wanted to pay his bill. He couldn't be tied up with an emergency for half the day like yesterday.

He walked down the hall and opened the door to something much much worse—Seth Dickson stood next to Marshal Reeves.

* * *

Lalita heard the doorbell and wondered who would be dropping by so early. *Tate will be furious if he's called out to deliver a baby. This town could use more doctors.*

Hurriedly, she slipped into her high-top shoes and snugged the laces. Checking the mirror, she gave her still damp hair a little shake and grabbed her hat to put on after it dried. She was wearing the same thing she had on the day before. Maybe Tate would buy her a real wedding dress, but his crazy desperation didn't give her much confidence of that. *And I refuse to wear one of Augusta's dresses to get married in.*

As soon as she opened her bedroom door, she heard the voices. She recognized Tate's and Dickson's, but a third resonated with a deep timbre that seemed familiar, but she couldn't place it. *Now what do I do?*

The voices were getting louder.

"Marshal, how can you give any credence to this man's story when I've told you that this wasn't the only time he tried to waylay Miss Torres, and that he even attempted it in a church? He has her scared. Of course she would defend herself against his unwanted advances."

"Doc, was she or wasn't she mostly unclothed, even showing off her limbs, outside the house?"

"She was in the carriage house, attempting to unharness the buggy while I was called on an emergency. She had never done it before and didn't want to spoil her new dress. I believe Mr. Dickson only appeared at my house because he saw me heading out of town. He was not invited onto my property."

"Heck, Doc." It was Dickson speaking now. "You protect that little chit as if she were yours."

"She is mine, Mr. Dickson. She's my patient. Any patient in my care is also under my protection."

Dickson blew out an exasperated breath. "The only person in the town that believes she is your patient is you, Doc. Marshal, maybe the doctor has acted more untoward than I have. Why, he even punched the preacher when he suggested she shouldn't be under his roof."

Lalita couldn't help it when a high-pitched chirp of indignation leaped out of her mouth. She clamped a hand to her lips, listening, but there was nothing but silence below.

Finally, Tate restarted the conversation, obviously flustered with the knowledge that she was listening. "Dickson, you know that's not true; that punch was meant for you. You were the one harassing—"

"Doctor," the marshal broke in, "I'd like to speak to the lady myself. Would you please ask her to come downstairs?"

Lalita sucked in a breath and started down. At the bottom of the stairs, she heard Mrs. Kettler coming in the back, and for just a second, she considered making a break for it. The whole scene of speeding through the kitchen, dodging Mrs. K. and turning over a stool or two to make it difficult for those who would race after her flashed before her eyes. *If Tate ran out to the buggy, and I ran around the house and jumped in, could we get away?* The answer, of course, was no. Maisy, with a buggy attached, could not outrun the marshal on a horse.

Turning to go down the hall, she could see the trepidation in Tate's eyes. She held her chin up and came to his side. Dickson gave her a smile and a tilt of his head, but Lita didn't acknowledge him. She focused on the marshal in a jacket and vest, his hat in his hand at his side. Only the badge gave him distinction from every other man in town. "Marshal, what can I do for you?"

Marshal Reeves gave her a weak smile. "Miss Torres, Mr. Dickson claims that you... that you... well, that you assaulted him."

Lalita turned a steely glare on Dickson. "Did he? Did he also tell you that he had me pinned against a fence and that he was touching me inappropriately?"

Dickson broke in. "No decent woman wears what you were wearing without expecting a man to act on it."

Tate stepped toward him. "Are you calling her indecent, Dickson?" He fisted his hand. "I still owe you a punch to the jaw."

The marshal pushed the two apart. "Dickson, wait outside."

Dickson stood a moment sliding the brim of his bowler between his fingers before turning and letting himself out. The marshal let out a breath. "Now, Miss Torres, did you assault Mr. Dickson?"

"I did what was necessary to get out of his clutches. Where I come from, that's called self-defense."

The marshal studied her a long moment, but Lalita refused to break eye contact. "I can't help noticing, Miss, that the buggy's out front ready to go, there's a picnic basket sitting by the door, and you have your hat. May I ask where you were heading so early this morning?"

She gave a quick glance to Tate just behind his shoulder who gave a tiny shake of his head. "I was just going out for a drive, Marshal. The fresh mountain air is good for recovery."

"Alone? Surely if Dickson had been nigh unto molesting you, you'd not venture out alone."

"Well, no," she stammered, "the doctor was going to accompany me."

The marshal turned to Tate with eyebrows raised. "Just the two of you, alone and unchaperoned?"

Tate swallowed. "No, Mrs. Kettler and Nellie were coming as well."

The marshal picked up the small basket and looked under the cloth covering. "Seems a bit sparse for four."

Lalita put her hat nervously on her head. "Nellie doesn't eat much, and I'm on a diet. Is there anything else we can do for you?"

He set the basket on the stool by the door and looked from her to Tate and back again. "Dickson wants to press charges, Miss Torres. As the marshal, I am obligated to arrest you until the judge is in town to decide the case."

"That's ridic—"

"It's just his word against—"

The marshal held up a hand. "There is a caveat. He says he'll drop the charges if you agree to marry him."

Tate blew like a volcano. "What? Marshal, can't you see how he is warping the circumstances to suit himself? Well, two can play this game. I'll charge him with trespassing."

"As I understand it, you weren't here, so how do you know he was trespassing?"

Lalita's eyes flashed. "Well, I was here, Marshal. I can attest to the fact that he came right into the carriage house uninvited."

The marshal shook his head. "It would be your word against his, and he would win."

Her hands flew to her hips. "And why is that?"

The marshal seemed to be losing patience. "I can think of three right off. One, you're a woman. Two, you showed up here out of the blue, and nobody knows you and nobody is looking for you. Three, you've got Indian blood."

Lalita looked to Tate wide-eyed as the marshal went on. "Dickson, on the other hand has some evidence of your vulgar exhibition. He claims you have quite the tattoo on your shoulder. You could prove him wrong right here and now, and I'll tell Dickson to run on home and stop bothering you."

Lalita looked back to the marshal and slowly licked her lips. "I was in a private building trying to deal with a horse harness I've never undone before. My only audience was supposed to be the horse."

The marshal stepped closer. "Do you want to know what I think, Miss Torres? I think your memory loss has to do with trying not to be found. I think you're a soiled dove that got into some trouble, and now you're taking advantage of the doctor's good graces."

Lalita's mouth fell open, but it was Tate that spoke. "Marshal, this woman came to me completely unconscious. The Hill brothers brought her to me in that state. She did not pick my house as a hide-out."

"Maybe not, but once she woke up, I'm sure she saw the advantage of staying with you. And from what I hear, you've been providing her with all kinds of gifts."

He turned his attention to a flabbergasted Lalita. "I don't know why Dickson wants to marry you, but to each his own. It will make less paperwork for me should you decide to go that route. Now," —he clapped his hands once— "since you're all dressed up and ready to go out, you need to decide if you'll be going with me to the jail or with Dickson to the Justice of the Peace."

Tate didn't know what to do, but he couldn't let Dickson marry Lita. "Marshal, may I have a word with Miss Torres in private?"

The marshal took a step back and waved them into the parlor. Taking her by the elbow, he guided her to the far corner. "Lita, you need to go with the marshal."

"But—"

"I know." He looked over her shoulder to make sure they weren't being watched, then lifted her hand to his lips. "I'll go out right now and hire a lawyer."

She kept a tight hold on his hand, her face contorting with tears. "I've never been in jail."

He stroked the side of her head. "Of course you haven't, darling," he whispered, "and with any luck I'll have you out of there before the day is out."

"Tate, just tell Dickson that we were going to get married this morning. Won't he—"

Tate shushed her. "I don't know what he'll do," he whispered, "but once that cat is out of the bag, we won't be able to put it back in, and if he still wants to charge you—"

"We'll be in exactly the same place as we are now. I'll be in jail, and you'll be trying to get me out."

"Doctor," the marshal called from the hallway, "Dickson interrupted my morning coffee. My patience is wearing thin."

"Well, good morning, Marshal," Mrs. Kettler's voice sing-songed. "I'm sure the doctor will be with you shortly. In the meantime, would you like a cup of coffee and a biscuit?"

His voice moved down the hall. "I'd be glad to take you up on that, Mrs. Kettler. Your biscuits are a well-known treat."

Tate exhaled and tried to regroup his thoughts. "The difference is between a doctor acting on behalf of a patient or a man acting on behalf of his lover." At her wide eyes he explained. "It won't matter that we haven't known each other in that way yet. As soon as the word is out that we planned to marry, all manner of rumors will fly about what has been going on behind these closed doors."

"But didn't you expect rumors to fly with our sudden marriage this morning?"

"A few certainly, but once a couple is married, decorum demands best wishes be said, and life goes on."

Lita wiped a tear from the corner of her eye. "So you think that if you're acting as my doctor only, you can make a better case?"

He nodded.

She inhaled a big breath and let it out. "All right then, I guess I may as well go, so you can get me some help."

"Help is here, Miss."

Both Tate and Lita looked to the parlor door to see a tall fellow with his dark hair parted down the middle, a neatly trimmed black mustache tickling his upper lip.

He hung his hat on the rack by the door. "I hope I'm not interrupting. I was about to ring the bell, but the fellow sitting on your porch said to go on in."

Tate's heart plummeted even as he walked forward to greet the doctor he'd sent correspondence to.

Correspondence about Lita's fragile state of mind.

Chapter 26

Dr. Jeremiah Fischer watched from the front porch of the Cavanaugh residence as Tate, with the young lady beside him, urged his horse and buggy to follow the marshal on horseback. The man who'd introduced himself as Seth Dickson brought up the rear on a horse of his own.

Jeremiah scratched his head at Tate's hurried explanation as to their sudden departure—something about a misunderstanding that should be straightened out by nightfall—but Tate had told him to make himself at home until he returned, so he decided he may as well do just that.

Turning, he went back inside just as the housekeeper was coming down the stairs with a young girl who was crying. "She can't go to jail! She's going to be my mama!" Jeremiah's ears pricked at this, but the housekeeper didn't seem to be in accord with this proclamation.

"Nonsense! She would not make a suitable mother. She's far too permissive. You'd be spoiled rotten in a matter of weeks. If she is finally out of this house, then that's a good thing."

They didn't appear to notice him in the hallway, and the girl wailed louder as the housekeeper pulled her into another room.

Jeremiah followed, the mystery of it all pulling him to the dining room doorway, where the little blonde sat with her head bent over her arms, weeping as if she'd lost all that she held dear. He pulled out the chair across from her, and she looked up, startled.

"Don't be afraid." He smiled. "I'm a friend of your father's." He extended a hand to her over the table. "I'm Dr. Jeremiah Fischer."

She hesitantly put hers out to him, even as she shuddered in her sorrow, and he gave it a firm squeeze. "And what's your name?"

Mrs. Kettler entered with a plate of eggs and toast and set it before the girl. "This morning, her name is Miss Weeping Willow, but never fear, she'll be as fit as a fiddle soon enough, once she spends the day helping me clean. Have you had breakfast, Doctor? There's plenty."

"Why no, I haven't. Thank you."

The housekeeper bustled back to the kitchen, and Jeremiah looked to the girl who only stared at her plate of food, her cheeks wet with tears.

He leaned forward. "It's perfectly all right to be Miss Weeping Willow, but I think that's probably not your real name, is it?"

She shook her head, her lip trembling. "It's Nellie," she said quietly. "Although sometimes Papa calls me Miss Nell."

Jeremiah straightened. "Well, Nellie, I'm pleased to meet you again. I think I may have seen you once or twice as a baby. Your papa and I are old friends, and I knew your mama, too, when she was—" He suddenly thought better about elaborating on that topic. "When you all lived in Denver."

She picked up a piece of toast and nibbled. "I don't remember living anywhere but here."

"Naturally."

Mrs. Kettler returned with a plate of food and set it and a cup of coffee in front of the doctor. "Thank you, Miss..."

"Mrs. Kettler. I've been Dr. Cavanaugh's housekeeper ever since... well ever since he had need of one."

Jeremiah nodded. "I see. Well, thank you again for the breakfast."

She gave a nod and scurried back to the kitchen. Jeremiah turned his attention back to the youngster across from him. "So," he began, cutting off a bite of ham, "you've had some bad news this morning." He placed the bite in his mouth and chewed while he awaited a reply.

Nellie blew out a sigh. "Yes. Very bad news. Our Lalita is going to jail."

Jeremiah made a mental note of "our Lalita" as he sipped his coffee. "I didn't catch the reason... did she break the law?"

The poor girl started to cry once again. "I don't know. Mrs. Kettler wouldn't tell me."

Jeremiah's heart clenched at the sadness she felt. "There, there, now, your papa's working right this minute to clear it all up."

She looked up in surprise. "He is? Will she be home soon, then?"

"Let's hope so, and I'll help however I can."

The girl brightened and took another bite of her toast, so Jeremiah availed himself of the eggs on his plate. After a few moments of silent eating, questions began to push once again toward his mouth. "So Lalita is your good friend, then?"

Nellie actually smiled. "She is my best friend. She is so much fun, and she's teaching me to sew, too! Papa said at first that she was staying with us because she had nowhere else to go, but now he wants—" Her face became suddenly like flint, and she went back to eating.

"What does your papa want?"

Nellie shook her head, still looking at her plate. "I promised not to tell."

Jeremiah hitched a brow but let it go. After he'd swallowed another bite, he tried coming at the topic of Lalita Torres from another angle. He wondered if she had made the same claims of the future to the little girl that she'd made to Tate. "So from what your papa said, it seems that Lalita showed up here quite out of the blue. Did she say where she came from?"

Nellie drank her milk then wiped her mouth on a napkin. "Mm, she talks about Missouri a lot."

"I see. Has she tried contacting her family?"

Nellie slipped out of her chair and picked up her plate and glass. "She says it's no use. They're not there anymore."

Jeremiah nodded as Nellie took her dirty dishes to the kitchen. He sat, sipping his coffee, wondering if Tate would mind if he visited Lalita at the jail. He had been so intrigued by the doctor's letter, he'd caught the next train to the area. Her delusions, if he could treat them, could be the very thing he needed to break into publication. And if her mental disorder had somehow landed her in jail, it would make an even more dramatic story.

He finished his coffee then informed Mrs. Kettler and the young Nell that he'd be stepping out.

* * *

Still in shock, Lalita was sitting on the small, hard bunk in her cell. Thankfully, there was only one other person in the jail at the time, his snoring broadcasting the fact that he had yet to awaken.

Seth Dickson had played his part in this charade like a pro. Limping and wincing into the building, he asked her one more time, before he put his name to the assault charges, if she'd really rather go to jail than his home. Her steely glare hadn't seemed to penetrate his thick skull one iota, however, as he was smiling as he signed.

After the jail cell door had clanked shut behind her, she'd heard him tell the marshal to be sure and call him when she changed her mind. The marshal had seemed as disgusted with his ploy as Lalita, warning that this whole thing could backfire on him.

Lalita didn't have to wonder at the meaning of that. *If the judge finds me guilty, I could be sentenced to prison.*

Even though it wasn't yet mid-morning, she felt weary. She looked over at the blankets and wondered when they'd been washed last. She leaned back against the brick wall, hoping that Tate had found her a lawyer. She did not want to spend the night here.

Voices brought her out of a fog, and she sat up, realizing that she must have dozed off. The door to the marshal's front office opened, and he walked in followed by the doctor that had just shown up at Tate's house right before they left. She rose as the two came toward her cell.

The doctor smiled as he swept off his bowler. "Miss Torres, I'm wondering if I might keep you company while Dr. Cavanaugh is working toward your release."

Lalita didn't know why that brought tears to her eyes. She nodded, and the marshal unlocked her cell, letting the tall, impeccably dressed man in. He bid her sit, and he took one of the straight-backed chairs that had been affixed to the floor on either side of a small table bolted down in similar fashion.

She sat back down on the bunk. "I'm sorry that your visit has been complicated by all this. Tate said you came down from Denver. Did you work together?"

Dr. Fischer clasped his hands on the table. "Not exactly. We met in one of the men's clubs, and then later, I treated his wife."

Lalita's eyes narrowed. "Why wouldn't Tate treat his own wife? Since he's a doctor too."

The dark-haired man smoothed his mustache with a thumb and forefinger and brought them together at his chin. "We are in different fields. I'm a psychologist."

A light came on in Lalita's head, and all at once she realized why Dr. Fischer had paid them a visit. "You didn't come to see Tate, did you? You came to see me."

He studied her for a moment before resting his hand once again on the table. "Yes. Dr. Cavanaugh wrote me a letter about you. I was so fascinated by what he wrote, I had to come see you for myself."

Lalita blinked. *What does Tate want me to say to this man?* She knew he'd written the letter before he believed her story. He'd wanted to help her, but now that help could be detrimental. She mustered up a smile. "I'm afraid you've made a long trip for nothing, Dr. Fischer. When Dr. Cavanaugh wrote to you, I was still having some memory problems and general confusion that has mostly cleared up now." She rose, hoping he'd see it as a dismissal of sorts.

He didn't. "So you're feeling much better now? Tell me, how did you end up in Dr. Cavanaugh's care?"

"That's where I still have a few holes in my memory, but I was evidently knocked out by a close bolt of lightning when I was up on Pikes Peak." Now feeling awkward, standing, she walked to the bars. "Some men brought me to the doctor, and I've been there, recovering, ever since."

Dr. Fischer slid out from behind the table. "You were *knocked out* by the lightning." The lanky fellow sat on the table itself. "You didn't ride it a hundred years into the past."

She turned to face him, giggling. "Did I really say that? Oh my, no wonder the doctor was worried about me for a while."

She leaned back against the metal, feeling more trapped by Dr. Fischer's scrutiny than the bars themselves.

188

He folded his arms across his chest. "So what is your assessment of the town? Is it similar to other places you've been?"

"Oh, it's much more beautiful than most, wouldn't you say?"

The doctor's eyes narrowed a hair. "Do you keep a book of predictions that you claim are things that have already happened?"

Lalita feigned shock. "Oh dear, I do hope Dr. Cavanaugh didn't trouble you with any of those! For a few days, I thought my dreams were memories." She grinned. "And I've been known to have some pretty wild dreams."

He uncrossed his arms and gripped the edge of the table. "But you've made a complete recovery in less than a week from some of the strangest delusions I've ever heard of."

Lita pushed away from the bars, feeling more than a little annoyed. "Yes, evidently." She rubbed her hands together, feeling her smile starting to droop. "If I've answered all your questions..."

The doctor didn't move. "So why are you here? I had assumed that your mental condition had somehow gotten you in trouble, but if you are completely recovered, then—"

Lalita sat on the bunk once more. "Not completely recovered. As I said, there are still a few things I can't remember." She rubbed her temple. "But that has nothing to do with why I'm in jail. I'm here on assault charges."

Dr. Fischer's brows did a speedy climb. "The blond man who—"

"Yes. He had me cornered in the carriage house, and I gave him my knee."

The doctor grimaced. After a moment or two, he shook his head. "Well, Miss Torres, I wouldn't be too quick to claim recovery. In this world of male judges and juries, delusion may be your best defense."

*   *   *

Tate was waiting in the office of Claude Watt, Attorney at Law.

Having risen early to get Lita down the road, he hadn't really realized that he was premature for most business until he arrived at the office and found it locked. Making note of the opening time on the sign, he took the opportunity to break his fast at Cliff House before returning.

There was another lawyer in town, but he had found Mr. Watt to be professional and trustworthy when his wife had taken her own life, handling all the necessary documents with efficiency and the utmost discretion.

He'd only arrived five minutes past the hour, but in that time someone had slipped in ahead of him. As the clock ticked toward ten o'clock, Tate ground his teeth, trying to resist the urge to ask the woman at the desk a second time when the attorney would be free. *She didn't know the first time. She won't know now.*

He closed his eyes and rubbed his brow. *As soon as the reverend suggested you would ruin Lita by keeping her in your house, you should have driven her to the Justice of the Peace.* He blinked his eyes open, reminding himself that with the wagon accident, he would have had no time to do that anyway. *Was that just yesterday?*

Exasperated with the delay, he blew out a breath and rose just as a door opened down a short hall, and a man came out, followed by Mr. Watt. Both were dressed for business, although Watt's suit seemed to speak of more money in its tailoring.

The two exchanged goodbyes; then Watt's eye landed on Tate. "Ah, Dr. Cavanaugh, to what to I owe this visit?"

Tate extended his hand to the balding lawyer, whose graying mustache had been twisted into an impressive handlebar. "Mr. Watt, I was hoping to speak to you on a matter of some importance."

Watt nodded, then moved to his secretary's desk. "Maggie, when's my next appointment?"

The brunette stopped typing and checked a book on her desk. "Nothing until afternoon—Mr. Ellis at two o'clock."

Watt nodded and waved Tate back to his office. "Have a seat." He sat behind a large, mahogany desk and leaned back with his hands clasped at his waist. "What can I do for you, Doc?"

Tate sat in one of the leather chairs that faced him, trying to hide his desperation behind an air of professionalism. "I'm here to solicit your representation for a patient of mine—a Miss Lalita Torres."

Watt leaned forward and began to write on a pad of paper in front of him. "Why does the lady need representation?"

Tate took a deep breath before beginning.

* * *

"Are you sure you want to do that?"

Jeremiah Fischer looked at the chess board and saw immediately that his queen was in danger. "Ah, I see. Well, I concede the next move to you."

Lalita took the opposing queen with her bishop. "Since I've never played with you before, Dr. Fischer, I don't know whether to chalk that up to a lack of skill or a lack of mental focus."

Fischer smiled. "Ah, I think the acceptable excuse in the presence of a lady would usually be distraction, but since I am happily married, I will have to concede to the lack of skill."

She laughed. "You are slick. I think you left out one possibility. Distraction by vocation. I think you are trying to puzzle me out, and that leaves precious little brain power for chess."

He couldn't help but smile as he pondered his next move both on the chess board and in getting her to open up to him.

He'd never met a woman quite like Lalita Torres, and he felt certain she was not what she was pretending to be. Besides the shorter hair, she carried herself differently. Most women sat as if on exhibition in a museum—rigid and stiff—their smiles practiced, their gestures under-pronounced. Their clothing and elaborate hats say "look at me," while their demeanor says, "but not too long."

Not so Lalita Torres. She walked, sat, even slouched, in a stylish dress that seemed to be lacking the stiff undergarments that packed other women in and held them up should they grow weary. Though she had a nice figure, he could tell she was not cinched in as his wife insisted on being until she could barely breathe. No, this woman moved freely, unaware that her freedom was provocative, her expressions too unrestrained, her words bolder than was considered good politesse. *Perhaps it's the Indian heritage.*

He knew she was hiding something, but at the same time, it seemed obvious that she wasn't used to hiding. Her voice across the table brought his mind back to the game. "If you don't hurry up, I'm going to fall asleep over here. Dr. Cavanaugh got me up rather early this morning."

He moved a pawn forward. "Oh? Did you have plans other than jail today?"

Lalita's eyes showed a moment of sadness before she looked down at the chess board. "We did."

"An early morning picnic?" At her questioning stare, he went on. "I noticed the basket by the door."

She took his pawn with one of her own. "Are you sure you're not a detective instead of a shrink?"

Fischer cocked his head, squinting, "A shrink?"

The brown eyes across from him blinked twice. "You've never heard that term for a psychiatrist?" She bent her head over the game board. "It's pretty common in Kansas City."

Fischer sat back and crossed his arms? "How does the term apply?"

She didn't look at him. "Uh. . . I think it comes from 'head shrinker,' but I'm not really sure."

"Well, that's hardly flattering."

Lalita shrugged like an insolent teenager. "Don't ask me. I didn't come up with it."

Fischer moved his rook. "I'm not so sure."

That brought her gaze back to him. "Huh? What do you mean?"

"Your good doctor mentioned that you often spoke words, phrases, even whole paragraphs that he couldn't comprehend."

She looked back at the board, making a quick move that put her bishop in danger. "I told you, that was before—when things were foggy."

He took her bishop. "And yet, you just confused me."

She sat back, and he could see he had her riled. "Well, isn't that just typical of this oppressive era. A woman couldn't possibly utter something that a man might not know about."

"Which era do you prefer, Miss Torres?"

Her glare was interrupted by the marshal, carrying a plate of food. "I'm sorry, Dr. Fischer, but I'm only allowed to serve the prisoner. You'll have to find your lunch elsewhere."

Fischer rose, grabbing his jacket off the back of the chair. "Ah, yes, well I don't suppose you'd allow me to return this afternoon, Miss Torres?"

"I think I'll be resting after lunch, Doctor. I'm suddenly tired."

He smiled. "As you wish. Here's hoping that Dr. Cavanaugh can secure your release in a timely manner."

Leaving the jail, Fischer donned his bowler and made his way to his rented buggy, pondering the woman he'd left behind. He could see why Tate had been baffled. She was a riddle even without any confessions of time travel. Unhitching the horse, he climbed aboard the buggy and pointed her toward the business district to find some lunch, itching to speak with Tate.

*   *   *

"What did you find out?" Lalita was on her feet the moment Tate, followed by Claude Watt, came through the door.

Tate gave a sideways glance to the marshal as he unlocked her cell and waited until he was back in his office before speaking. "Miss Torres, this is Mr. Watt. He has agreed to represent you."

Lita looked nigh unto panic. "Do I need representing? I thought you were going to get me out of here."

Tate nodded, resisting the urge to take her in his arms. "That was our hope, but we are having a difficult time reaching the judge in Colorado Springs. There is evidently a trial underway, making it impossible to gain an audience to determine bail. Mr. Watt will keep trying, but—" Tate found it difficult to go on. He swallowed hard. "But should the hour get too late, you may have to spend the night."

Lita's eyes misted over, but she bravely blinked the tears away. "Okay."

He took her by the elbow and steered her toward the table and chairs, at the same time waving his newly acquired lawyer to the other side. "Mr. Watt needs to ask you questions about the incident in the carriage house, and in the meantime, I'm heading over to the saddlery to see if I can talk some sense into Dickson."

He paused but a moment, then called for the marshal to let him out.

* * *

Mrs. Kettler had hurried Nellie through the store, sending her mood straight into pouting. *Lalita lets me look at things.*

Only when Mrs. Atkins stopped Mrs. Kettler right next to the apples to ask her about something she'd heard at the Ladies Aid meeting, did Nellie get to pause, although she would have chosen the side of the store that held penny candy sticks if she planned on lingering anywhere at all.

Her attention was caught however at the name Torres. Mrs. Kettler was filling in everything Mrs. Atkins hadn't heard about Lalita's trip to the jail, and unlike what she told Nellie on almost a daily basis, she was not thinking before she spoke. Nor was she being kind.

All sorts of "secrets" tumbled out of Mrs. Kettler's mouth, including the beautiful flowers on Lalita's shoulder, and instead of wishing for their own as Nellie did, they said terrible things about her friend and said she was a bad woman who deserved time in jail.

And once again, Nellie wanted to cry.

* * *

Tate strode into the saddlery, the smell of leather hitting his nose like a locomotive. William was cutting a thick piece with a knife, while Max was sitting on a stool stitching a saddle that looked nearly complete.

They looked up when he entered, and Tate forced a smile he didn't feel. "William, Max..." He craned his neck trying to see into a back room. "I don't suppose your father's here?"

Seth Dickson appeared through a side door before either of his sons could answer. "Doc, what took you so long? I thought sure you'd be here before lunch."

Tate's anger only surged with Dickson's flippant attitude, but he didn't want to have it out with the man in front of his sons. His lip twitched. "Is there somewhere we can talk in private?"

Dickson walked across the room to pick up a carved piece of wood that would form the seat of a saddle. "Sorry, Doc, I don't really have the time. What with business and" —he looked back at Tate over his shoulder— "other plans."

Tate stepped forward. "These other plans... have you shared them with your sons?"

Seth looked from one to the other. "Not yet, but they'll find out soon."

Max and William exchanged baffled looks, the older pausing in his work. "What kind of plans, Pa?"

Any other time, Tate would be loathe to get in the middle of a family disagreement, but Dickson not only put him in a position to be in the middle, he handed Tate a match to light a fire under it. *I gave him a chance to talk privately.* "Your father plans to marry Miss Torres."

Both boys' eyes grew wide, and Max immediately rose, grabbing his crutches leaning nearby. "You want to marry her? You're old enough to be her pa!"

Dickson visibly bristled. "Not quite, Max."

Max employed his crutches, maneuvering through the saddles in various stages of construction. "Well, you're too old for her anyway. I was thinking that as soon as I got out of this cast—"

"Pa may be too old, but you're too young, Max," William interjected. "I'm a lot closer to her age, I'd wager."

Max spun to face his brother, and Tate almost regretted getting the two involved. "You? You've never even spoken to her. I... we've... "

Tate followed and clapped a hand onto Max's shoulder. *Oh Lord, forgive me for chaffing these young men's hearts.* "So how do you feel about her being your ma?"

Both boys looked horrified.

Dickson's jaw went tight. "All right, Doc, outside. Now." He breezed past Tate and out the side door. Tate followed with Dickson leading him a good thirty feet from the saddlery to a small grove of aspens that had survived the building of his corral.

Dickson turned and his usual good mood was nowhere to be found. "Doc, I need a wife, and I know my boys have both got stars in their eyes with regards to Lalita, but—"

"That's Miss Torres to you, Dickson. I don't recall her giving you leave to be so familiar."

Dickson finally found his smile. "Doc, if I didn't know better, I'd say you've got stars in your eyes too."

Tate ground his teeth. "She's a patient, and it's my job—"

Dickson put a hand to Tate's shoulder. "I know, son, and you've taken good care of her. But I swear on my granny's grave that I'll take care of her too. The Good Book says that God looks at the heart, and that's what I strive to do. She's an Indian and a ruined one, too, I'll wager, but the Lord forgives, and so do I."

Tate was seething. "You are not endearing yourself to her by throwing her in jail."

The man shook his head. "Don't I know it, but she'll come around. She just needs to see that her options are limited. A few days in the hoosegow ought to do the trick."

A declaration of his love for her was bursting out of Tate's heart, and a speech about her options was on the tip of his tongue. Unfortunately, it was his fist that seized the moment.

Chapter 27

Lalita and Tate drove the buggy in silence. After he'd paid her bail and his own fine for "brawling," they were finally heading home with Tate's bank account considerably smaller. She was glad to be out of the jail, but she knew it wasn't over yet. She still had to go before the judge.

They met another couple in a buggy, and Tate touched the brim of his homburg, but the gesture was met with icy stares. Lalita's chest squeezed as Tate gripped the reins, his jaw set. "I'm sorry, Tate, I've brought you nothing but trouble."

He took her hand on the seat beside him and flashed her a weary smile. "No, Lita, you've brought me more joy than I've had in years. We'll get through this."

"Can we still get married?"

He slowly shook his head. "You're not allowed to leave Manitou until after sentencing."

"That's too bad." She leaned her head back and looked at the late afternoon sky. " 'Cause if we had gotten married this morning, tonight would have been our wedding night."

Tate stiffened, and Lalita guessed she must have crossed that Victorian line again that she was forever stumbling over. She was too drained to be miffed about it, however. "I'm sorry, I keep forgetting I can't... just say things I'm thinking."

Tate threaded is fingers with hers. "No, Lita, when you're just with me, you can say anything. I was just... surprised that you'd be looking forward to our wedding night."

She shifted on the seat to look at him. "Are you kidding me? Why wouldn't I look forward to it?" Her eyes grew wide. "Is there something you haven't told me?"

He looked at her, alarmed. "No! Everything is... as it should be."

She blew out a breath. "Whew! I thought you were going to tell me you lost something vital in a war or something."

There was a moment of silence before Tate laughed out loud. Lalita started to giggle, and the two laughed most of the way home. As he was driving up the hill, he finally found control. "Lita, you say things no one would ever say. With you around, I think I'm going to be laughing for the rest of my life."

"But that's a good thing, right?"

He looked into her eyes. "That's a very good thing."

The two were quiet for several minutes, though smiling. With their hands entwined under the fabric folds of her skirt at her side, she returned to the original topic. "So why would you think I wouldn't be looking forward to our wedding night? You're a great kisser; I can't wait for the rest."

Tate seemed nervous. "Women rarely concede to being eager for their marital obligations, and I thought—"

"Obligations!" She blinked, wide-eyed. "It will be my honor, and hopefully my pleasure, to... to... What's an acceptable term?... To... *know* you, Tate. It's not my obligation."

When he didn't respond, a look of amazement on his face, she added, "Just to be clear, I meant 'know' in the Biblical sense."

He blinked the dazed look from his face and chuckled as he turned Maisy into the driveway to the carriage house. "Yes, Lita, I understand your meaning."

"My century is too permissive, but yours is way too uptight."

Tate pulled into the empty carriage house, and Lalita looked around the space. "No Harold waiting for us today."

"It looks that way." He rose and stepped down, and she started to follow, but he stopped her. "Just stay there a minute."

Puzzled, she watched him walk back to the large doors and close them, securing them with the board brace. Her eyebrows raised when he did the same with the side door, effectively locking them in. Stepping back up into the buggy, he sat and patted his lap. Lalita smiled and took off her hat, laying it on her vacated spot as she accepted his invitation. He removed his as well as she slipped her arms around his neck. "You're a bad boy, Tate Cavanaugh."

He nibbled her earlobe. "Just trying to prove that I'm not 'uptight.' "

She licked her lips and his met hers with longing and passion. She ran a hand into his hair as his hands roamed over her back. After several heated minutes, Maisy snorted and lurched the buggy forward. They jerked apart, and Lalita laughed. "I think Maisy is hungry."

"I imagine she is." Tate pulled Lalita back and continued kisses down her neck.

She put a finger under his chin, bringing his eyes back to hers. Her brows lifted. "She's not the only one, I think."

His smile, compounded by the black eye that was just starting to show, was absolutely devilish. "Again, your fault. You were the one who wanted to discuss our wedding night."

She slid off his lap and stood. "And you were the one who said we can't have one yet, so I think we better go in and see how Nellie is."

He sighed. "I suppose you're right."

Lalita took the opportunity to watch Tate undo the harnesses; then he showed her where Maisy's feed was located and how much to give her along with her hay. "I hope you won't have to do all this," Tate was saying as he escorted her out of the building toward the house, "but it's good to know just in case."

"I don't mind doing it." She stopped at the door, and Tate stopped with her. "In case you haven't noticed, I'm not like the girls around here."

Tate just grinned as he opened the door and ushered her in.

* * *

Tate heard Nellie running down the stairs as they entered the kitchen, and no admonitions from Mrs. Kettler could slow her down. "Lalita! Papa saved you!"

Lita bent down and gave her a tight hug. "He did, indeed. No moth-eaten jail blankets for me tonight."

As the trio spilled out of the kitchen with Nellie chattering all the way, he could see Mrs. Kettler at the top of the stairs, her lips drawn tight. His eye was starting to ache, and he realized he must look a sight, but seeing Nellie holding Lita's hand as she excitedly asked one question after another put a smile on his face, and the joy he felt simply couldn't be contained. "Mrs. K., dinner smells wonderful. When do we eat? I think I could eat a side of beef."

Mrs. Kettler slowly descended with an unmistakable air of grandeur. "There's a meat pie in the oven." She looked after Nellie and Lita who had just disappeared into the parlor. "Will Miss Torres be dining with you? Should I stay as a chaperone?"

Tate stopped, considering. A blow had been dealt to Lita's reputation today, and even his own. Then he heard the voice of Dr. Fischer in the parlor and knew that conversation could turn to things Mrs. Kettler need not know about. "That won't be necessary, Mrs. Kettler. Miss Torres is still my patient."

Mrs. Kettler's expression showed her distaste, but she turned and continued to the kitchen.

Tate moved down the hall to the parlor where Nellie and Lita were holding hands and spinning in a circle, laughing. Tate smiled, envisioning his future with this woman as his wife and the mother of his child. Then his eye landed on the amused Dr. Fischer, and his smile faded. *I know I invited him, but now how do I get rid of him?*

* * *

Tate let Nellie stay up later than usual, both because she was so excited to have Lalita home, and it kept the conversation off the letter that he had sent to Jeremiah. When both girls started to yawn, however, he conceded their need for rest and sent them upstairs to bed.

He was feeling pretty tired himself and was about to ask Jeremiah if he had acquired any accommodations in the town, when the man pierced him with a stare and wasted no time starting the conversation he must have been waiting for all day. "Tate, what's going on here? Your letter sounded desperate, but now that I'm here, I get the feeling you both wished I were gone. Is the girl suffering from flights of fancy or not?"

Tate cleared his throat and straightened in his chair. "I'm truly sorry that you made the trip clear down here. I had no idea you would jump on the first train without calling me first. I'll be glad to pay for your train fare—"

Dr. Fischer interrupted him with a wave of his hand. "Nonsense. I can afford the fare, and your mountain town makes a delightful vacation if it turns out to be just that, but I was hoping to... whet my psychological appetite on your riveting case."

Tate shifted in his seat. "Yes, well, Miss Torres has made a rather rapid recovery in the last few days. Most of her idiosyncrasies have normalized, and she only suffers now from a spotty memory concerning the day of the accident that put her in my care."

Fischer leaned forward, clasping his hands over his knees. "So she's given up all of it—the idea that Manitou is stuck in the past while the rest of the world moved on, the time travel, the predictions of the future—all of it."

Tate's mental list of his recent lies haunted him, but he saw no other way to get the man to hop on a train and go back to Denver. He nodded, but the doctor seemed to be waiting for some other explanation. Tate tried to accommodate him. "Since I don't know exactly what happened to her up on Pikes Peak, it's a difficult thing to speculate about her recovery. All I know is what I have observed; every day she has improved."

Fischer leaned back, his eyes narrowed. "I hate to say this, Tate, but I don't believe it. It's too fast, and you have obviously developed feelings for the girl."

Tate started to sputter. "Where would you get... of course I was obligated to help her today... and Dickson is insufferable. How could you think—"

"Tate, have you looked in a mirror lately?" Fischer smiled. "That shiner says it all."

Tate rose, uncomfortable with Fischer's scrutiny. "You're jumping to conclusions." Turning, he walked to the picture window on the front of the house and let down the sash. "You know I have a temper, and Dickson rubs me the wrong way every time he opens his mouth."

"While I don't know Dickson, I do know your temper." Tate turned back, hoping to see that he was succeeding in changing his opinion, but Jeremiah's face wore a lop-sided smile. "And what I know about your temper is that it only blows when it's personal or when you are championing another. When your family was bullied and persecuted, or when your wife was shunned by the society matrons. Your temper doesn't just blow at rash or irritating words; it takes a personal jab directed at someone you care about to set that volcano off."

Tate took a step forward and pressed on. "Of course it's personal. The poor girl is alone here and has been through some sort of trauma that she can't recall, and ever since, I have been judged for keeping her here and protecting her. Excuse me if I'm a bit raw."

Fischer seemed to chew over his words, and finally he rose. "All right, Tate. You've had a long day. I've got a room at Barker House, so I'll take my leave of you for tonight." He slipped into his frock coat and bowler that were hung by the door. "If I'm welcome for breakfast, I'll see you then."

Tate wished he'd take his breakfast in the dining car of the Rio Grande, but being rude would only raise his suspicions higher. "Certainly. I look forward to it."

With the click of the door, Tate walked to the end of the parlor where a mirror hung above the piano. He winced at the sight. Thanks to an ice pack prepared by Lalita after dinner, the swelling had been somewhat reduced, but the black and purple would most certainly be with him most of the week.

He hoped the same would not be said of Jeremiah Fischer.

Chapter 28

Lalita was heading down the stairs in one of Augusta's outfits made from a small floral print, when the doorbell rang. She ran her hands down the shirtwaist that she had taken in at the sides, then looked further down to the green border she had added to the skirt's hem to give it more length. After Tate's outlay of money for bail and brawling, she didn't want to ask him for more fabric for another dress just yet.

Tate came out of the parlor with his newspaper in hand to answer the door. Her heart sank as Dr. Fischer stepped over the threshold, but Tate seemed to be expecting him. She stood at the bottom of the stairs, wishing she had waited upstairs for Nellie.

She forced a smile as the two men reached her, and for the first time, Lalita really noticed the difference in their frames. Tate was of a medium build with a strength that would go undetected unless you had been on the receiving end of being lifted out of buggies, or you had occasion to caress his biceps the way she had when they snuggled together in the parlor. Dr. Fischer was tall and lanky, and Lalita wagered that Tate could beat him easily in an arm wrestling match. She smiled a real smile, wondering if she could arrange it.

Dr. Fischer took her smile and ran with it. "Miss Torres, you're looking rested. I hope today will be a more pleasant one for you than yesterday."

"You and me both."

Nellie appeared on the stairs in a black and gray checked dress that Lalita immediately wanted to add some color to, but Tate waved them toward the dining room. As Nellie reached the bottom stair, Tate placed a hand on her head. "Good morning, Miss Nell. I trust you slept well."

When she shook her head, looking troubled. Lalita stepped back to the stairs. "More bad dreams?" She had gone to Nellie's room once when the little girl had called out in the night and sat with her until she'd fallen asleep again.

Nellie nodded. "I kept looking for you, but I couldn't find you." She looked to Tate. "And someone beat you up until you were black and blue all over."

Tate lifted her up and held her tight. "A dream is just a dream, Nellie. Lalita is here, and I just have the one bruise to show for my bad temper."

The three joined Dr. Fischer at the table that was already filled with a steaming bowl of scrambled eggs, plates of bacon and biscuits, not to mention butter, jam, coffee, milk, and juice.

After Tate said the blessing, Fischer unfolded his linen napkin and laid it on his lap. "If I thought it would do any good, I'd try to talk your Mrs. Kettler into moving to Denver. Our cook left us last month, and Bess hasn't found a new one to suit her yet."

Lalita dished up eggs for herself and Nellie. "Is Bess your wife?"

"Yes. And I have a son named Tobias, who is a few years younger than Nellie."

The talk turned to politics and the economy, and Lalita wondered how she could leave the house without it being obvious that she was avoiding their guest. A bike ride was out, at least until after all the talk about her time in jail yesterday had died down. She also doubted that Tate would let her take the buggy. Even if he trusted her with it, as a doctor, he might need it at any time. "I guess Nellie and I could walk to town," she muttered as she reached for another biscuit.

"Do you have some shopping to do, or are we boring you?"

She looked up into Dr. Fischer's questioning face. *Did I say that out loud?* "Oh, no, I'm sorry, I just don't know much about the politics of this time." It nearly killed her to play dumb, but she knew it was the necessary role at the moment. "I mean of any time. I'm not really into politics."

Tate set his cup down a bit too hard on the saucer, and she put herself to the task of buttering her biscuit.

204

"I wouldn't expect you to; women don't have a head for politics. But just what are you 'into,' Miss Torres?" She heard a definite smile in Dr. Fischer's voice.

Tate jumped in before she could answer. "She's an accomplished seamstress; she's been teaching Nellie to sew. And she has an interest in history, which I think may explain her earlier confusion."

Lalita smiled tightly before taking a bite of her biscuit now coated with strawberry jam. It was imperative to keep her mouth occupied. Otherwise, she would no doubt fill this man in on all she did know about the politics of this country and a few others.

"She knows all about history!" Nellie chimed in. "Even stuff that hasn't happened yet."

Lalita coughed and put a hand over her mouth in an attempt to keep half chewed biscuit from landing on Dr. Fischer's plate.

Her eyes watered as Tate handed her a glass of juice, all the while directing his words to Nellie. "You mean in school, right sweetheart? Lalita has told you things you haven't learned about yet in school."

As Lalita downed her juice, she was sure that Dr. Fischer couldn't possibly miss the pointed look that Tate was giving Nellie. Nellie blinked several times before nodding and asking to be excused, and Lalita saw the look of trepidation cross his face. *Poor Tate doesn't know if we're better or worse off with her in the room.*

Tate worked up a smile and gave Nellie the permission she wanted before lifting his cup to his lips.

The doorbell rang, and he wanted nothing more than to rush out of the room to answer it, but that would leave Lita alone with Jeremiah. He forced himself to sit and let Mrs. Kettler receive whoever was at the door.

She returned a moment later with an envelope that merely had "Dr. Tate Cavanaugh" scrawled across it. Hoping it was payment for a bill, he opened it and pulled out the pages within. Unfolding them revealed not cash nor a cashier's check for services rendered, but a list of names. His eyes scanned back to the top for the explanation.

"*Dr. Cavanaugh, we the concerned citizens of Manitou Springs implore you to put one Miss Lalita Torres out of your house immediately. The keeping of this harlot in your home is not becoming a respected doctor. If you choose to ignore our plea, there will be repercussions.*"

The names were numbered to fifty in two columns on the first page and continued to eighty-one on the second. He quickly folded the pages and stuffed them back in the envelope.

He attempted to look pleasant, but he was certain it was not coming off well. Dr. Fischer confirmed it. "Bad news?"

Tate shook his head. "No, not at all. Just a small misunderstanding about a bill." He poured himself another cup of coffee, wondering at what point he had given in to lying as a way of life.

He glanced at Lita, whose expression seemed as concerned as Dr. Fischer's, but it was even more important to keep the letter's contents from her. He slid the envelope into the back pocket of his trousers, intending to stash it in his office at the earliest opportunity.

Everything was escalating faster than he could handle it. He needed an ally, but he wasn't sure if the man sitting across the table from Lita was the one for the job. *Would he believe us if we told him the real story or not?*

As he ate the last bite of his eggs, he tuned in to the conversation that was going on at the table and realized that Lita was getting riled.

"So you seriously think that we should bring back the ducking chair as a vital part of our justice system?"

One look at Jeremiah's cocky smile, and Tate knew exactly what the man was doing. "Absolutely. What better way to cool the hot tempers of nagging women than a cold plunge into the river."

"Nagging women!" Lita was leaning over the table. "And what about those who knee lecherous men in the balls? I suppose I should have been—"

There was a gasp from the kitchen, and Jeremiah's eyes went wide. Tate took hold of her elbow. "Lita!" She clamped her mouth shut and looked to him, her eyes flaming. "I believe my old friend is just trying to goad you." He shifted his gaze to the man who was biting his lip to keep from laughing.

"He's just trying to find out your boundaries. It's not an uncommon way that potential suitors have used in the past to test a woman's manners and personality, but I hadn't realized it had found its way into the field of psychology." Tate held his gaze in challenge.

Jeremiah straightened. "I'm sorry, Tate, I just didn't realize how easy it would be." He shifted his gaze to a still fuming Lalita. "Miss Torres, please forgive me, but you're an enigma, and what I want to know is were you this outspoken before your head injury or lightning jolt or whatever left you unconscious?"

Tate watched her try to rein in her ire. "If you'll excuse me," she said tightly, "I'm going to check on Nellie."

Tate blew out a breath as she left the room then leaned forward, his forearms on the table. "You're not going to let this go, are you?"

"What was in the letter?"

Tate reared back. "What? What does that have to do with—"

"If there's one thing I do well, Tate, it's read people. Your expression and subsequent distraction would seem to indicate something more serious than a minor misunderstanding over a bill."

Tate tried to smile. "How do you keep your job with so many wild assumptions made each day?"

Jeremiah's smile and shake of the head was laced with frustration. "Tate, except when I spoke with Lalita in the jail—"

"You went to see her in the jail?"

Jeremiah was smug. "Yes, and you just proved what I was about to say. Knowing your background, I can see why you feel a need to protect her, but you guard her and what she says like you were getting paid to do it. So when I can start a conversation with the lady right beside you on a topic sure to bring out her true inclinations without you even realizing it, whatever has distracted you has got to be dire."

Tate closed his eyes for a moment and rubbed his brow. Then he rose from the table and waved Jeremiah to his study. When the door was closed, Tate still spoke in low tones as he pulled the envelope from his back pocket, handed it to

Jeremiah, and went to sit behind his desk. "It was a petition by eighty or so townspeople demanding I put Lalita out of my house." At Jeremiah's furrowed brow, he continued. "Somehow the rumor has gotten started that she is... a harlot. Dickson may have started it himself, as he seems to be of that opinion as well."

Jeremiah's eyes went wide as he unfolded the pages. "But I thought Dickson wanted to marry her."

"He does, but he so magnanimously declared that he would forgive her." A flame came to Tate's eyes. "He said he was trying to get her to say yes to his proposal by limiting her options. This may be his way of doing it."

"What a cad!"

"Indeed."

There was a moment of silence as Jeremiah read the letter for himself; then he refolded it and shifted uncomfortably. "I assume that you believe her not to be a harlot."

Tate straightened. "She is not."

Jeremiah cocked his head. "She is brazen enough—"

Tate rose. "Her upbringing was different—we could even say deficient in proper decorum—but you will have to take my word that she is not a harlot. And if you do not, I will ask you to leave my home immediately."

Jeremiah pushed out of his chair and rose, staring Tate down. "I will take your word if you will admit that you have feelings for her. Let's have some truth between us."

Tate deliberated a moment, then nodded.

Jeremiah smiled and stuck out his hand. "How can I help you?"

Jeremiah followed Tate's lead and sat back down, but not before getting a glimpse of a decorated book in the drawer where he stashed the envelope. The colorful, calligraphed title faced him: *Lalita's History Book.*

Tate blew out a breath. "Yes, I'm in love with Lalita. In fact, we had planned to drive to Colorado Springs and be married yesterday morning before Dickson and the marshal changed our plans."

Jeremiah hitched one leg over the other. "What's the rush?"

Tate licked his lips, and Jeremiah could see that he was only going to get as much truth as Tate was willing to give him. "After the incident with Dickson, it seemed the only way I could protect her from further unwanted attention from the man."

"Why not just announce your betrothal and court the woman?" Jeremiah crossed his arms over his chest. "Surely Dickson wouldn't try to interfere with that."

Tate shook his head. "No, probably not, but to do that, I'd have to put her out of my house. I could pay for a room at a boarding house for the six months of courtship that Reverend Niemeyer demands, but..." Tate ground his teeth.

Jeremiah prodded the conversation forward before Tate closed down. "You're afraid to do that because..."

"You know what I'm afraid of." Tate pushed away from his desk and rose, walking to the window. "You saw how easy it is to move her out of what's considered proper. It's as if she—"

"Doesn't even know what 'proper' is." He uncrossed his arms and legs and rested his elbows on the arms of the chair, his hands clasped on his stomach. "I thought the same thing when I was talking to her yesterday in the jail. She speaks her mind, she plays to win, she's confident without staging. She's the most unnaturally natural woman I've ever met. And that includes my wife."

He paused a moment while Tate nodded; then he pressed on with new concerns. "So how will that work as a respected doctor in a small community? I know you're thinking that your name will give her acceptance, but that petition may indicate that she will not be accepted, and she may take you down with her."

Tate's jaw squared. "I won't make the same mistakes with her that I made with Augusta—I will not push her into changing who she is to fit in. I lost one wife that way. I'll not lose another."

Jeremiah leaned forward. "Tate, surely you're not blaming yourself for Augusta's death. The woman had a classic case of melancholia. True, I advised you not to take her out of my care, but your point was well taken that she needed to get out of Denver. And your letters indicated that there had been some improvement." He rose and crossed the room, clapping a hand on Tate's shoulder. "So, my friend, release yourself from that burden of guilt. You did not drive your wife to take her own life. And you will not drive Lalita to the same end if you take a firm hand with her and rein her in as a husband should."

Tate gave him a thin smile. "I'm not her husband yet, and I'll be unable to marry her until after her hearing."

Jeremiah sat on the edge of Tate's desk. "Do you really think Dickson will take his bluff that far? My guess is he'll drop the charges before risking sending her to prison."

Tate slowly shook his head. "I have no idea. His mind works in ways that mine can't fathom."

Jeremiah pondered his friend's dilemma. He could see the attraction of someone like Lalita Torres, but to his mind, she was nothing but a mountain of trouble to a professional man, with or without delusions. *If Tate were smart, he'd let the Seth Dicksons of the world have her.*

He assumed that Tate no longer believed her to be delusional, otherwise he wouldn't be considering marriage, but there still was something he wasn't telling him. Of that he was certain.

Chapter 29

Lalita had decided a walk was just what she needed, so after she had tied a length of wide, red ribbon around Nellie's waist with a bow in the back, they had started down the hill hand in hand. "It's not all that far to the Pilson's. I wonder if it would be okay to just drop by to see the baby?"

Nellie released her hand to watch a honeybee on a wildflower by the road. Lalita stopped with her, and after a moment Nellie looked up. "How do bees make honey?"

The bee had flown away, so the two continued their walk. "Well, the bees have an enzyme in their mouths that mixes with the nectar of the flowers. They go back to their hives and spit it out. The worker bees flap their wings really fast in the hive to evaporate most of the water, and when they're done, it's honey."

Nellie looked concerned. "It was in their mouths?"

"Yep, pretty weird, huh? God has a crazy imagination."

"Do bumblebees make honey?"

"Nope. Only honeybees. That's why they're called honeybees, I suppose."

They walked on with Lalita telling Nellie about all the insects that could be found in Kansas and Missouri that didn't seem to be in Manitou.

"Bugs that light up at night?"

"Uh, huh, those are called fireflies, and there are great big, ugly bugs called cicadas that crawl out of the ground in the spring and break out of their hard brown shells, leaving them hanging on trees and fence posts. And they are really loud. They make a sound something like this."

Lalita demonstrated, and Nellie's eyes grew round. "I wish I could see one!"

"Well, if I still had my phone, and we weren't about a hundred years too early for the internet, I could show you a picture just like that." She snapped her fingers. She let out a big sigh as they turned the corner at the bottom of the hill. "I do miss my phone."

Nellie giggled. "If I were you, I'd miss fireflies!"

Lalita nodded. "Yeah, you're right. As cool as my phone was, fireflies are way cooler."

"Cooler? Do they shiver?"

Lalita laughed. "No, I'm not sure when the word 'cool' came to mean something neat." Nellie still looked bewildered. "I mean something... special."

A swallowtail butterfly was meandering on the breeze, and Nellie stopped to watch. "You know, I think you might like to be an entomologist when you grow up."

"A what?"

"An entomologist. Someone who studies insects."

Nellie jumped over a rock in the road. "Could I really?"

Lalita did a quick calculation of the date thirteen years from now. "Well, as a woman in 1905, you might be breaking into a man's field, but I say go for it!"

She took Lalita's hand again, grinning up at her. "Okay, I will!"

As they walked, Lalita contemplated all the ground that would be gained for women in the coming century, and the fact that even in her time, women didn't always get paid the same as men for the same work. "There's a long row to hoe, Nellie girl."

Nellie frowned. "I do not want to be a gardener!"

Lalita laughed.

*　*　*

Tate and Jeremiah were reading different parts of the same newspaper in the parlor, but Tate was having a hard time keeping his mind on what he was reading. It wasn't unheard of to not be called out of his house by mid-morning— he'd even had whole days occasionally where his medical services weren't needed—but with the petition's threat of "repercussions" fresh in his mind, the silence of the phone seemed ominous.

And even though he'd given permission for Lalita to take Nellie on a walk, he was now regretting it, imagining all kinds of ways those repercussions might be dealt out to his girls. Finally, he laid the paper down and rose, striding to the front window.

Jeremiah turned his section over. "Why don't you just go look for them. You're going to work yourself into a heart attack."

Tate swiveled away from the window. "You think I'm being ridiculous."

Jeremiah folded his portion of the paper and laid it on a small table next to him. "Not at all. One man has gotten too familiar with her, and you have eighty people threatening who knows what. I'm surprised you let them out of the house."

Tate paused for only a moment before heading for the door. He'd let them go to get them away from the all too perceptive Dr. Fischer, but he reprimanded himself for that hasty decision. He nabbed his homburg off the hat rack. "I'll be back when I find them."

Jeremiah rose. "If you don't find them in half an hour or so, come back by and see if they're here."

Tate nodded, his chest feeling so tight he could barely breathe as he stepped out the door.

* * *

Jeremiah waited until he saw Tate driving his buggy down the hill before he made his way down the hall. He could hear Mrs. Kettler humming in the kitchen and faltered for a moment considering his plan. He knew it was unethical and a breach of Tate's trust, but he rationalized that should he find anything worthy of writing about for psychiatry journals, he would change the names.

He moved stealthily through the dining room and as quietly as possible, slipped into Tate's office, closing the door behind him. Moving quickly to sit in the leather chair at his desk, he opened the center drawer and pulled out the book with Lalita's name on the front cover. He opened it and began to read.

Only a few of the names on the first page meant anything to him at all, but he was arrested by dates for World War I and World War II. There were other wars listed as well: Korea, Vietnam, Dessert Storm, Afghanistan, Iraq. And there was a date written twice as large as anything else—9-11-2001.

The next few pages were filled with names. He recognized the first half of the list as presidents listed in order from Washington to Harrison, but there were twenty-one names beyond Harrison, and with the exception of Grover Cleveland that was next in line, he didn't know a one of them.

Jeremiah leaned back in the chair, his mouth agape as he flipped the page and read about The Roaring Twenties, The Great Depression, Al Capone, a singer named Elvis, a black preacher who was killed called Martin Luther King Jr., Mother Teresa, a strange style of music called "rap" that didn't really sound like music at all, an irrational fear that gripped the country called "Y2K" and the rise of something called "the internet" that connected the world in ways never imagined before.

He turned another page to find sketches labeled "car," "plane," "television," "modern refrigerator." That one had an arrow pointing to an indentation on the front that was labeled, "ice maker." Jeremiah stopped, Jules Verne novels coming to mind. *Could she be an author, and Tate misinterpreted her imagination early on?*

There were a whole series of "telephones" with dates beside each different type. The last one was just a rectangle with rounded corners labeled "smart phone." A list beside it seemed to be an advertisement for its virtues: phone, camera, photo album. The phrase "gateway to knowledge" made him smile, and terms like "Angry Birds," "Bad Piggies," and "Beach Buggy Blitz" just wrinkled his forehead.

On the other side of the rectangular object was drawn a picture of the backside of a pair of trousers with an arrow from the "phone" to the back pocket. *Oh, now that's just ridiculous.* He chuckled. "Even in fiction, no one would believe that," he muttered aloud.

Checking his pocket watch, he realized that if Tate took his advice, he could be back at any minute. He slid the book back in the drawer, hoping to get another look at it later.

After he was back in the parlor with the newspaper, he chuckled again, resigned to the fact that he'd get no story for publication from the Cavanaugh household. He snapped the paper open. *Tate, you've just got a little woman with a big imagination.*

* * *

Lalita and Nellie were waiting in the Pilson's parlor where they'd been directed by the housekeeper. Lalita was always in awe of the luxury exhibited in the furnishings, and she wondered if there was a room somewhere that had furniture that the children were allowed to sit on. She ran her hand over the velvet cushion. *Toddlers obviously don't spend time on these.*

They'd been left alone for so long that Nellie was starting to fidget, and Lalita wondered if they had come at a bad time. Finally Millie entered the parlor wearing a striped day dress in black and gray, looking nervous, but carrying no baby.

"I'm sorry to keep you waiting. I needed to call my husband… Miss Torres, could I speak to you privately."

Lalita wondered if she were having other medical issues she was embarrassed about. "Sure thing. Nellie, stay here just a minute, okay?"

Nelli looked bored, but nodded. Lalita expected to follow Mrs. Pilson up the stairs and was surprised when she led her past the stairway and into a larger, even more formal, sitting area with a grand piano. She did not invite Lalita to sit, however. She merely closed the French doors behind them and blew out a tortured breath. Lalita took a step toward her. "Is everything all right? How's the baby?"

Millie turned away, wringing her hands. "Anna is fine. I just can't let you and Nellie see her today."

Lalita reached out a hand to her arm. "That's okay. We shouldn't have just dropped in on you. If she's sleeping, we'll come back another time." She reached for the French doors. "And next time we'll call first."

Millie spun back. "I'm afraid that's impossible as well. My husband has forbidden you to enter our home. He'd be furious if he knew I was talking to you now." Lalita was sure the shock on her face was evident. She had no idea what to say.

Millie looked near tears. "Someone came by last night and spoke with my Edwin, and when he left, Edwin said you were not to enter our home again, and that we would find a new doctor, as well. I asked him why, and he said that you were—" She cut herself off with a hand to her lips.

Lalita felt near tears herself. "Go on, Millie," she whispered. "What did he say?"

The distraught woman cleared her throat. "He said that you were a soiled dove, and that by keeping you under his roof, Dr. Cavanaugh had soiled both his house and his medical practice."

A fire burst into flame inside her as she remembered the last time she'd heard the term "soiled dove." She sucked in a deep breath and let it out, trying to remain calm. "Millie, was the man who came by Seth Dickson, by any chance?"

"I don't know. I was upstairs with the baby. I only know someone was here because I heard the doorbell and a man's voice in the foyer." Her eyes narrowed. "Why do you think it was Mr. Dickson?"

Lalita put her fingertips to her temple and closed her eyes for a moment. "I have my reasons." Opening them again, she sputtered into laughter. "Oh my, wouldn't my friends back home have a jolly time with this. There, I was teased for still being a virgin."

Millie gasped. "Surely not! Are your friends so heartless to want you ruined before you have a chance to wed?"

Lalita gave her a weak smile. "Yes, yes they are. Although they think of it more as becoming experienced rather than ruined." She shook her head, realizing she was not helping her cause any by rambling on about a different time and culture.

She turned once again to the doors. "I don't want to get you in trouble with your husband, Millie, so I'll go, but I do ask that you put in a good word for Dr. Cavanaugh. He's a good doctor and a good man, and he doesn't deserve to be disrespected just because he was kind to me."

Millie nodded, and Lalita let herself out, found Nellie, and the two stepped out into the late morning sun. Lalita looked to the peak that overlooked Manitou, and for a moment she regretted ever laying eyes on it. "Nothing but trouble," she muttered as a tear broke loose and coursed down her cheek.

*   *   *

Tate saw them heading toward the hill from the west as he was reaching the turn from the east. Dragging along in silence, he could tell that something was wrong even from a distance. Tying the reins to the arm rail, he jumped down and jogged to meet them.

It was obvious that Lita had been crying, and he wanted to take her into the comfort of his arms, but he didn't dare out in public. He had to think of her reputation. He swept up Nellie to keep those arms occupied. "What happened?"

Nellie held him tight around the neck. "Oh, Papa. Mrs. Pilson said we couldn't see the baby today, and that made Lalita very sad. I tried to tell her we could go back another time, but she still cried."

Tate knew Lita well enough to know that was only a small part of the story. "Well, come on home. It's nearly time for lunch."

He lifted Nellie into the buggy and offered his hand to Lita, taking the opportunity to caress her fingers with his thumb as he helped her up. It wasn't enough—not nearly enough to stop the ache in his heart for what his little mountain town had done to them both over the last few days, but for the moment, it would have to do.

*   *   *

Lunch was a solemn affair.

Tate had taken Lalita aside while Nellie was washing up and heard the full, awful story of Lalita's conversation with Mrs. Pilson. He'd nearly stormed out to find Dickson, but Lalita was right—trying to talk sense into him the day before had gotten him nothing but a black eye.

They ate in silence under the watchful gaze of his friend, and as soon as Nellie was finished, Tate excused her from the table and asked her to play in her room until he came to get her.

It was time to talk strategy.

Tate took a long drink of water, unsure of how to begin.

Jeremiah began for him. "So what happened? You two have been acting like your best friend died all through the meal?"

Tate set his glass on the table, his smile grim. "I'm sorry for our poor company. Lalita had an upsetting encounter this morning." He briefly shared what had occurred at the Pilson's, then filled in Lalita on what he had told Jeremiah about their plans to wed.

Jeremiah had listened attentively then sat a moment rubbing his chin. "I think I'd bring the man up on charges of slander. Libel, even. You've got it in writing."

Tate inwardly groaned as Lita looked confused. "What do you mean? What do we have in writing?"

Jeremiah looked sheepish. "You didn't tell her that part?"

Tate shook his head as Lalita's wide-eyed gaze turned to him. "What haven't you told me?"

Tate laid his hand over hers on the table. "The letter I received over breakfast this morning wasn't about a bill. It was a petition signed by eighty or so people demanding I remove you from my house."

Lita gasped as though stabbed. "Eighty people who now think I'm a 'soiled dove'?"

"Eighty people is still a small percentage of the town. I haven't studied the names yet, but I'd wager Dickson went to people who don't even know you to spin his lies."

Lalita's brow pinched. "No one really knows me, Tate, except you and Nellie and Mrs. Kettler." She lowered her voice to a whisper. "And Mrs. K. doesn't like me all that much."

"It's true, Papa." Everybody turned to see Nellie in the doorway.

Tate let out an exasperated breath. "I thought I asked you to play in your room for a while, Miss Nell."

She took a hesitant step into the room. "I couldn't find Arabella, and I just came down to see if I left her in the parlor." She took another small step and cupped her hands around her mouth. "But it's true." She glanced toward the pantry hall that led to the kitchen. "She doesn't like Lalita. I heard her tell Mrs. Atkins in the store."

Tate put out his arm with a hitched brow, an invitation for her to come closer. He spoke quietly, the other adults leaning in. "What else, sweetheart?"

Nellie's eyes were wide with disbelief. "She said Lalita's flowers were bad and showed that she was a bad person." She looked to Lalita and smiled. "I think they're beautiful."

"Flowers?" Jeremiah inquired as Tate got to his feet, but he had no intention of telling him about Lita's shoulder bouquet.

"Excuse me, but I need to have a talk with Mrs. Kettler. Why don't you all move to the parlor."

As the adults headed Nellie out of the dining room and down the hall, Tate tried to get his emotions under control. He knew to let her go could result in more gossip against his household, but he would not—could not tolerate this kind of malicious tongue wagging by his own employee. To lose her would also probably mean he'd lose Harold's assistance in the carriage house, but it couldn't be helped. Tate tugged on the hem of his vest with conviction and strode into the kitchen to fire his housekeeper.

Chapter 30

Jeremiah stopped the buggy in front of the mercantile and took in the view for a moment before stepping down to the street and offering a hand to Lalita. As soon as she hit the ground, she was moving toward the store. He stopped a moment to rub Maisy's nose before hitching her to the post and walking to the door of the store himself.

He waited just inside, not wanting to draw attention to the fact that they were together. He could have waited in the buggy, but he had an almost compulsive need to study her. She handed her list and empty basket to the girl behind the counter and scanned the room with an apprehensive eye.

He had heard Lalita and Tate arguing in the hallway as he sat in the parlor reading the newspaper after breakfast. She said she needed some things from the store. He said with no one calling for a doctor, they had to be frugal. She said if she was going to be cooking, she had to buy some different things than were in the pantry. He had finally agreed but begged her to keep purchases to a minimum. She expected him to drive her, but Tate was hesitant to leave the phone. And that's when she'd cursed the nineteenth century for its lack of "cell phones."

Finally, Jeremiah had volunteered to take her, quite happy to have the lady to himself. After two days of Tate waiting by the phone, and Lalita trying to fill Mrs. Kettler's shoes, the tension between the two of them practically filled the house. He'd hoped by getting her out, that tension would be released in enlightening conversation, and although he tried to get her to talk, all he got was short answers and a cordial facade.

He watched her nervously tapping her toe beneath the purple striped dress she was wearing. He noted that, with the exception of the dress he'd first seen her in, everything she wore had a different fabric border around the bottom, and after hearing the sewing machine going for several days, he realized that she had been remodeling all of Augusta's dresses to fit herself. It seemed almost profound, in a way, as this woman was as far removed in personality from Tate's late wife as any woman could be.

She paid the woman with the bills that Tate had given her, and he headed outside to ready the horse.

What was supposed to be a research trip had turned into something else, and he had asked himself several times in the last few days why he just didn't go home. He liked to think that in some small way, he was helping his old friend work through a crisis, but he knew there was more to it. And it had to do with the little woman heading his way with a basket full of groceries.

He smiled as she approached, and he was happy to see her smile back, looking more relaxed now that the deed was done, and they were going to be heading back home. He took the basket from her hand and stashed it behind the seat. He turned to help her up, but she was already sitting in the buggy, completely unaware that she'd just committed a breach of etiquette. He smiled to himself, as he walked around the buggy, knowing he should have expected it.

He let Maisy set her own slow pace as he tried once again to engage the unusual woman beside him in conversation. "Were you able to purchase everything you wanted?"

"Mostly. I still haven't got a good grasp on what's available in this ti—" She blinked. "Town. The selection is a bit different here."

"Oh? What were you looking for that they didn't have?"

"Whipped cream. I didn't really expect it, but I had hoped."

"A ready-made product? How would the store keep it sufficiently cold?"

She blew out a breath. "That, Dr. Fischer, is the million-dollar question that must wait for an answer."

Jeremiah was intrigued. While he couldn't decipher the larger mysteries surrounding the woman beside him, she seemed far less on her guard about the seemingly innocuous questions that told him more than she realized. "To make fresh whipped cream, don't you merely beat cream and add sugar? When it's that easy, why would you—"

"Easy? Have you ever tried to use a hand-cranked egg beater to whip cream? The picture is not in the dictionary under 'easy,' I guarantee you."

Dr. Fischer smiled at her phrasing, even as he pressed her further. "Hand-cranked? Isn't Tate's kitchen equipped with an electric model? I bought one for my cook several years ago."

Lalita's face brightened into a look of happy surprise. "There is such a thing?"

He grinned. "Quite. I'm surprised you've not seen one."

"I've seen one, I just didn't realize..." She looked back at the shops they were leaving behind. "Do you think I would be able to buy one here?"

"I would think so. Do you want me to turn around?"

She thought a moment before shaking her head. "No, Tate asked me to only buy what I needed. It will have to wait."

Jeremiah was confounded. "You have me a bit confused. When I first mentioned the device, you acted like you didn't know that it existed, but then you said you'd seen one."

She floundered for a response. "Well, what I meant to say is... I've wondered... I mean it seems logical, doesn't it, in this day of... of safety razors and flush toilets and modern electricity and all that, that something like an electric mixer would have to be invented. So when I said I've seen one... I... I... imagined what it might look like with turning beaters" —she started demonstrating with her hands— "and... and buttons to make it work..."

"You imagined it."

"Believe me, if you had struggled with that hand beater, you would start dreaming about a better way."

He laughed. "Perhaps you're right. 'Necessity is the mother of invention.' "

Her explanation was the poorest lie he'd ever heard, but if he challenged her further on it, she'd close the door of communication. Instead, he took the opportunity to move the conversation toward a topic he was more than a little curious about. "You seem to have a very vivid imagination, Miss Torres. Do you write fiction?"

She laughed. "Heavens no! I read fiction on occasion, in between dusty history tomes, but I don't think I have what it takes to write it."

Jeremiah had a difficult time hiding his surprise. "So you've never even considered writing something along the lines of a Jules Verne novel?"

When she laughed this time, she nearly snorted. "What would make you say that? That's not me at all! I find real life much more interesting. Give me a good documentary any day of the week."

"Documentary?"

Her smile slipped even as her laughter was squelched in an instant. "You've heard of a documentary... haven't you?"

The way she squeaked the question, made him wonder if it was something risqué. He shook his head. "What is it?"

Lalita knew she was digging herself in deeper every moment she was with this man. Her mind flew. *Okay, what's the history of film?* "So," she began slowly, trying to feel him out, "you've probably heard of the new moving pictures..."

"Not terribly impressive, if you ask me. 'Much ado about nothing.' "

Lalita inwardly sighed with relief. "Well, 'documentary' is kind of a new term for non-fiction motion pictures. History, how things work, etc." She paused and swallowed.

Dr. Fischer nodded. "I see. It has been *documented* by facts. Well, the cameras will have to improve. They just give me a headache."

Lalita smiled, thinking about the last 3D movie she had gone to. "I'm sure they will. They're just getting started, really."

The doctor turned the corner to ascend the hill toward home. "There's that imagination again. Where did you get such a large dose of it?"

Lalita wished she were home. "Dr. Fischer, if you're referring to Tate's letter, please remember that I had a head injury. Think of what I said at that time as nothing more than fuzzy dreams."

The doctor nodded, but Lalita didn't think her answer really satisfied him.

They drove up the hill in silence, but as they pulled into the carriage house, he spoke again. "If it is nothing more than an injured girl's ramblings, why would Tate keep it?"

"Keep what?"

The doctor turned to her. "Your history book. He has it in his desk. Why would he keep it?"

Lalita felt heat rising in her face. "I don't know what you're talking about."

Dr. Fischer gave her a slight smile. "Of course you don't." He turned and hopped off, and Lalita stepped down with as much calm as she could. *He read it. He must have.*

Walking to the side door, she called back over her shoulder. "If you wouldn't mind bringing the basket in when you're done unhitching the buggy, I'd appreciate it."

Forcing herself to walk, she made her way to the back door. She found Tate in his study, staring out the window. "We're back. You should probably go help Dr. Fischer with Maisy."

He nodded, and Lalita hoped for a kiss as he rose and came around the desk, but his focus was on the door. She turned and blinked as she watched him leave, a foul mood threatening. She tried to shake it off as she moved to Tate's desk chair.

Opening the center drawer, she took out the book with her name on the cover. She realized now that even though writing it was therapeutic for her, it was a dangerous thing to do. She'd burn it at her first opportunity.

She was about to close the drawer, when the corners of several old photos caught her eye. She pulled them out. The one on top was of a couple in wedding attire, and Lalita recognized a younger Tate. She knew the somber expression was due to the need to be still for the longer exposure time, but she'd seen that look too many times this week. She let her gaze move to the woman. *So this is Augusta.*

Even though, she too, had a solemn expression, she was obviously a beauty. Fine features were framed by curls underneath a simple veil that fell over her shoulders. She held a bouquet, and Tate's hand was on her shoulder just like— She turned the photo abruptly over and slid it back in the drawer. Blinking back unexpected tears, she tried to focus on the remaining photo in her hand. There was handwriting across the top that said "The Cavanaughs, April 18, 1886."

Her eye found Tate in this group shot that must have been
taken on the same day as the wedding photo. She lingered
on him a moment, then let her gaze explore the rest of the
faces. Her brows flew up as her mouth dropped open. Tate was
surrounded by people that looked like her.

Chapter 31

Tate was longing for some private time with Lita, but instead, he was once again sitting in the parlor with Jeremiah while Lita and Nellie cleaned up in the kitchen. She had seemed on edge for days, but especially short-tempered since she and Jeremiah had returned from shopping. He wondered if Fischer had said anything to upset her, or if it was the news that Lita's court date had been set for early the following week.

After a bit of political hashing, Tate brought up the topic that had been on his mind ever since he'd gotten word from his lawyer that Lita's time before the judge was at hand. "Jeremiah, I know you planned on leaving at the end of the week, but would it be possible to stay through the hearing? I'm not certain we will be allowed to offer any kind of testimony, but if so, your statement as a psychologist would carry some weight, I should think."

Jeremiah seemed to deliberate, and Tate was embarrassed for even asking. *He has patients he needs to get back to.* "I'm sorry, I shouldn't have asked."

Jeremiah held up a hand. "No need to apologize. My hesitancy comes from wondering if my testimony would be a help or a hindrance. Because most of what I've learned about your Miss Torres is that she rarely tells the truth."

Tate blinked. Obviously their cover-up of Lita's real story hadn't fooled his perceptive friend in the slightest. "Jeremiah, there are circumstances that are best not discussed if Lalita and I are to have a normal life together. But that doesn't change the fact that Dickson was acting inappropriately when he cornered her in my carriage house."

"Maybe. Maybe not. We only have her word, and as I said, her word is not worth much in my book." Tate's eyes flamed, and Jeremiah hurried on. "You wanted my professional opinion, so there it is. I've heard very few sincere words come out of her mouth, and the ones that do are more than a little perplexing."

Tate nodded, trying to keep a cool head. "I understand your confusion. I felt the same way at first, as you well know from the letter I sent you, but..." He licked his lips wondering if he could really trust him with the truth. "Will it be good enough for you if I say that something happened that changed everything—that all her idiosyncrasies and ramblings suddenly had a context that gave her credibility? Would you accept that from an old friend and not ask any more questions?"

The tall man leaned an elbow on the arm of his chair and propped his chin against his fist. "I could as an old friend." He rubbed his thumb along his jaw. "But you're asking for more than that. You're asking me to speak as a professional in my field in front of a court of law." He tapped a finger against his lips for a moment before straightening in his chair. "For that I'd need it all. The whole truth."

Tate blew out a breath. If Dickson didn't back down, and Lita stood before a judge, he had a feeling she was going to need all the help she could get. *But will he keep the secret?* Tate could see no advantage for him to tell anyone. To bring it to light would only harm his reputation as a psychiatrist. Tate met Jeremiah's expectant gaze and began.

* * *

Lita and Nellie stood drying the dishes in silence. She knew she should try to put on a happy face for the little girl, but she just couldn't. Knowing that Tate's family was Native American, and he never mentioned it, was eating at her.

As she had studied the picture, she could see that it was his grandmother who was the only family member who was full-blooded. The older man in the picture was white and their half breed son had married a white woman. Tate's siblings, a younger man and even younger girl, looked like Lita—just a touch of their heritage showed through—but Tate looked like he had married into this group instead of being born to it. One would never know by looking at him that he had the same amount of Native American blood that she has.

And with that portrait crammed in a drawer, he obviously wants to keep it that way.

Lita couldn't help feeling marginalized. *If he's embarrassed of them, won't he be embarrassed of me?*

She slid the last plate into the cupboard, turned, and leaned against the counter. Nellie hung her towel up, and Lita tried her best to muster a smile. "Hey, kiddo, thanks for your help. Why don't you get ready for bed, and I'll come up and read to you in a bit."

Nellie nodded, smiling. "I'll put Arabella in the nightgown you made for her!"

Lita felt suddenly overwhelmed with angst and squatted down to take Nellie in her arms for a hug. "Great idea!" She released her and blinked back the tears that were threatening. "I'll be up in a minute or two."

As the girl hurried from the kitchen, Lita shed her apron and hung it on a peg. She was about to head out of the room herself when there was a tap on the back door. Sweeping the curtain aside, she saw a tall, broad fellow in a baggy suit jacket and dusty bowler, holding a crate. His black hair was as slicked as his mustache twisted.

She opened the door, and the big man smiled. "Evening ma'am, I have a delivery for the doc—some medical supplies from Denver."

She moved aside to let him enter. "Oh, okay, just put them anywhere. Do you need to be paid?"

"No, ma'am, that's already been taken care of." He set the crate on the floor and rose smiling, holding something Lalita hadn't seen since her trip up Pikes Peak.

She reached for it. "My purse! Where did you find it? How did you know?"

His smile grew into a grin, "My brother and me, well we were the ones that brung you down the mountain to the doctor. Your bag got left behind in our wagon, and then supplies got piled on top. We just found it this afternoon."

She opened it and peered inside. "Well, thank you so much for bringing me to Dr. Cavanaugh and returning my purse. I appreciate it."

He just stood there smiling, and Lalita wondered if she needed to give him a tip. She started to pull out her wallet, but realized that none of the bills would match the currency of the time. *I don't need to be arrested for counterfeiting.* She gave him a nervous smile, thinking of going to get Tate, when he suddenly spoke.

"You know, I didn't really expect to find you still here. I was just going to leave your things with the doc and hope he'd know how to get them to you."

"Really? You've not heard anything about me?"

"No, ma'am, but I've been on the road with deliveries for a while." He smiled again, grabbing the door knob. "Well, I'll get out of your way. Tell the doc 'hello.' "

As soon as the door closed, Lalita was fishing in her purse for her phone. She knew it was mostly useless now, but it did still hold pictures. Lots and lots of pictures. It was dead, but thankfully, she had been fortunate enough to be thrust back to a time with electricity. And she had a charger.

Even though it was only useful as a paperweight at the moment, she still wanted to show it to Tate and talk to him about the photos she'd found in his desk. She started down the hallway, knowing that couldn't happen with Dr. Fischer still lurking about. *I wish that man would go home.*

A sudden need for fresh air had her moving past the stairs and down the hall to the front door. The voices in the parlor stopped her in her tracks. Dr. Fischer was speaking. "The list of people... did you know them?"

"Some." Lalita strained to hear Tate but couldn't make out his next few sentences.

"So having it in writing became crucial." Dr. Fischer must have been facing the doorway, as she could hear him plainly. "And once you were struck with the reality of it, the people on the list suddenly became important to you, and that made you see her... differently?"

Lita sucked in a little breath waiting for Tate's response.

"Yes, I could no longer deny the truth." Tate was suddenly loud and clear. "Everything changed at that moment."

Lita didn't want to hear anymore. With her heart breaking, she moved quickly back down the hall and up the stairs. She had feared it, but now she knew for sure; the petition made Tate re-think his love for her. The truth was that his career was at an end as long as she was in his house. *Everything changed. He said it himself.*

Heading for her room, she just got the door closed before she broke down in sobs.

*   *   *

Jeremiah had no idea what to do with what Tate had just told him, but one thing he was sure of—Tate believed it. "So how does this riding on lightning bolts work? Seems pretty dangerous to me."

"I have no idea. She obviously wasn't hit directly. She says she remembers a bright flash before everything went black."

Jeremiah leaned forward, struck with a new thought. "Do you think it's happened before... to others?"

Tate ran a hand through his hair. "Who knows? There are a certain number of people who go missing each year without a trace."

It was a compelling idea, and it would explain many things about the enigmatic woman, from her short hair to her speech to her improper behavior, but Jeremiah wasn't ready to confess belief in time travel just yet. "What did you say the murderer's name was—the one that matched Lita's prediction?"

"Lizzie Borden. I don't think I'll ever forget that name."

Jeremiah searched his memory but couldn't recall hearing anything about it. "And when did it supposedly occur?"

"On the morning of the fourth. Lita wrote it down on the third around midday."

Jeremiah didn't remember the name from her book, but at the moment, he couldn't recall any but Mark Twain. "And have you verified Mr. Allen's story?"

Tate nodded. I made some calls to some colleagues back east. It's real, and it happened just like Lita said—both parents were killed with an axe. Lita says all the evidence points to the daughter Lizzie, but she won't be convicted."

"Really?" Jeremiah was surprised at the extent to which Lalita was willing to put this story of hers to the test. "Well, I guess time will tell."

Tate looked at his pocket watch and rose. "Yes, but we don't have time enough to prove her story before the court date." He glanced toward the door. "I need to go up and tuck Nellie in. What do you say? Will you testify on her behalf?"

Jeremiah was still reluctant to commit before having another look at her little book. "Do you still have her predictions?"

"Yes." Tate hesitated in the doorway. "Is that what it will take to get your support?"

Jeremiah nodded. "That, and my own calls to verify the axe murderer story."

Tate turned. "Follow me."

Pretending to know nothing of the book and its whereabouts, Jeremiah followed him to his study. Tate sat behind his desk and pulled open the center drawer. His brow wrinkled, and he pulled out all the papers within. "I'm sure it was right here earlier today." He closed it and went through the other drawers, all without result. "Lita must have it. Sometimes she adds to it." He rose. "Let me tend to Nellie, and then I'll ask her about it."

Jeremiah gave a nod, kicking himself for letting Lalita know he'd seen it.

* * *

Lalita managed to get through one book, and even though she knew Nellie was disappointed that she didn't read another, she had escaped with the confession of a headache.

Lying in bed, she scrolled through the pictures on her phone, tears streaming down the sides of her face. She skimmed through photos of family, friends, pets, and school, sinking deeper and deeper into depression. Finally, she turned it off with a brusque move of her thumb and set it down on her bedside table to continue charging.

Wiping the tears from her face, her mind spun with what to do. Tate no longer cared for her, or at the very least, he wasn't willing to give up his medical practice for her. To save his practice, she would have to leave. *But I have no money—at least none that's usable— and since everyone thinks I'm a slut, they probably won't hire me.* Seth Dickson's proposition came to mind, and she closed her eyes tight before flopping to her side. *That just can't be my only option. Think, girl.*

What she needed was respectability, and in this time, at her age, and with her ancestry, she wasn't sure how to get it outside of marriage to a white man. She almost laughed, thinking about the fact that her "white man" was hiding who he really was. *He's no whiter than me.* She could understand why he might hide that fact from the general population, but why her? *Why wasn't it one of the first things he told me when he talked about his family? Why the big secret?*

The only conclusion she could come to was shame. *It's okay, somehow, to marry someone like me, but not be someone like me.* His words, "Everything changed" pierced her heart yet again, and tears flowed anew.

She knew she'd have to leave more than his house. It would kill her to be so close to him and Nellie without being a part of their family. *There might be more options in Colorado Springs, but how would I survive while I looked for a job?* She wondered if Tate might make her a loan. She huffed out a breath. *With what? Thanks to me, he's almost broke.*

Her mind shifted to her other possible future. Prison. If Dickson didn't back down, and she got a judge with the attitude of the marshal, she wouldn't have to worry about altering any more of Augusta's clothes—she'd be wearing horizontal stripes. *And stripes are not the new black, in my book.* She punched her pillow hard. *Why does everything come back to Dickson?*

She tried imagining a future with Seth Dickson but only felt a wave of nausea. There was no doubt he was still a good-looking man, but he had to be over forty. And there was just that way he had of looking at her that gave her the willies. *He doesn't love me. He doesn't even know me. He just wants to get me out of my clothes.*

Fisting her hands in the sheet, her adoptive mother's frequent admonition came to mind. *"You don't always get to choose your garden. Bloom where you're planted."*

All those times that she thought her life was hard, she hadn't had a clue. But she wasn't a quitter. Whatever happened to her—wherever she ended up—whoever she kissed

232

goodnight—she knew she was a survivor. *With or without Tate, I'm going to make it.*

* * *

Tate knocked lightly on Lita's door after Nellie had informed him of Lita's headache. He wanted to kiss it away, and he had some headache powders she could take as well. There was no answer, so he assumed she'd fallen asleep.

He also wanted to ask her about the book and tell her that he had enlisted Dr. Fischer as an ally to testify. He had wanted to give her hope, but he didn't want to wake her. He'd get the book from her in the morning and tell her the news over the big breakfast he planned to make for her. He'd sulked around the house long enough. Time to sit down and make a plan, and if that plan meant moving to a new town and start over with his medical practice, then that is what he'd do.

He smiled, thinking about Jeremiah's suggestion that he make an appointment with the judge to get married as soon as he arrives in town. They would have the morning as newlyweds before she would have to appear before him on assault charges. Dickson's scheme would be undone, and Tate didn't think he'd go through with it just for spite.

And if he did, they still had Jeremiah's testimony to fall back on. Whether he testified that she was a woman of character or one with mental deficiencies, it didn't matter, as long as he agreed to be her doctor. For the first time in a week, Tate felt hopeful.

The doorbell rang, and Tate hurried down the stairs. He opened it to Haskel Emory, a middle-aged man with thinning brown hair, carrying his wife Josephine—two of the people who had signed the petition against him. Tate opened the door wider. "Haskel, what's the trouble?"

Emory's wife moaned, and he stepped inside. "I don't know, Doc, but she's in terrible pain."

Tate waved him into his examination room as Jeremiah came to the door of the parlor. "Anything I can do?"

"Not until I can ascertain the problem." Tate turned to follow Mr. Emory. "Stay close, though."

Tate pulled his stool to the side of the bed and studied the woman's face contorted with pain. *She looks as though she's going through the contractions of childbirth.* He looked down her slender body. *But that is obviously not the problem... Unless it's an early miscarriage.*

"Haskel, is your wife pregnant?"

"No, I don't believe so."

Josephine shook her head with her eyes closed, confirming her husband's answer.

"Mrs. Emory, can you tell me where the pain is located?" Her hands unclenched from her skirts and moved to her abdomen. As he gently pressed in various spots, his worst fears were confirmed when she screamed out with the pressure he applied on the lower right side.

He sat back, wishing for a different diagnosis.

"What is it, Doc?"

He patted Mrs. Emory's hand. "I'll just be a minute, then we'll see what we can do about reducing your pain."

Rising, he faced her husband, and taking him by the arm, he led him across the hall to the parlor and spoke in a low voice. "I believe it's appendicitis. There's no other recourse but surgery. If it bursts, she'll die from the infection."

A look of panic came to the man's face. "And if you cut into her, she'll probably die anyway."

"I won't lie to you, Haskel, there is a risk of that, but we know she has no chance at all without the surgery, and the risk goes up the longer we wait."

The man's nostrils flared as his breathing accelerated, staring at Tate's shoulder. Finally he lifted his head and nodded.

"Good, let's move then. I'll need your assistance to get her undressed." He looked over Haskel's shoulder to Jeremiah. "Dr. Fischer, will you fill the largest pot you can find in the kitchen with water and fill up the autoclave, then wake up Miss Torres. We'll need to sterilize the area as fast as we can."

As the psychiatrist sprang into action, Tate and Haskel went back to the exam room to find Josephine clutching her skirts over her abdomen, tears running down the side of her face. Tate sat on the stool next to her and covered her hand with his. "It's going to be better soon, Mrs. Emory. Your husband and I are going to move you, bed and all, into the parlor temporarily while we set up for your treatment in here."

She gave a tiny nod, and the two men rolled the bed across the hall. Tate turned off all the lights save one small lamp. "Try to rest, and we'll be underway momentarily."

Fischer met them with the kettle of water, and Tate directed him toward the sterilization machine and told him how to get it running after he had added his surgical equipment.

Tate set them to work scrubbing down the surfaces of the room with carbolic acid before he opened a closet with double doors that revealed a tall wooden table. They moved it into the center of the room, and Tate adjusted the separate head and foot rests with cranks to bring it into a laying down position. After throwing a thick wool pad on top, followed by a waterproof cloth, he instructed Mr. Emory to wipe it down with the carbolic acid as well.

"Now we scrub the floor, and when we go back in, Dr. Fischer and I will be scrubbed and gowned and carrying Mrs. Emory, unclothed and wrapped in a sterile sheet." He gathered these things from the cupboard as he spoke. "Doctor, run upstairs and see what's keeping Miss Torres. I'd like her to assist me."

Fischer put a hand to his head. "Oh! In all the commotion I forgot to wake her." He jogged out of the room, and Tate set Haskel to the task of swabbing the floor while he took the linens and surgical gowns into the parlor.

Gently rolling her to her side, he spoke softly. "Mrs. Emory, I just need to get to your buttons."

As he started unbuttoning her shirtwaist, she whispered through clenched teeth. "What are you going to do?"

He hated to scare her, but he had to tell her about the impending surgery. "I believe you are having an appendicitis attack. That simply means that your appendix has become inflamed and infected, and unfortunately, it has to come out."

She let out a sob, and Tate wanted to console her in a more tangible way, but he knew the best thing he could do for her was get her prepped for surgery as quickly as possible. He kept working on the buttons. "You're going to be fine. I have had experience with this surgery, and I have done all we can to make a sterile environment to keep infection at bay."

Rolling her to her back once more, he began to work the sleeves off her arms as her husband came into the room. "I'm all done, Doc."

Tate rose and began to roll up his sleeves. "Good, she will feel better about all of this if you undress her."

Haskel moved to her side. "Everything off?"

Tate nodded. "Everything. Put this sheet around her. I'm going to scrub and get dressed." He moved out into the hall as Jeremiah came flying down the stairs. "Is she coming?"

Jeremiah stood at the bottom looking baffled. "She's not in her room. I can't find her anywhere."

Chapter 32

"This town could use a few more streetlights," Lalita grumbled as she stumbled over a stone on the street. A nearly starless night, she was relying on lights shining out of the houses to guide her, but they did nothing to illuminate her path, making it slow going.

Determination to do whatever she could to save Tate's medical career was fueling her trek toward the house that stood next to the saddlery, but that didn't mean that a good, long pep talk wasn't fueling the determination. "Tate's too kind to tell me this is what needs to be done, and even if he... he has had a change of heart about marrying me, he cares about me enough to not want me to be with someone who calls me a 'squaw.' "

She stopped as she suddenly realized why that term had gotten Tate's fist swinging. "Oh my gosh. It was because of his family." She began moving slowly, a new revelation dawning. "He just wanted to protect me because I remind him of his family. Maybe he never really loved me; maybe he just mistook a need to watch over me for love."

With no money of her own, she had needed that place of safety, but hopefully, if Dickson agreed to drop the charges and help rebuild her reputation, she could find someone who would hire her.

With a hand on her shoulder bag, she turned a corner, and her destination came into view. *Tate has taken care of me; now I have to do this for him.*

* * *

It was fortunate that Tate had performed this particular surgery several times, as the need to find Lita was vying for his attention. He couldn't even send Jeremiah out to search for her, as he needed him to assist.

Mrs. Emory had responded well to the chloroform, and the inflamed appendicitis had been removed—none too soon in Tate's estimation. He was now closing the incision in between two sheets covering her upper and lower body.

"Where do you think she would have gone?" Jeremiah asked behind his mask as he gathered the bloodied gauze by Mrs. Emory's feet.

Tate shook his head as he tied another knot. "I don't have any idea. It doesn't make any sense."

"Who does she know in town?"

"The Pilsons, although I doubt she'd go there after her last visit. She knows Reverend Niemeyer and the Allens, but she doesn't know where they live."

Jeremiah held out the treated aseptic gauze pad with a gloved hand as Tate set down his needle and scissors. "What about Dickson?"

Tate's eyes grew wide over his face mask. "Why would she go there?"

"Just a hunch. She seems like the kind of woman to take matters into her own hands."

Tate positioned the pad while Jeremiah brushed adhesive on gauze strips to create surgical tape to hold it in place. Tate couldn't imagine why Lita would go to Dickson's, but his pulse jumped to a higher level at the thought. "What do you think she'd hope to accomplish?" He pulled the two bed sheets together and pulled off his gloves.

Fischer followed suit after depositing the wads of used gauze in the pan that Tate held toward him. "I don't know. What are the possibilities?"

While Tate checked Mrs. Emory's vitals, he pondered that question. "I could see her trying to talk sense into him—maybe even tell him that we had planned to marry."

"What about his offer? She's watched you sit around all week with no work."

Tate scrawled the results of Mrs. Emory's pulse and blood pressure on a pad of paper, not liking this train of thought.

"And then I practically scolded her for wanting to buy a few sundries. She thinks I'm penniless." He pulled off his surgical mask and gown. "But I can't see her actually accepting Dickson because I'm having a financial crisis. She has more heart than that."

Fischer untied the cloths wrapping his shoes. "Exactly, Tate. I'm not suggesting she'd leave you because you're poor, but that she believes she is the reason for your sudden poverty."

The woman's husband appeared at the door, and Tate waved him in, his chest so tight he could barely breathe. "I believe your wife is going to be just fine, Haskel. She will need to stay here for a few days, though. You are welcome to wheel the bed back in and stay the night."

Haskel came to his side and stroked his wife's cheek with tears in his eyes. "Thanks, Doc. You're a good man and I—" He fought for control. "I am so sorry that I signed that petition. Josephine was just furious about it, and when this came over her, she wouldn't hear of calling any other doctor."

"All is forgiven." Tate clasped his extended hand. "And now I must ask you a favor. I should stay here and watch your wife for the next several hours, but... my Miss Torres has gone missing."

Fischer stepped forward. "Just tell us what to look for and what to do."

Tate spent the next several minutes explaining the dose for pain medication should she wake up before he got back and wrote down the phone numbers of the other doctors in town in case of excessive bleeding at the incision site. Then grabbing his jacket and hat, he hurried through the house and out the back door.

Clouds had rolled in, blocking out any celestial light, but he could still see where he was going by the light from his house.

As he strapped Maisy into her harness and hitched the buggy, he tried to think of any other reason that Lita might go to Dickson. Lightning flashed, thunder clapped, and he remembered her term for thinking in new directions— *brainstorming.*

"What does she have to offer him besides herself?" he asked aloud as he backed Maisy out. All at once it dawned on him that her little history book was missing. Snapping the reins, he sent Maisy trotting down the hill. *Knowledge.* The sky broke open, and it started to pour. *She might offer what she knows of the future in trade for her own.*

* * *

Lalita stood frozen on Dickson's porch. The thunder and lightning had sped her steps toward shelter, and now that she was under the eaves, the downpour was keeping her there. Her plan had seemed sound right up to the moment that she stepped onto the porch; then the memories of their carriage house encounter had flooded her.

Shaking it off she pulled out her phone, started an audio recording, and slipped it back into her purse. She lifted her hand to knock, when the door suddenly opened. A surprised Seth Dickson stood in trousers but no shirt, his suspenders hanging at his sides. His astonishment quickly turned into a grin. "I heard someone on my porch, but I never imagined it would be you, Miss Torres." He ran a hand through his hair. "What can I do for you?"

Lalita swallowed and tried to lick her lips, but her mouth was suddenly dry. "Mr. Dickson," she squeaked, "I wonder if I might have a moment of your time."

He stepped aside and waved her in. "Honey, you can have all the time you want."

She waffled a moment, but a sizzling crack of thunder had her scurrying into the house. The Dickson residence wasn't as nice as Tate's, but it seemed serviceable. Dickson ushered her into the parlor, and Lita observed that it could use a good cleaning as she lowered herself to sit primly on the edge of a chair.

He seemed to notice her scrutiny. "If I'd known you were coming, I'd have had the boys clean up a bit." He pulled a shirt off the back of a chair and slipped it on.

Lalita tried to smile. "How is Max? It must be annoying to have your leg out of commission in the summertime."

"Yeah, well, he's getting along." He tucked in his shirt and pulled the suspenders to his shoulders. "That isn't the reason for your visit tonight, though, is it—to inquire after Max." He sat on a worn out chair across from her.

She chewed her lower lip. "No. I came to ask you to drop the charges."

Dickson's chin ticked up. "So... you'll marry me?"

She slowly shook her head. "No, Mr. Dickson. I can't. I don't love you."

"Pshaw, that'll come later. You'll see."

Lita pulled her shoulder bag to her lap. "What if I offered you something else? I have inside knowledge of some economic boons that you could take advantage of, and I also know of some coming economic crises that you could avoid."

The man leaned back and crossed his arms. "I didn't realize that you were a financial advisor. How did an Indian woman get a job like that?"

She pulled out her history journal and held it to her chest. "It's not exactly my job, Mr. Dickson. I know about these things because up until I ended up unconscious on top of Pikes Peak, I... I lived in the 21st century."

Dickson stared at her a moment before snorting out a suppressed laugh. "Oh my, you are a peach." He leaned forward, his forearms on his legs. "So what is it you think I'd be interested to know?"

"I'd need your word that you'll drop the charges first, even without marrying me. In writing."

The man couldn't stop grinning. "Well, okay then." He jumped up and went to a desk in the corner and pulled out a piece of paper and a pen. After a few minutes of writing, he held it close to his lips and blew gently.

Stepping toward her, he held it out, but when she reached for it, he pulled it back. "Not quite yet, Miss. I think you made a promise of your own."

She realized she needed him to say it out loud. "Would you mind reading to me what you wrote?"

His smile took on an unattractive smugness. "I'd be delighted." He cleared his throat dramatically. "Should Miss Torres provide me with information that would certainly lead to wealth, I promise to drop the charges against her."

She nervously opened her book. "Well, the first thing you need to know is that next year there will be a downturn in the economy, and there will be runs on the bank. Your cash will be safer under your mattress than a bank in 1893."

"I see." He pulled the desk chair over and sat close to her. "And what about the 'boon' you spoke of."

Lalita narrowed her eyes. It was obvious he didn't believe her, so why was he still listening? "In 1896, there will be another gold rush. This time in the Yukon."

He sat back. "The Yukon! That's the news you think you can bribe me with? I have a business that keeps us in food and clothes. I wouldn't travel to the Yukon for all the money in the world!"

"Well," Lalita scrambled, "you wouldn't have to go yourself. You could just hire someone to go for you—someone who could be there right from the beginning to stake some of the first claims."

Lalita tried not to blink as he looked into her eyes, a smirk lingering. "Do you know what I think?"

She shook her head. "No, Mr. Dickson, your mind is a mystery to me."

He laughed again. "You're a mystery to me as well, but I think you came with this horse hockey as an excuse." He ran the back of his finger along her jaw. "I think you just wanted to come see me for me."

Suddenly his arm came around her as he pulled her face to his. One touch of his lips, and she was sliding down off the chair and to the floor, her hat tumbling behind her. Trying to scramble to her feet, she got tangled in her skirts, and then she was being lifted into the air. She grasped her book with both hands as the shoulder bag slid off her shoulder. "But I have proof! Just let me show you. I brought my phone."

"Hush, we don't want to wake the boys."

Lalita disagreed. "Max! William! Help!"

Dickson carried her through the house with his arms around her waist until he had her on the wash porch. He set her down on her feet, and she spun to face him as she hooked her bag over her head and slid the book inside. She said a silent prayer that her phone was still recording.

Dickson's earlier joviality was nowhere to be seen. "Now, are you going to be quiet, or do I need to take you on out with the saddles."

She took a step back and shouted louder. "Max! William! Help!"

With two long strides, he took hold of her waist and threw her over his shoulder. As he pushed through the screen door, she yelled some more. The rain was still coming down, and the cold water penetrated the cotton of her dress in a matter of seconds as she pounded her fists against him. She tried to kick, but he held her legs tight.

The smell of leather was overpowering as he opened the door to the saddlery. He switched on a light and closed the door behind him before setting her down. She quickly moved to the other side of a saddle perched on a stand, breathing hard. "Mr. Dickson, I have proof that what I say is true. I have a 21st century phone with me. You won't believe what it can do." She trusted that he wouldn't comprehend that it was recording his every word. She reached for her bag. "In fact, I've got pictures that will blow your mind."

His hand shot out and grabbed her wrists, and in another moment he had her hauled around the saddle. "Who knows what kind of little revolver you might have in there. I think it's best if you keep your hands where I can see them." He pulled them to his chest and wrapped his arms around her, pinning her against him. He looked down at her and smiled. "Now this is better."

"Tate and I are going to be married," she blurted out as he ran his hands over her back. "That's why I can't marry you."

His hands stilled, his mouth smirking unbecomingly. "Oh, I know he's sweet on you. Anyone can see that."

Lalita shook her head. "Then why would you..."

A corner of his mouth twitched up. "It won't be the first time I take the doctor's woman."

He lowered his mouth toward hers, and she pushed hard on his chest. "What do you mean?"

He pulled her back against him and whispered in her ear. "Augusta. My wife died because of Dr. Tate Cavanaugh, so I took Augusta."

Lalita was appalled. "You... you kissed Augusta?"

He buried his nose in her hair. "Oh, I did more than kiss her. She was wearing the dress you were wearing when the doctor set Max's leg, and she smelled like honeysuckle."

Lalita thought she was going to be sick. "Did she... was she willing?"

He backed her against the wall. "She said she wasn't, but then all women say that, don't they?" With his body pressed against her, and her arms trapped at his chest, he began to run his hands through her hair by her face.

She squirmed against him, kicking at his ankles, but his heavy work boots absorbed what little impact she could make. "You just want revenge on Tate; you don't want me at all."

He laughed. "Oh, I want you, and since there's always the chance that you'll go to jail..."

His rain-slicked hair reminded her of something, and her eyes grew round. "You go to church!"

He sneered. "So do you, my little soiled dove."

Lalita managed to turn her hands around and dig her nails into his chest. "I am not a soiled dove!"

He jumped back but grabbed her wrists again. "Hey now, that's enough of that." His voice deepened into a husky snarl. "I don't mind a bit of a tussle, though. The late Mrs. Cavanaugh didn't have an ounce of fight in her." He looked deep into her eyes. "She was as limp as a rag doll. Nearly took the fun out of it." His expression changed to one of disgust. "Then the pathetic creature took the doctor's razor to her wrists a few days later."

Lalita's jaw dropped. "She... she killed herself? Because you—? I thought she fell in the bathtub!"

The door opened, and William stepped in, dripping wet and scowling. "Pa, what are you doing?"

"Never you mind. Go back to bed."

Max stumbled in on his crutches. "No, Pa, leave her alone!"

Lalita wrenched her arms free and ran toward the sons. They moved aside to let her through. As she ran out into the stormy, dark night, she hoped the boys could slow their father down.

She splashed through the rain until she reached the street that was fast turning to mud. She heard a horse snort a ways up the road and could make out a buggy through the driving rain. Lightning flashed and she jumped, screeching.

"Lita!"

She wiped the rain off her face as she slogged forward. "Tate?"

Without warning, hands gripped her shoulders and pulled her back. Her boots stuck, and she sat down hard in the mud.

Another flash of lightning revealed Tate with his fist drawn back, and then she heard the fight commence. After a few punches, the two were brawling on the ground.

Lalita got to her feet and stumbled out of their way, straining to see Maisy. She heard the sizzle as tingles ran down her spine. The flash was blinding just before the dark.

* * *

"Lita! Lita!" Tate stood calling in the rain after finally throwing the punch that knocked Dickson out. William provided an umbrella and a lantern before dragging his father to the house, but he couldn't find her anywhere.

Hopeful that she had just run home, Tate turned Maisy around and headed there himself, certain that he'd pick her up on the way. He couldn't fathom why she would leave without him, but he reasoned that it must have to do with Dickson. He couldn't stand the thought of what he might have done to her to make her so frightened. Urging Maisy around a corner, he had a sudden remembrance of waiting out the storm at the church and her fear of lightning. He blew out a breath. *That's probably the reason for her flight.*

The longer he drove without seeing any sign of her, another possibility crept into his thoughts, and his heart slammed into his chest. Running a hand through his wet hair, he refused to entertain the notion. He parked Maisy in front of the house and raced to his door, taking the steps two at a time.

He burst in and was met by a wide-eyed Dr. Fischer coming out of the exam room. "Did you find her?"

Tate leaned his mud-slicked back against the door, the chill of that question seeping deep down to his bones.

Chapter 33

Lalita groaned and rolled over, feeling like her skin was cracking off. She blinked her eyes open in the early light and sat, her head pounding. Closing them again, she tried to remember, but nothing she dredged up explained why she was sitting outside with dried mud all over her body when the ground around was dry—dusty even.

She got her aching body into an upright position, and when the world stopped spinning, she looked around. She was in front of a two-story, four-square house that seemed familiar. As she stood there staring, the door opened, and a young man walked out.

He startled when he saw her and rushed forward. "Ma'am, are you okay?"

She looked into his blue eyes, and a name popped into her head. *Max.* "I... I think so, although my head sure hurts."

"Come on in the house, and I'll call the doc."

She wasn't sure why, but she knew she did not want to go into that house. "Thanks, but I really just want to go home."

"Okay. Where's home?"

The fog in her head was starting to lift, but nothing was completely clear. "Dr. Cavanaugh."

The young man smiled, and Lalita frowned, unsure of what seemed wrong about his face. "That's who I was going to call... Would you rather I took you there?"

She nodded.

He took a step back toward the house. "Just let me hitch up the wagon, and I'll tell Pa where I'm going."

He disappeared around the house, and Lalita just considered walking home. Two wobbly steps toward the street changed her mind.

As she waited once again for the ground to stop shifting, a voice behind her made her skin crawl. "Well, don't you look like somethin' the cat dragged in." She held her head and turned slowly to look into another familiar face, and this one came with memories. She stepped back, surprised to see that Dickson didn't follow. "Actually you look like you got fished out of the creek. Ran into some trouble, did you?"

Lalita nodded slowly. The minute the man before her came into complete focus, she planned on turning and running as hard as she could.

He squinted at her. "I guess you've got limited English." He looked to the left as the horse-drawn wagon drove around the house. "Well, Max will get you to the doctor."

Before she knew what was happening, he was lifting her up to the front of the buckboard, and she sat by Max. *Does all this mud make me unrecognizable?*

They rode in silence, and Lalita couldn't help feeling that the town looked different; then she was struck with another memory and turned to the young man beside her. "Max, your cast... your leg couldn't have healed that fast. You were on crutches just last night."

Max looked at her, surprised. "You must have me mixed up with someone else. There's nothing wrong with my leg—either one of them."

Lalita blinked and turned her attention back to the road, feeling completely off balance. "It must be my head," she mumbled.

The boy nodded and didn't say another word until he pulled up in front of the Cavanaugh residence. Max helped her down, and more mud crumbled off of her as her feet hit the ground. She looked down at the dress she'd lengthened and wondered if it would ever come clean.

Max escorted her up to the door, and when Lalita reached for the knob, he put his hand on hers. "I think we better ring the bell."

He poked the button with his finger while Lalita explained. "It's okay, I've been living—"

The door was opened by Tate, although Lalita had never seen him with his hair so short and slicked down. *Did he get an early morning haircut?* She wondered that he hadn't been looking for her, but then realized he probably thought she was still in bed. He looked surprised, and she knew she had some explaining to do.

She was about to begin, when he turned his attention to Max. "What do we have here, Max? Is the young lady injured?"

Young lady?

Lalita jumped in, suddenly feeling near tears. "Doc, I'm so sorry. I should have never gone out alone."

The doctor put a hand to her shoulder and stepped back to allow her entrance. "What happened, Miss?"

She scowled at his formality, but realized he must be doing it for Max's sake. "I. . ." She looked back at Max. She didn't want to elaborate on his father's bad behavior in front of him. "Thanks for the lift, Max. I'll be okay now."

He nodded and jogged down the steps as Tate closed the door, guiding her into the exam room. He pulled his stool over to her and bid her sit. "Now, can you tell me what happened to you and if I can be of assistance."

Lalita didn't want to sit. She wanted his arms around her. "Tate, we're alone now, you don't have to be so proper."

His eyebrows lifted, and she blamed the mud for his distance. "I'm sorry I'm a mess. I'll get in the tub in a minute." She pulled her purse over her head, causing more mud to hit the floor. "Sorry, I'll clean it up. I just need to show you what I got from Dickson."

"Seth Dickson?"

She gave him a look. She was in no mood for him to be suddenly dense. "Of course, Seth Dickson." She stuck her hand in her bag and pulled out her phone. She sighed. It was dead. "Damn it!"

As she went back to digging in her purse once again, Tate laid a hand on her shoulder, gently pressing her to the stool. "Please have a seat. There's no reason to be upset. I'm here to help you."

Lalita stopped searching for her charger to look up into his concerned face. A face that looked so professional, so calm, so not like her Tate at all.

She was still staring when someone appeared at the door. Lalita gave a screech and leaped to her feet. She knew this woman, although only from a picture.

Augusta.

* * *

Tate didn't know what to make of the woman who had shown up at his door. She acted like she knew him—had even called him by his first name, but he didn't recognize her—even after a bath. She was obviously of Indian ancestry, although probably no more than his brother and sister. He sat in his leather chair in the parlor, the corner of his mouth quirking up. *No more than me.*

Perhaps she had been a friend of one of his younger siblings, but how she came to be here with nothing but the dress on her back—covered in mud, at that—and a bag with a few strange items in it, was anyone's guess, and she wasn't providing any explanations yet. The appearance of his wife had seemed to send her into some kind of shock.

He could find no head injury, although she had bruises on her wrists and soreness around her rib cage that suggested that she had met with violence of some kind. She had not wanted to talk to the marshal, however, so there wasn't much he could do for her except give her headache powders and a cool cloth for her head and let her rest in his exam room in one of Augusta's nightgowns.

Augusta had taken the girl's dress outside and was beating it with the rug beater to get all the mud off. *How did she get in such a state, and what does Seth Dickson have to do with it?*

Sitting in the parlor across the hall, he cataloged the injuries he could assess in his medical journal along with what she had said when she arrived. He looked at the name at the top of the page. *Lalita Torres.* She had seemed on the verge of tears when he had asked her name.

Augusta appeared in the doorway with the dress over her arm, looking disturbed. "Tate, except for the border around the bottom, I have a dress just like this."

He gave her an indulgent smile. His wife was prone to anxiety over the littlest things. "Is that right? Well, it must have been popular in Denver. I have a feeling that's where this woman is from."

She stepped into the room. "No, Tate. It was tailor-made, and it is exactly the same right down to the lace on the collar."

Tate was having a hard time getting concerned. "It just shows that you women think alike."

She turned. "Well, I'll try to get it clean..."

"That's all you can do." He had a flash of Augusta wearing the dress she was talking about, but he decided that it must have been some time ago. *All she wears these days is gray.*

She lingered at the door, twisting a blond curl near her face around her finger. "Has she said any more?"

Tate shook his head. "She's resting."

"How long will she be here? I should cancel with the Harrisons."

Tate closed his eyes, trying not to appear vexed. "There's no need to cancel yet. Their party isn't until tomorrow."

Nodding, she left the room, and Tate returned in thought to the mysterious patient across the hall.

*   *   *

Lalita was lying with her eyes closed, but she wasn't sleeping. Or maybe she was, and this was a nightmare. She couldn't decide.

With the easing of her headache, her last memories had returned. She remembered running from Dickson in the rain, Tate throwing a punch, and then the lightning flash. If she wasn't sleeping or just plain crazy, it had happened again. She had been thrown back in time.

She didn't know how far back, but it would have to be less than three years; Max had looked younger, but not drastically so. *I'll know more when I see Nellie.*

The big question, of course, was how close was Augusta's death? She didn't know if she should warn Tate, although she didn't know specific dates, and why would he believe her anyway? Her phone with all the evidence was dead and the charger was missing. *Is this now my responsibility—to make sure Augusta doesn't die?* She knew that Tate wasn't even happy with Augusta, but how could she let her die if she could somehow prevent it? *If she dies, and I could have done something, I may as well be a murderer.* She rolled to her side. *But if she lives, I lose Tate.*

Tears came to her eyes as she recalled his very professional examination of her body—so close she could smell his aftershave, but as far away from her emotionally as he had ever been. *He doesn't even know me, and if Augusta lives, he never will.*

She clenched her eyes tight against the tears. She knew that no matter how hard she cried this time over what she had lost, Tate would not scoop her up on his lap and comfort her.

This time she was all alone.

Chapter 34

"I'm pleased to meet you, Nellie. How old are you?" Lalita sat on the side of the exam room bed, trying to control her emotions.

The youngster held up three fingers but was instantly corrected by her father. "Put up another finger, Miss Nell. You just celebrated a birthday, remember?"

The cute curly-headed blonde, with one arm wrapped around her doll, added her pinkie to the finger count, and Lalita couldn't help but smile. She noted that the doll looked newer than the last time she'd seen it. "Did you get Arabella for your birthday?"

Nellie nodded and held it out for Lalita's inspection. She gave the doll a good looking over then handed it back to the little girl who hugged it to her chest as she left the room.

Tate sat on the stool and put his stethoscope to Lalita's back. "I didn't realize that you and Arabella had already met. Nellie must have sneaked in here without permission."

Lalita realized her error and scrambled to get Nellie out of trouble. "Oh, no, I'm the one who sneaked. To the bathroom, that is. I... I was embarrassed to ask. I talked to Nellie and her doll for just a minute on the way."

He put a finger to his lips and the bell of his stethoscope on her chest. Lalita sat as still as a stone, looking at those lips he'd drawn her attention to, remembering how they felt against hers. He smiled and removed his finger. "I do need you to breathe, Miss Torres. Deeply. Just don't talk for a minute."

She closed her eyes and breathed him in, and she couldn't help it when she choked on a sob.

He removed his stethoscope and gripped her upper arm. "Are you quite all right? Is there more you wish to tell me about last night's assault?"

She shook her head, unable to speak for the lump in her throat.

He sat back on the stool studying her. Finally he spoke. "Are you hungry? Augusta can make you a tray."

She nodded, and he patted her knee and rose. She heard the clanging bells of the wall phone, and he started toward the door. "It will be just be a minute or two," he threw back over his shoulder as he left the room.

Even though she rose and moved closer to the door, straining to hear, she couldn't make out anything until "I'll be there as soon as I can."

With the clack of the receiver being placed in its holder, she scurried back to her bed and sat as he appeared at the doorway. "I have an emergency to take care of—a railroad incident— but my wife will see to your needs while I'm gone." He left and returned a split second later. "Your heart and lungs sound fine, by the way, so as soon as you feel up to it, and your dress is dry, you can be on your way. Just leave your address with Augusta." He gave her a smile. "And it was nice to meet you, Miss Torres."

He turned away, and Lalita clutched the nightgown over her heart, certain that it would never be fine again.

* * *

Lalita had no intention of eating alone in the exam room while her adorable Nellie and that Debbie Downer mother of hers ate in the dining room. She headed toward the kitchen as soon as Tate was out the door.

Augusta seemed surprised that she was out of bed, but allowed her to carry the bowl of potatoes to the table. They sat, and Augusta offered a stilted blessing over the food before cutting up Nellie's meat and pouring gravy over her potatoes. Now that Lalita was sitting across from her, she recognized the gray outfit Augusta was wearing as the one she'd turned into riding bloomers.

"So," Lalita began, feeling awkward, "how did you and the doctor meet? It was back in Denver, right?"

Augusta narrowed her eyes. "Were you friends of the Cavanaughs? Tate seemed to think you came from Denver also."

Lalita decided then and there that she was a friend of the Cavanaughs. She remembered the name of his sister from the family portrait and nodded. "I was a friend of Nettie's." Never had she considered herself a compulsive liar until she had started zipping around through time.

Augusta seemed to relax a little bit. "I liked Nettie, although that brother of his was more than I could take most of the time. He had such a chip on his shoulder and was so jealous of Tate." Lalita nodded as if she understood completely, and Augusta continued in a low voice. "And I never thought Tate's mother cared for me."

Lalita reached across the table and touched Augusta's arm. "Surely you're mistaken."

Augusta raised her cup to her lips. "No, she made it very plain." She took a sip and set it back down. "I was not what she expected. She thought a doctor's wife should be more... more high society." She scooped up a bite of potatoes on her fork. "And frankly, I don't know why anyone would want to be friends with those people. They'll eat you alive and spit out your bones."

Lalita was astonished at the fervor behind her words. "I didn't realize... Does Tate expect this too?"

Augusta paused a moment, chewing, and Lalita could see that she was trying to form an acceptable answer. Finally she wiped her lips and spoke. "He has become more understanding over time, but he still thinks he has some kind of societal role to live up to."

They ate in silence for a few minutes; then Augusta asked her a question. "What happened to you last night? The bruises on your wrists... Someone mistreated you."

Lalita couldn't tell her that Seth Dickson had attacked her a year from now. She pulled something out of the air. "I had a falling out with the man I was traveling with. He said he wanted to marry me, but it turns out, he just wanted to rob me. We were camped along the creek, and when I woke up and saw him digging through my purse, we had a tussle, and I fell into the water."

Augusta reached for her hand. "Oh, you poor dear! He took your money?"

Lalita nodded. "I don't have a thing." She felt tears forming that were not by any means an act. "Your husband said I could leave anytime, but. . . "

Augusta gave her hand a squeeze. "You've got nowhere to go. Of course you're welcome to stay until arrangements can be made. Perhaps your family can wire you some money."

Lalita gave her a tiny smile. "Perhaps. They were pretty angry with me for going off with. . ." —she said the first name that popped into her head—"Alphonse."

She grimaced at the name, but Augusta took her expression as a commentary on her situation. She leaned forward over her plate as if struck by an idea. "You know, sometimes I need help around the house. Sometimes I. . . I can't do everything that's expected. Would you be willing to stay and help me? I'm sure Tate would pay you, and then you could get back on your feet again."

Lalita swallowed. She had actually been hoping for a hand-out so she could get a room at a boarding house and look for a job. *Can I stay here with Tate and Nellie and his wife and not fall completely apart?* As she looked into the pleading blue eyes across from her, another piece of her memory fell into place. *She didn't die by accident. She killed herself.*

"Yes," she heard herself saying. "Yes, I'd be glad to help you."

* * *

Tate had to make a stop at the pharmacy to pick up a few antiseptic supplies that he was running low on before heading to the railroad accident site.

As he was settling up with the cashier, his ears pricked at a rattling cough from somewhere in the building. Collecting his supplies, he quickly searched out the source. He discovered the woman on a side aisle with a handkerchief held to her mouth as her lungs spasmed relentlessly. She looked up as he approached and tried to catch her breath.

"Mrs. Dickson, that cough doesn't sound good. Have you seen a doctor?"

She shook her head and tried to speak in between coughs. "No, I haven't found the time." She lifted up a bottle she'd picked up from the shelf nearby. "I'm getting supplies for my mama's cough remedy, though. I'll be right as rain by tomorrow."

Tate knew that a mixture of laudanum and olive oil might give her a bit of relief, but from the sound of her cough, he suspected something more serious. "I'm on my way to see about a railroad accident, but I would advise you to call another doctor as soon as you get home. That cough is nothing to put off."

He turned to leave but remembered the mention of Seth Dickson's name by his early morning patient. He debated for a moment then went on. *If the woman knows nothing about her, it will just raise suspicions in her mind.* He climbed aboard his buggy and gave the reins a snap. *And what this town doesn't need is more unsubstantiated rumors.*

He couldn't help but wonder about Miss Torres's bruises, however, and he regretted giving her permission to leave before he returned to discover more about her situation. He knew that many men considered themselves the master of their domains, and they remained so by any means necessary, but he had not been raised that way. His father had always stressed that women were a gift to men and should be treated as such. *"Any man who would raise his hand to a woman is not a man"* was heard often in the Cavanaugh household.

He considered his own "gift," and his brows grew together at the thought that Augusta would leap on any excuse to back out of a social obligation. *Is it really so hard to put on a smiling face for a few hours now and then and be sociable?*

He had hoped that the smaller social circles of Manitou Springs would be less daunting and would draw Augusta out, and although she had fewer bouts of melancholy since leaving Denver, she was by no means cured. He sighed. *I imagine she will work herself into either an anxiety attack or a completely despondent state before the Harrison gathering tomorrow evening.*

As he headed out of town, breathing in the fresh spring air, he urged Maisy to a trot, wondering if he should buy Augusta a new dress for the occasion as an incentive to keep their commitment. *Or maybe some perfume.*

* * *

Lalita had spent the day getting to know a younger Nellie and Tate's moody wife. She had helped Augusta hang the laundered clothes on the line and played a mini game of hide and seek with Nellie among the hanging sheets and dresses. Augusta had started to slide into a funk shortly after and had gone to lie down.

When she hadn't reappeared by the time Lalita's stomach started to growl, she and her four-year-old companion had gone into the kitchen to investigate the possibilities for a meal. There, she found what remained of the roast in the ice box and half a loaf of bread. She made them both a sandwich and wished for fries and ranch dressing to go with it. She settled for apple slices.

She entertained the youngster for most of the evening and was beginning to wonder if Augusta was ever going to come down, when she had a disquieting thought: *Maybe this is the day.* Racing up the stairs, she checked the bathroom, but found it empty. Moving down the hall to what Mrs. Kettler always referred to as "Augusta's room," she found the woman sitting in a small upholstered chair, staring out the window. The same chair that Lalita had sat in to stitch the buttons on her new dress just a week ago.

Lalita put a hand to her racing heart. "Augusta, aren't you hungry? Nellie and I had a sandwich; I'd be glad to make you one too."

The woman slowly brought her attention to Lalita, and it was if she were looking at a completely different person than she had eaten lunch with. "How do you do it, Lalita?"

Lalita stepped on into the room. "How do I do what?"

"You've lost everything, and you've just jumped into something completely new—completely unexpected, and you just... just deal with it."

Lalita walked to the bed and sat on the edge. "If you could do anything, what would you do, Augusta?"

She turned to look back out the window. "I'd go home."

"Home? Denver or somewhere else?"

She gave a little laugh. "Somewhere else."

Lalita reached out a hand to her knee. "And what would you do there?"

Augusta straightened and lifted her chin. "Reign."

Lalita paused, wondering if she heard correctly. Then she heard the sprinkles on the roof. "Ah, well, that will settle the dust."

Augusta's chin fell toward her chest, and Lalita leaned to see her face. Her eyes were closed. "So. . . how about that sandwich?"

*　　*　　*

Tate tiptoed up the stairs, exhausted, around eleven o'clock.

It had been a long drive up into the mountains to reach the site of the blasting accident. Thankfully, he hadn't been the only doctor called, or he'd be there yet. Several had lost their lives and many would have weeks of recovery due to one man's careless cigar stub.

As he neared his bedroom, he was surprised to hear humming coming from the bathroom across the hall. *It's rather late for a bath, Augusta.*

She usually liked to hear about his time away from the house, even though she often seemed averse to venturing out herself. He knocked lightly. "Augusta, I'm home. Do you want me to wait up for you?"

The humming stopped abruptly, but she didn't answer. "Augusta?"

A moment later the door opened, and he found himself staring into the dark brown eyes of the mysterious Miss Torres in one of his wife's wrappers. "Oh! I'm so sorry, I didn't expect. . . Do you still feel dizzy?"

She shook her head, and the layers of her hair, cut uncharacteristically short for a woman, bounced with the motion. "No, can I talk to you a minute?" She looked down the hall and lowered her voice to a whisper. "In private?"

Tate nodded and waved her back down the hall to the stairs, wondering if he might learn the reason for her bruises. When they arrived in the exam room, however, the topic on her mind seemed to be his wife.

"Doc, you need to lighten up a bit on Augusta and these social engagements she hates so much."

Tate couldn't hide his surprise. "Have you become her confidant in less than a day?" He crossed his arms. "We can discuss my marriage when you explain your bruises."

She held up her wrists, letting the sleeves slide down. "These? Sure." She told him a story of a man, an assumed marriage, and a robbery with such speed it made his head spin. Then she went on to tell of his wife's proposition. "So your wife kind of hired me to help her around the house. If you don't want to pay me, that's fine. Room and board will be enough for now."

He stared at her blankly, wondering how a story she was too choked up about this morning to speak of at all, could come tumbling out of her mouth now with all the emotion of reading a shopping list. *Maybe I'm just too tired for this conversation.*

She continued to look at him with anticipation. "What do you think, Doc?"

He walked to the stool by the bed and sat, rubbing his fingers back and forth over his forehead a few times. "I imagine it's a good idea. She does seem to struggle with... life." He searched her eyes. "And if she asked you herself, she must trust you." *Maybe this is the answer to Augusta's melancholy—a female companion.* He straightened. "I'll pay you $3.00 a week plus room and board." He suddenly had an idea. "And if you accompany us to social engagements, I'll give you $1.00 bonus once a month."

He thought he was being quite generous, but the woman's brow knitted. "But the society parties are the very thing she hates, Tate—I mean, Doc. You're better off just letting her off the hook there. Believe me, in a year, you won't even care."

Tate found himself feeling nettled. "Miss Torres, I appreciate the fact that you have made friends with my wife, but if you are to be my employee, I will thank you to keep your opinions about how I handle my family to yourself."

He watched the woman in front of him close down—from the narrowing of her eyes to the pursing of her lips. "Fine, but you may live to regret it, Dr. Cavanaugh." She spat out his name like it left a bad taste in her mouth. Spinning abruptly, she headed for the door.

Tate sat a moment, his tired brain rehashing his conversation with the woman who was now heading up his stairs. Unable to put the pieces of the puzzle together, he dragged his weary body after her and went to bed.

Chapter 35

Even though Lalita had shared quite a few breakfasts with Tate and Nellie, never had she shared one that included Augusta, and the prospect of them all sitting around the table like one big happy family made her stomach turn over. She flipped the sausage patties in the skillet. *Happy is probably an overstatement.* She looked over to where Augusta sat in the chair by the door in another drab outfit, staring out the window. *She's even lower than yesterday.*

She knew from a quite audible early morning spat between Augusta and Tate that he had all but forced her up and out of bed this morning. Her complaints of a headache were met with derision instead of the compassion that Lalita had come to associate with the doctor.

Lalita had hurriedly dressed and had breakfast mostly prepared by the time Augusta had dragged into the kitchen. She had acknowledged Lalita's presence as though it were an everyday occurrence to see her there, before sitting without another word to watch the birds at her feeder.

Lalita wished she knew how to help the woman, but at the moment she was trying to keep pancakes from burning on the temperamental stove.

Nellie wandered in with her dress unbuttoned halfway down the back, her hair looking like she'd just rolled out of bed, and Lalita sent her toward Augusta. "Good morning, Nellie. Go ask your mama to button you up."

Nellie walked dutifully to her mother and turned around, and Augusta pulled her view from the window to accomplish the task, although at a snail's pace. When she was finished, she ran a hand over Nellie's hair a few times before looking once again out the window.

As Lalita piled the pancakes on a platter, she decided to try an experiment. "Augusta, I talked to your husband last night, and he agreed to pay me to help out around the house. I'd thought to assist you with your bath and preparations for this evening's party, but he had such a strenuous day yesterday that he said he would like to just stay home and spend the evening with you and Nellie."

Augusta looked to her surprised. "He said that?"

Lalita vacillated for a few seconds before nodding. She hoped she could get him to say that, but she hadn't had a chance for the actual conversation yet.

The change in Augusta wasn't exactly dramatic, but she did rise and walk to the stove to transfer the sausages to the plate that Lalita had gotten out for that purpose, then followed her to the dining room with Nellie on her heels.

Tate was sitting at the table already reading the newspaper, but with the ladies' entrance into the room, he laid it aside and rose. He held a chair for Nellie and Augusta in turn, and Lalita waited to see if he'd do the same for her, or if she was expected to eat somewhere else. Augusta cleared up any confusion when she motioned for her to take the seat beside her.

Tate stepped in like the proper Victorian gentleman that he was, and Lalita couldn't help but smile wistfully remembering how that very proper gentleman had locked the carriage house door and necked with her in the buggy. She felt a blush rush to her cheeks and quickly bowed her head for the morning prayer. Tate blessed the food, but Lalita was praying fervently that he would not bring up the evening party before she had a chance to talk to him again.

While they ate, Tate gave them an overview of the railroad accident, and Lalita was surprised when Augusta participated in the conversation, expressing her concern over those injured and worse. "Was there anyone we know among the dead?" Augusta asked lifting her coffee cup to her lips.

Tate shook his head as he chewed and swallowed. "No, although Charlie Haynes got hit with some flying debris that grazed his skull. He's a very lucky man. Another inch, and he'd be on the deceased list."

"Bryant Dickson wasn't up there, was he? The rumor mill says that he had a falling out with Seth and left the saddlery to work on the railroad."

Tate shook his head again. "I didn't see him among those injured, but that doesn't mean he wasn't there."

"Bryant Dickson?" Lalita inquired. "I didn't know there was a Bryant."

"He's the eldest of the Dickson boys," Augusta supplied. "Very headstrong. He and his father butt heads quite a bit."

Tate helped himself to another pancake and drizzled on Lalita's creamy home-made syrup. "Speaking of the Dickson's, I saw the Mrs. in the pharmacy yesterday, and she sounded just awful." Lalita raised her head, her pulse kicking up a notch. Tate continued. "She had a terrible cough. If I hadn't had an emergency to attend to, I would have insisted on an exam right then and there."

Goosebumps rose up on Lalita's arms. "Did you see her when you got back?"

"It was quite late when I got back, as you well know, Miss Torres." He lifted his cup from the saucer. "I told her to call one of the other doctors in town."

Lalita persisted. "Do you think she did that?"

Tate stared at her. "I'm sure I have no idea." He finished the last bite of his pancake and pushed away from the table. "If you will excuse me, ladies, I have some bookwork to see to while the phone isn't ringing."

Lalita knew that Tate needed to see Mrs. Dickson sooner rather than when it would be too late to help her. She rose and blocked his way into his office. "Why don't you just give her a call, Doc? Just a friendly checking-on-you kind of call to see if she actually did as you suggested."

Tate cocked his head at her. "Do you have some connection to the Dickson's? It seems unlikely that you are related."

She knew he was referring to her Native American features. She couldn't resist a jibe. "I'm not related, but looks can be deceiving, can't they, Doc?"

He paused and licked his lips, accepting the challenge in her eyes with his own. "To be sure," he said quietly. "I am more than willing to help anyone who asks," he said as he made to step around her, "but they have to ask."

Lalita couldn't let him disappear into his office. "Tate, you have to go see her. If you don't, she'll die."

At that, Augusta rose and came to her side while Tate narrowed his eyes at her. Lalita looked at the floor, realizing she had no idea how the story of Mrs. Dickson's death had played out. "Maybe it's already too late."

She felt a finger lift her chin, and Tate looked into her eyes. "Are you feeling all right, Miss Torres. Perhaps you've pushed yourself too hard after your ordeal yesterday morning. I advise you to go have a rest."

Lalita scowled. She was finding this earlier rendition of Tate to be quite annoying.

Augusta put an arm around her and tried to lead her away from her husband, but Lalita knew what was at stake for all of them if Mrs. Dickson died. "No, I'm fine. This is really, really important!"

Augusta was stronger than she looked. "Of course it is, dear, and we'll make sure someone checks on her, won't we Tate?" Lalita heard a grunt that could be either a denial or agreement behind her as Augusta practically drug her out into the hall. When she heard Tate's office door close, Augusta released her and put her finger to her lips. With a quick glance back to see that Nellie was still eating, she bent her head toward Lalita's. "You seem very sure that Mrs. Dickson is in dire need of a doctor," she whispered.

"I am," Lalita affirmed. "I can't tell you how I know, but I do. If she doesn't receive care, she will die." She puffed out a breath. "Actually, she may die anyway, but we have to try."

Augusta nodded as Nellie appeared in the doorway. Putting a hand on the back of Nellie's head and an arm around Lalita's waist, she moved them forward. "The dishes can wait. I believe we women should take a walk on this beautiful spring morning, don't you Lalita?"

The women donned hats and headed out the door after Augusta wrote a quick note for Tate, leaving it among the dirty dishes on the table.

Lalita felt a mixture of things as they stepped out onto the dirt street. She knew in her heart that this was the right thing to do. Her knowledge gave her the power to change things for the better for the Dicksons and the Cavanaughs.

What it would mean for her own future was anybody's guess.

* * *

Tate had worked in his office for only thirty minutes when the phone rang. Entering the dining room, he was surprised to see that the table had yet to be cleared. He listened for any activity in the house but heard nothing but the jangling phone.

He grabbed up the receiver. "Dr. Tate Cavanaugh."

"Tate, it's Augusta."

Tate slid a hand into his pocket. "Augusta! Where—"

"We're at the Dickson's, and Lalita's right. Mrs. Dickson's cough is quite bad, but she's still trying to do the laundry, and she says that she has not called a doctor."

Tate was tempted to be annoyed that his wife had taken it upon herself to indulge her new friend's whims, but his medical training won over mere human emotion. "I'll be right there."

* * *

Lalita paced nervously on the porch of the Dickson house waiting for Tate's assessment of Mrs. Dickson's health. Augusta and Nellie sat in the porch swing watching her. Finally Augusta spoke. "Mrs. Dickson acted like she had never met you, and yet you seem as worried for her health as if she were your own mother."

Lalita stopped and forced herself to stand still by the railing. "I just hate to see anyone suffer."

"I see." Augusta didn't seem convinced.

Tate appeared at the door, talking with Seth as they both came out onto the porch. "Doc, I had no idea. I knew she'd been coughing, but I can sleep through anything, and she insisted that she was fine."

"She may have been frightened of a tuberculosis diagnosis, Seth, and I don't believe that is the case here. Pneumonia can be just as serious, however, but thankfully, much has been discovered about the illness in recent years, and we have some new medicines to work with." Tate put a wider-brimmed hat on his head than Lalita was used to seeing him in, and she had a sudden flash of Doc Holiday in the movie *Tombstone.*

The two men walked down the steps, and the women followed. "I gave her a dose, and I'll be back to check on her this afternoon. Make sure she rests while I'm gone." Tate lifted Nellie up into the buggy and gave a hand to Augusta and Lalita all the while continuing to talk. "Don't hesitate to call if you feel she is getting worse before I get back."

Augusta pulled Nellie up onto her lap as Tate jogged around to the other side. No one said a word for a few blocks, and Lalita could see the stubborn set of Tate's jaw out of the corner of her eye. It was Nellie who broke the silence. "It's a good thing we went to check on her, isn't it, Papa?"

Tate shifted his fingers on the reins and flashed a tiny smile her way. "Yes, sweetheart, it was a good thing." Some of the tension seemed to leak out of him. "I don't know how you knew, Miss Torres, but another day, and it might have been too late."

Lalita didn't know what to say, and thankfully Augusta jumped in. "Lalita is a sensitive soul. She feels things more deeply than most." She laid her hand over Tate's on the reins, and Lalita could see the surprise that move brought to Tate's eyes. "You should listen to her next time."

"I.." Tate fumbled for words as he tentatively took her hand in his. "I suppose you're right."

Lalita turned away before she was tempted to cry.

* * *

"But I thought you didn't want to go to the Harrison's party." Lalita was confused by Augusta's announcement after lunch that they needed to go through her wardrobe and find something for Lalita to wear for the occasion.

"Now that Tate will be busy this evening monitoring Mrs. Dickson, you and I can go, and it will be more fun."

Lalita shook her head. "I still don't understand."

Augusta pulled her up off Nellie's bedroom floor where they had been playing with paper dolls, and bid her follow. Lalita thought she had Augusta figured out, but this threw a wrench in her social phobia theory.

Augusta led her through her bedroom and into the dressing room that was in between her room and Tate's. "I'm afraid all my dresses will be a bit short on you, but maybe we can find one that I can't fit into anymore, and you can add a border at the hem like the one you're wearing." She paused at the closet door. "Where did you get that dress, by the way? I have one that's nearly identical, and I thought it was being made exclusively for me."

Lalita gave her a nervous smile before turning her attention to the dresses hanging in the closet. "Oh, you know how those tailors are. You just gave him a great idea, and he ran with it, selling it everywhere."

Lalita knew all of Augusta's clothes like they were her own, and she also knew that very few would fit without alterations or her waist being cinched in to the point of asphyxiation.

Augusta pulled out the familiar trunk, and she bit her tongue against declaring looking through it a waste of time. Augusta straightened and huffed out a breath before opening the lid. Right on top was the corset that had nearly suffocated her on her jaunt with Tate to see the marshal. She dreaded trying to wear it for a whole evening.

Augusta, however, picked it up and threw it aside. "I was as slim as a stick when I wore that. I think there's a bit larger one at the bottom." She dug down until she pulled out an ivory corset with delicate lace trim. "We'll try this one." She moved to close the door then came back to Lalita and turned her around to start on her buttons.

Lalita didn't know what Augusta would think of her pink bra and panties—not to mention her floral tattoo—but she had nowhere to escape to, and for once, she had no good lies coming to mind to get her out of it.

Lalita sensed Augusta hesitate a moment as she reached her bra strap, but then she kept going. When she pushed the sleeves over her shoulders, Lalita assisted with pulling them off her arms, letting the dress slide down her body to the floor. Lalita slowly turned to see Augusta practically beaming. Lalita just stood there, confused by her reaction.

Augusta clasped her hands at her chin. "Where is it?"

Lalita folded her arms under her breasts, feeling a bit weirded out. "Where is what?"

"The mark of the lightning," she said in a hushed voice; then she turned and pulled down her high collar to reveal what looked like a reddish birthmark in the shape of a lightning bolt on the back of her neck.

Lalita swallowed and pointed to a red flower on her shoulder. "I had the tattoo artist work it into the design. If you look close, you can still see it, though." Her mind was abuzz with questions. "How do you have the same birthmark? What... what's going on?"

Augusta gripped her shoulders. "I rode the lightning too. In my time, it was an experiment, and some even rode it back in time to experiment on others. Were you ever a ward of the state?"

Lalita's jaw dropped. "For a bit, yes. How..."

"It's an injection. They pass it off as immunizations."

"Why?" Lalita was feeling dazed.

"They looked at it as kind of a history randomizer. The courts began to use it for exile, sending those convicted of violent crimes into prehistoric times. And then there were those that used it for revenge or"—she hesitated just a moment as she released her hold on her shoulders—"to get rid of the ruling party."

Lalita's eyes grew wide. "You weren't commenting on the weather yesterday. You said you would 'reign' if you went home. Were you a queen?"

Augusta nodded. "Something similar." She went to her closet and pulled out a robe and handed it to Lalita. She slipped it on and sank to the edge of the bed. Augusta sat beside her. "The funding had been cut, and we were trying to round up the renegades, but one night they infiltrated the Ballustadia. I was captured and injected."

Lalita's head was spinning, and she felt again like she had the moment she had realized the truth in front of the Antlers Hotel. "But wouldn't they have to wait for a storm?"

Augusta shook her head. "They could recreate lightning in their dome. In fact, according to the history books, Nikola Tesla began the work that the riders would later build upon. We know now that Nikola Tesla was a rider himself. I was hoping that he could send me back, but I have to wait seven more years before he will even begin building his laboratory." She rose and walked across the room. "That's why I traveled to this area, but I don't know if I can wait that long." She paused and heaved a heavy sigh. "Sometimes... when my depression is very bad, I think about—"

"Slitting your wrists?"

Augusta spun back to face her. "How do you know that?"

Lalita pushed up off the bed and crossed to where Augusta stood wide-eyed. "Because you did it, or I should say you will do it. And not too far in the future, either. When I was here in 1892—"

"I knew it! You've been here before! That's how you knew about Mrs. Dickson!" Augusta's brow knitted with questions. "But there's no simulator here... You were struck by the real thing."

Lalita put a hand to her temple. "Twice. So it's the... the..."—she moved her hand to her tattooed shoulder—"the lightning mark that keeps us from getting killed, along with sending us to another time?"

"Yes, without it, you would have died."

Something was on the edge of Lalita's brain, but she couldn't quite grab hold of it. She began to pace, chewing on a fingernail. "You said they could send people back to specific times, so it doesn't have to be random. How do they choose?"

Augusta put her hands to her head. "They place a kind of helmet on you that points your mind to the time."

Lalita stopped pacing. "But I didn't have a helmet. How did I end up in 1892, and even more curious, why did I only bounce back a year the second time?"

"I don't know."

Lalita remembered the Victorian house at Rock Ledge Ranch that she had seen just before the ride up Pikes Peak and took a step toward Augusta. "They only need the helmet if they want to make you go where you don't want to go. Otherwise, it's just a matter of thinking of the time. When I went back a year, I had just been told by Seth Dickson something that had happened a year earlier. I didn't know an exact date, so I just went to a time that was close."

Augusta closed the gap between them. "So I could go back anytime? I was afraid to try. As much as I hate this oppressive Victorian era, I know it could be much worse." She half-smiled. "Tate thought my fear of lightning was just one of my 'irrational phobias.' "

Lalita nodded understanding but then had a disquieting thought. "You could just do that? Just leave Tate and Nellie?"

Augusta took her hands. "You say that I do that anyway, at one of my low points. To just disappear would be better, wouldn't it?" She squeezed Lalita's hands as tears came to her eyes. "There's a man back in my time that I love. Tate has taken care of me, and I appreciate that, but my heart has always belonged to someone else. I'll never be able to give him that."

Augusta released her hands and took a step back, a look of epiphany on her face. "Your dress is my dress. You've lived here. With Tate."

Lalita sucked in a breath and let it out. "We were going to be married," she said in a rush." Her throat constricted, and her next words were high and tight. "Now he doesn't even know me, and he is so different, it's like I don't know him either."

Augusta moved toward her, and the two women embraced. "My death changed him then."

"Yes." Lalita clung tightly to the only woman to truly understand her since she "rode" the lightning on Pikes Peak. "He said he pushed you into being something you weren't. I think he blamed himself for your death."

Augusta pulled back to look in her eyes. "Then it is good that I go."

"But," Lalita sobbed, "how can you leave Nellie?"

"There's help for depression in my time. Here, I will only hurt her." A tear rolled down her cheek. "I have hurt her. You love her, though, don't you? I will entrust her to you."

Lalita nodded, unable to speak.

The two pulled apart, and Augusta smiled. "Now we wait for the perfect storm."

Chapter 36

Despite the medication that Tate was giving Mrs. Dickson, she took a turn for the worse, and her fever spiked to 102 degrees the following afternoon. As he worked to bring it down with ice compresses, he considered Augusta's assessment of Miss Torres as "a sensitive soul."

He'd asked Seth Dickson how he knew her, and he said he'd never laid eyes on her until she showed up caked with dried mud in front of his house. Tate frowned remembering his leering smile as he had commented, "That little squaw cleans up real nice."

Mrs. Dickson, too, had expressed no knowledge of her before she had shown up with Augusta to check on her. *So how did Miss Torres know how serious her condition was, and why was she so concerned?*

A spasm of coughing racked Mrs. Dickson's frame, and he clicked open his pocket watch to check if he could give her a draft to ease her cough. *I should wait at least a half hour.*

Max poked his head in the door. "How's Ma? I heard her coughing again."

Tate didn't have good news to share about her current condition, but he didn't want to worry the boy. "Sometimes things get worse before they get better. Right now, we're at worse." He forced a smile. "I'm expecting better to come along soon."

Max nodded solemnly. "If you don't mind, I'd like to pray for her."

"A grand plan, Max." Tate rose and waved toward his chair. "Have a seat while I get a bit of fresh air."

As he walked out onto the front porch, he saw his girls approaching up the street. He walked to meet them contemplating the speed with which Miss Torres had become a part of their home. Indeed, she took over in the kitchen as if she was already well-acquainted with it, and he had even seen her using the sewing machine on one of his brief stops back at the house.

When he drew near, Nellie ran to him, and he swept her up. "How's my angel this afternoon?"

"Very well, thank you," she giggled as he tickled her ribs and planted a kiss on her cheek.

He turned his attention to the two women. He could see that Lalita had acquired one of Augusta's brighter dresses. He glanced down to the slightly ruffled piece that had been added to the hem and noticed that the same color had been added to the sleeve edges and to her hat. Augusta, on the other hand wore a striped outfit in two shades of brown. He smiled as they reached Nellie and himself. "Well, you two look fashionable today." He glanced to the basket over Augusta's arm. "I don't suppose you've brought me a bite to eat?"

"We have," Augusta confirmed. "Lalita is a much better cook than I am. She made fried chicken and biscuits that will melt in your mouth."

Tate raised a brow and looked to the now blushing, dark-eyed woman at her side. "I can't wait to try them." He turned and led his crew to the Dickson's big front porch, where Augusta sat with him on the swing while Miss Torres held Nellie on a wicker chair opposite. He dove into the meal with gusto and had to agree with his wife's appraisal.

After a few moments of eating the best biscuits he'd ever tasted, their baker spoke up. "How's Mrs. Dickson?"

Tate swallowed a bite of chicken and chased it with a gulp or two of water. "She has a fever and the rattle in her chest hasn't cleared. I'm continuing to give her bacteriolysins... Time will tell."

"Time will tell." Miss Torres sighed and looked to his wife. "Gosh, I'm tired of that phrase."

Tate looked questioningly to Augusta, whose lips curled up in a slight smile. "I'm afraid our new friend is impatient."

Tate swallowed another bite of chicken. "Oh? What are you impatient about, Miss Torres?"

Before she could answer, Max appeared at the screen door. "Doc, Ma is mumbling stuff I can't understand. She isn't making any sense."

Tate handed the basket back to Augusta and went in the house. After washing his hands at the kitchen sink, he went upstairs to check on his patient. A quick evaluation revealed that her fever had risen to a dangerous level. "Max, run a cool tub of water. We need to get her fever down."

* * *

The two women sat on the porch waiting for news while Nellie drew pictures in the dusty yard with a stick. Augusta shaded her eyes from the sun as she looked at her daughter. "What's she like in a year?"

"Beautiful, funny, full of laughter." Lalita smiled. "She's a sweet girl."

Seth Dickson's voice erupted from the upstairs window. "Damn it, Doc, there's got to be more you can do."

"I'm doing all I can, Seth. Perhaps if she hadn't waited—"

"Does the medicine work or not?"

"Sometimes even the best of treatments can't overcome the colony of bacteria that—"

"I think I should call another doctor."

"That is certainly your prerogative, although I don't think he will do anything differently than I'm doing. The best thing we can do right now is get her fever down. If you will assist me in getting her into the tub..."

The argument stopped, and Lalita rose, intending to warn Augusta concerning Seth Dickson, when something Nellie was pulling out of the dirt caught her eye. A long thin black cord with a plug on the end. Lalita smiled. *My charger.*

She started down the steps. "Leave the basket inside for Tate, Augusta. We need to go home; I have something I need to show you."

*   *   *

Lalita felt a hand gently shaking her shoulder and blinked her eyes open. Augusta was looking down at her. She sat up. "What's wrong? Is Tate back yet?"

"No. I called before I went to bed, and William told me that they had gotten her fever down a few degrees but it hasn't broken completely."

A low rumble rolled outside, and Lalita's head snapped to look out the window. "Is it—"

"Yes." She swept the sheet aside. "We must hurry."

Lalita pulled her legs up and hugged her knees. "What about Nellie? I should probably stay here with her."

"I've made arrangements." She put a hand impatiently on Lalita's arm.

Lalita swung her legs over the edge of the bed but still didn't get up. "Don't you at least want to say good-bye to Tate?"

"I've written him a letter explaining everything." She pulled Lalita to her feet and continued pulling her until she was across the hall and in the dressing room.

"Should we leave him my phone and the charger, so he knows what you are avoiding by leaving?"

Augusta stopped pulling and switched on the light. "No, that could just cause more trouble. Tate might attack Dickson, and he'd be the one in jail when you get back."

"Augusta, isn't it dangerous for me to go? What if we also *attract* the lightning? I mean, I've been struck twice; what are the odds of that?"

"Of course we attract the lightning, but you can't stay in this time any more than I can."

Lalita suddenly realized what Augusta meant by when she "got back." "But I want to stay with Tate and Nellie, right here, right now."

Augusta grabbed the dress that Lalita had arrived in from the closet and held it out to her. "This is the wrong time for you and Tate. You said yourself that you can hardly recognize him, and he will not be ready for you either. He needs that year of pain to welcome you into his heart just the way you are. If you are pushed together now, when the time isn't right, it could ruin it for all time."

Lalita felt panic crawling up her throat as she reached for the dress. "But what if I don't... What if I go too far and miss him altogether?"

Augusta put her hands on her hips. "You were willing for me to try it. Did you really believe in what you said, or were you hoping to just get rid of me?"

Lalita squared her jaw, tossed the dress to a chair and pulled her nightgown over her head. "If I had wanted to just get rid of you, all I had to do was sit back and watch."

Augusta smiled as the first sounds of rain splattered on the roof.

* * *

Tate was dozing in the rocking chair by Mrs. Dickson's bed when he heard the door creak open. Max and William tiptoed in. Tate leaned forward, his hands clasped between his knees. "Couldn't sleep?"

Max shook his head, and even in the dim light, Tate could see he was fighting tears. William put a hand on Max's shoulder but looked to Tate. "Pa's still working. I know he's just trying not to think about Ma, but it isn't right him not being here."

Tate pushed up out of the chair. "Everyone has their own way of dealing with these sorts of things."

"Pa's way is blaming everybody else," Max blurted, pulling up a small chair on the other side of the bed. "He knew Ma was sick, but he just kept her working."

William squatted down and took his mother's hand. "She still feels warm, but maybe not as hot as this afternoon."

Tate nodded. "I've given her another draft of medicine even though it's early to do so. I believe tonight is the turning point, so there's really nothing to lose by giving her more than the recommended dose."

Max looked up with hope in his eyes. "She sounds less rattly when she breathes, doesn't she, Doc?"

Tate didn't really think she sounded much better, but he swept up his stethoscope and listened to her lungs as she slept.

He could still hear crackles indicative of the infection. *Do I dare give them false hope?* He looked up at the two young men who would obviously be crushed if their mother died. *Hope is always a good thing.* "I believe you're right, Max." He reached across the bed and patted his hand. "Keep those prayers coming."

* * *

"Where are we going?" Lalita asked as she and Augusta walked swiftly under one umbrella in the lightly falling rain.

Augusta lifted her lantern. "Toward the storm. Right now we're only on the edge."

Lalita shivered and pulled the wool shawl around her. "So higher up in the mountains? That seems to be where the lightning is flashing."

They walked in silence, and Lalita breathed in the wet pine scent that filled the air, thinking about Tate and Nellie and wondering if she would ever see them again—wondering if she would just start over in a different time. She tried to focus every thought on 1892, picturing the Cavanaughs she had come to know and love in that time.

Her thoughts were interrupted by a whimper from Augusta. Lalita moved the umbrella to her other hand and put an arm around her. "Are you all right? Are you having second thoughts?"

"It's... it's just a shame this storm didn't align with my depression. It would make leaving so much easier."

Lalita was a bit surprised. "Really? You're not depressed? You haven't exactly been cheery since I've been here."

"Oh, my dear Lalita, it can get much, much worse."

Personally, Lalita didn't know how the woman could leave her own daughter, depressed or not, but she also didn't want to jump back to 1892 and still find Augusta there. "Well, I'm sorry, but if you want this to work, you need to focus on your own time and the man you left behind."

Augusta nodded, wiping her eyes with a handkerchief. "His name is Halen, and he is the Vice Principia of the United Nations of North America."

"And what is your title?" Lalita asked, jumping over a puddle in the road.

"I was the Royal Vicerine of Scandia."

"Wow, that sounds impressive. I'm just curious... why did you hate the social scene here so much? Seems all those rich folks would be right up your alley."

"Tate thought I was scared of them, but by not participating, I was being judicious. A tasty rumor about Mrs. Ellinwood today could easily be a scandalous rumor about Mrs. Cavanaugh tomorrow. They believed that money gave them importance, and therefore, earned them friends. But it's really knowledge, ideas, invention, and most of all, caring for each other that propel people into meaningful relationships. It's something the rich rarely understand, unless they've spent some time being poor."

The rain started to fall harder, the wind was picking up, and the thunder was growing louder. Lalita counted three seconds from the flash of lightning until the accompanying boom. "So did you spend time being poor?"

"It's required of every Duke and Duchess in Scandia to work a minimum of one year in factories or farms, earning a modest wage, before accepting the title of Viceroy or Vicerine. Some can't make it a month and are therefore disqualified."

Thunder rolled, and Lalita's heart jumped. A part of her wanted to turn back. *If this isn't the right time for Tate and me to get together, I could just stay out of his way for a year.* "Augusta..." She heard fear in her own voice.

Augusta put a hand to her back. "Hush, you are not the type to give up and be disqualified. Stay focused."

Lalita started to slow her steps. "I don't really need to do this. I can just wait a year for Tate. In fact, I can spend that time learning how to fit in, so I won't cause the kind of ostracism he was facing when—"

Augusta stopped and turned to her as the wind whipped at their skirts, nearly pulling the umbrella out of Lalita's hands. "That is the very reason you mustn't stay. You would be changed in a year, and whether Tate realized it or not, it was your uniqueness that he was attracted to."

The crackle started, and Lalita knew it was too late to turn back. She closed her eyes tight, and the umbrella was wrenched from her hands. Her mind shouted, *August 12, 1892!* as she was blinded by a flash so bright she thought she would be disintegrated on the spot. What followed was a darkness so deep, it swallowed her whole.

Chapter 37

Tate, carrying Lita, kicked his back door hard until Fischer opened it, his expression telling him that they both looked a fright. "What happened? Is she all right?"

Tate walked through the kitchen, not caring that he was tracking mud through the house. "I don't know. She's breathing, but she's unconscious and soaked." He felt a strong déjà vu. "I need to get her warmed up." He stopped at the bottom of the stairs. "How's Mrs. Emory?"

"She woke, and we gave her the pain medication. She's sleeping now."

Tate started up. "I can't thank you enough for taking care of her."

"So why was she out in the rain?"

Tate faltered, feeling suddenly disoriented. "I don't know. Hopefully she'll be able to tell us when she comes to." He carried her up the stairs and into the bathroom, laid her gently on the floor, and started to run a hot tub of water before sloughing off his mud-covered jacket.

Fischer spoke from the doorway. "You lost your hat."

Tate squatted down and began to unlace Lita's boots. "Lita hated that bowler anyway."

Fischer smiled as he reached for the doorknob. "Holler if you need anything. I'll go check on Mrs. Emory again."

Tate nodded, slipped off her boots, and moved up to her torso, pulling a jackknife out of his pocket. *The dress is probably ruined anyway.* He made a slit through the hem of the shirtwaist, and grabbing both sides, tore it up the center. *All those little buttons would have taken forever.* As he struggled to get the wet sleeves off her arms, he considered employing the knife again, when her eyes fluttered and a sigh escaped her lips.

"Lita, can you hear me?"

Pulling a washcloth from a cupboard, he held it under the warm spray filling the tub, and kneeling beside her, wiped the mud splatters off her face. Her eyes blinked open. For a moment, she seemed frozen, then she focused on his face and started to cry. "Oh, Tate, I made it back to you. I made it back!"

He pulled her to sitting and wrapped his arms around her, rubbing his hands up and down her cold arms and whispering words of comfort. "Shh, it's all right. Why were you out, darling? I was so worried. I know you had talked about going to see how Max was doing, but the middle of the night is hardly the time for a visit."

When the sobbing slowed, he shut off the bathtub faucet and went back to work getting her undressed. "And that lightning scared the dickens out of me. I thought I had my eye on you, then I lost you in the dark." He finally got the sleeves worked off her arms then helped her slip out of the sodden skirt, leaving her in a wet, clinging chemise with her pink underclothes showing through, and he smiled. "I've never been so glad to trip over someone and land face down in the mud."

She half-smiled as she trembled; then her expression changed again to one of horror, and she gripped his hand. "Oh, Tate, Augusta..."

Tate's brow furrowed as he pulled her up off the floor. "Augusta? Why—"

She clung to him. "Oh, Tate, did she leave you a letter when she left?"

"Yes." He paused, looking puzzled. "But I've told you this, sweetheart. I even let you read it, remember? She told me you were coming back, but I had completely dismissed the idea as the ramblings of a madwoman and forgotten it by the time you were delivered to me by the Hill brothers. Once I got a good look at you"—he kissed her temple—"and realized you were a woman, I knew you were the one who had disappeared with her."

"So... did Mrs. Dickson live?"

Tate nodded, still looking concerned. "Thanks to you."

She pulled back and looked into his eyes. "If I didn't have to convince you of the truth about time travel, and Seth Dickson wasn't harassing me to get back at you, what have we been doing the last three weeks?"

He smiled, wiped the mud off her nose, and kissed it. "Falling in love, darling."

Epilogue

Sunday evening found Tate settled next to Lalita on the settee in the parlor with his arm thrown around her, her head on his chest. It had been a very long weekend.

Dr. Fischer left the day before with his wife, Bess, and Lalita learned that the couple had been merely vacationing in Manitou Springs—not investigating her mental state.

The time line changes were coming back to her in a series of dreams until she could hardly keep the differences straight. She wrote down her "original" three weeks with Tate before they disappeared altogether.

The tale of Josephine Emory's appendicitis had flown around town with amazing speed, and people dropped in most of the weekend to offer their well wishes. When they saw the way that Lalita cared for Mrs. Emory, and with Mrs. Pilson gushing over her assistance with her baby delivery, her presence in Tate's home was no longer questioned. With or without training, she had become Tate's nurse.

Now that they were all gone, and Nellie was in bed, Lalita was listening to the silence of the house and the beating of Tate's heart under her ear. She knew she should be able to relax. Mrs. Dickson was alive, Augusta had returned home, she wasn't heading to jail, and most importantly, she was in the arms of the man she loved. But something was still eating at her. "Tate, why didn't you tell me that you're as much Native American as I am?"

She felt him tense. "How did you...? Fischer!"

She shook her head against his chest. "I found pictures in your desk drawer. Why didn't you tell me? Are you... ashamed?"

He rubbed a hand up and down her arm. "No. Absolutely not." He paused, and she waited. Finally he spoke. "Maybe a hundred years from now, Indians—Native Americans—are accepted as a vital part of the population, but in this time, we haven't gotten there yet."

Lalita puffed out a breath. "You'd think so, wouldn't you? Oh, I know acceptance isn't nearly as difficult in the 21st century, but there's still room for improvement."

Tate took her hand laying on his thigh. "My grandmother was a healer and used the old ways passed down through her tribe. She trained my father, but he wanted to also incorporate new medical knowledge. There weren't very many white men who would let him treat them, however. He soon found that he could only treat the Native Americans, and they were frightened of what they called 'white man's medicine.' "

He paused and rested his lips against the top of her head. "So," she prodded, "because you looked like your mother, you had more opportunities."

He nodded. "My brother was jealous and thought I'd abandoned them when I left home. He thought, like you, that I was ashamed of them, but I just knew my... my... destiny lay in a different direction."

"I guess I can understand that. But why didn't you tell me?"

He held her tighter and sighed. "Habit, I guess. I truly didn't intend to hide it from you." He encouraged her to sit, so he could look in her eyes. "It may have been just my good luck that you had my time in your head when you were struck by lightning, but I think there was something more at work when you were brought to me. Your heritage was of no concern to me. You are everything I want; everything I need."

With a finger under her chin, he placed his lips against hers, and Lalita felt the same. When she had first thought herself "stuck" in this time, she had been devastated. She soon realized, however, that every century had its own set of joys and sorrows, trouble and triumph. *With someone you love to share your time, any time will do.*

"So when are we getting hitched?" Lalita asked when their lips finally parted.

Tate grinned. "If I wasn't so bone weary, I'd take you to the judge right now."

Lalita smiled, rose, and pulled Tate up from the sofa and out into the hall. "To bed with you then, sweet prince. You're going to need your strength tomorrow."

"Oh?"

"I have a big day planned."

He stopped her at the bottom of the stairs and pulled her into his arms. "Just what do you have in mind?"

"Taking Maisy out for a drive, shopping, wedding bells, and..."

He leaned his forehead against hers. "And..."

"I don't know, I thought maybe we should stay in the Antlers Hotel at least once before it burns down. You know, for purely historical reasons."

"Historical. Just as long as you don't write about it in your book."

"Of course not." She turned and ran up the stairs with a sudden burst of energy. "Things of that nature go in my diary," she flung back over her shoulder.

And somehow, Tate found the energy to chase her.

Thank you for reading *JOLT*. I hope you enjoyed it! If you liked this book, please consider reviewing it at Amazon or Goodreads. Your reviews help other readers find new favorites. Thanks for your support!

About the Author

I live with my husband and several spoiled cats in beautiful Colorado Springs where we get to look at Pikes Peak every day!

I've worn many hats in my life, but I spend most of my creative talents these days on writing and art. You can read more about what I do at jodibowersox.com. You can also follow me on BookBub, Goodreads, Linked-In, Pinterest, Etsy (Pikes Peak Unique), Facebook (jodibowersoxartistry), and Twitter.

In addition to romance, I have published a short Bible commentary and a compilation of plays and skits. I also have children's books published under the name J.B. Stockings. I'm available for school presentations on art and writing.

**Read on for a sample from the second book in the
Lightning Riders Series, *JUMP*:**

Prologue

1907 Manitou Springs, Colorado

"Papa, do something!" Nellie paced the small dining room with squalling baby Sadie at her shoulder, tears coursing her cheeks.

Tate was doing all he knew to do. His teen-age son, Jackson, was standing wide-eyed in the doorway with Tate's medical bag in hand, but he knew there was nothing in it that could help.

Nellie had been preoccupied with a crying baby in the parlor when Tate's son-in-law had risen from the dinner table to retrieve their apple pie dessert from the kitchen and collapsed before he reached the door. Not detecting a pulse, Tate had begun chest compressions, but after over ten minutes of cardiac stimulation, the man wasn't coming back to them. *Dear God, don't take Nellie's husband. Please.*

Lita, on her knees beside him, put a hand to his shoulder. He paused merely a moment to wipe the sweat from his brow, then began again. Nellie's sobs pushed him on, even though in his heart, he knew this was over. Paul was gone.

"Tate," Lita whispered, "it's been too long."

The catch in her voice told him she was crying too. He stopped and sat back on his heels with an anguished sigh.

Nellie stepped toward them, screaming, "No, Papa, don't stop! You're a doctor; you can't   you can't just let him die!"

Lita rose and went around the fallen man, taking the wailing baby from her distraught daughter's arms. Nellie fell to her knees, placing her hands on her still husband's chest, frantically trying to continue what Tate had ceased to do. "Is this right, Papa? How hard do I push?"

He gently stroked her head as he fought tears. "Nellie, Paul's gone."

She tossed her head defiantly, loosening several wavy strands of blond hair from her upswept hairdo. "No. We have to just keep working."

Tate noticed that the small lightning-shaped mark below her ear had turned a bright red. He started to rise, trying to pull Nellie up with him. "No!" she protested. "We can't give up!"

Stepping over the body, he turned Nellie away and wrapped her in his arms. "Nellie, dear, we knew this could happen. We knew that Paul's heart wasn't strong." Even in this new twentieth century, medical advances could do little to repair the ravages of rheumatic fever.

Nellie's sobs shook her petite frame. "But I thought we'd have more time than this! Oh, God, I need more time!"

Tate met Lita's sorrowful gaze. Ever since she had come into his life, the subject of "time" had held special significance. And for the first time, he wished he could do for Nellie what Lita had done for him: go back in time and change the past. Turn sorrow into joy.

Lita had bounced little Sadie into a slightly better mood. Nellie's grief wouldn't be so easily assuaged.

Chapter 1

Nellie startled awake and felt acutely the night she had spent sitting in the upholstered chair by the open window. It was the early morning birdsong that had brought her out of her grim dreams. Dreams of a frantic search for Paul. Dreams that usually ended in a funeral.

The last one had been different. She had been watching the Paul that she knew as a child in school. She was a transcendent observer to his rambunctious boyhood pranks and energetic games where he always seemed to be sprinting. This dream ended with the boy in bed, a red flush to his cheeks and hushed voices whispering concern.

She'd never actually seen this, as she was only five when the love of her life had fought for his own, taken to the brink by rheumatic fever. She pondered the two types of dreams and concluded that they were basically the same. The fever at ten had led to the funeral at twenty-five.

She shivered and clutched her shawl tighter around her nightgown. Wanting to divert her mind from the dreams, she looked around the room she had grown up in. It had been months since she sold the house that she and Paul had called home—months since she had returned to live with her father and Lita as a widow, although she'd be hard pressed to say how many. The days all seemed to run together now.

She heard Sadie crying across the hall, but it was as one detached. Sadie's bassinet no longer resided in Nellie's room. The baby's colicky nature had been hard to deal with before her husband's death. After, Nellie simply couldn't cope. Sadie looked too much like her dark-haired, dark-eyed Paul.

Tate had removed the baby to his and Lita's room where nearly every night the child screamed as though in pain. Tate practiced the medical wisdom of the day on her, while Lita suggested remedies from her past, which were actually remedies from the future.

Lita had spent many hours telling Nellie stories of her life in that future that had occurred in the last decade of the twentieth century and the first fifteen years of the twenty-first, as well as what she knew of the happenings between now and then. It had been their family secret—this ability of Lita's to ride the lightning—a secret that she dared tell no one. Nellie's father had told her it was a treasure they must hold very dear. He emphasized that the one who flaunts a treasure is only inviting a thief, and he'd given her a jewel in a small polished wooden box as a reminder.

That secret had carried her through every season of her life, the mystery lighting her from within and spurring her to thoughts that were, frankly, far ahead of her time. Most thought of her as odd, and some went so far as to call her touched. Paul had called her special and wanted her to be his treasure. *He said we had a love for the ages—the kind of love that only happens once in a lifetime.*

Nellie rose stiffly and wandered to her dressing table to sit once more. She turned on the Tiffany lamp in the still dark room and stared at her care worn image. Never would she estimate the age of the woman she saw there as twenty. To her weary eyes, she looked a good decade older.

Reaching for that box her father had given her so many years ago, she opened it and stared at the gem within. She lifted the red, chiseled prize out of the box and held it in the soft glow of the lamp, not feeling the magic she had felt as a child. Turning it over in her hands, she was suddenly struck with the fact that it was only made of glass. *Not much of a treasure, Papa.*

Setting the bauble back in the box, she thought it somehow appropriate that her "treasure" had turned out to be as fragile as her wedded bliss.

She allowed herself a daydream of her honeymoon. Lita had told her what to expect and how to guide her new husband into a night of shared pleasure. Their joining had been beyond anything she could have imagined, and that's when Paul had noticed the birth mark that only seemed to show up with intense emotions.

Leaning toward the mirror, she looked for the faint jagged mark on the side of her neck, just below her ear. She ran her finger over the spot, recalling the day that Lita had first seen it when Nellie had been crying over a scraped knee. As Lita had run through the house calling for her father, Nellie had stood on the piano bench to look in the mirror. She had seen a bright red bolt of lightning not more than half an inch in length, and she had been instantly frightened that a storm might sweep her off to another time as Lita had experienced only a few years before.

Nellie's mother hadn't left her much when she deserted her to return to her own time, but she had somehow passed this on to Nellie, and for thirteen years, she had obediently stayed safely inside and away from windows whenever there was even a hint of a possible storm. She had been as frightened as Lita to be swept away from those she loved.

But now, her mind started turning on a different track. Lita had always reassured her that her mother didn't leave on purpose, even though she had another husband she loved in a different time. Nellie had never questioned that until now. The new hole that loss hollowed out in her gave her a new perspective. *Is there a way to determine the course through time? If Mama learned a way to go back to him, how could she not go? Maybe she sought out the lightning.*

Pushing away from the dressing table, she walked back to the ever brightening windows. *What if I could get back to Paul? Could I brave a storm to see him again?*

* * *

Lita slipped back into bed beside Tate as the first rays of dawn eased over the horizon. Never had she been so exhausted. Whatever ailed the nearly six-month-old Sadie was about to take them all under.

Jackson had been a very happy baby, and Tate reported that while Nellie hadn't been quite as easy, she had been nothing like their new granddaughter. The crying only stopped when the child was asleep, and that never lasted more than two hours at a time. She also spit up what seemed like most of her milk and rice cereal and sometimes refused to eat altogether.

After Nellie had lost her milk in the midst of her grief and depression, they had tried what this era offered as substitute: thinned, boiled cows' milk with sugar added, Carnation evaporated milk, and even goats' milk, but none seemed better than the other for their constantly wailing baby.

Lita felt sure she had some kind of digestion issue, and while Tate agreed, he didn't really know what to do for her. He'd studied medical journals late into the night and made calls to doctors around the country and still had no solutions.

She knew that Nellie needed attention as well—the depression that had plagued her mother seemed to be settling on her in full force—but Lita simply didn't have the time or energy to deal with them both. It took her and Tate, and sometimes Jackson, to deal with the baby.

Tate hooked an arm around her and hauled her against him. She wished she had the energy to enjoy the feel of his body spooned with hers.

* * *

"Nellie." Tate rapped quietly on her bedroom door with an elbow as he held a bottle for the nursing baby in his arms. "Nellie, I need your help."

He waited several long moments, looking down into the eyes of his granddaughter. He rapped again, louder. "Nellie," he hissed, "I'm coming in." After another pause, he grasped the knob with the hand under the baby's bottom and pushed the door open, not caring if Nellie was presentable or not. She lay in bed, staring at the ceiling.

"Nellie, you need to get up and take care of Sadie. I've been called out on an emergency, Jackson is working for Mr. Hammil at the autoshop, and Lita was up half the night with Sadie. I won't wake her when you could just as easily take care of your child."

Nellie looked his way, her vacant stare turning sorrowful. "Oh, Papa, I can't."

Pulling the bottle from the baby's lips, he set it on the night stand and flung the covers off of her, remembering with regret, doing the same for Augusta on more than one occasion. "You can, and you will." He tried to soften his expression as he turned Sadie to his shoulder to pat her back. "I'm not trying to be mean, Nellie. I understand better than you think, but I need you. We all need you." He reached for her hand to pull her to sitting. "And most of all, Sadie needs you."

Nellie swiped at her eyes, and Tate fought with guilt. It broke his heart to see his sweet girl sinking into the same melancholy that had enveloped her mother, but they were all exhausted. Nellie had to pitch in.

Slowly rising, she swept up her wrapper laying on the arm of the chair and slipped it on. She reached hesitantly for the child, but Tate shook his head. "Go take care of your morning ablutions."

Nellie nodded, heading out of the room, and Tate swept up the bottle and sank into the chair. He'd need another cup of coffee before setting out to see about Mr. Burrel's foot that had been stomped on by his bull. He rubbed his free hand over his weary face. *Maybe two.*

Nellie returned, and Tate rose, finally hearing the burp he'd been waiting for. He paused a moment, but when the child didn't spit up, he shifted her to Nellie's arms. "Holding her more upright while she eats, and even after, seems to improve her chances for keeping her milk down." He moved toward the door. "Don't disturb Lita unless you absolutely have to." He turned back to give his daughter a pointed look. "She deserves some rest." Nellie gave a tiny nod and sat in the chair by her bed as Tate turned to leave the room.

Heading to the kitchen, he poured himself a cup of tepid coffee and drank it down as he moved through the wash porch to the screen door on the back of the house. Setting the empty cup on the table by the door, he donned his fedora and set out, praying that Nellie was up to the task of caring for her baby.

* * *

Nellie stared ahead, trying not to look at her child. Her dark eyes were too much—her thick ebony hair so like her father's, Nellie thought her heart would break to touch it.

She felt rather than saw when Sadie rejected the nipple in her mouth, and she forced herself to look at the face of her daughter. She seemed content for a minute or two, then her sweet face crumpled into sadness as she pulled her legs up and began to fuss. Nellie looked to the open door. She really didn't want to disturb Lita's sleep. She knew how much Lita had done for her.

She tried putting the bottle back to those pouting lips, but Sadie no longer wanted it. Rising, she turned the baby to her shoulder, patting her back as she moved swiftly out of her room and down the stairs, feeling panic rise within her. Heading down the hall and into the parlor, she slid the pocket door shut and tried to shush the now wailing little one. *If only she wouldn't cry. I could handle it if she wouldn't cry.* She began to pace the room. *Papa says she didn't get worse after Paul died. He says she always cried a lot, but that's not true. This is worse. I know it is.*

The child paused and burped, bringing up what felt like most of the bottle of milk running down her back. Nellie closed her eyes and held her breath, hoping that with the expulsion of the meal, she would feel better. Only thirty seconds passed before her hopes were dashed.

As the child began to cry again, Nellie sank to the floor weeping. "Oh, Paul, I need you!"

The parlor door slid open, and Lita appeared in her wrapper. The dark circles under her eyes told the story of too many sleepless nights.

"I don't know what to do!" Nellie wailed nearly as loud as Sadie.

Lita bent to receive the baby, and Nellie sat wiping her eyes and blowing her nose on the handkerchief that Lita handed her. "Go change, and then we'll give her a warm bath. Sometimes that helps."

Nellie got up and headed for the hall when the doorbell rang. She didn't want to be the one to answer, but she could hardly expect Lita to do it with a crying baby. Not really caring that she looked like something the cat dragged in and smelled like something the cat threw up, she pulled open the door to see Daisy Cummings, who had been a year ahead of her in school.

The expression on her face was better than a mirror. "Oh, Nellie... I..."

Nellie swept a strand of hair behind her ear and went into her practiced spiel. "My father isn't in right now." She gave a big sniff. "If you're needing medical assistance of any kind, I can tell him you came by, and he will call you as soon as he can."

The fashionably dressed Daisy held out her calling card, trying to unobtrusively look into the parlor where all the screaming was coming from. "My mother would like more of the pills Dr. Cavanaugh gave her for her heart flutters." She brought her eyes and her wrinkled nose back to Nellie. "If you don't mind giving him that message."

Nellie took the card. "Certainly. Good day, Daisy."

She started to close the door, but Daisy put out a hand. "Nellie, is your baby all right?" She reached out to touch her elbow and dropped her voice. "Are *you* all right?"

If Nellie thought Daisy held any real concern for her or her baby, she might have invited her in for a heart-to-heart. But she didn't believe that. Not for a minute. Daisy was gathering information—gossip for the working girls downtown to chew on for the rest of the week. She could just hear it now. *Crazy Nellie smelled like what?*

Nellie couldn't begin to muster a smile. "Sadie is a baby, Daisy. Babies cry. And I am a very tired mom. No newspaper headlines here."

Daisy blinked her eyes wide. "I've never heard one that cried like that!"

The crying grew louder as Lita brought Sadie to the door. "I'll tell Tate you called, Daisy," she said, closing the door in her face.

Nellie knew that half a year ago, they would have laughed about Daisy's saucer-eyed expression for days. Today, however, they merely turned and dragged themselves to the stairs.

* * *

Jackson left Mr. Hammil's auto shop feeling restless. It had been months since he'd been able to spend any time with his friends, and the last thing he wanted to do was go home to

Nellie's screaming kid. He'd done his share of babysitting, and he was fed up. His feet were taking him in the direction of home, nonetheless.

"Jack!"

He looked back over his shoulder to see his good friend Pete jogging to catch up with him, his red hair set aflame by the sun heading toward the peaks. He stopped beside him, catching his breath. "Jack, where ya been? Does Hammil have you working all day and all night?"

Jackson turned and continued walking, and Pete fell into step beside him. "Nah, I've been busy with other things— helping my dad."

"Really? So are you going to be a doctor mechanic or a mechanical doctor?"

"Something like that," Jack mumbled.

"Ralph says you've been babysitting your sister's brat."

Jackson ground his teeth. "I've been known to help out in a pinch. Babies are hard work."

"They're a damned nuisance, if you ask me."

"Well, who asked you?" Jackson shot back, not really sure why he was irritated. He'd thought the same thing nearly every day since Nellie had moved back home.

"Ah, Jack's a baby lover. I bet you're really working for your ma and your sister, and you're studying to be a nursemaid."

Jackson punched him in the arm. "I am not. You don't know what you're talking about."

"Don't I? Folks is inside your house all the time with your pa being a doctor. Word gets out."

Jackson could feel his face heating up, but he couldn't think of anything more to say. It was the truth—he was fast becoming a nursemaid. He knew way more about babies than he ever wanted to know.

They approached the drug store, and Pete stopped. "Let's get a phosphate."

Jackson knew he'd be late for supper if he did. "Nah, I gotta get home."

Pete put his hand to the door. "I suppose you've got diapers to change."

Jack was suddenly furious, but not with his sassy-mouthed friend. He was mad at his parents for forcing him to do girl stuff, he was mad at Nellie for having such a troublesome baby, and he was even mad at Paul for dying, although he knew that one was a trifle unreasonable.

Pete had already gone in, and he could see through the glass that he was joining up with a couple of his other buddies. He found himself opening the door, and the bell dinged, signaling his decision to all those gathered at the soda fountain. A cheer went up as Pete waved him over, and Jackson silenced the dissenting voice in his head as he slipped onto a stool and ordered a strawberry phosphate.

*   *   *

"I've called a leading specialist in gastrointestinal abnormalities to try and find a solution for whatever ails Sadie," Tate announced over supper as he passed rolls to Nellie. It was a rarity for her to join them for a meal these days. He paused, hoping to see some spark of interest. Not seeing any, he pressed on. "I hope Dr. Englewood will review her case and return my call in the next week or two."

"What do you think is wrong with her?" she asked flatly, setting the basket in the center of the table without taking a roll.

Tate spread his roll with butter, elated with her question. "I think it's an esophageal sphincter issue. I suspect it's not closing properly, letting stomach acid back into her esophagus."

"Can anything be done for it?" she asked quietly, not meeting his gaze.

"That's what I hope Dr. Englewood can tell me."

The back door opened, and after a moment, Jackson appeared in the dining room.

Tate straightened and lifted his chin as his son sank into a dining room chair beside Nellie. "You're late for supper, young man. Is Mr. Hammil working you so hard?"

Jackson helped himself to a piece of roasted chicken and a roll. "I stopped at the soda shop after I was done sweeping. Where's Mom?"

"Your mother's resting." Tate tried not to be irritated at his son's lackadaisical attitude. "Supper is served promptly at 6:00. I expect you to be here."

A swoop of Jackson's brown hair slipped toward his eye, and Tate made a mental note to get the boy to the barber soon.

"I haven't seen Pete in ages, what with all the baby business. I needed a break."

Tate had no doubt that he did, but his attitude could use some polish. He was about to rub a shine on it, when Jackson continued to spew forth thoughtless words. "So, sis, what brings you out of your room? I told mom weeks ago if she wanted you to come out, she needed to stop taking food up there."

Nellie scowled, tossing her napkin to the table. "Did you? How understanding of you."

Tate didn't want her to retreat back upstairs. "Jackson, apologize. That was not... kind."

Jackson took his time chewing and swallowing. "The reverend always says we should speak the truth. So that's what I'm doing."

Tate was sorely tempted to wallop some truth on his backside, but with their lack of sleep they were all short-tempered. "Speak the truth in *love*, Jackson. You are missing the love part."

Tate held his gaze until the young man gave a little snort of concession. "I apologize," he muttered.

It was a sorry excuse for an apology, but Tate was too weary to demand more. He turned back to his meal, surprised when Jackson went on. "I apologize for my 'lack of love,' but where is hers? She has let us deal with her squalling baby for months while she hides out in her room."

Tate nailed him with a not-now look. "Jackson."

"No, I'm tired of playing nursemaid. Men shouldn't be tending babies. All my friends are laughing at me."

Tate rose, leaning forward, his knuckles on the table. "In this house men and women are equal. Your mother would say that being a 'nursemaid' is not 'gender specific.' "

The young man dared to defy him, crossing his arms over his chest. "But it's *her* baby."

Tate headed around the table. "I thought you were too old for the woodshed, but I guess—"

"Papa, I want you and Lita to adopt Sadie."

Nellie's words stopped Tate in his tracks. "Nellie, you don't know what you're saying. You've been through a trauma, and—"

"No, I've given it a lot of thought." She pushed back from the table and rose, her chin ticking up. "I'm not a suitable mother."

Jackson shook his head, muttering something unintelligible.

She looked down at him. "I don't expect you to understand. I just can't... I may be leaving soon. She's better off with Papa and Lita."

"Leaving?" Lita had appeared in the doorway, her long black hair in a simple braid down her back. "Where would you go?"

Nellie swallowed. "I don't know. Somewhere with less memories. I could go back to school—get my entomology degree... or someplace completely different."

Tate put a hand to her shoulder. "Honey, we would support you in a degree, but I don't think you could handle the studies right now." Nellie closed her eyes, looking as if she could come apart, and Tate wondered if he should place a call to his old friend and psychologist, Dr. Jeremiah Fischer.

"I just want to know," Nellie began slowly without opening her eyes, "if you will always take care of Sadie if I can't." She blinked her eyes open, looking between him and Lita. "Please, tell me you'll raise her as your own."

"Oh good grief," Jackson spouted behind them.

Tate sent him a quelling look designed to remind him of his earlier woodshed threat, and the boy clamped his mouth shut.

Lita put a hand to Nellie's cheek. "She's our granddaughter, Nellie. Of course we'll take care of her." She pulled her into a hug. "But you're going to get better. You'll see. This will get easier. You just need time to heal. We all do."

The crying started upstairs, and Tate gave a sigh as he pulled both women to his chest.

Buy *JUMP* today on Amazon.com or, for a signed copy, JodiBowersox.com.